In the Shadow

of the

Blue Ridge

by

Carolyn Tyree Feagans

In the Shadow of the Blue Ridge

Library of Congress Catalog Card Number
98-60606
ISBN: 1-890306-10-X

Third Printing

In the Shadow of the Blue Ridge is a novel, packed with factual happenings, both locally and nationally; however, all characters and names of main characters within are fictitious.

Warwick House

Publishing

Dedicated to...He who is no respecter of persons...

and...

...to my grandmother, Grace, from whom Hallie emerges...
...to my mother, Margaret, who Lauralee's childhood mirrors...

and...

...to those special people of the Blue Ridge, past and present...
...the strong Scotch-Irish descendants...
...and especially the Monacans...

Foreword

Until recently, people living in Central Virginia wanting to learn more about their local habitat could only read historical chronicles written by authors with old-time Lynchburg names like Cabell, Blackford, Christian and Yancey. These tomes are well worth reading, but admittedly are only for those who are willing to trudge through heavy, halting dialogue. Native readers, not so inclined to dusty history books, can now be treated to a potpourri of local literature of poetry, genealogy, architecture, fiction and history, ranging from ethnic groups (Indians, Quakers), churches, Civil War, county histories, local cemeteries and on and on. At Lynchburg's bicentennial celebration, many examples of these were included in a time capsule which will be opened in the year 2086!

One piece missed in the capsule will be *In the Shadow of the Blue Ridge*, the third work by Lynchburg's novelist, Carolyn Tyree Feagans. Along with the creation of other literary authors blooming in the community, now we have a legitimate, local novelist, one who grew up here, who understands its social dynamics, who lived through the latter half of the twentieth century as a *part* of local history, a person who can humanize it all with her pen.

Nationally when you recall historical fiction, authors' names like Irving Stone, John Jakes and Howard Fast leap to mind.

Like these more famous people, Carolyn Feagans has deftly learned how to flesh out Central Virginia's historical skeletons over the past century with interesting stories; so what would be historical obfuscation to some, now has a more narrative flow. The author has a marvelous grasp of not only local events, but also our natural surroundings like fauna and flora. Her text, rich with outdoor descriptives, winding through mountain trails, is embellished with a backdrop of local wildflowers, trees, animals and seasonal changes.

Skillfully using nature's backdrop, the story begins during today's time period with an older woman recollecting her life on Oak Mountain in Amherst County. As this ninety-seven-year-old native, Pocahontas "Poky" Fitzgerald, shares her life's story with Grae Branham (Monacan descendant), they revisit her log cabin where she lived most of her life. The reader is then treated to the experiences Poky lived through as an Indian descendant (Cherokee), raised by a Negro midwife. Becoming an apprenticed midwife herself allowed her to cross cultural barriers to care for the variety of indigenous persons living there.

Slowly and tantalizingly, a love story emerges between Barclay Branham and Addie Jane Taylor (the parents Grae never knew). This is a romance fraught with cross-cultural conflict, yet beautifully intertwined with human emotion.

Parallel to the drama in the Blue Ridge is another family story taking place in what is now downtown Lynchburg. The Lynchburg Daniels family is skillfully connected to Oak Mountain, providing an interesting contrast of mountain life and Lynchburg times.

Blended into the stories in Lynchburg and Oak Mountain are songs, Biblical scripture, national and local happenings. Those of us who grew up in the area will nostalgically recall the 40's, 50's and 60's when we shopped at Snyder and Berman's, lunched at Patterson's Drug Store on Main Street and enjoyed the latest movie at the Paramount Theater. Those who did not grow up here will learn to appreciate the transformation of businesses, entertainment, social customs and attitudes over the years.

Finally, *In the Shadow of the Blue Ridge* is a book of healing. Happiness, frankness, sadness and truth emanate, and a healing portrayal of the life of persons who were once looked down upon. Although history gives us facts and dates, the author's text fills in the gaps with emotion so the reader experiences how it feels to be regarded as an "Issue" during an era of social contempt.

Years from now our children will read in local history books about the revival of the Monacan Tribe in the latter twentieth century. More is discovered each year by academics who rush to explain the archeology and culture of the ancient Monacans — the Monacan mystique. Thanks to *In the Shadow of the Blue Ridge*, the author has folded the Monacan's twentieth century story into dialogue, so now our children can appreciate the human side.

To understand...*Shadow...*, is to understand the drama of social change right in our midst. Now we can grab it and hold on to it.

Dr. Peter W. Houck
Historian

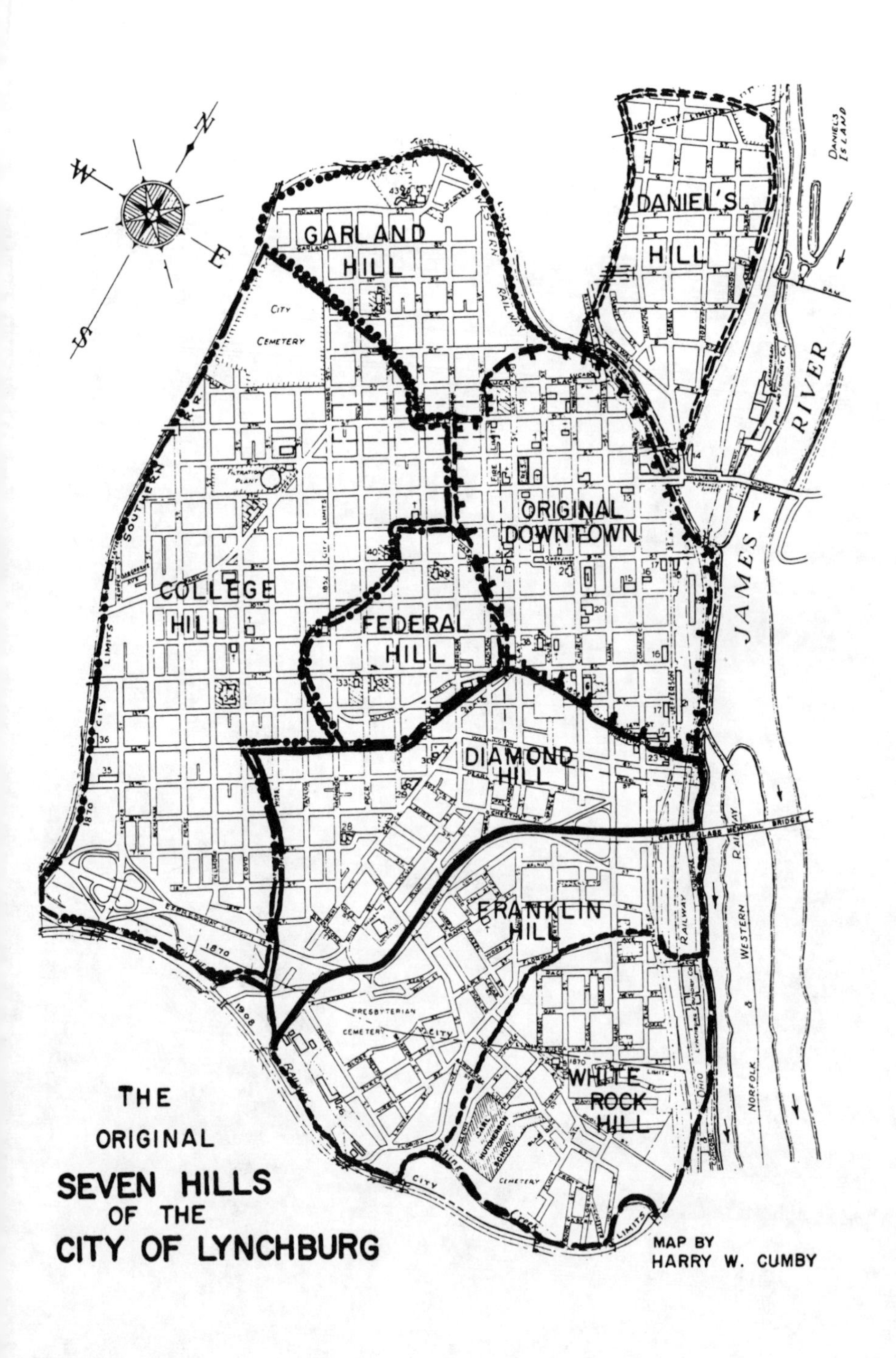

THE ORIGINAL
SEVEN HILLS
OF THE
CITY OF LYNCHBURG

MAP BY
HARRY W. CUMBY

In the Shadow of the Blue Ridge

THE JEEP CHEROKEE climbed up the steep mountainside, passing a familiar brown sign...*The Blue Ridge Parkway*...and dodged a young doe timidly crossing its path. The striking young driver smiled and again looked up into the rearview mirror. She sat still and erect on the back seat in spite of her painful arthritis. *Ninety-seven years old today!*

"You all right, Miss Poky?"

The old woman didn't answer. Thin, wrinkled and weathered from a lifetime of cold mountain winds and hot sunny days, she stared out the window. She was silent, obviously escaping reality, walking the corridors of time. The late morning sun illuminated the autumn forest with its emblazoned foliage that boasted translucent yellows, vivid golds and deep crimsons that overshadowed the dark pines. It was mid October, and the Blue Ridge was peaking! Young Grae Branham didn't quite appreciate this magic vista, but *she* did. Her clouded eyes, seemingly estranged from the modern world, skillfully captured the essence of it all, bringing it home for her to sift through, compare and remember. It was in such an autumn that Barclay and Addie Jane had fallen in love. The trees had cast this same vibrant spell. She remembered the two young people holding hands, walking off into the rainbow of trees on Oak Mountain. An elusive smile crossed over her deeply creased wrinkles.

The green Cherokee leveled out on the smooth parkway and began weaving around its numerous curves, hugging the precipitous ridges that allowed for panoramic views. A large tulip poplar extended out toward them from the mountainside. *"Poky, come down'ere right'is minute!"* Her mother's voice echoed from the rustling yellow leaves just as it did so many years ago. She stared at the young man behind the wheel, so much like Barclay...how could it be? But he wasn't Barclay!

"You enjoying the ride, Miss Poky?"

She nodded, reentering the present, and leaned toward the window. "See them trees...look at'em yonder...so many'uv'em..." She chuckled, "...can't keep'em down."

"Which trees, Miss Poky?"

She pointed a gnarled forefinger toward rows of paradise trees lining the parkway, now reddened with their fall attire.

"Those scrawny little things? I don't even call *them* trees...just a nuisance, they are. Understand the parkway personnel fight a losing battle with them, keep chopping them down and they spring back up faster than they can cut them down."

Again she chuckled in the back seat. He eyed her closely, seeing for the first time more than a wrinkled old woman. A hint of humor? Cunning discernment flickered as a candle in a darkened room.

"What's so funny, Miss Poky?"

"Son, I need t'tell ya' th'story'uv th'ailanthus sometime. Some folk call'em paradise. Up on Oak Mountain, they burn'em in wood stoves. Some folk call'em stink wood 'cause'uv how it stinks so when it's burned, but I call'em *the tree of heaven.*"

Realizing she was keenly alert and most likely a rare source of information on the past century, he quickly responded, "First, I'd like you to tell me another story, Miss Poky...the story of my parents."

Her countenance didn't change, and she spoke calmly, "Possible t'get a lil' fresh air? It's a might cold in'ere. If'n I didn't see them autumn trees, I'd think it was winter."

Amused, he turned the air conditioner down and gave his right signal for the pull off just ahead. Parking against the curb, he opened the back door, allowing for a wide sweeping view.

She sighed, "Been a long time, son. Nigh thirty years since...since that time. Your folks an' me...well'sa...they were a part'uv me. Might as well start from th'beginnin'." She inhaled the crisp fresh air, her bony chest heaving beneath her black wool sweater, and settled back. "A wind's blowin' up from th'valley...feel it...."

CHAPTER ONE

1898

HISTORY WAS TRAGICALLY about to be made on that eventful night of February 15, 1898...quarter to ten. A horrendous explosion erupted in Havana, shaking the entire city as windows were shattered in all houses. The Battleship Maine was blown up! Two hundred and sixty young men were suddenly buried at sea.

But thousands of miles away, a full moon illuminated the otherwise darkened Blue Ridge, creating a picture of perfect serenity. Thus is life! Climactic catastrophes envelop individuals or hosts of individuals in one area as calmness and joy caress another...a counteraction maybe. It was so on that historic night as the moon's silver rays shone down upon the folds and crevices of the hills known as Oak Mountain, casting its shadow about. The humble cabin sat slantingly upon a rugged ridge, and now stood out with its rough-hewn logs chinked with mountain mud, and its proud chimney sending up curls of hazy blue smoke. Winter winds moaned softly through thick pine boughs as if they understood, and greyish white clouds slipped silently by, reluctant to tarry, it seemed. Two men lounged on the small wooden porch, quietly hunched over, a part of their still surroundings except for an occasional tobacco spit.

Suddenly, a shrill scream escaped the crude, thin walls.

"Don't figger on much longer...this'uns takin' on...."

"Gonna be that thar son you been'a hankering for, Maxie."

The tough mountain men allowed a fleeting smile to cross their otherwise stern countenances.

For seven long years, Maxie Fitzgerald had waited for a son. Four times before he'd sat out here on his own porch through all kinds of weather...only to have another girl...and each one stillborn. He thought on these things now. His woman just won't much at havin' young'uns. If'n he didn't have no luck this time, why he might be takin' things into'is own hands! He pulled his tattered hat down over his ears as the winds were getting up some, though it was tolerably mild for February.

Inside the nearly bare cabin, methodical movements were taking place as the wizened old midwife scurried to and from the hot wood stove, where two large kettles of spring water sat boiling. She moved to the bedside of the thin, worn-looking face grimaced with pain. A fairly young woman, with little rivulets of sweat glistening on her high cheekbones, lay very still. A woman well acquainted with hardships and grief, although her years were few, now struggled again for courage to face the unknown. Suddenly she clutched frantically at the damp twisted sheet.

"It's gonna be all right, Mrs. Fitzgerald...it's gonna be all right."

The young mother turned her tired eyes in appreciation to the old Colored midwife, but they couldn't hide her disbelief. The night wore on, and morning hours took over as winter winds increased outside, rattling window shutters and moaning its eerie message. The hours crept upward...3:00 AM, and all energy was drained from her, but she would not give up. This baby must be born! It must live! She turned her matted head toward the midwife who now sat sleepily beside her, and saw also her ill-tempered husband beyond sound asleep in the shadows, and she was glad. If the baby...if things didn't turn out...well then, he wouldn't carry on so. She'd learned through the years how to cope with her place in life by creating her own escape, her own world, and it was to this world that she now sought refuge — a beautiful world filled with warmth from the all enveloping sunlight that pressed down upon the serene meadow...her meadow surrounded by swaying pines. Its warmth and beauty were so encompassing that she felt herself a part of it. The heavy pine scent mixed with sweet honeysuckle fragrance floated heavily about her. A busy hummingbird hung in midair about a wild cherry tree. Ah, what peace! She sighed, and a deer appeared out from the pines, so graceful, stopping suddenly, glancing to the right and to the left before advancing forward to the center of the meadow, there to graze at a leisurely pace. A gentle breeze delicately touched each blade of emerald green grass causing the entire meadow to move evanescently before her eyes. Suddenly her meadow vanished as a searing pain ripped through her body, and throughout the next hour, she rode the powerful gripping waves of childbirth. Just before darkness gave way to the first rays of light, a daughter was born...but this child let out a gusty cry that could be heard beyond the cabin walls, out into the cold winter morning.

Maxie Fitzgerald raised his bearded head questioningly.

"Another girl, Mr. Fitzgerald, but she be alive an'a fine lookin' lil' gal, too." The midwife grinned from ear to ear.

He grunted and turned over.

Four days later, the young mother still lay on the iron bed in a frightening weakened state, the anxious midwife fussing about her and the infant every waking minute, but time was running out.

What was she to do? The midwife thought over and over. She *must* do something! But how could she? She couldn't leave the two of them here alone...and Maxie Fitzgerald...she figured he was gone for good. She knew his kind. While pondering these troubling thoughts, she suddenly heard a gasp. The young mother was reaching out with her thin arm hanging limply from the covers.

"What is it, child?" She bent down close to hear what she was trying to say. Difficult as it was to make out the hardly audible voice barely above a whisper, she understood.

"...call her...call her...Indian name...she must know...." Her words trailed off as the young mother closed her tired eyes for the last time. The midwife just sat there in shock, staring down at the small silent form...with the tiny infant still hungrily sucking at her breast. She gently pulled the baby away, but it held on tightly as if it knew it was a final break.

The cold winter winds left Oak Mountain, and the mountain ridges began to thaw, sending forth springs of water that seeped through rocky crevices, creating a picturesque sight as the stone cliffs glistened in the welcomed sunlight. Normally, the mountain folk would be happily basking in this long awaited spring, but the country was at war. Most went quietly about their way, hoping it wouldn't touch them, if it hadn't already. It was the explosion of the Maine that caused it, and though no one knew for sure whether or not it was planned or accidental, it was too late now. On April the twenty-fifth, the United States had formally declared that a state of war existed with Spain!

A blue jay rested atop the mountain laurel that hugged the cabin. The midwife quickly shooed him away, "Off with ya'...always'a skeerin' th'nice lil' birds away!"

She turned and went back inside, listening carefully for any sound. She smiled. The infant was still sleeping...such a good little'un...no trouble a'tall. So why couldn't she raise her?

AT THE FOOT of Oak Mountain, vast lands stretched forth from the Blue Ridge for miles and miles to the east, flat and tiresome for the most part, however, interspersed with periodic slight hills, sunny meadows and crystal clear streams. Rivers, some placid and others foaming from dangerous rapids, crossed its path on their individual courses to the grand

and mighty Chesapeake. One of these rivers, fearlessly winding through the Blue Ridge and gently meandering down through the valleys, was a proud river called the *James,* after James I, King of England. The largest river in Virginia, it originated from numerous cold mountain streams in western Virginia and West Virginia. These streams that cascade down from lofty mountains, merge and form such rivers as the Cowpasture, Calfpasture and the Bullpasture. Ultimately they join and become the powerful James that encompasses nearly three hundred miles on its path to the Chesapeake. Sometimes with fury, but mostly gentle and always proud for its part in history, the James held a prominent place in serving its local master, a relatively young town called Lynchburg that had actually just celebrated its centennial only twelve years prior. Many an eyebrow had been raised at the name of *Lynchburg*...wondering from whence it came! Lynchburg, the nearest town to Oak Mountain but still aways to travel at that time, was renowned for its wealth from its abundant tobacco trade, and it relied upon the James to transport its many cargoes of tobacco, either by bateaux or the canal. Rising up from this river, the small town climbed the abundant hills, claiming them as it grew. Caught up in its heyday, the thriving town bustled with success, but today it had a low-lying undertone that hung over it as the townsfolk went about their usual business, but talked in hushed tones.

"It was that explosion that did it...the explosion of the Maine...that was it!" a thin, weathered farmer stated as he threw a large heavy sack of grain onto his parked wagon and covered it with a thick canvas.

The storekeeper nodded, "...that's right all right...you heard tell of the Smith boy being on that battleship...."

"I sure did. Hard to believe one of our own Lynchburg boys would be way down there on that ship. Nicholas Smith was his name, won't it?"

"That was it. Didn't know of him, but I used to know his uncle back when we were young."

"'Tis a shame...'tis a shame." He tipped his worn hat to the bearded storekeeper, who kindly waved him off. The wagon rolled down Main Street, bouncing over the granite blocks in the misty rain.

The Lynchburg boys were preparing to leave. It was May the ninth and early that Monday morning, the excited boys were hurrying to and fro. Lynchburg was now beginning to realize that there really was a war going on, especially those whose sons were going to the front lines. A large crowd gathered on Church and Ninth streets and around the depot waiting to see them off. You could hear the slogan *"Remember the Maine"* being bounced around by the restless young soldiers. It was a popular war cry now. About seven o'clock, the Hill City band began to play. Shortly thereafter, the command was heard, "Fall in," and a detachment of Confederate Veterans under Colonel Langhorne escorted the young soldiers to the depot. These same old veterans had marched to war thirty-seven years ago. What was going on in their minds? It was a scene that brought tears to eyes to see these war-scarred heroes leading their sons into war. Cheers went up from the thousands of spectators that had come to bid them farewell as they marched by. Soon they were aboard the Chesapeake and Ohio headed for Richmond, and all that could be seen was their waving arms as the loud, lumbering train disappeared.

The boys arrived in Richmond and headed immediately to Camp Lee at the old State Fair Grounds. As they proudly marched through the narrow streets, they received hearty cheers, much to their delight. All eyes were glued to the bright and merry faces of the young soldiers, obviously enthusiastic about what faced them. Maxie Fitzgerald cheered along with the rest. Nobody noticed him.

The next day, a solemn aura hung over the hills of Lynchburg...their boys gone...their future uncertain. The older folk struggled to push their memories aside. Memories of another war...not that long ago. But this war was different! It wouldn't be fought on southern land or on northern land, for that matter. It was far away in a place they couldn't even envision.

"Mama, listen to this...." Fifteen-year-old Carrie Daniels lifted the newspaper and read...'*The Home Guard and Zouaves presented a handsome appearance as they moved steadily along the streets with heads erect. The Fitz Lee Rifles, having no uniforms or accoutrements of any description, were not much on looks from a military point of view; but it is predicted that they will fight to kill.*'

"Oh, Mama, I'll just die...simply die...if anything happens to him!"

Ethel Daniels looked anxiously at her daughter. "Now, Carrie darling, don't carry on so. I'm quite sure Will Morgan will return as handsome and charming as ever. You need to put that paper down and get on your studies. Get your mind occupied."

The young girl started upstairs. She didn't want to worry her mother too much in her condition. She pushed open the heavy oak door to her tidy Victorian bedroom and flung herself down on the soft feathery bed covered with Grandmother Daniels' wedding ring quilt. "He will come back!" she told herself aloud as she gazed out the wide bay window, noticing the cloudless sky, glad it wasn't still raining. Oh, why did it have to be this spring? She looked out over the flat rooftops of the downtown buildings and on down below to the lazily flowing James. She was glad they lived here atop this hill on Court Street. She used to imagine that she was the queen and all the buildings down below her kingdom. What silly ideas children have! But at least children don't have these mixed up, sad feelings. Being grown up wasn't exactly what she'd expected, and she didn't know whether or not she liked it particularly. She looked out beyond the river, past Amherst Heights, on out to the misty blue mountains. They always made her feel better...made her feel peaceful.

"Mercy me, child, what ya' doin' layin' 'round on a pretty day like today?"

Carrie quickly turned her face away from Aunt Bertha, afraid she'd see her tears.

"I'm to be studying, Aunt Bertha. Mama said so."

"That's good, child...books is good for ya'. You know my Sister Jane be comin' tomorrow with that baby."

"That's right!" She perked up. "I can't wait to see her baby."

"It ain't her baby. Sister Jane's a midwife, you see, an' she got left with this baby when its mama died, an' its pa up an' run off."

"The baby's not Colored...but Indian, you say?"

"Sho thing...that's what Sister Jane be sayin'. Name's Pocahontas. Ever heard'uv such a thing? My sister named'er, you see. Just before her young mama, who was an Indian, left this'ere world for a better place, she says t'my Sister Jane, 'Call'er an Indian name.' Now Sister Jane didn't know no Indian names 'cept for Pocahontas. So Pocahontas she be!"

Carrie smiled weakly, "Seems like a lot of name for a little baby."

"'Tis a fact." She left the room, and Carrie stared back out toward the distant mountains where that little Indian baby would be coming from tomorrow.

SISTER JANE WAS up before daybreak the next morning, readying herself and baby Poky (she'd already shortened it) for the long trip to Lynchburg. She hated leaving Oak Mountain, but this was gonna be a good thing for her an' Poky, she told herself...an' she was sho gonna enjoy bein' with Sister Bertha. That extra money was gonna come in handy, too. 'Course she didn't much know 'bout them fine livin's in Lynchburg that Sister Bertha done told'er 'bout, but it would jest be for a couple'uv months 'fore th' missus delivered. Imagine bringin' a body all th'way from these'ere mountains just so's t'be sure that th' young'un would be birthed right!

The ride proved to be as long and tiring as she'd anticipated, but she was mighty glad and obliged to Z.B. Tomlin for offering to carry her in. Baby Poky seemed to be enjoying it all the same and slept the best part of it, the bumps and jostles putting her to sleep. Finally as the wagon descended the Amherst Heights hill, the river came into view, and the bridge spanning it, then the town. What a sight! It had been a long time, just a girl she'd been. My...such a change...a city had sprung up and rose proudly from the banks of the river, climbing the steep hills. "An' look at them houses!" she whispered to herself. "Now who in thunder needs sech'a house? Why, it'd be room in one 'uv'em for me an' most 'uv my neighbors."

The wagon rumbled across the bridge, and Sister Jane stared up at the tall sides spanning the bridge. It reached the other side and laboriously pulled up the hill behind the panting horses. Sister Jane marveled at all the activity surrounding her, particularly the trolley car that barely missed them as it boldly flew past, loaded down with passengers. She glared at the well-dressed people crowded onto it, ladies with wide brimmed hats and parasols and men sporting smart looking derby hats. So folk really did live this'a way! Suddenly she felt as if she didn't belong here, and wondered what she'd done. She was pondering it all when the wagon wheels finally stopped in front of a stately red brick house. She gazed up at the formal two story house with its fine white laced curtains blowing gently in the open windows. The elegant, ornate black ironwork that graced the long porch and the upper portion of the house resembled giant filigree, artistically embracing each pillar of the otherwise stern countenance of the house. Impressive but somewhat intimidating double oak doors faced them. An immense tulip poplar with a base the size of a tractor wheel guarded the house, extending to the uppermost eaves in its noble endeavor. Sister Jane noticed how it seemed to reach out to protect the home. She liked that. Suddenly the large oak doors swung open and Sister Bertha stood in their midst smiling from ear to ear.

ONE WEEK PASSED, and Sister Jane was comfortably settled in, enjoying her sister's companionship. She and Poky had temporarily moved into Sister Bertha's room at the back of the house leading out from the kitchen. Poky stirred a certain amount of interest in the household, particularly from little Hallie, the youngest of the Daniels family, but also Carrie, helping to take her mind off Will Morgan, much to her mother's joy. Not that Ethel Daniels wasn't concerned herself about the young man's potential danger, but Will Morgan was not for her Carrie, and the sooner this infatuation passed, the better.

Young Hallie was definitely taken with little Poky, with her jet black hair, olive skin and expressive black eyes staring out just above the already prominent high cheek bones. It was obviously novel to her to have someone in the house younger than her. Poky was enjoying all this new attention in no small manner, as well.

It was Saturday morning and already the feel of summer was in the air even though school wasn't quite over. Carrie and her mother had taken little Hallie to have her portrait made, even though she'd resisted all the way. Ethel Daniels made sure that all her children had their portrait done at six years old. It was tradition in their family. Their brother, Carlton, had gone with their father on 'men business,' he'd boasted to the girls.

Bertha had talked Sister Jane into going downtown for a little excursion with Poky. It was a cloudless day, full of sunshine, and they were thoroughly enjoying it as they took turns pushing the bulky wicker carriage that was beginning to show wear. It bounced over the uneven granite blocks, causing Poky to grin with excitement.

"It was sho nice 'uv th' missus t'lend us this 'ere carriage."

"Miss Ethel is a nice lady...won't find no better. 'Course this old carriage done seen its day...gone through all of 'em. Guess this little'un comin' will be th' last."

"She be'a lucky lady...t'have such'a fine family."

"She sho is."

The carriage picked up speed going down the steep hill, and they both held on tightly as Poky squealed with delight. Leveling off, they breathed heavily as they approached the Firemen's Fountain and paused to refresh themselves. The stone fireman kept his sentinel perched high above them while holding onto the water hose, his constant companion. The cascading fountains of water flowed unceasingly from three different levels, sending forth a welcomed spray all around its base, and the sisters lingered in its mist. Poky grinned and squinted her dark eyes as minute drops of water fell into her carriage.

"Sho feels good. S'pose we could've walked down them steps if'n we had a mind to and didn't have this'ere carriage." She pointed to the numerous steps leading up to the courthouse on Court Street.

"You're right, Sister Jane. Reckon we should've, too, since they done worked so hard buildin'em. 'Course it's been awhile now...nigh 'bout fourteen-fifteen years I s'pose. Use'ta run down that hill. But I was'a bit younger, too," she chuckled.

"More'n a bit." Sister Jane laughed.

"No use'n you laughin', Sister. I's fifty-one an' you's two years older'n me. An' that brings me to some'in I's been worryin' 'bout. What you gonna do with this'ere baby anyhows?"

"I aim t'keep'er an' raise'er."

"...but Sister Jane, you ain't up t'that!"

"Sister, I been birthin' other folks' babies all my life an' ain't never got t'keep none...never had no baby'uv my own. Now I'm gonna keep Poky. She gonna be mine!"

"You ain't skittish 'bout raisin' a baby at your age?"

Sister Jane shook her head.

"Well'sa, don't reckon nobody else wants'er."

"That's right...nobody but me."

"...but what folks gonna say 'bout you havin' a *white* baby?"

"Poky ain't white."

"She sho ain't Colored."

"Well, she just part white, but her mama was Indian. 'Course her daddy, Maxie Fitzgerald, always bragged he was Scotch-Irish...a shame for th'Scotch-Irish I say."

"An' s'pose he up an' comes back?"

"Don't worry. He *ain't* comin' back." She turned to the tombstones all lined up evenly facing them on display by the Lynchburg Marble and Granite Works located right next to the steps. "He might as well have one'uv them tombstones over him right now. He's well as dead I figure. He ain't comin' back!"

Sister Bertha shook her head and proceeded to push the carriage across the street and on down to Main Street. They passed by Mr. Joseph Cohn's Clothing Establishment, noticing all the fine clothing hanging in the tall windows, particularly the handsome derby hat placed strategically in the forefront.

"Yonder looks like Mr. Daniels' hat."

"It sho do."

"Right airish if ya' ask me."

"What ya' talkin' 'bout, Sister Jane? Mr. Daniels don't put on no airs. He jest'a gentleman, that's all."

"Maybe so. What 'bout that liniment you s'posed t'pick up for th'missus?"

"I'm fixin' t'do that right now...yonder's W.A. Strother. Th'missus always gets her liniments from them 'cause she say it's special like. We also get all'uv her flavorin' extracts from'em. Th'missus sho can be particular...she can," she chuckled.

Sister Jane chose to wait outside the drug store with Poky. She rocked the wobbly carriage back and forth, noticing Poky was almost asleep. The fresh air and bouncy ride had about done its job.

"Well'sa, we best be gettin'on back up th'hill." Sister Bertha joined her, the screen door slamming behind her.

"Sister Bertha, can't we walk down a bit. I wants t'see th'river again. It looked like'a fine river just a flowin' nicely when we come over th'bridge th'other day."

"Sho can. No bother. I better be sheddin' this'ere shawl then. Sister Jane, you ain't missin' th'country already, are you?"

She grinned at her. "You know I ain't fond'uv th'city, Sister. An' this city...where in tarnation did it ever get sech a name...*L-y-n-c-h-burg*...conjures up things in my mind I'm askeered to ask 'bout, an jest soon not think about!"

Sister Bertha laughed aloud. "I knows what ya' mean, Sister...but you know it ain't like that. 'Course some say there was a law roun' these parts called th'Lynch law. Mr. Daniels done told me all 'bout it. You know he likes sech things...readin' 'bout history an' all...keeps up with everything...smart man...Mr. Daniels...."

"What ya' talkin' 'bout...*Lynch law*?"

"I don't rightly know. Seems like nobody really knows what happened, but Mr. Daniels says 'twas in th'time'uv th'Revolutionary War, way back. Seems some rough'ens, part'uv th'Tories he say, commenced t'causin' a heap'uv trouble roun' here. Some folks believe these Tories were tied up to a tree an' got thirty-nine lashes jest like in th'Bible. They say they could stop th'floggin' by cryin' out *liberty*. An' they say this'ere tree was on Mr. Charles Lynch's place, an' that's how th'name came about...Lynch law. Some even say there was some lynching. Now, other folks don't go along with this a'tall. Mr. Daniels say he reckon nobody really knows what happened.

"So say Mr. Daniels...." Sister Jane mimicked.

"Now this Charles was th'brother'uv Mr. John Lynch...who our city was named for...." Caught up in her story, Sister Bertha continued on, proud of her knowledge of the city.

"Sounds like you gettin' t'like history a bit yourself, Sister. Must be rubbin' off on ya'."

They walked on down closer to the smooth flowing river, and paused to enjoy its beauty. The sun shining down on its glassy surface created a glistening picture that caused one to squint in the overpowering effect. Tall sycamores, ghost trees of the Indian legends, lined the river bank, stretching forth their heavy arms out over the lapping water guarding the river's edge. Directly behind the tall white trees rose a wild and abrupt bluff which began Amherst Heights. It jutted out with rocky ledges and precarious cliffs, daring one to challenge it. The proud river, lofty trees and dramatic bluff presented a striking scene, but Sister Jane's eyes looked on beyond, overtop the bluff and on out to the misty blue mountains in the distance...and her heart yearned.

"Looks a far piece to th'mountains."

"Ain't that far, Sister Jane. Now take a gander at that."

"What?"

She pointed to two small boys down on the riverbank with reed poles in their hands, and one was pulling in a fairly sizable fish. "Now that's somethin' t'do. Probably a catfish. Wouldn't mind bein' down there myself. But we better be gettin' on back." She turned the carriage around to head back up the hill. "Gotta get them vittles goin'." Reluctantly, Sister Jane followed.

By the time they reached Court Street, perspiration stood out in shiny little beads on their copper skin, and Sister Jane's large chest heaved in and out. She commenced to coughing, but Poky still slept.

"You still havin' them asthma attacks?"

"Some...but I'm all right. Been usin' pokeweed mostly for it. But when it gets real bad, I fix up my potion...put'a few pieces'uv th'heartwood'uv a pine in 'bout a pint'uv gin, leave it be till they turn brown, then take'a spoonful'uv it twice a day...an' first thing I know, I feel like a new person."

"Look yonder...would ya'...." Sister Bertha pointed to the majestic court house that stood atop the hill before them. Three little girls were dancing around on its porch playing *ring-around-the-rosy.*

Sister Bertha hollered out, "Hallie Daniels...you come on down'ere right now. You's got t'get cleaned up for dinner. Get off that there porch. I done told ya' 'bout that."

The little girl skipped toward them with a broad smile on her pixy face. "Can I push the carriage, please, Aunt Bertha?"

" 'Course you can, sugar." She smiled lovingly at the child. "This one's already taken in by yo' little Poky. Can't keep'er hands off'er."

"I knows that...but looks like you got a family, too, Sister Bertha."

Sister Bertha grinned proudly.

Lacking a few days of being right on time, Mrs. Daniels gave birth to another healthy son, and Sister Jane accepted all the credit, packed up her bags and headed back to Oak Mountain with Poky. A very proud Mr. Daniels drove them this time.

The next few months passed quietly, and in the heat of the summer, the brief war ended. It was August, and the Lynchburg boys came home...all of them! Cuba had received its freedom from Spain, and the United States ended up with Guam, Puerto Rico and the Philippines. Things resumed to normal again. Lynchburg was blessed in that it didn't lose one of its soldiers in the war...but, of course, there was Nicholas Smith.

CHAPTER TWO

THREE YEARS DISAPPEARED as Poky consumed Sister Jane's every moment. Lovingly, she watched her run up and down the mountainside, keeping company with any and all creatures that happened her way. Already she demonstrated an unusual sensitivity to all aspects of life, the plentiful animals, the lush mountain plant life and even the minute insect kingdom that carefully hid itself from sight. Sister Jane watched her proudly and often wondered about her unique insight as one wiser than her years.

When Sister Jane went out into the countryside at all hours, day or night, with her little black bag, Poky, wearing a serious expression, trotted along beside her. The mountain folk marveled at the little tyke. Times were hard, and Sister Jane had to scrape together whatever she could, but still she was happier than ever before. She had Poky and Poky had her!

Sister Bertha had begged them to come back to Lynchburg for a visit...just a short one. Little Hallie particularly wanted to see Poky again. But Sister Jane never seriously entertained the request. No, she would stay put on Oak Mountain where she belonged. Her only concern was if anything ever happened to her...what would become of Poky? Every time she had another asthma attack, she worried more. She'd taken to using more pokeweed than ever. It seemed to be the only thing that would combat the awful stuff now. Not even her potion helped.

It was on such a day that she was thinking on these things that the news hit. Another summer had ended, and fall was in the air. That cool, crisp air that seemed to invigorate the soul was a welcomed relief after the hot, humid summer and added a zest not previously felt. In fact, it had forced her to start a fire in the wood stove just so she could give Poky her weekly bath. The warmth radiating from it felt good as she wiped out the galvanized tub and slid it back under the bed. Poky was already lying back on the bare floor with her clean clothes on and playing with Coon, her favorite pet. There was a knock at the door. Sister Jane opened it, and Maude Jones stood in the doorway, filling it with her large, robust frame.

"TH'PRESIDENT'S BEEN SHOT!"

"What?"

"I say th'president's been shot in New Yawk...Buffalo, New Yawk. Been shot by some assassin!"

Sister Jane clutched her breast, "Lawd have mercy!"

"Gotta go...." Maude spun around and left on her mission to spread the news.

It was days later before she got the details. Again Maude Jones stopped by, this time with a newspaper stuck in her coat pocket. Sister Jane welcomed her in and anxiously waited as she carefully removed her coat and spread out the worn paper before her on the kitchen table. Obviously, she enjoyed her important role as news carrier. She began to read slowly, stumbling over difficult words... '*"President McKinley was shot an' seriously wounded by a would-be as...sassin while holding a reception in th' Temple of Music at th' Pan-American Ex...Ex...position a few minutes after 4:00 this afternoon. One shot took effect in th' right breast, th' other in th' ab...abdomen.'* His stomach it was...got shot in th'stomach an' th' breast!"

"How is he...th' president?"

"Still livin'. Think maybe he's gonna be all right now. Listen t'this...tells how't happened... '*"Buffalo, September th' 6th... While President McKinley was receiving in th' Temple of*

Music on th' Ex...position Grounds this afternoon, he was approached by a man with a dark mustache an' with one hand covered with a handkerchief. As th' man ex...tended his hand to th' president, ap...apparently with th' intention of shaking hands with him, he fired a shot which entered th' president's right breast, lodging against th' breastbone. Another shot was fired at once, which entered th' president's abdomen. Th' sharp crack of th' revolver rang out loud an' clear above th' hum of voices. There was an instant of almost complete silence. Th' president stood stock still, a look of hes...itancy, almost of bewilderment, on his face. Then he retreated a step while a pallor began to steal over his features. He slumped forward gasping, 'Am I shot?' Th' mul...multitude, only par...tially aware that something serious had happened, paused in surprise, while necks were craned an' all eyes turned as one toward th' rost..rum where a great tragedy was being e...nacted. Then came a commotion. With th' leap of a tiger three men threw themselves forward as with on impulse an' sprung toward th' would-be assassin. Two of them were United States Secret Service men who were on th' lookout an' whose duty it was to guard against just such a ca...lamity as had here befallen th' president an' th' nation. Th' third was a bystander, a Negro, who had only an instant previously grasped in his dusky palm th' hand of th' president.'" Maude paused for Sister Jane's reaction.

"Ain't that somethin'?"

She continued, *"As one man, th' trio hurled themselves upon th' president's as...sailant. In a twinkling, he was borne to th' ground, his weapon was wre...wrested from his grasp, an' strong arms pin...ioned him down. Th' president pointed to his would-be assassin im...ploringly, 'Let no one hurt him,' he whispered* to *his secretary: 'My wife...be careful, Cortelyou, how you tell her...oh be careful.'"*

"How terrible...but thank God...they got'im!"

"They got'im all right...an' they was gonna lynch'im...but th'police saved'im."

"Who was he?"

"Some young feller...only twenty-eight years old...you ever hear tell'uv sech!"

"Terrible...terrible thing...but ya' say th'president's gonna be all right?"

"That's what I heard. Gotta get another paper. Couldn't get over to th'store yet. I'm sho glad we live here on Oak Mountain...an' not in New Yawk!"

"You're right 'bout that, Maude. 'Course it was 'cause he was th'president that he got shot...just like Abraham Lincoln."

"I know...an' he's a good man jest like Abraham Lincoln, too. A God-fearin' man, they say."

"I can't help but wonder what that Negro bystander must be'a feelin' right about now. To think he'd jest shook his hand. Some'in' to sho tell'is grandchillen."

But as the two ladies talked, the president had taken a turn for the worse. Again Sister Jane was bathing Poky when she got the news.

"Now Poky, fetch that soap, don't leave it under th'water so long. Gonna melt...an' I told ya' how 'spensive it is. 'Course I don't mind payin' for it, sugar. I want you t'have th'best...an' *Cuticura Soap* is th'best! Gonna make your little skin so soft an'beautiful."

Poky giggled and pulled the soap back out of the water. "Mama, can Coon get in with me?"

"Not hardly, child. Don't want no raccoon in the tub with my baby. Coon don't need no bath anyhows. He all right."

There was a loud knock at the door.

"Who is it?" Sister Jane called out while struggling to get up from the slippery floor.

"Maude...Maude Jones...."

"Come on in, Maude."

The door opened and Maude stood with the paper raised in her right hand.

"President McKinley is DEAD!"

"Lawd have mercy...HE DIED?" Sister Jane reached for a chair.

"He sho did. Listen here whiles I read it to ya'...." She grabbed another chair and commenced reading as Poky splashed in the warm water.

"*Milburn House, Buffalo, September 14— Th'president died at 2:15 this Saturday morning. He had been unconscious since 7:30 PM. His last conscious hour on earth was spent with his wife, to whom he had devoted a lifetime of care. Th'phy...sicians had rallied him to consciousness an' th'president asked almost immediately that his wife be brought to him. Th'doctors fell back into th'shadows of th'room as Mrs. McKinley came through th'doorway....*"

Her reading was interrupted with sobs.

"You all right, Jane?"

"I'm all right...it's just so sad...."

Maude read again...*"as Mrs. McKinley came through th'doorway. Th'strong face of th'dyin' man lighted up with a faint smile as their hands were clasped. She sat beside him an' held his hand. Despite her physical weakness, she bore up bravely under th'ordeal....*"

"Mama?"

"Yes, sugar."

"Can I get out?"

Sister Jane rose to assist her in getting out of the tub. "Maude, will ya' wait jest'a minute till I get Poky dressed? I want t'hear th'rest."

Poky finally skipped out to the porch with Coon scrambling behind her. Maude shook her head, "...a raccoon for a pet...don't that beat all? Well, here's th'rest." She began to read..."*Th'president, in his last period of consciousness, which ended about 7:40 PM, chanted th'words of th'hymn, 'Nearer, My God, to Thee,' an' his last aud...ible conscious words as taken down by Dr. Mann at th'bedside were: 'Good-bye, all, good-bye. It is God's way. His will be done.'*"

"Amen...amen," Sister Jane repeated softly.

Maude sat quietly for a change.

"You're right, Maude. Mr. McKinley was a God-fearin' man."

That evening after Poky was put to bed, Sister Jane sat out on her porch, rocking to the tune of the cicadas. She kept thinking of President McKinley and his poor wife, and she began to hum...*"Nearer, My God, to Thee."*

A couple of days later, Maude returned with more news of the national story. Sister Jane finished peeling the last of her potatoes and pulled up a chair beside her. "They done buried him?"

"Says here...*'Solemn service in the Capitol. Thousands of people pass by to look upon the face of the dead president.'* Can you believe it? Says that so many people crowded in after they'd been waitin' since early mornin' that some'uv th'women an' children got hurt right bad. Ain't that somethin'?"

"Sho is."

"'Course it's nice to show Mr. McKinley respect. He deserves it. They even showed'im respect over in Lynchburg, too. Yes, ma'am, th'Mayor called a mass meetin' in his memory. I do think that's th'right thing to do in a time like this."

"You're right, Maude. Now we got a new president...."

"Yes, ma'am...Mr. Theodore Roosevelt...mighty fine name...don't ya' think?"

"Ain't he right young?"

"Forty-two th'paper says...ain't old as my Tom! Hope he 'kin fill Mr. McKinley's shoes."

Sister Jane commenced to coughing. Maude stood up. "You all right? You been lookin' right poorly these days."

"I'm...I'm all right..." she answered between wheezes. Quicker than a flash, Poky was at her side patting her on the back. The coughing ceased, and Poky smiled.

"You take care'uv your ma, Poky."

Days grew shorter and each one cooler. September eased into October, and Oak Mountain was suddenly arrayed in all its splendor. Sister Jane and Poky exclaimed over the colorful foliage as they walked the mountainside. Poky was particularly drawn to the vivid red Virginia creeper that ceaselessly crept over massive grey boulders and wound itself up and around spindly yellow maples for all to behold.

"Grab that basket there, Poky. We gonna gather us some chestnuts today. They's plenty'uv'em, too, an' we'll make us a fair piece'uv money I figure." She carried two bushel baskets herself as they headed out from the cabin toward a stand of chestnut trees not too far in the distance. Poky loved to gather the prickly little nuts, and Sister Jane always made it a game, more fun than work.

But soon October came to a close, and the vibrant parade of colors vanished. A close to the national drama took place, as well. President McKinley's assassin, Leon Czolgosz, was put to death in the electric chair.

SEASONS PASSED INTO years, and Poky celebrated her seventh birthday in the year 1905. That severe winter finally ended, and she and Sister Jane rejoiced in yet another spring that caused Oak Mountain to come alive!

All morning Sister Jane had been working her herb garden, now she rested. Rocking back and forth in the porch rocker, she inhaled the sweet scented apple blossoms that surrounded her. The apple trees were in vibrant bloom...a time she much enjoyed each year...and the dogwoods were blooming, also, splashing the dark forest with their fragile white lacework. Suddenly a strong warm mountain breeze caused a breathtaking scene as it lifted thousands of white feathery petals from the apple trees, filling the air with their floating presence. Sister Jane smiled at this act of nature and once again considered herself blessed to live on Oak Mountain. She looked out beyond the apple trees to the chestnuts and poplars that towered above them. She could see Poky clear up in the top of the tallest poplar.

"Poky!" she hollered out loudly, "come down'ere right'is minute!"

"But, Mama," the small child hollered back, "it's so pretty up here...prettier than down below...I'm up'ere with th'birds...."

About that time, there was a loud SNAP and a wood splintering sound...and Poky was falling!

Sister Jane stood frozen to the porch.

She stopped falling, and her small body limply draped a sturdy bottom limb. Sister Jane hastened to her, crying wildly..."Poky...my baby...Poky...."

She reached the tree and looked up into the dark eyes of her Poky.

"I'm all right, Mama...don't worry...it jest knocked th'breath plum' out'a me...that's all."

Sister Jane's tears became tears of joy. So were the next few years...filled with such episodes of growing up on Oak Mountain. But as childhood has a way of doing, it subtly slipped by and vanished before her eyes.

Such was the day on April 15, 1912 when Sister Jane awoke to a beautiful spring morning arrayed in all its glory. She quickly finished the breakfast dishes, kissed Poky good-bye and followed her out to the porch to watch her leave for school. Poky walked down the path by the cabin that led to the road on below. She didn't skip anymore. Instead she walked with purpose and resolution. When she reached the bend in the path, she turned and waved. Sister Jane waved back and felt a sharp pain. She realized Poky was a child no more.

Suddenly a blue jay flew down from a nearby chestnut and perched itself on the porch rail, eyeing her cautiously.

"Don't worry none, old blue jay, I'm gonna be all right. I reckon yo' babies done growed up, too...jest up an' flew off I s'pose...an' you doin' all right...."

She slowly moved to the rocking chair and commenced to rock. The grove of apple trees on the north side were in full bloom again, and she welcomed their sweet fragrance drifting about. She glanced down beside the porch and to her delight, the first lilac bud had blossomed. Poky would be so happy when she got home from school. It was her bush, given to her by Maude Jones. She had admired Maude's big lilac bush so that Maude had given her a slip from it a couple of years ago. Poky had faithfully watered it that first year, and the second, and now finally she had a lilac bloom.

Within this tranquil setting, life took its course, and Sister Jane commenced to coughing. She coughed and coughed, echoing throughout the spring filled forest.

She was still sitting in the rocking chair when Poky returned from school...but her cough had ceased. At the tender age of fourteen, Poky found herself alone in the world.

Sister Jane lay in the pine coffin placed in the center of the small front room, her work-worn hands folded over her large bosom. The dull silver pieces, laying atop her once vibrant eyes, were a stark realization of death. Poky sat gravely beside the coffin, nodding to all who came to pay their respects; but inwardly, her young mind was racing...thinking of how she was going to survive. The perfume of lilac permeated the humble dwelling as the soft, lush purple flowers overflowed from a milk bottle on the table. Maude had brought them over, and Poky picked her own little lilac to place with them.

The next day, Sister Jane was buried under an apple tree out aways from the cabin, but within sight of the front porch where she loved to sit. Poky stayed on at the cabin, refusing to leave. Maude Jones offered to board her, but Poky would not leave her home or her mother's final resting place. Maude contented herself with stopping in daily to check on her, conveniently bringing odds and ends, leftover foods and whatever she thought pleasing to the young girl. Though Maude had a reputation on the mountain for crudeness, she had a soft spot in her heart for Sister Jane's orphan.

Poky decided not to return to school. She'd had enough of readin' an' writin' an' 'rithmetic, she figured. She was well read now and could do most any math necessary to figure out her livelihood. Besides, she needed her time more at home to work with her herb gardens. Already, the mountain folk were depending on her herbs just as they had Sister Jane's. Not only this, she was being called upon whenever a new baby needed to be birthed, as well; and by carrying on her mother's trades, she soon became self sufficient, no longer needing any handouts. Amazingly, the wisdom of this young girl, just fourteen, was already sought from day to day. The calming quality that filled Poky's cabin and her quiet patient life was like a magnet drawing in those with troubled lives...and there were more than enough of those on Oak Mountain. It never occurred to Poky to question her plight in life or to feel discontent; although in the beginning following her mother's death, she experienced loneliness...much loneliness. Then she discovered Sister Jane's old black Bible and began reading it every morning. Soon she was reading it every evening as well, finding answers to the many troubled questions that the mountain folk posed to her. She was delighted to find all the promises in it and was soon sharing them with those who entered her door.

One day she noticed the guitar hanging on the wall. It had hung there from the large nail for as long as she could remember, but Sister Jane had discouraged her from ever handling it, treating it as an evil object to avoid. But why did she keep it? She knew it had belonged to her father...the father she'd never known. Sister Jane only said...'Best to keep it for a rainy day, might bring a few pennies, never know.' But Poky was glad it hadn't been sold, although she'd thought of it a few times herself. It was a part of her past...a past she didn't know.

She reached up for it now and blew off the dust. Grabbing a dishrag, she commenced to wiping it. Its shrill tones reverberated off the cabin walls each time she hit a string. Right then and there, she decided she was going to learn to play it. The following week, she asked ol' Billy Watkins if he'd be so kind to teach her a few chords. Ol' Billy won't much at hard labor or any labor for that matter, but hardly anyone on Oak Mountain could match his nimble fingers on a banjo or guitar. After a few times, she commenced to teaching herself more than a few of her favorite tunes. The old guitar became her constant companion. Many an evening after a long hot day of working in her gardens, putting up jar after jar of her prized herbs or vegetables, the surrounding mountains absorbed the soothing sounds coming from the porch of the little cabin. And it was a good thing, too, for Poky would never know the joy of an earthly companion. And thus it was that Poky Fitzgerald became a permanent fixture on Oak Mountain.

CHAPTER THREE

1933

TROUBLED TIMES! Youthful America was struggling for survival. As raging waters seek out every crook and crevice, filling them beyond endurance, thus was the Great Depression. It reached into every home near about and touched every life, young and old. Its devastating tentacles poisoned all that it touched. Homes were wrecked, lives were destroyed, millions tasted hunger for the first time, and America groaned as a mother in travail. Soup lines were formed across the great land, Hoovervilles sprung up displaying wretched people barely existing in rusted out cars, orange crates and piano boxes, hobo jungles provided necessary survival ingredients to such vagrant travelers, great city parks and harbors witnessed scores of homeless people asleep on the cold sidewalks and, unfortunately, not infrequent mornings discovered an absence of some that could be seen floating in the harbor waters...too distressed to fight anymore. The wealthy jumped out of high windows, unable to face their great losses. Its tentacles not only wrapped around the great cities, but also reached out and found those small towns that previously existed practically unnoticed. And thus Lynchburg was found...and Hallie Daniels Frederick.

Even before the axe fell in the form of the Great Depression, the Daniels family had suffered many trials. The past three decades had taken both of Hallie's parents and her brothers. The baby boy that Sister Jane had so proudly birthed died from a severe case of whooping cough at the tender age of three. Her older brother, Carlton, had been tragically killed in a hunting accident. Her parents died naturally, but heart broken from the loss of their sons. Through surprising financial setbacks, the Daniels' estate had fallen into ruin, and Hallie and her older sister, Carrie, were left practically penniless. Carrie, depressed from it all, had moved away from Lynchburg with her husband to Richmond. There they had chosen to build their lives with hopes of more opportunity. Carrie seemed bent on putting as much distance between her and her past as possible. Only Hallie, now the youngest of the Daniels family, remained to eke out an existence. Life might have been kinder to young Hallie had it not been for the fact that she was determined to ignore her parents' wishes and married the gregarious but irresponsible Jon Franklin Frederick. What monies she'd inherited were long gone, and now she faced this dark period of history with little hope.

"Mama..." her eldest child called.

"Coming...hold on a minute...I'm getting your father's warmest scarf."

Jon Junior, a lanky teenager, paced the floor, anxious to be off. Already he was getting warm from the hot coal stove. Covered from head to toe, with both legs wrapped in croaker sacks ready to face the freezing temperatures, he wiped his forehead.

"Here you go." His mother handed him a red and white wool scarf, which he wound tightly around his neck.

"Now, son, please don't stay out in the cold too long. Remember last time...and watch those slippery sidewalks. They're nothing but sheets of ice."

"Don't worry, Mother. I better hurry...else I'll be late." He pulled open the door, and blustery cold air blew in behind him as he left. Hallie moved to the window, watching him leave with his head bent against the cold, his chin tucked in the scarf. Her heart ached for him. Too young for the burdens he carried...but she was grateful that old man Pantanna had given him a chance to work out their grocery bill. Again, it had run up too high. If only it was summer...or even fall...but it was so cold for delivery boys now...and Jon Junior seemed to keep a cold. She walked over to the secretary and sat down to write Poky, reaching for her tablet and pen...but no thoughts would come. She was tired. She looked at the portrait hanging on the wall beside the secretary. Her portrait. The innocent little girl's pixy face stared out at her. Was she ever so young and free from worry? It seemed so long ago...and she was reminded that it was long ago. She had a birthday coming up...forty-one years old. She stood up and wiped the dust from the portrait with her hand, recalling that day like it was yesterday. She and her mother and Carrie all going downtown to have her portrait done — family tradition her mother insisted. She smiled. What would her mother say now if she could see her circumstances? Suddenly there was a knock at the back door. She moved toward it, pushed back the curtain and peered out the window. All she could see was a pile of old clothing...then realized there was a person there. She opened the door.

"Ma'am, would ya' be s'kind to give me a little somethin' to eat?" the disheveled man begged.

"Step inside out of the cold, mister." She motioned him in, and he followed.

"Have a seat at the table there...I just happened to have a little cabbage and pork'n'beans left over and some rolls...take off your wraps and lay them over the chair yonder."

"Thank you, ma'am...you're ever so kind."

Hallie commenced to heat the leftovers and placed them in front of the humble beggar. She eyed him cautiously, not from fear but curiosity. She always wondered about these vagrants...and how they survived, and she never failed to feed them...hoping that someone would do the same for her Jon...wherever he was. She sat down at the table across from him as he devoured the food, obviously the first he'd had in awhile. The heavy bearded man looked up. "I was hoping you'd be the kindly type, ma'am...when I knocked, that is. You never know, 'specially down here. Ain't as many of us out needin' something to eat." He started to wipe his mouth on his sleeve, then looked up embarrassed and reached for the napkin.

"You're not from here, are you?" Hallie asked, pretending not to notice.

"No, ma'am. On my way further south. Been up around Pittsburgh mostly. Lot more of us there. Before that I was in New York. Now, that's a place to go hungry for sure...so we had a code we worked out among us...."

"A code?"

"Yes, ma'am. We marked the buildings, the brick apartment houses, you know, with chalk...usually the back door. By the codes...we let each other know which houses would give us food...and which ones wouldn't...."

"Clever."

"Yes, ma'am. It was. We always looked out for one another. 'Course when no food was to be had, sometimes we'd drift back to the sally...."

"The sally?"

"The Salvation Army, ma'am. We call it the sally."

"I see. How long you been out of work?"

"Goin' on nigh two years. 'Course I pick up a little here and there. Times are hard...but maybe they'll be changing now with this here Roosevelt."

"I certainly hope so. How're you traveling?"

"Boxcar mostly. Gettin' mighty crowded these days though...."

Hallie nodded sadly. That was the worst of it...these hard times...the degrading of America's men. Again, she thought of Jon. The front door opened and closed. Jamey and Lauralee appeared in the kitchen doorway, rubbing their cold hands together. They'd set a crumpled sack on the floor between them.

"These are my children. Say hello, Jamey and Lauralee...this is Mr...."

"Mr. Lawrence, ma'am...the name's Lawrence. I'd best be gettin' along now. Thank you kindly for your good food." With that, he stood, obviously feeling uncomfortable being so long apart from normal family life. Once he'd gone with a wrinkled brown bag concealing a sandwich and a small piece of cornbread, Jamey spoke up, "Mama, why're you giving food away? I thought you said we didn't have hardly enough left for us...."

"That's true, son. But if we expect God to take care of us, we certainly have to be sensitive to those around us with less."

"I learned about that in Sunday school last week," Lauralee piped in."

"Well, I'm proud of you, Lauralee...you've been listening."

"But he didn't look much like Jesus."

"Jesus?"

"Miss Hall said what we give to the poor...we're really giving to Jesus."

"Miss Hall was right. It's the same as if we actually were giving it to Jesus when we gave the food to Mr. Lawrence. Jesus looks at it that way."

"Maybe we should've given him more, Mama."

"Maybe," she agreed and turned to the large dirty bag propped beside the door where they'd left it. "Got some coal, I suppose?"

"We were real lucky, Mama," Jamey answered proudly, "that old freight must've thrown off more than it hauled. Got almost a whole bag this time."

"Thank you, children. But do be careful around those tracks. You know how I fear trains...."

"Don't worry, Mama. I'm always careful, and I don't let Lauralee get near the tracks. I pick it up and toss it to her, and she fills up the bag. We got it down pat now." He winked at his little sister.

"That's right, Mama. We got it down pat."

Hallie began washing up the dishes. "Lauralee, how would

you like to have a new pair of shoes?"

"Really, Mama...can I...please?"

"Well, it just so happens you were the lucky little girl chosen at church...and a Mr. Statler will be coming by this Saturday to pick you up and take you to be fitted. Mr. Statler is a fairly new member in the church." She stacked the dishes neatly in the dish drainer.

Lauralee commenced to jumping up and down for joy, and Hallie's heart was gladdened. Thus she suppressed the feelings of frustration at the thought of more charity.

"Gosh, Mama, why her? I need shoes more than her!"

"Now, Jamey. We'll see about your shoes later on. We can't just now. You're older and should be more understanding about these things. Your brother, Jon Junior, needs shoes worse than any of us...and he isn't complaining...."

"Where is he?"

"Delivering for old Mr. Pantanna."

"When can I do that? I never get to do anything but pick up coal!"

"Certainly delivering groceries in this kind of weather is not anything to yearn for."

"Mama, look what I got."

"Lauralee, you ruined another penny!"

"I told'er, Mama...but she wouldn't listen. Anyhow, it's just a penny."

"Jamey, pennies make nickels and nickels make dimes."

"I know, I know, Mama...."

"Lauralee, please don't put anymore pennies on the tracks! Those tracks are for streetcars...not for pennies...."

"I won't, Mama...but look how pretty it is...all flattened out...and you did say I could spend my money from Mrs. Doughty the way I want to...."

Hallie shook her head, "You're right, of course, but you must consider carefully how you use your money. Times are hard, and there are people without any money...a lot of people...like that Mr. Lawrence who just left."

"He looked awful dirty and all hairy."

"He can't help it, Lauralee. But he seemed to be a good man on the inside...and isn't that what really counts?"

"Yes, ma'am. Can I go to the picture show on Saturday, Mama? I have my money. Mrs. Doughty got me to go for her *True Story* magazine two times this week."

"My goodness. Why she wants to read such...."

"She said she forgot to get the last issue and so she had to buy both."

"Just junk reading, that's all...but the money's good for you, Lauralee. If this cold lets up some, I suppose you can go."

Lauralee skipped off and Jamey followed, "Gonna work on my school paper."

Hallie nodded and dried her hands on the dishtowel hanging on the wall, walked back over to the secretary, and picked up her tablet again to finish her letter to Poky. The radio was playing softly in the background, and she heard those familiar words that seemed to be of everyday life now.

They used to tell me I was building a dream
And so I followed the mob
When there was earth to plough or guns to bear
I was always there — right there on the job
They used to tell me I was building a dream
With peace and glory ahead
Why should I be standing in line just waiting for bread?
Once I built a railroad, made it run
Made it race against time
Once I built a railroad, Now it's done
Brother can you spare a dime?
Once I built a tower, to the sun
Brick and rivet and lime
Once I built a tower, now it's done
Brother, can you spare a dime?
Once in khaki suits — Gee, we looked swell!

Full of that Yankee Doodle-de-dum
Half a million boots went sloggin' thru Hell
I was the kid with the drum
Say don't you remember, they called me Al
It was Al- all the time
Say, don't you remember — I'm your pal
Buddy, can you spare a dime?

The pensive words held her captive, unable to write until it ended. She sighed and began in her neat and still fashionable style....

Dear Poky...

Again the front door slammed. "Mama...."

"In here, Jon Junior...you're back so early?"

"Mr. Pantanna didn't have but two deliveries today. He said time's getting worse. Folks not buying."

"I see."

"Mama?"

"Yes, dear." Noticing the urgency in his voice, she looked up.

"I've gotta do something...find a job somewhere...."

"I know, dear, but I'm sure things will change soon. You'll find something."

"I don't know. I'm beginning to doubt it, and this delivery job just isn't gonna do it." He slumped down in a chair.

"Well, it's better than nothing."

"I'm gonna lay down a bit, Mama. Feel like my cold's getting worse." He proceeded to unwrap the croaker sacks from his stiff legs.

"Take some aspirin first, son." She turned back to her letter. She'd tell Poky of her trials. Poky always made her feel better in her letters. Just thinking of her long time pen-pal cheered her, and her mind wandered back all those years to Court Street when she was just a child, and Aunt Bertha's sister, Sister Jane, brought Poky to visit them. She smiled to herself. What a cute little baby she was! She'd won her heart then and still held it. Though she didn't see Poky again as a child, they were encouraged to write one another as soon as Poky learned to write. She recalled that first letter and how hard it was to read. She was a teenager then, and Poky was only about five or six. But it didn't take long...and her letters were a never ending joy, full of details of mountain life which Hallie yearned for herself. However, she never had the opportunity to go until Sister Jane died. She remembered again with fondness that trip to Oak Mountain. It was their second meeting...her's and Poky's. She was home from college just before she dropped out to marry Jon. Aunt Bertha received word of her sister's death, and she carried on so, her father decided to take her to Oak Mountain. They allowed her to go with them, and as long as she lived, she'd never forget that scene. The corpse, the large silver pieces and Poky's solemn vigil. Of course, she wasn't her real mother...but the only mother Poky had ever known. There with all the mountain folk coming and going, paying their respects, she had certainly felt like a stranger. She sensed that Poky, even midst her grief, understood and felt for her. Every time their eyes met, Poky had smiled at her, endearing their friendship even more, forming a bond that would last a lifetime. It wasn't until much later that they'd learned about Poky remaining alone, a fact that caused a deep sense of guilt thereafter for both Hallie and her father. Now as she picked up the tablet, she began again her letter to Poky... *'My heart is heavy. Times are getting harder, and the future looks dim. Jon Junior can't find work and is burdened as well. I don't know what I'd do if it wasn't for the church. They've been paying half our rent for the past six months. There're so many kind folk in the church, old families that knew my family years ago...but there's an ache in my heart when I have to receive charity. I know I have too much pride...and I know God doesn't like pride...but it's hard to hold your head up when you feel so dependent. Maybe if I had more faith like you, it would be easier. Poky, I do wish I could see you. I know a visit with you would be a healing touch. Of course, it's out of the question...there's certainly no extra money for a trip. Forgive me for laying my burdens on you. I sure hope you're faring all right during these hard times.'*

POKY BENT HER hooded head against the blowing, blinding snow as she forged ahead on foot, pushing out of her path pine boughs already laden with a heavy wet blanket. A frozen twig reached out for her, jabbing at her right eye. She winced, clutched her worn black bag and kept on going, carefully picking up her heavy brown boots which left obvious footprints in the new fallen snow. However, the tracks were quickly filled in with fine wet flakes. Her visage was that of a sorcerer or witch with her long black cloak and conspicuous bent over body. Every now and then her prominent nose and high cheek bones were visible, contrasting against her black attire. "This trail is too growed up," she mumbled. "Come spring, I'll need t'sickle it down some. A body can't see where they're goin'." But she knew the trail well without looking. She'd often been summoned to the Branham household, which was on the adjacent mountain called High Peak. Trudging down the side of Oak Mountain, across the narrow valley that separated the two, she soon began her ascent up High Peak. Fortunately, they didn't live too far up. How many children would this make? she pondered. Lemme see...should make 'bout five. Four boys already an' th'two that'd arrived too soon an' didn't make it. Maybe this'un will be a girl...be nice for th'missus. She sho could use some help. Poky shook her head against the cold wind and her thoughts. These were hard times t'birth a baby. Th'country all messed up an' all, folks goin' hungry, committin' suicide an' sech. Hard to understan'! Why in th'world would ya' do a thing like that? Jumpin' out'a windows from them skyscraper buildings jest 'cause they done lost all their money! Folks were messed up all right, puttin' more stock in things than life itself!

She heard a bobcat in the distance, and wondered if it was the one she'd spotted day before yesterday. The moaning wind drowned out its eerie call, and she remembered the keen, steady gaze of that cunning creature so like her own mama cat back home. It was mating time, and she figured that call could'a been part of its courtin'. She smiled and returned to her former thoughts. She was glad she was here on Oak Mountain. It was'a sight better'n city life nowadays...accordin' t'what th'papers say an' what Hallie writes. Leastways here on Oak Mountain, a body has a place t'lay his head an' don't get kicked out, an' folks have vittles from summer cannin'. What would she do without her garden? She couldn't imagine. Poor Hallie an' all her young'uns an' no home'uv her own...an' no husband neither. Where on earth could that man be? Maybe he'd up an' run out on'em for good like her daddy had done, leavin' her an orphan. But Sister Jane was there. This snowstorm reminded her of th'many times she'd struggled along side'uv her, bumping into her black bag. She hugged it to her now. How she missed her! Yet an' still, she had a good life, no use complainin'. She had her home an' friends an' food t'eat...more'n a lot'uv folks now. Again she thought of Hallie. She recalled what the preacher had said just th'other day..."Why, Miss Poky," he'd said, "I do believe you were put on this here earth to help other folk". She kind'a liked that...yes sir, she liked that a lot. When th'weather breaks an' spring commences t'warm these mountains, think I might jest take a trip. I might jest take a trip t'Lynchburg for a spell!

"WHERE'S POKY?" The eldest of the four boys demanded of no one in particular, knowing that no one had the answer.

"I don't know where in tarnation she is! Can't go birthin' no baby at my age...don't know nothin' 'bout it," Mr. Branham fumed, excited and distressed at the same time at the idea, while pacing the usually clean swept front yard, now covered with snow.

The youngest, almost ten, was oblivious to the whole affair and sat contentedly on the wooden crate by the front door, sucking on what was left of the prized black licorice given to him by his Uncle Pete three days prior. With black juice oozing down his chin, he asked, "Why can't mama have th'baby on'er own? Why she gotta have Poky anyhows?"

"That's what midwives are for, stupid...got *you* here, didn't she?" Jack Jacob, the oldest, answered crossly, "...an' you better get your coat on 'fore you catch your death in this'ere snowstorm."

"Ain't no snowstorm...just a nice batch'uv snow fallin' for me to go sleddin' on tomorrow."

"Is so a snowstorm," George Lewis, next to the oldest, added proudly. "The snow's fallin' an' the winds blowin'...that's a snowstorm sure 'nough."

"Cut that fussin' out," Mr. Branham chided, "...got more important things to figger on."

"Tha' she is!" Jack Jacob let out down the front yard, slipping and sliding half the way in his effort to meet Poky, who was just coming up the path, huffing and puffing and brushing snow off her covered head.

"Careful there, young feller...gonna break your neck...."

"Miss Poky...hurry...mama's awful sick. This baby's done it. Pa said so."

Poky caught the fear in the young fellow's eyes and hurried up to the porch with Mr. Branham helping her up the slippery steps. "So glad you're here, ma'am."

All the years of experience at her fingertips, Poky quickly set about the familiar duties, shooing off the clan to other parts of the small cabin, placing a big iron pot of water on the hot wood stove and wiping the sweaty forehead of the obviously weary mother, who smiled up at her weakly.

"Gonna have that girl, Mrs. Branham?"

"No matter...just get it here, Miss Poky," she winced in pain.

"We'll do just that!"

Later, as she sat beside the small, frail mother who'd drifted off into a restless half sleep, she felt a kinship. Neither knew for certain their heritage, but both knew they were part Indian. She'd been told her own mother's folk were Cherokee...a scattered few that decided to settle in the Virginia Blue Ridge while on one of their many treks back and forth from North Carolina to Washington to see the president or some government official...and maybe so. But these folk that lived in the High Peak settlement knew they were of Indian descent, but they weren't quite sure which tribe, and it didn't matter particularly. They knew they were different and everyone else knew they were different...and because of that, they were ostracized! Driven from society, forced to band together midst the folds, ridges and protected hollers of the Blue Ridge. Poky felt for them deeply. Though she, too, was part Indian, she'd escaped their cruel plight...because she was Sister Jane's child. The Colored folk loved her. The white folk accepted her as ol' man Maxie Fitzgerald's offspring. And even though his reputation was certainly tainted, the Fitzgeralds had been around Oak Mountain for a long time. But these folk, branded as *Issues*, were outcasts. Poky swallowed hard. It jest won't fair!

The first rays of light fell upon the snow laden cabin, and a fifth son let out his lusty cry.

"What's this one gonna be called, Mrs. Branham?"

"*Barclay...Barclay Branham.*"

"No middle name?"

"No middle name...don't need none."

"That's fine an' dandy, Mrs. Branham. I'll get his pa."

When Poky returned home, a pleasant surprise awaited her...Hallie's letter. Quickly fixing herself a cup of hot tea spiced with her own herbs, she sat down to enjoy the letter. Each word from Hallie convinced her that she must make that visit when the first signs of spring occurred.

THE ICE MELTED, and a few warm February days were welcomed in downtown Lynchburg with people turning out from everywhere, walking the streets...window shopping...a favorite pastime of the era. It gave them a sense of joy to look, wish and think that one day things would be better.

Mr. Statler stepped briskly down Main Street on his way to G.A. Coleman & Company, an established shoe store, with Lauralee in tow, trying hard to keep up with his sweeping stride. Every now and then he half turned to see that she was still there.

"Come along, child," he chided as she slowed to stare at a beautiful blue silk dress draped over a bald child mannequin in a passing window, her heart tugging. But she hurried to catch up...she was gonna get new shoes!

The heavy door closed behind them, and Lauralee stood glued to her spot staring at hundreds of shoes, all shapes and sizes.

"This way, child," Mr. Statler urged impatiently.

"Good morning, sir. It's a pleasure seeing you today and on such a fine day, too, I might add," a dark, lean clerk with a curling mustache said as he appeared from around shelves loaded with men's shoes, "...and who do we have here?" He looked questioningly from the tall gentleman, handsomely attired, to the poorly dressed child, who stood timidly peering up at him.

"The child needs shoes as you can see, sir. Would you be so kind to fit her? I'm acting on behalf of First Baptist, another one of its many charities, of course."

"Of course."

Lauralee quickly looked up, recognizing that word. She felt her face grow hot. Mama had said charity wasn't good. She followed the clerk to a row of chairs, wondering why mama had sent her. The joy and anticipation of the new shoes began to dim, and suddenly she wished she wasn't there. Looking back toward the door, she realized that was foolish. Mama wanted her to get new shoes...and she was gonna get them! Obediently, she tried on the shoes the clerk placed before her...a dainty pair of black slippers, with shiny gold latches, that fit perfectly. She reluctantly smiled up at the hurried Mr. Statler.

He nodded, "We'll take those."

"Certainly, Mr. Statler, and it's sure a benevolent deed you do today...obviously the child has needed shoes for some time." He frowned at the dirty, torn shoes he placed in the box. "They always like to wear the new ones, you know."

Lauralee looked down, trying not to hear, and her heart seemed to skip a beat at the sight of those dainty new slippers on her tiny feet...it was worth it.

That night as she placed them carefully beside her bed, she knelt to say her prayers. Hallie knelt beside her. "Don't forget to thank God for your new slippers. You know the Bible says all good things come from God."

"I know, Mama...but He sure has a funny way of giving them."

"What do you mean?"

"Like Mr. Statler...how come he bought me the shoes when he didn't like me?"

Hallie stiffened. "Why do you say that?"

"I could tell, Mama, the way he looked at me...and talked to me. Are we really poor, Mama?"

Hallie pulled her young daughter to her. "We are going through hard times, dear, just like lots of people. But we're not supposed to like people or not like people by how much they have. You know God looks on the heart...not on the outside...."

"I don't think Mr. Statler does, Mama. But that's all right. I got my shoes and...I don't mind."

As they bowed their heads and Lauralee prayed..."*Now I lay me down to sleep, I pray the Lord my soul to keep...*," Hallie choked back her tears.

THOSE WARM FEBRUARY days did their job of melting the snow on Oak Mountain, as well as drawing out the mountain folk to soak up the sunny rays, even though winter still held its bite. Poky inhaled the sharp chilling air, and decided to call on the Branhams...to check on little Barclay. She'd go directly after lunch. It'd probably be even warmer then. Gently closing the door behind her, she plopped down in her second hand stuffed chair and picked up her favorite book, *Pilgrim's Progress.* It was her fourth time to read it. Given to her many years ago, it had become her favorite outside of the Good Book. She still remembered vaguely the old itinerant preacher traveling through Oak Mountain on his tired old mule with his Bible on one side of his saddle bag and *Pilgrim's Progress* on the other. It wasn't new then. He'd read it a plenty before giving it to her. She'd resisted, not wanting to take his only copy, but he'd adamantly insisted on her having it. She often wondered what ever happened to the old preacher. She figured God wanted her to have the book, and the preacher was just about the only way she would've gotten it. The first time she'd tried to read it, it was a struggle to understand it, but now she practically felt a kinship to Christian; a lot of his troubles were just like her own. She began to read the part about Mistrust and Timorous and those lions they fled, but not Christian. '*The lions were chained, but he saw not the chains. Then he was afraid, and thought also himself to go back after them, for he thought nothing but death was before him. But the Porter at the lodge, whose name is Watchful, perceiving that Christian made a halt, as if he would go back, cried unto him saying, "Is thy strength so small? Fear not the lions, for they are chained, and are placed there for trial of faith where it is, and for discovery of those that have none. Keep in the midst of the path, and no hurt shall come unto thee."*' She smiled, remembering how that passage had encouraged her when she was so young...and somewhat timorous like the fellow that fled the lions. 'Course nobody ever believed she could be timorous...but she knew. After Sister Jane died, she woke many a night in the dark, frightened and alone. But she'd kept in the midst of the path...the Lord's path...and truly no hurt had come to her. She continued to read about her friend, Christian. '*Then I saw that he went on, trembling for fear of the lions, but taking good heed to the directions of the Porter; he heard them roar, but they did him no harm. Then he clapped his hands, and went on till he came and stood before the gate where the Porter was. Then said Christian to the Porter, "Sir, what house is this? And may I lodge here tonight?" The Porter answered, "This house was built by the Lord of the hill, and He built it for the relief and security of pilgrims."*'

She closed the old book and sighed. She'd had many lions in her days since then. Her faith had been tested, but it was God's promise that had always sustained her... *'I will never leave thee, nor forsake thee.'* But with His promises came commandments. Just like in Hebrews before He promised to never leave nor forsake, He said... *'Let your conversation be without covetousness; and be content with such things as ye have.'* Now that was somethin' t'mull over. These'ere folk that're jumpin' out'a windows 'cause'uv things are sadly mistaken...thinkin' them things gonna make'em happy. God never meant it that'a way. Oh well...she rose to fix her dinner.

The path was much different now, quite pleasant, in fact, as she painstakingly made her journey down the rugged mountainside and across the narrow valley. Though it was February and most of the mountain creatures still chose their snug secluded dens, a few did venture forth, fooled by the unexpected warmth. Poky heard a rustle in the nearby brush, and quickly turned, but the intruder had apparently vanished. Picking up her stride across the welcomed but soggy valley, she yearned for the upcoming spring...just weeks away now and these mountains would once again return to their lively, bustling nature. Hardly able to wait, she thought of the garden she'd plant. She wanted to plant more this year if possible...more needy folk, and it did her good to help out. She'd take lots with her to visit Hallie...and she could bring some over to the Branhams, give her a reason to visit little Barclay. Poor Mrs. Branham had such a brood to feed and one more now, and Zeke Branham seemed like a hard man, a good man most likely, but a hard man just the same. Some of the womenfolk like her must surely face a difficult life. She reckoned there were some blessings in being alone after all.

Her knock reverberated off the rough-hewn door, and she heard a baby's cry. She was smiling when Mrs. Branham slowly opened the door, and the afternoon sunlight fell into the darkened cabin.

"Why, Miss Poky...do come on in."

"Jest thought I'd mosey over an' check on our lil' man here...." Glancing down into the oversized drawer made into a comfortable crib, she felt the kinship she had with all her babies. The tiny infant made her think of the blessed Christmas story, looking as if he was wrapped in swaddling clothes, too.

"How's he doin'?"

"Fine, Miss Poky, just fine...th'best one so far...he's a good baby."

Taking in the untidiness of the cabin, Poky asked, "Mind if I help out a bit...know ya' must be all tuckered out...no daughters...all boys, an' I know they ain't much good at women things."

Mrs. Branham laughed, "You're sho right about that, an' I'd be obliged for ya' to help. But first you gotta hold Barclay since he wouldn't be here if'n it won't for you." She reached down, and tenderly handed him to Poky, who proudly drew the little fellow close to her, feeling the intense pride as always with the babies she'd birthed.

"Barclay...Barclay Branham...you've got a fine name, lil' feller. Where'd ya' get sech a nice soundin' name, Mrs. Branham? I never heard tell'uv it before."

"Just before his birth, I was over at my cousin Lew James Adcock's in Amherst. He got'im one'uv them nice radios...a big thing...stands up on th'floor an' all...me an' him listened to it practically all morning. You know, they got 'lectricity where he lives. Well, I heard this here feller on th'radio called *Barclay*...an' I decided right then an' there that my baby was gonna be called *Barclay*...sounds strong an' clear an' has class...don't you think so, Miss Poky?"

"I reckon I do...class...that's it...I knew it was somethin'. Be sure ya' spell it right on th'birth certificate now. Don't wanna mess up a nice name like that."

Mrs. Branham hung her head.

"Did I say somethin' wrong?"

"Nothin', Miss Poky. I jest wish they wouldn't put mulatto on it. He ain't Colored. Look at that skin. Look at them cheek bones. He's *Indian* all right. Don't get me wrong, Miss Poky. I ain't got nothin' against th'Colored, an' I loved your Sister Jane like everybody else...but Barclay ain't Mulatto or Colored!"

"I know that, an' you know that, Mrs. Branham...but th'gover'ment says it has t'be that'a'way, so I wouldn't fret about it if I was you. Won't do no good."

"It ain't Roosevelt's gover'ment. It's th'Virginia gover'ment."

"I know. But maybe Roosevelt will change that, too. He's makin' a lot'uv changes with his new deal."

"That's how Cousin Lew got his new radio at Wards...they was havin' a sale...a *new deal sale....*"

Poky laughed, "I ain't surprised. Everything is th'new deal. Gonna get me one'a them radios one day when we get 'lectricity."

"Times is hard, Miss Poky. Zeke ain't been able t'find work like before. 'Course we'll make out I reckon...like we always do. But I sho hope Roosevelt can do somethin'."

"I do, too, Mrs. Branham, but I figure we better pray an' trust the good Lord. He's th'one really in control, ya' know."

"I'm doin' that for sho, an' I'm fixin' to get back to church soon's I can."

"St. Paul's...th'mission?"

"That's right."

"Ya' know, Mrs. Branham, I've been meanin' t'visit St. Paul's. But I've been at th'Methodist Church nigh since I was'a little'un...you know how it is."

"I hope you do, Miss Poky, 'cause we'd love to have you. You're just like one'uv us."

Weeks passed. The first of April arrived, and true to her word, Poky showed up at the little mission in the hollow, St. Paul's Episcopal Church. Before she rounded the bend in the narrow country road, she could hear the joyful singing emanating from the small new chapel nestled among aged grey boulders of the Blue Ridge and a babbling creek that rose with rage whenever the rains suddenly came. Built only three years prior, right after its predecessor had sadly burned, it still gleamed with fresh white paint. As the quaint little church came into view, Poky noticed the curl of smoke rising up from its chimney, blending with the hazy blue mist that generally hung over the Blue Ridge often until late morning. It was a welcomed sight. The early spring morning still held a raw chill that reached into her familiar black cape and didn't stop until it totally penetrated each and every bone. Approaching the backside of the chapel, acknowledging the spray of weeping willow with its bright green new growth gracing the rear of the church and now gleaming in the fresh sunlight that pierced the blue haze, she was anxious to join in the spirited singing and hurried her step. The sight of the little chapel, perched upon a large flat granite boulder, gave her goose bumps...surely it was founded on the rock! She smiled to herself as she walked around to the front door, slowly pushing it open. The bold words grasped her... *'When we've been there ten thousand years, bright shining as the sun, we've no less days to sing God's praise than when we'd first begun....'*

The upright piano in the corner silenced, and the congregation sat down, along with Poky on the last pew. So caught up with the spirit of the place, she was astonished when the last amen was said. It couldn't be over already! But another good hour was spent with folk milling around inside and outside, discussing what had gone on the week before and what might happen in the approaching week. Poky had never felt such bonded love, such closeness within a group, such security. Suddenly she wanted more than anything to be a part of this close knit group. She was standing there alone under a tall sycamore tree when Mrs. Branham came up with little Barclay all bundled up in her arms, with the boys following.

"Miss Poky, so glad t'see ya'."

"Same t'you, Mrs. Branham. I told ya' I'd be visitin'. Hello, Jack Jacob, George Lewis, Herman Ray an' Paul David...now I know why Barclay don't have no middle name." She chuckled. "You must be plum' tired'uv sayin' all them names."

The proud mother smiled while unraveling some of the layers of coarse muslin, displaying the small round head that held those dark penetrating eyes.

"He's puttin' on weight, fillin' out all right."

"Already weighs more'n Paul David did at this age."

"Gonna be a big feller, he is."

CHAPTER FOUR

LEONARD EVANS AND Mr. Davis chatted on while Poky leaned stiffly out the car window, anxious to catch the first glimpse of Lynchburg.

"They just keep goin' up. Can't keep them prices down. What can you do? Gotta have seed!"

"You're right about that. Folks gotta eat."

As the Model-T picked up speed, coasting down the steep hill toward the bridge, all Poky could see was a heavy rolling mist rising up from the easy flowing James, concealing the small town.

"Mighty foggy 'round the river."

"Sure is, Leonard. Can't see a thing."

"Always like this?"

"Oh no, Poky, sometimes it's clear as a full moon on fresh fallen snow."

"Now I don't know 'bout that, Leonard." Mr. Davis grinned.

The Model-T chugged slowly across the viaduct, through the heavy fog and abruptly appeared on the other side with Lynchburg rising sharply before them. Wakening to the warm morning sun, the quaint town yawned with early risers anxiously coming to market with their particular wares. A lumbering wagon rumbled past, and a hurried trolley clanged noisily by, half full of sleepy townsfolk dressed for a new day. They pulled up behind a slow moving wagon loaded down with milk, obviously a dairy farmer from across the river. Poky's eyes widened with all the excitement, and she again recalled Sister Jane's description of the town many years ago. It was even more exciting!

After a slow, but interesting ride down Main Street, with store owners unlocking their doors, lifting shades and placing "OPEN" signs strategically in windows, the street took on a different appearance. Small residential houses now lined it. Shortly after passing Pearl Street, Mr. Davis stopped in front of an humble two-story house on the lower end of Main Street that looked as if it had once been a store of some description. An upstairs porch perched awkwardly above long narrow columns. Obviously, it could stand some repair with shutters hanging carelessly crooked and paint peeling in several places.

"This it, Miss Poky?"

"We just passed *Pearl*...s'posed t'be between *Pearl* an' *Chestnut*...an' it does look like'a store instead'uv a house...must be...."

Just then a door opened, and Hallie waved to them.

"Thank you ever s'much, Mr. Davis. There's Miss Hallie now, just a wavin'. I'm certainly obliged t'you." She was already tumbling out of the car, pulling her large black valise behind her.

"Think nothin' of it, ma'am. Glad to be of service to you, and hope you have a nice visit here in the city."

Hallie was quickly descending the steps while pulling a yellow shawl around her thin shoulders, with Jamey close behind her. "Poky, you made it!"

"I told ya' I'd be here, didn't I?" She laughed with joy.

Jamey came up behind her. "Want me to help with your suitcase?"

"That'd be right nice'uv you...you must be Jamey...I didn't 'spect you t'be so grown up lookin'."

The young boy grinned under his heavy load.

"Now don't strain yourself there, son, an' don't think I'm comin' t'stay forever. That ain't filled with my belongin's, mind ya'. Got them in here." She patted a brown paper sack tucked under her arm.

Jamey looked at the valise questioningly.

"It's full'uv goodies for you folks."

Hallie smiled. "This way, Poky." She led her up the steps and into the house.

Later that evening when all was quiet finally, Hallie and Poky sat opposite each other sipping Poky's special brewed tea in the cozy living room, mixed with worn but elegant Victorian furniture and cheap odds and ends. The wind rattled loose window shutters as April struggled with March for ownership.

"Why didn't ya' tell me 'bout Jon Junior in ya' letter?"

"I didn't know then. It was quite sudden."

"An' ya' say he jest left three days ago?"

"That's right, and you're a Godsend, Poky, helping to take my mind off him. I thought I'd experienced heartbreak when Jon left...but I never really knew heartbreak until this...seeing my first born leave home. I can't explain it. Everywhere I look, I see him, or the absence of him. I go into the bathroom and see the empty spot where his shaving soap and razor always laid. I go into the boys' room and see his bed all made up, empty now...."

"What made'im decide t'go?"

"He's such a good boy, Poky. Of course, he wouldn't want me calling him a boy if he could hear me." She smiled. "But he's thinking of us, Jamey, Lauralee and me. You see, he'll get thirty dollars every month, and he'll send all of it home except for five dollars which he'll keep for his own personal needs and such. That's the way it's set up...the way the government set it up."

"This'ere CCC...what's it stan' for anyhow?"

"Civilian Conservation Corps...part of Roosevelt's New Deal. He says they'll be working in the forests making parks and such, conserving our natural resources. But at the same time, they'll be helping out their families back home...and also themselves. They'll teach them skills. Of course, it's just temporary employment," she sighed, "but at least, it's employment. I'm really glad for Jon Junior most of all, though. He's been so restless and down, not being able to find work and help out. This will give him something to be proud of finally. It's just so hard seeing him leave."

"Never havin' any young'uns, 'course I can't completely sympathize with ya'. But I know it must be hard."

Suddenly Hallie felt sorry for her dear friend not knowing the joy of motherhood. "But Poky, you do have so many children. You've said so yourself...all those little ones you've brought into the world."

"Speakin'uv that, I have'a new one, an' he's real special like. Name's Barclay Branham...fine lookin' lil' feller. Wish ya' could see'im. Got th'prettiest eyes ya' ever did see...an' even though he's just an infant, he looks at me like he knows me already."

Hallie smiled. "I'm sure he does."

"He's from th'High Peak area 'cross th'holler from Oak Mountain. I been knowin' his folks for some time, has four older brothers. His people, I mean th'whole lot'uv'em, they stay t'themselves. Can't say as I blame'em, th'way folks treat'em, but they've accepted me like one'uv their own."

"How do folks treat them?"

"Bad, Miss Hallie, badlike. Treat their dogs better. Folks say they're different, got'a different ancestry or somethin'. 'Course I know they're Indian or leastways part Indian. But other folk don't wanna believe that. They call'em names."

"Names?"

"Yes, ma'am, call'em *Issues* mostly."

"Issues? You mean like the term "free issue" used to describe the Negroes that were freed before the war?"

"I don't know. But that's what th'folks livin' in th'settlement are called, an' it ain't meant nice like for sho. They mean it in'a bad way." She looked around and half whispered, "It's like callin'em 'Indian bastards' or somethin'. 'Course th'settlement folk hate this name, hate it worse than all th'others they're called."

"I can see why. What a shame. Makes you wonder how people can be so cruel."

"Always been people like that, Miss Hallie, from th'beginnin'uv time been folks like that. I hope you don't mind me askin', Miss Hallie,...but have ya' heard anything a'tall from your Jon?"

Hallie's face whitened. "No, Poky, not a word."

"What ya' reckon got into'im, Miss Hallie?"

Hallie seemed to drift off. "Well...Poky...you'd have to know Jon. He was so full of fun and laughter when we met, but then when the children started coming, he seemed to change. Just wasn't one for responsibility, I guess. Seemed to burden him more than most people. And then when times got hard...well, he just sort of pulled a wall in around him. When he left, saying he was going to look for work...I wondered then if I'd ever see him again...."

Poky listened.

"I don't know whether he's dead or alive. Been over a year now. Sometimes I think I could accept it better if I knew he was dead...but then by not knowing, I still have hope."

"That's good, Miss Hallie, hope...we need hope. Hope an' th'good Lord will keep us goin'."

"I know, Poky. I just wish I had your faith."

"Nonsense! Th'Lord gives to us all. You jest gotta trust Him. That's one'uv my favorite verses... *'Trust in th'Lord with all thine heart, an' lean not unto thine own understandin'.'* God never meant for us t'understan' everything down here. That's how he tests our faith...we gotta trust Him."

Hallie smiled at her friend through teary eyes.

"You gotta trust his promises, Miss Hallie, like th'one that comes after my favorite verse I jest said...in Proverbs... *'In all thy ways, acknowledge Him, an' He shall direct thy paths.'* If we look t'Him in everything we have t'do, He's promised t'show us th'way."

"That's certainly comforting because I often feel like I don't know what to do next."

"I know 'xactly what ya' mean. How're th'other two copin' with Jon Junior's goin'?"

"They miss him for sure. No doubt there's insecurity, what with their father leaving and now Jon Junior, whom they both looked up to, but they're doing all right. Lauralee, you know, is a busy little bee, very active, and she's so close to me. It's Jamey I'm more concerned about, particularly his attitude lately. I sense bitterness and maybe anger...something I never had with Jon Junior."

"Well, all folks handle problems an' disappointments different like, an' he's had a lot'uv disappointments for a young feller."

"I know, and he was always the closest to his father...at least as close as Jon would let him be. Jon was never real comfortable with the father role. Guess my folks were right after all."

"Well, some folks have a hard time meetin' what life dishes up, others jest ride their troubles out with ease, seems like. We're all different, ya' know."

"Oh, Poky, it's just so nice having you here. I do hope you can stay a good while."

"I figure a couple'uv weeks at th'most, then I best be gettin' on back up t'th'mountain. Folks will commence t'missin' me most likely." She chuckled.

"I'm sure they will. I want you to go with us to church next week and meet my friends. They'll love you."

"You mean that big, fancy lookin' church you sent me a picture'uv?"

"That's right. First Baptist. It's not far from here, and we walk every Sunday morning."

"My, my...that'll be somethin' t'tell th'folks back home."

Hallie just smiled.

The days all but flew by with each one shortening the delightful visit with Poky. One week passed. Saturday morning arrived, and Lauralee bounced into the kitchen where

Hallie was stirring the steaming oatmeal, its sweet aroma filling the small kitchen. Poky was mixing up her tea.

"Mama, can I go to the picture show today, and can I take Poky with me, please? I know she wants to go. She already told me so."

Poky looked up sheepishly.

"You did?"

"Well, sort'uv. Always did wanna see one'uv them movin' picture shows I hear tell'uv. They say they're big as this'ere room."

"Bigger, Poky. Especially the screen at the Paramount. That's my favorite. Can we go, Mama, please?"

"May we?" Hallie coached.

"May we go, Mama?"

"Well, of course you may go, dear. I'm glad you can share the picture show with Poky. Do you know what's playing?"

"I think it's called *She Done Him Wrong*."

"You mean the one with Mae West and Cary Grant?"

"Yes, ma'am."

"I reckon that's all right. That Mae West...she's something. Too bad *Little Women* isn't playing. It just came out, you know. You'd love it, Poky."

"Don't matter none, Miss Hallie. I jest wanna see a picture show, that's all."

It was the Saturday matinee, and movie goers filed into the ornate movie palace of the twenties, a fine specimen of Art Deco now only a few years old. The Paramount Theater offered an escape from reality and a world filled with fantasy. As soon as one entered its royal doors, they were able to forget for a little while the troubles awaiting them outside. Artistic carvings, glittering lights and lush inviting carpet met each guest in the glamorous lobby that smelled of hot popcorn before they entered the darkened theater with its anticipated pleasures.

Sandwiched in among the line of guests, Lauralee and Poky moved along happily. Lauralee slipped ten cents for herself and fifteen cents for Poky under the glass opening of the ticket booth, and soon the heavy doors closed behind them. Their eyes slowly adjusting to the darkened interior, Poky blinked while staring unbelievably all around her.

"My gracious!"

"Isn't it pretty, Poky?"

"Never seen nothin' like it. Must'uv cost a mint!"

People quickly crowded around the snack bar for popcorn, soft drinks and candy.

"We don't need none of that. We've got our bag of chocolates." Lauralee nodded at the brown bag protruding from her purse. They'd stopped by Kresge's on the way to buy the bag of chocolates, big hard chunks of it and only a nickel for the whole bag.

"There sho are a lot'uv goodies in city life, more'n I 'spected...Oh my!" Poky gasped as they stepped into the darkened theater and faced the large gaping screen. Long flowing graceful curtains were slowly closing before it. Lauralee led them down the dark carpeted aisle. Poky was amazed at how soft everything sounded, like Oak Mountain after a heavy snow.

Soon the magic began, and the dim lights completely darkened, leaving them in total blackness for an instant. Suddenly a bright spotlight lit up the empty stage, and soft melodious strains of music filled the large auditorium. Poky looked around her, up to the balcony and then back around, leaning forward, trying to figure out where the music was coming from. To her amazement, she watched as a beautiful lady, dressed in a flowing honey gold gown and seated at a fancy organ, rose from a hole in the floor!

She turned to Lauralee with her mouth wide open, and Lauralee laughed aloud.

The lovely lady kept ascending until she was completely visible and played on while Poky, smiling from ear to ear, sat back enjoying herself immensely. Lauralee tried watching both at the same time, the organist and Poky. This had always been her favorite part, the reason she preferred the Paramount to the Isis, the Academy and the Trenton, even though her mother's friend worked at the Trenton and once was very kind to her. Often she'd walk downtown and stand around in front of the various theaters, reading the marquees out front, even when she didn't have any money. On one such occasion, this friend, after watching her for some time standing first on one foot, then the other, savoring each sign, said, "Go ahead in." She did, and she would never forget that, although thereafter she didn't stand around as much in front of the Trenton. Mama wouldn't want her accepting charity.

The movie began, and Poky was glued to her seat, lost in another world. Her eyes danced with the screen, hardly answering Lauralee's questions and forgetting totally about the brown bag and big chunks of chocolate.

That evening, Hallie, Poky and Jamey sat in the kitchen sharing Poky's brewed tea. Lauralee was in bed early with a stomachache.

"I've told her time and time again not to eat that whole bag of chocolates."

"It's my fault, Miss Hallie, since I didn't eat none, she had th'whole bag t'herself. But I couldn't see nothin' but those people up there, bigger than life people, movin' all over that big screen...'specially that fancy lady, don't know if I'd call'er a lady or not. What's her name? Mae somethin'. I plum' forgot about th'chocolates."

Jamey laughed. "It's not your fault, Poky. It's not the first time she's done it, won't be the last either."

Suddenly there was a loud clanging noise outside. Poky jumped up to look out the window. Amused, Jamey glanced at his mother.

"Sounds like'a train comin' through! I still can't get used'ta that trolley comin' right up t'your front door almost an' stoppin'."

"Would you like to ride on one, Poky?" Jamey asked, "...costs only sixteen cents."

"Jamey, sixteen cents is not a small matter these days, you know."

"That's all right, Miss Hallie. I've had enough excitement for one trip already...what with th'picture show today. Thank you jest th'same though, Jamey."

"Well, I'm glad you had a good time." Hallie stirred sugar in her tea.

"I sho did...all 'cept for when we passed by that line'uv folk standin' there waitin' on soup. That made me feel downright poorly, almost didn't want Lauralee t'lay that twenty-five cents up for th'picture show, but I knew she had'er lil' heart set on it."

"I understand how you feel, Poky. But during these dark times while we eke out a living, I feel it's even more important for the children to have some ray of sunshine in their young lives...and it's picture shows for Lauralee. She thrives on them, you know."

"Yeah, she sure does," Jamey added. "I'd rather play a good game of ball myself or go for a spin in Lewis Taylor's dad's new Ford with that V-8 engine. Now that's something!"

Poky patted Jamey on the back and laughed. "Miss Hallie, I do believe you got th'right idea. There's time enough for facin' life's troubles when ya' grow up. Let'em be children...let'em have fun."

"Changing the subject, Miss Poky," Jamey interjected, tiring of the present conversation, "what'd you think about that earthquake that hit California last month? Think we could get such a quake as that?"

"Don't figure on it, Jamey. Seems we fare better'n most when it comes t'sech as that. It's th'mountains, ya' know...th'Blue Ridge...that protects us. But I sho do feel for them folks that lost their people...over a hundred I believe."

"Paper said one hundred and twenty-five and over five

thousand hurt. That's hard to believe."

"Not really, Jamey, when you consider such a large city as Los Angeles..." Hallie concluded. "...living here in Lynchburg, it's hard to imagine, but over two million people live in that area."

"Well, I'm glad to live here in Lynchburg."

Poky smiled at him. "Don't blame you, Jamey...an' I'm glad t'live on Oak Mountain myself. There are folks livin' in places I fear that are downright scary...like over there in Germany since that feller *Hitler* took over last month...an' right away went an' cut out th'freedom'uv press. What's he thinkin' 'bout anyhow?"

"That's a bad situation." Hallie rose for more tea. "...imagine ordering a national boycott against Jews...and Jews of all people...*why Jesus was a Jew!*"

"It affects all th'Jews, too, even th'lil' children." Poky sighed. "Now how can ya' boycott children?"

"Who knows? But I wonder what's really going on." Hallie reached into the cabinet, pulling out a newspaper. "I saved this, bothered me so, I just stuck it away. Listen to this." She opened the wrinkled paper and began to read..." *'The patriotic society of national German Jews took action similar to that of the Central Union, protesting against reports of atrocities as "foreign attempts to blackmail Germany which we, as Germans, oppose with the same determination as our non-Jewish compatriots. The statement of the Central Union said. "Certain foreign newspapers are spreading stories to the effect that mutilated bodies of Jews are regularly found at the entrance to the Jewish cemetery in Weissensee, a suburb of Berlin; that Jewish girls are forcibly herded into public squares and that hundreds of German Jews have reached Geneva, nine-tenths of them, including many children, terribly maltreated. All such reports are pure inventions. This union emphatically declares that German Jewry cannot be held answerable for such irresponsible distortions which deserve the utmost condemnation.'* "

"Only God knows th'truth."

"That's right, Poky...but where there's smoke, there's usually fire, you know. Let's just hope that none of that is true. It's too horrible to think about. But making that *Hitler* dictator is bad business, I'm sure."

"Of course it's bad business, Mama. Any dictator is bad business. That's why we have a democracy, the best form of government."

"I know, Jamey. It's just that lately my faith in our government has been shaken. Hoover did us in...but looks as if Roosevelt might pull us out before it's over."

"Did you know President Roosevelt passed through Lynchburg, Miss Poky?" Jamey asked. "Passed through on a special train in January...slowed down at the Kemper Street station, but kept on going. I sure would've liked to have seen him."

"Now that would be somethin'...to see'a president."

"Be even better to talk to him. Maybe Jon Junior can fill us in on things now that he's in the CCC's."

"Maybe, maybe not," Hallie responded. "Jon Junior's probably just busy planting trees and such. Only those high up in the government know what's going on...and I wonder if they do!"

"Well, the banks did open back up after that bank holiday, Mama. Maybe not all of them, but most...and all of ours in Lynchburg reopened, Miss Poky."

"I read they did, Jamey. Don't have t'worry none 'bout th'banks myself. Keep my money in pickle jars."

Jamey laughed. Often he felt adults boring, and often he stayed in his room when they visited, but not so with Poky. She stirred his youthful curiosity as a fresh, crisp breeze in autumn.

"Well, I don't know 'bout you folks, but think I'll turn in for th'night. My eyelids are a might heavy. Maybe I'll dream 'bout th'picture show an' that lovely lady risin' up out'a that hole!" She stood up.

The next morning, Lauralee's stomachache was worse, and

Hallie thought it best to keep her in bed. Even though she and Poky put off their plan to attend church together until the next Sunday, she tried coaxing Jamey to go ahead, but to no avail. It was hard enough to take him, much less to send him. The second week seemed to pass even more quickly than the first, with Hallie and Poky dreading the inevitable departure. One day they walked up Main Street to window shop and admire all the bright spring colors in the windows. Poky's eyes bulged at their sight, never having seen so many store bought items at once. Another day they walked up to Bragassa's Toy Store on the corner of Twelfth and Court, and Poky marveled again at the shelves of shiny new toys. Hallie wanted to price a new pair of skates. The price tag read one dollar and thirty five cents.

"A little too much for now. Will have to wait awhile, maybe by summer."

"Can Lauralee skate?"

"Oh, yes, quite well. She uses her friend, Kate's, sometimes."

When they returned home, a letter was waiting...a letter from Jon Junior. So excited, Hallie ripped into it.

"Listen Poky, I'll read aloud...'*I'm here at Camp GWNF-1, F1 or Camp Roosevelt as we call it. It was named that because it's the first CCC camp. So, I guess you can say, we're kind of special. Although, I didn't think so when we first arrived and had to march through woods for what seemed like forever to find absolutely nothing. It's way out in the sticks. A place called Edinburg is nearby...at least the 'burg' part was comforting. It's actually in the George Washington National Forest on a mountain called Mt. Kennedy. That night when the lights went out, I thought I'd fallen off the face of the earth — couldn't see my hand in front of my face....*'"

Poky laughed. "Jest gettin' a lil' taste'uv mountain life."

Hallie nodded and kept reading... "'*but I must have been awfully tired because I slept like a baby, even when my roommate (he's from West Virginia) snored ferociously. The first day, we spent putting up our own tents which are shaped like pyramids, and making the camp ready. I hardly had time to breathe, and that night my back was some kind of sore. I might add that at first I was taken to Fort Monroe to get shots before coming here, and my arm felt like a pin cushion. Every morning, we get up with the chickens; breakfast is at 6:00 AM. Our barrack's leader marches us to the mess hall; we carry our mess kits with us and are served first-come, first-serve. And, Mama, the food doesn't taste a bit like yours! Although, we have plenty of it. After breakfast, we wash our kits in a tank of hot water, and then we go back to straighten up our tents and get ready for work. I feel like I'm in the Army!!! They issue us tools and tell us what truck to get on. I've been working on the road crew, building roads for a parkway to go through mountains. Imagine that! We're actually having to carve this road right out of the rock! But it's important work, and I'm glad to be on the road crew. Guess I better close for now, time for lights-out. Y'all take care and you will be getting the twenty-five dollars soon.*

Love to all,
Jon Junior'"

Hallie wiped her eyes.

"Sounds like th'boy's farin' pretty well, Miss Hallie."

"I know. Even though his description is graphically negative, I hear the lilt in his voice. Jon Junior's all right."

"Wonder 'bout'em buildin' them roads through th'mountain, though. Sho hope they don't come up Oak Mountain with'em. First thing ya' know folks be comin' from everywhere jest to see what's up there...an' folks on Oak Mountain ain't gonna cotton t'that."

It was Sunday morning, and Hallie, Poky, Lauralee and Jamey set out walking toward First Baptist Church on the corner of Eleventh and Court. The day was particularly warm for April, a day made for walking.

"My, it's nice walkin' on these'ere wide sidewalks, a body don't even stumble."

They turned up Twelfth.

"I remember Sister Jane talkin' 'bout these'ere hills in Lynchburg. 'Course, we don't have hills on Oak Mountain!" she chuckled.

"Yes, I recall, Poky. You're right, they aren't hills...they're mountain ridges, and if you happen to stumble on one of them, it might be your last."

Poky laughed aloud.

"There's Bragassa's, Poky," Jamey spoke up. "Understand you liked it in there."

She walked over, and pressed her nose against the glass. "Just one last look t'take with me." Lauralee ran up beside her.

"A child's paradise, for sure." Hallie sighed.

"Mama, there they are! The skates. Look how shiny they are, Mama. I bet they're fast...."

"Come along, Lauralee. We mustn't be late for Sunday school." They turned up Court Street, and the massive brick edifice towered above them with its tall steeple piercing the clear blue spring sky. Poky stood in awe, and then noticed all the well dressed folk filing into the church. She looked down at her old black dress and suddenly felt uncomfortable. Hallie noticed out of the corner of her eye.

"Some members here are quite well-to-do, and then there are others like myself; but, you know, I don't think God sees that."

Poky smiled. "'Course not. He's no respecter'uv persons ...says so in th'Bible." She quickly marched up the hill beside Hallie to the black wrought iron gate, and paused as many had done through the years...such an impressive place of worship! An aura of royalty seemed to surround the High Victorian Gothic style, impressively designed by a New York architect, as it sat loftily, gracing the hill of Court Street and lending class to the small town of Lynchburg. Its graceful one hundred and eighty foot steeple demanded one's attention, pointing them in the proper direction. Above its base were decorative motifs of voussoirs, foils and gargoyle faces that caught the interest of the children particularly. Its hard pressed red brick and slate roofs lent solidity and timeliness as it was proving to be. Dedicated in 1886, it was already pushing fifty years old. And the looks of it was cause to believe it would be around for many, many years to come, far surpassing the gentle folk who filed in today and who would have long since passed on to their eternal destination. Because the church was perched atop a hill with steeply graded streets, it was surrounded by an iron fence that was set in heavy retaining walls made from stones from across the James River. Just now, Jamey was leaning against the wall, busily engaged in conversation with a slight girl with medium brown hair pulled back in a knot. Even with this severe style, the girl radiated beauty. Poky nodded to Hallie.

"See you after Sunday school, Jamey."

He absently waved to his mother, and again she was reminded of the strong resemblance to his father.

"Mama, I'm going to my class." Lauralee scampered off.

"Okay, dear, don't forget to put your offering in."

"I won't," she answered as she disappeared.

Hallie and Poky entered the large sanctuary.

"Oh my goodness!" Poky exclaimed as she looked around and up at the dominate stained glass windows ablaze with the early morning sun rays falling through them, creating a widespread kaleidoscopic picture. Soft organ music filled the sanctuary, adding to the aura of reverence as they moved down the aisle and found a seat. Poky noticed Hallie nodding to several people. Obviously, she was well thought of in this impressive place, Poky thought to herself, and felt more comfortable. Once seated, she stared up at the high darkly stained ceiling with its lofty arches rising forty feet above the floor, and the two massive beams apparently supporting the building. She took in the gently inclined floor, the cushioned pews that curved around the pulpit and the choir...my goodness! Adorned in elaborate robes, the choir stood in the high balcony, seemingly suspended in midair behind the pulpit. And above the choir, magnificent organ pipes aspiringly reached up to the ceiling. The elevated choir captivated Poky most of all, and she turned to Hallie with a wide grin as they began to sing. Lifting their voices in unison, Poky couldn't help but join in, humming away.

The service seemed short for Poky and all too soon was concluded. Afterwards, the crowd thronged the aisles, fellowshipping one with another. Hallie was immediately caught up in conversations while Poky lingered, watching intently the sea of faces, smiling cordially when they looked her way. She stepped back to make room for people to pass and gently bumped into one of two smartly dressed middle-aged ladies deep in conversation. Engrossed in their subject and unaware of her presence, they continued talking in hushed tones, but not too hushed for Poky..."a *poor aristocrat...that's what she is!"*

Poky followed their gaze to her adored Hallie.

"Oh, Mabel, you're too much!" The two ladies moved off and disappeared through the crowd. Poky remained in her spot still bristling, then nodded her head with a smile and mumbled, "The lady's right."

IT WAS MONDAY, a week since Poky had left them, and Hallie missed her greatly. She'd decided to visit old Mrs. Turbin up on Harrison Street. The old lady looked forward to her visits. By all known sources, Mrs. Turbin was quite wealthy, but partially crippled and alone, except, that is, for her cook. Therefore, Hallie felt sorry for her and tried to call on her from time to time. Today, she took Lauralee along.

She lifted the solid brass door knocker and let it fall, resounding loudly. It was three fifteen in the afternoon, their appointed time. One didn't visit Mrs. Turbin without an appointment. The massive oak door opened slowly, and Mrs. Turbin's cook nodded and led them into a dark parlor shaded by heavy damask drapes. Soon the tall, elegant Mrs. Turbin appeared, leaning heavily on her gold embossed cane. She sat down across from them in her usual chair.

"Francine, would you kindly serve Mrs. Frederick and her nice young daughter, Miss Lauralee, some raspberry sherbet?"

"Certainly, ma'am." The heavy set Francine scurried off to the kitchen while Lauralee winced. Hallie sent her a reprimanding look. Soon the dreaded raspberry sherbet sat before her, and she reluctantly tasted it. She quickly blurted out, "Can I have a drink of water?"

"Yes, you *may*have a drink of water, "Mrs. Turbin answered.

Lauralee glanced at her mother with raised eyebrows as she proceeded to the kitchen.

"Mrs. Frederick," the noble old lady inquired, "have you ever had the honorable privilege of visiting The Hotel Mons in Bedford?"

"No, ma'am, I haven't. I have heard of it, however. You're speaking of the hotel up in the mountains...at the Peaks of Otter?"

"Yes, ma'am. It is a lovely place for certain. The Mr. Turbin and I made several nice visits before he succumbed. I do so wish I could visit once more...but I guess it is simply out of the question in my crippled state. I saw an advertisement in the paper just the other day. They will be reopening for the season soon. If you ever have the opportunity, dear, you must visit."

"I will, Mrs. Turbin, for sure." Hallie thought to herself how far apart their two worlds were.

After an hour or so, they departed. Lauralee skipped happily down the uneven sidewalk, with Hallie trying to keep up.

"How come, Mama, Mrs. Turbin seems so unhappy when she lives in that nice, big house with a cook and everything?"

"Lauralee, things don't necessarily make for happiness."

"I know, but she lives in a *mansion*."

Hallie smiled in agreement. Truly the stately house on Harrison Street was just that.

CHAPTER FIVE

THE PICTURE WAS a melancholy one. It was early evening, with the sun, just behind the rounded ridges of the Blue Ridge, casting its last fiery rays. The Blue Ridge has been described by countless people down through the ages, and in countless ways. Of course, it is always changing depending on the particular season, the particular day, the particular time of day and most importantly what the day has created. Perhaps the day chose to bring warm sunshine, perhaps a persistent misty rain or gently falling snow, or just a dismal gloom to overshadow all. But one word most accurately describes the Blue Ridge in the evening when one slows one's pace and leaves off daily chores...and that is *melancholy.* It creates a pensive mood that reaches deep down within one's soul and conjures up safely hidden feelings or thoughts from the past.

It was such thoughts that surfaced as Poky walked slowly out to the edge of the mountain, her lone figure creating a silhouette against the distant ridges. She listened to the wind blowing up from the valley, up through the mountains, the updrafts. It was a wistful sound, but a sound Poky loved. Shadows began to fall about her, but still she lingered, remembering her childhood, wishing she could return somehow to the warmth and bliss of youth when the joys and security surrounded her in the presence of Sister Jane. She pulled her woolen shawl tightly about her shoulders against the cool updrafts and headed back to the cabin.

The oil lantern blown out, she climbed into bed, snuggling deep into the softness of the feather tick mattress, and lay very still. She waited, knowing full well it was coming. Suddenly a shattering crack of thunder reverberated throughout the cabin, and she jumped under the covers. It's springtime, she thought. It is time. The lightning flashed, illuminating the small cabin, thus creating an eerie illusion as Poky peeped from beneath the covers. It proved to be a highly electrical storm and though her faith was strong, her human strength was no match for the overwhelming power of the early spring storm, and she cringed. Then it struck with a tremulous force. She jumped out of bed and ran to the window. In the brilliant white light, the old chestnut, tall and bare, was toppling over. Clutching her gown to her, she felt as if part of her was crashing to the ground along with the old tree. So many times she'd climbed it throughout her childhood or sat beneath its lofty branches. Already dead for many years from the blight, it still had stood as a silent reminder of bygone days for both her and itself. Her heart saddened as she recalled the many bushels of chestnuts she and Sister Jane had gathered from its bounty and sold through those early years, enabling them to have things otherwise not possible. Not only had it been their provider but their friend, sharing its shade with its strong, outstretched limbs. But then the horrid blight had visited Oak Mountain along with the rest of the eastern United States and mass murdered the faithful old trees, including her friend. But never did she think to cut it down. Oh no! Year after year, it had stood. But now! She slowly returned to bed.

Sunshine filled the cabin the next morning. Such is life, she thought, recalling the old chestnut. Whenever she felt a bit sad, she'd open up the door to her jewels, so many jewels. They were all stored away in her memory bank. Just now, she pulled out the ones associated with her recent Lynchburg trip and thought of Hallie, Jamey and Lauralee...and the picture show. Ah! What'a lovely lady in that flowin' honey gold gown risin' up out'a nowhere. She envisioned the soaring steeple atop that magnificent church on Court Street...but still she smiled. She was glad to be back home, back on Oak Mountain. She decided to get up and visit little Barclay.

The walk after breakfast was invigorating. Though it was April, spring was coming slowly to the Blue Ridge, and the mountain ridges were still thawing out, sending forth springs of crystal clear water. Poky stepped up to the Branham door, knocked and waited. Mrs. Branham opened it slowly, looking more worn and weary than before.

"You all right, Mrs. Branham?"

"Oh, Poky, do come in. I'm fair to middlin' I guess. Haven't gotten my strength back yet from my lil' feller there." Poky followed her eyes to the darkened corner of the room where the young child sat propped among pillows.

"My goodness, how he's grown!" She grabbed him up immediately, holding him tenderly to her. "I knew he'd know me."

Mrs. Branham leaned against the iron bedstead in the living room. Obviously space was at a premium for the growing family.

"You sure you all right? Maybe you ought'a see 'bout a doctor."

"Oh, I'll be all right directly. All my babies took their toll."

"Well, I don't know. You lookin' mighty pale t'me, hate t'see ya' feelin' so poorly."

"I'm obliged to ya', Poky. You've perked up my spirits already just seein' ya'."

Barclay was staring up at Poky with an inquisitive look, and she proudly smiled down at him.

Spring slid easily into summer, and Poky was busy about her vegetable garden, weeding and wistfully thinking of its upcoming bounty. Though the Great Depression wore on, making history throughout the country, folk on Oak Mountain still fared better, seemingly cut off from the real tragedies wreaking havoc in the cities. Poky figured as long as she had Bertha, her Guernsey cow, named after her Aunt Bertha, long since passed on, her ten hens and Elijah, her old rooster, she'd be all right. Enough for herself and a little left over for sharing. It's nice to share, she thought. Why, just th'other day, the paper was sayin' how th'depression's bringin' out some good things in folk. People bein' nicer t'one another, givin' out food an'sech, stickin' together. Now that was good. She kept thinking on these things while staking her tomato plants in the late morning. She tied the already tall plants to the slender stakes with some old twine and then proceeded to sucker the plants, breaking off the new growth, just leaving two or three strong stalks so the plants would produce nice, large tomatoes. She felt content, didn't really have a hankering to change anything. She commenced to thinking aloud..."Now, th'Smiths over th' next holler aimin' t'get *'lectricity* soon as th'REA strings up th'mountainside. That would be somethin'! No more lanterns, jest cut on'a switch. Don't know whether I'd go to th'trouble'uv gettin' it, though, mighty 'spensive they say. 'Course it'd be nice t'have one'uv them new radios. Be company all day long. But I don't know that I'd want company all day long, been s'used t'bein' by myself. And if I want company, I can mosey over to a neighbor. Matter'uv fact, think I'll call on Mamie Smith today. Mamie says she gonna get herself one'a them *'lectric* stoves, too. 'Course, I wouldn't want one'a them things. Like my old wood stove jest fine, couldn't bake up a batch'uv biscuits no better if it tried, an' I know it couldn't turn out'a hoecake like mine." She continued talking to herself as she tied up the last tomato plant.

Poky crossed over the south meadow toward Hidden Hollow where the Smiths lived. She stopped to enjoy masses of milkweeds growing tall and straight with numerous butterflies alighting on them to feed. She remembered Sister Jane telling her about the beautiful monarch. How they're hatched on the milkweed and feed almost totally on milkweed leaves, and how the bitter liquid in the leaves not only feeds the beautiful monarch but gives it protection, too. She'd wondered about this as a child, but now found it to be like one of

Jesus's parables. The lovely butterfly is so enticing to other creatures until they try to eat it. *Too bitter*! So they avoid eating the bitter monarch. Just like things in the world. Often, they look so good, so enticing, but the taste is bitter. "This is what th'Good Book teaches," she said aloud midst the milkweeds as she strolled through, stirring up the graceful orange and black butterflies that went about their business. She figured she'd come back later to this fine patch of milkweeds and gather some of the tender leaves. They'd cook up nicely, she thought, better'n spinach most times. Be nice an' healthy for Mrs. Branham. She'd take her a pot, too. Starting down the mountain ridge, she could feel the temperature rising and enjoyed the change, seeing the hollow curled up beneath her. The Smith's chimney came in sight, then the two-story white frame house. It looked like it needed more whitewash, though. The Smiths were generally particular about keeping their house freshly whitewashed, but some things were being neglected during these hard times. The front door cracked, and then Mamie popped out on the porch, all hundred and eighty pounds of her. Though past sixty, she didn't look a day over forty-five, with her rolls of lily-white flesh. Her salt and pepper hair was pulled back in a knot, accentuating her round, plump face even more, and her beady little eyes sank deep into this plumpness, almost disappearing. A wide grin lit up her face. "Well, Poky, how in th'world are ya'? Come on in an' sit a spell. Been fixin' to call on ya'. I was gonna come last week, but then we had that gully-washer, you know. And I was a bit skittish 'bout crossin' th'creek, was up mighty high. Have you et?"

"Done had my dinner. Fact, I brought you a mess." She handed over a small sack of yellow neck squash. "These done come up already, believe it or not."

"Why, thank you, Poky, that's mighty neighborly of ya'. Appreciate it, too. You know Gordon, Jr.'s been on his back nigh three months now, couldn't get much of a garden in. Got a few tomatoes an' string beans, though."

Poky wondered if it was all his back or just a little laziness there, too. She'd heard of his constant injuries. Seems ever since his daddy passed away a couple of years ago, he'd gone to ailin'. "Where is Gordon, Jr. now?"

"Been feelin' some better lately, went over to Charlottesville to visit Nancy Joe." She stashed the squash away in the pantry.

"How is Nancy Joe an'er little one? Must be nigh 'bout six months old now. I recall he was born right about th'time lil' Barclay Branham was."

Mamie twirled around. "*Barclay Branham*, what kind'a name is that? Sounds mighty fancy for them."

"What ya' mean...*them*?"

"My goodness, Poky. You know what I mean."

"I think I do, Mamie."

"'Course they're all right, I'm sure. It's just that they're different."

"What's wrong with different? I'm different."

"But you know how folks feel about them."

"That don't make it right."

"Guess not, but if we go spendin' time with'em, first thing ya' know, they'll be callin' us names, too. Best to leave'em alone. Come on an' sit down. I aim to hear all about your Lynchburg trip...from th' beginning to th'end."

Poky spent the next hour sharing her glorious memories of the trip. On the way back home, she recalled the comments about Barclay. Oh well, Mamie always was right high-minded. Can't blame'er, though. She got it naturally from'er folks I understan'. They got a little somethin' an' it went right to their heads. But she liked'er in spite'uv her airish ways, she thought as she passed through the milkweeds again on the way back to her cabin. "Shucks, I'm not gonna worry 'bout what Mamie says," she muttered, and stopped to pick a few milkweeds.

JON JUNIOR EXCITEDLY dropped his mother's letter in the box, and headed for the mess hall. Wouldn't she be impressed! Luck was surely with him just as the guys said. Who would've believed it? He was thinking again of the events of the past few days and how he had been transferred from Camp Roosevelt to Big Meadows in the Shenandoah National Park...and just in time for the *president!*

It was August 12, 1933, and everyone was rushing about in preparation for the president's inspection visit. Everything had to be in top order, and the CCC boys were scurrying about, each trying to outdo the other in handling their particular task. Jon Junior was not assigned to any personal duty that would bring him even close to the president or the members of his cabinet, but he was determined to see him one way or the other. And he had his chance when they sat down to dinner outside. Though CCC enrollees were all crowded around the tables, he and his roommate, Robert, took turns holding each other up on their shoulders. That's when he actually saw President Franklin Delano Roosevelt, he later wrote to his mother, sitting there at the rough-hewn table, eating dinner out of the same regulation aluminum mess kit that *he* used every day.

Hallie finished reading the letter aloud to Jamey and Lauralee as they sat down together at the end of the day. '*...and he looked just like any other person....*'

"Imagine that," Jamey spoke up, "...seeing the president and saying he looked just like any other person...."

"Well, he is just like any other person."

"Oh, Lauralee, what do you know?"

"Please children, let me finish the letter...'*I'll be planting trees here in the park. We have thousands to plant! Think I'll like this job much better than the last one, though. At least, it should be a lot easier. But I must admit, I miss you all a lot, especially on Sundays, remembering all of us going to First Baptist together. Tomorrow is Sunday, and I'll be going to service, but I'll be thinking of you all back home.*'"

"When's Jon Junior coming back, Mama?"

"It will be awhile, Lauralee, a good while."

"Will he be back for Halloween?"

"Oh no, not for Halloween."

"Thanksgiving?"

"He may come home for Thanksgiving and Christmas, or at least one or the other, but not to stay. He has a year to serve."

"Wish I could go."

"Jamey, your time will come one day to fly your wings, too."

"I sure hope so. First Jon Junior joins the CCC's and now *you're* going to work at the bakery. All I do is baby-sit my little sister."

"I'm not that bad!" Lauralee stuck her tongue out at him behind her mother's back, but he ignored her.

"I'm sorry, Jamey, but we have to do what we have to do."

"I know, Mama. I just wish I could go to work instead of school."

"You have to go to school, and this job may only be temporary, you know."

"He ain't coming back, Mama!"

Lauralee glanced from him to her mother, knowing he was referring to their father.

"Jamey, please, and I wish you wouldn't use ain't."

"Well, he's not." He stood up to go to bed.

"Goodnight, Jamey."

"Goodnight, Mama."

SUMMER BURST INTO fall before anyone realized what was happening. Alas, October vibrantly exploded with vivid color, transforming Oak Mountain into a pulsating drama unequaled. Excitement surged through the tired veins of the mountain folk, and they were suddenly full of anticipation. It was time for sorghum molasses and apple butter making, quilting bees and such, a time of getting together, a time to forget one's problems before facing the hard winter ahead.

The day before the sorghum molasses making at the Smith's household, Poky called on Mrs. Branham to invite her to the quilting that would follow the day after. After some persuasion, the shy mother accepted. It was a neighborly act, Poky decided, an' Mrs. Branham certainly needed t'get out an' enjoy a little womenfolk fun. Stayin' there all th'time jest takin' care'uv Mr. Branham, those boys an' now lil' Barclay, it was enough t'get a body down, she thought. A sizable group gathered for the molasses making, and the menfolk enjoyed themselves immensely as always, trading hunting tales and such while the women assisted and in between, prepared for their quilting the next day. Poky joined in with the menfolk mostly, stirring the thick, dark syrup that boiled, bubbled and spewed out against the sides of the large metal pot, infiltrating the cool autumn air with its sweet fragrance. She'd loved making molasses ever since she was a teenager, and had always enthusiastically helped out with the sometimes monotonous job, realizing she would enjoy its sweet flavor for months to come. The weather cooperated with their efforts, providing a beautiful balmy day, causing the men to shed their wraps early and push up their woolen sleeves as the warm October sun smiled down upon the joyous affair.

"Poky, think we'll have enough molasses this year?"

"I reckon so. Campbell said th'cane harvest was right plentiful, an' from th'looks'uv that pile stacked up, I don't think there'll be a problem."

"Guess not, but ya' know how this stuff boils down...why, it takes 'bout ten gallons of juice t'make just one gallon of molasses, ya' know."

"I figure it'll be all right. Inez comin' to th'quiltin' tomorrow?"

"Wouldn't miss it for th'world!"

"Me neither."

The next day clouded up and sent forth showers periodically, but it didn't dampen the spirit of the quilting. Poky had met Mrs. Branham about halfway, and they'd walked together to Mamie Smith's place with Mrs. Branham's face shining with excitement.

"I thank you for askin' me to th'quiltin', Miss Poky."

"...just glad your sister could watch lil' Barclay. You need some time out, Mrs. Branham."

"Ah, yes." While wiping the raindrops from her face with her forearm, she smiled at Poky. Poky smiled back, but noticed the walk seemed to be unduly tiring her.

"This walk too much for ya'?"

"I'll be all right directly, just a mite weak."

"Well, we're almost there, just over th'next ridge, ya' know, an' down th'holler."

Poky knocked at the door, while Mrs. Branham stood timidly behind her. Mamie Smith appeared and directed them into the dimly lit foyer. "Come on in, Poky...an' you too...Mrs. Branham."

Mrs. Branham noticed the change in her tone as well as Poky, but tried to ignore it. All the ladies at the quilting had previously made one or more squares for the quilt, and Mamie had sewn them together for the top. The four-piece frame was set up, too, resting on the backs of chairs. The top and bottom linings were put together, and now they were ready for the quilting. The ladies respectively sat down around their piece of work and proceeded to stitch.

"Here's a seat, Mrs. Branham." Poky pushed a chair toward her, then sat down beside her, carefully eyeing the circle of faces. "You can help work on mine."

"Well, what kind'uv weather y'all think ol' man winter's gonna bring us?" Inez Jones began.

"Who knows," Mamie responded, trying to get situated comfortably in her chair.

"I'll tell ya' what kind. Gonna be a bad one. Th'squirrels been buildin' their nests down low like in th'trees...gonna be'a bad one, for sho."

"Poky's most likely right. She usually is," Mamie concluded.

"I hear tell June Matthews is fixin' to go off to college. Imagine that!" Lucille Brown announced while trying to hold her thread between her teeth, "...and her Pa is put out about it, too."

"Why on earth so?"

"Now, Mamie, you know how th'Matthews look on folks that're book read."

"That don't make no sense a'tall. College is good for th'young folk."

"I know, but Mr. Matthews says June will get all *biggety* and all."

"That's foolishness. More likely, he don't wanna spend none of that money of his. You know how folks say he squeaks when he walks."

"Inez, fetch me that bag of thread behind you there, please."

Inez reached behind her with some difficulty, struggling with her arthritis. "There you go. Ol' Arthur's been givin' me a fit these days. I'm feelin' better now...was afraid I wouldn't make the quiltin' last week. Was feelin' awful poorly."

"He'll plum' do it all right. You tried fixin' some tea from alfalfa? Use either th'seeds or th'leaves, don't make no difference. Both will work an' take care'uv ol' Arthur for you."

"That right, Poky? I'll give it a try."

"Poky, did ya' bring your guitar?"

"Naw, didn't wanna bring it out in th'rain...an' had my mind set on quiltin' anyhows."

"Do you play th'*guitar*, Poky?" All eyes turned to Mrs. Branham.

"I fool around with it, ya' might say, know a few tunes."

"That's real nice. Music makes a body feel good." She looked up uncomfortably at the circle of eyes, and looked back down at her stitching.

"How're your boys doin' in school, Thelma?" Poky asked quickly.

"Fair to middlin', I s'pose. Got a new teacher this year. A *Yankee*. Th'children ain't too taken with'er either."

"You gotta watch them Yankees...first thing ya' know...they come down here an' commence to takin' over...," Lucille added without looking up.

"Now, Butch, he's learnin' th'barber trade with his pa," Thelma continued. "Been workin' in th'shop most Saturdays. 'Course business is bad now. Folks got no money...cuttin' their own hair."

"Reckon so. Money's hard to come by these days. Folks doin' all kinds of things. Read it in th'paper every day," Mamie reported while pushing her glasses back up her nose, reluctant to lose a stitch. "Shucks, they even committin' suicide every day over it!"

"Just read last week they've had twice as many suicides over in Lynchburg this year...had eleven last year...an' already had ten in the first six months of this year. Hard to believe, ain't it?"

"Well, Inez, some folk, 'specially city folk, havin' it much harder than us...an' some folk just can't cope...that's all."

"You know, I read that same article in the paper, too," Mrs. Bates interjected, "...and it said that all those suicides were white people. I wonder why?"

"That's not hard to figure out," Mamie responded, "the Negroes don't have much to lose...least not as much as us white folks."

"Way I figure it," Poky added, "th'Colored folk been used'ta hard times more'n most of us. They done learned how t'cope with it. Lot of'em done learned how t'lean on th'Lord, too."

"You might have a point, Poky," Mrs. Bates concluded.

The mixed conversation bounced back and forth over the large outstretched quilt, and it became more and more apparent that Mrs. Branham was purposely being left out. So when Inez finished telling what her three girls had been about,

Poky quickly interjected, "Mrs. Branham here has a fine family'uv *five* boys, an' was a hopin' for a girl this time around, but got another lil' feller instead."

"Oh really," Mrs. Bates, a relatively newcomer to Oak Mountain, spoke up, "I bet some of them know my Kenny. He's in the fifth grade."

Mrs. Branham looked up and around the table hesitantly. "Don't think so. My boys go to th'*mission*."

"I see." Mrs. Bates, having heard of the mission, quickly changed the subject. "What time we havin' lunch, Mamie?"

"Thought about noon. Does that suit y'all?"

A chorus of *yes* was the quick response.

Mrs. Branham walked silently back home with Poky beside her, wanting to say something to break the awful silence, but at a loss for words. So they walked on with Poky occasionally remarking about a particular tree or plant until they said their good-byes at the crossing. They had put some distance between them when Mrs. Branham turned around. Instinctively Poky turned, too.

"I'd sho like to hear you play that guitar sometime, Poky," she hollered.

"I'll do it, Mrs. Branham. I'll come a'callin' in a few days...with my guitar," Poky hollered back.

They smiled at one another, waved and went their separate ways. It was nearly twilight when Poky reached home, took off her shawl, hung it on the nail behind the door and reached for her guitar. Although the rain had ceased about midday, and a mild wind was blowing, the still saturated forest reeked with its rich pungent fragrance that Poky loved. She went out to the porch, sat down in her rocker and looked out toward the old apple tree. Sister Jane's stone was barely visible as darkness fell over Oak Mountain. She began to softly strum...*'Down in the valley, valley so low, hang your head over, hear the wind blow....'*

CHAPTER SIX

HALLOWEEN IN LYNCHBURG was an exciting time for young and old alike, with practically everyone turning out for the annual parade down Main Street. Neighbors eyed one another, pointing and roaring with laughter. White folks, with blackened faces, dressed in their long underwear, marched unashamedly up the street. The Halloween of 1933 was especially lively with its slightly cool evening, the last of Indian summer. The full moon, casting shadows about the eerie sights that moved slowly along, added the required mood. There were awfully funny sights, as well, that brought instant laughter to a crowd that longed to laugh.

"Look, Mama, look!" Lauralee squealed with delight as the large bulky baby carriage wheeled past them. The so-called baby, sucking on a giant sized bottle, bulged out of the carriage. The rather fleshy, plump man wore only a huge white bonnet and an oversized diaper! His large fat knees jutted out high above the sides of the burdened carriage. His make-believe mother was almost as funny, stumbling along in heels apparently too small, trying to push the over-weighted carriage up the street. As soon as they passed by Hallie and the children, she tripped, and the curly black wig fell lopsided on a balding head! Everyone but Jamey laughed.

"Wouldn't catch me acting a fool of myself like that!"

"Oh, Jamey, it's all in jest. There's no harm in it."

"Look, Mama!" Lauralee squealed again as a grotesque witch idled over toward them, hoisting her wretched broom above her. Lauralee moved closer to her mother. Several characters followed, their faces blackened with stove pipe polish and singing without a bit of harmony, but still it was a merry tune.

"Let's head up the street, Mama," Jamey prodded. "They're selling popcorn up there."

"Popcorn! Can we get some, Mama, please? Can we get some?" Lauralee begged while pulling her own skimpy, black mask down over her eyes.

"Hold on. The queen's coming. Look, Lauralee. Isn't she lovely?"

Lauralee quickly jerked her mask off, admiring the beautiful young girl who sat high upon the slow moving float approaching them...the annually elected queen dressed in a flowing orange gown trimmed in black. It passed on.

"Can we get some popcorn now, Mama, please?"

"Calm down, Lauralee. We'll share a bag." Eyeing Jamey as they pushed their way through the crowd to the next block, she realized the popcorn wasn't the real motivator for Jamey. His eyes darted this way and that, obviously searching for someone.

Halloween passed. Thanksgiving arrived, and Jon Junior didn't come home. Lauralee pouted for awhile before realizing that Christmas was just around the corner. Though she loved Jamey, it was Jon Junior who had filled the empty spot when her daddy left. Jon Junior had held her, played with her and spoiled her, often bringing her little treats. But who could stay sad...it was almost Christmas! The townsfolk were busy making preparations, but the festive spirit was subdued. People were anxious about spending what little they had. It was going to be a lean Christmas all over the country.

"Mama, do you think Santa Claus will come this year?"

Hallie looked at her trusting daughter, still naive in this world so glum. "I think so, Lauralee...I think so...."

"Hope he brings me a *Bye-lo Baby*...I really do...it's the only thing I want."

"What about those skates up at Bragassa's?"

"Well...I'd like to have the skates...but I really want a Byelo Baby, Mama. Susan Jacobs has one, and they're so pretty."

"She talking about that doll again?"

"Now, Jamey."

"That's all I've heard for weeks. Every time we go by Bragassa's...*Look Jamey, look Jamey, look at the beautiful Byelo Baby....*"

"Jamey...."

"Don't worry, Mama. I understand we're in a depression and money's tight, real tight. I'm not expecting anything, you hear."

"Thank you, Jamey, but Santa may be able to manage a little something."

He smiled at her as he crossed the room. Lauralee giggled and followed after. They were going up to Mrs. Turbin's to see if she needed anything. Hallie had been doing this once a week ever since the poor old woman had suffered a slight stroke. Often she'd send Jamey and Lauralee on an errand, tipping generously. Hallie allowed them to keep the money. As they left the house, Lauralee piped up, "Hope she gives us a nice tip today, Jamey. We'll soon have enough to buy Mama something for Christmas. Think we can get her that statue of Mary holding Jesus?"

He nodded, "Maybe."

"Jamey, do you think Santa Claus knows we're in a depression?"

He looked at his little sister with amusement. "I don't know, Lauralee."

Hallie sat down to write Poky a Christmas card, filling the small card with news on the back and front...and then the *knock* came. When she opened the door, a uniformed officer, tall and slim with a kind face, stood before her.

"Mrs. Frederick?"

"Yes?"

"I'm Officer Dunbrick. May I come in?"

"Yes, why yes, of course." Immediately apprehensive, she led the way to the parlor.

"Please be seated."

"Thank you, ma'am." Sitting down and slowly removing his cap, he began with some reluctance, "I have some news for you, ma'am...I believe...about your husband...."

Hallie caught her breath.

He noticed and proceeded cautiously, "We just learned of this, ma'am, but it appears that your husband...Mr. Jon Frederick...came upon some difficult circumstances...and...."

She braced herself.

"*...and has been found dead.*"

She sat very still.

"Apparently Mr. Frederick was attempting to catch a ride on a freight train from New Jersey...when he fell...."

She gasped, "You mean he was *killed by a train?*"

"Yes, ma'am."

Stunned, she sat in silence. The officer awkwardly sat in silence, too. Then she asked quietly, "Where was the train headed?"

"This way, ma'am." He reached into his breast pocket and pulled out a worn cloth bag of a greyish color. "Fortunately, he had his name and address on him, and what's in this bag." He handed it over to her. "His remains will arrive here day after tomorrow."

Hallie quickly stood up. "Thank you, Officer Dunbrick, for personally coming." She was anxious for him to leave. She needed to be alone.

Seeing how strong the small lady was attempting to be, he felt very uncomfortable leaving her. "...if there's anything we can do...."

"I appreciate your kindness."

He followed her to the door with his cap in his hand.

That night after Jamey and Lauralee were fast asleep, Hallie reluctantly opened the small sack. A dollar bill, a few coins, a plug of tobacco and...a flattened penny fell out. Picking up the penny, she carefully examined it...one of Lauralee's. Then and only then did she cry. The tears went into the night as she grieved alone for wasted years, wasted talent...and most of all for a wasted life. Tomorrow she would face the task at hand, tomorrow she would have to tell the children, but tonight...she would grieve.

The funeral was small, very small and cold, so cold. A steady wind whipped at the grave covering as Hallie stood beside the open grave with her arm around Lauralee. Jamey and Jon Junior stood on either side of them. The tears were silent tears, even Lauralee's. It still seemed like a bad dream, and they would all wake up, and their daddy would be coming home like he used to. Hallie's church friends stood back, witnessing the forlorn scene, yearning to do something, but what?

Jamey and Lauralee returned to school, not mentioning what had happened, filing it away in their tender memories to sort through another day.

Hallie cleaned up the dishes while Jon Junior lingered at the kitchen table. He had another day at home before returning to camp.

"What're you gonna do with it?" He turned the small bag over and over in his hands.

"I don't know. Keep it. Maybe give it to you kids."

He dumped the meager contents out on the table, the coins rolled around in circles before stopping. "It's hard to believe a man can live that many years...and all he leaves is this."

Hallie knew he was thinking aloud.

"I'd like to keep something, maybe a few coins or even the tobacco...I think Lauralee should have the penny...her penny. Jamey and I could divide the rest, maybe."

"That's just what I was thinking, but you're wrong, Jon Junior, about one thing."

"What do you mean?"

"That's not all he left. He left treasures...you and Jamey and Lauralee."

Jon Junior stood up, walked to the window, and stared out into the bleak winter day. "No matter what he did or did not do, Mama...he was still my daddy. He might not have set the course for us or paved the way...but I'm gonna make him proud still...."

Hallie smiled.

"What about you, Mama? What do you wish to keep?"

"I already have it."

"What?"

"A memory."

Jon Junior paused before asking the question that had been on his mind for days. Hallie looked at him. "Mama, do you think he was coming home?"

"Yes, Jon Junior, I do...I have to believe that."

Christmas Eve arrived. The family sat around the sparse cedar tree adorned with delicate and familiar ornaments from Hallie's past. Although, they had gotten used to being without him a long time back, Christmas seemed to heighten the finality of it all.

"Mama, listen...." Lauralee jumped up and ran to open the door.

Familiar words floated in with the sharp cold air... *'It came upon a midnight clear....'*

Jamey, Jon Junior and Hallie gathered around Lauralee, listening to the carolers lifting their voices high into the darkened night as they stood rigidly against the icy wind. After singing two more carols, they left, declining Hallie's offer to come in, calling after... *"Merry Christmas and a Happy New Year...."*

"Merry Christmas to you," they called back and closed the door, suddenly feeling joyous and happy.

"How about some hot apple cider? Mr. Pantanna sent us a whole gallon."

"Sounds great. I'll get it, Mama."

"Thank you, Jon Junior."

As they sat sipping the steaming hot cider, the silence was broken.

"Someone's at the door." Jamey got up to answer. "Lauralee, it's for you." She rushed excitedly to see her Sunday school teacher, Miss Hall, standing there with a large box in her arms. She handed it to Lauralee.

"For me?" Her eyes grew larger as Miss Hall nodded.

"Can I...I mean, may I open it?"

"Certainly, it's yours."

"Please come in, Miss Hall." Hallie led her to a chair and rushed off to get another cup of cider. Lauralee began opening the box. She carefully laid the ribbon aside, and then the paper. She lifted the top from the box. "Oh...so pretty...Miss Hall...it's so pretty!" She stood up holding the dark blue silk dress against her, tenderly caressing the intricate embroidery at the top. "Look at its long puffy sleeves!"

"I don't know what's the prettier. That lovely blue dress or your rosy little cheeks." Miss Hall laughed.

"Oh my, Miss Hall, what a nice gift...." Hallie stood in the kitchen doorway all choked up. The Sunday school teacher rose and went back to the door, bringing back with her a large basket filled with groceries.

"From First Baptist, Hallie, for all of you...."

Tears swam in her eyes as she tried to thank her. After the teacher was gone, Hallie sat down before the basket. "You know what we have to do, don't you?"

Jon Junior, Jamey and Lauralee all nodded.

"Jamey, would you be the goodwill bearer?"

"Sure, Mama. You want me to go tonight instead of tomorrow?"

"It's Christmas Eve, and God just showered us with blessings. I think it would be nice to take it over on Christmas Eve."

Jamey went to get his coat while Hallie went through the basket, picking out a few items to share with the Colored family down the street that was more poverty stricken than them.

"We'll wait for Jamey to return."

As soon as he did, they all examined the contents left. Canned goods, a small hen, and fruit and nuts filled two long black stockings.

"Oh, I wish they were cream colored!" Lauralee whined when she saw the stockings.

"Lauralee! How dare you whine about what's been given us."

"I'm sorry, Mama. But you know I like wearing the cream colored rather than the black."

"We must be thankful for what we get, child."

Christmas morning dawned.

"Mama, Mama! He did it! He brought me a *Bye-lo Baby!* Isn't she just beautiful? Look, Jon Junior...isn't she beautiful?"

They all sat contentedly, watching her delight in the baby doll with its precious china face. Jon Junior smiled at her indulgently. Jamey shook his head at her antics, and Hallie basked in the happiness of the moment. The remaining gifts exchanged between them were few but meaningful. Hallie was surprised with the lovely scarf Jamey and Lauralee gave her, and Jon Junior presented her with a small Bible.

"Where did you get this, Jon Junior?"

He grinned. "Well, they gave it to me at camp, but I saved it for you."

"Mama, can I go show my new doll to Susan Jacobs, please Mama?"

Hallie frowned. "It's so cold outside." But knowing full well how proud she was of that doll, she relented. "Oh well, wrap up good and come right back." Excitedly, Lauralee jumped up to go.

"Jamey, you all shouldn't have spent your money on me.

I bet that beautiful scarf cost a lot."

Jamey grinned proudly. "We had something else in mind, but didn't have quite enough money. You like the scarf?"

"I love it, but...."

"Then you just enjoy it, Mama. We wanted to do it. Lauralee said she knew you'd love it."

Hallie smoothed the cream colored scarf. "Well, I certainly do."

Awhile later, Hallie was busy in the kitchen putting the hen on and humming a Christmas carol. Jon Junior and Jamey were leaning close to the radio trying to hear through the static...and the front door closed. They turned. Lauralee stood with tears streaming down her cheeks as she clutched the Bye-lo Baby doll to her. Something was wrong.

Jon Junior rose. "Lauralee, come here. What happened?"

Slowly, she walked across the room toward him holding the doll in her arms, its beautiful china face all smashed in. "I was running..." she sobbed uncontrollably, "...to show my doll to Susan...and I fell on the sidewalk...." With that she cried harder. Hallie stood in the doorway, helplessly watching Jon Junior hold her tenderly. Life is hard, she thought, even for the little ones.

MILES AWAY, POKY was joyously trampling through a few inches of crusty week old snow on the way to Barclay's. She held a small wooden sled tightly beneath her left arm while steadying herself with her wooden walking stick. It had been awhile since she'd seen him, just too cold to get out, but it was Christmas Day! She thought no matter what th'weather, she was gonna see'im today. She remembered those squirrels' nests. Sure 'nough, it had been a bad one already, she thought, an' th'worst was yet t'come. January through March. If it wasn't snow, it was ice or freezin' rain. But, oh well, makes a body 'preciate spring! Th'colder, th'drearier a winter, th'more excitin' spring! She was feeling all happy inside, and then she remembered Hallie's letter. Poor Hallie. Poor

Lauralee an' Jamey an' Jon Junior. Poor Jon Franklin Frederick...what a tragedy...God rest his soul! Well, leastways, they know now...no more wondering.

When she arrived at the Branham household, shivering and cold, they were all surprised.

"Miss Poky! What're you doin' walkin' in this'ere kind'a weather?" Zeke Branham demanded.

"It's Christmas Day, Mr. Branham. I've come a'callin'."

"Well, come on in out'a th'cold." He swung the door open wide and eyed the sled under her arm. Mrs. Branham sat up quietly on the bed.

"Poky, you should'na..." she half whispered.

"Nonsense. I made this'ere for Barclay...my first Christmas present for'im. It ought'a last a long time...made it out'uv my old chestnut that lightnin' brought down last spring."

"If it's made out'uv chestnut, you betcha life it'll be here long after we're dead an' gone." Zeke Branham laughed.

The boys all moved up close, checking it out. Paul David, who had been the youngest, now ten, spoke up first, "Barclay's a mite too little for that there sled right now, Miss Poky."

Poky looked over at him. "You're right, Paul David. Reckon I can leave you in charge of it till he gets bigger?"

The young fellow nodded, "Guess I might need to ride'er every now an' then to keep'er up an' runnin'."

"Guess you might." She smiled.

"Sit yourself down on th'end'uv th'bed, Miss Poky. Make ya' self at home. I know th'missus is mighty happy to see ya'."

Mrs. Branham smiled warmly at her.

"Thank you, Mr. Branham. You folks havin' a good Christmas?"

"Yes, ma'am," Mrs. Branham nodded toward four shoe boxes lined up on the kitchen table. Poky peered in them. Each one contained an orange, one apple, some walnuts and hard candy.

"That's mighty nice, but I only see four."

"That's 'cause Barclay's too young this year," Jack Jacob

quickly responded. "We'll share our'n with'im."

"Sharin's good, boys."

"Now Barclay's got th'best Christmas present of all," Herman Ray added, "that chestnut sled a'sittin' yonder."

"Where is Barclay?"

"He's nappin', Miss Poky," Mrs. Branham replied weakly.

"Ain't he gonna be fit to be tied when he wakes up?"

CHAPTER SEVEN

1936

(A lot happened between 1933 and 1936...the Social Security Act was passed, Will Rogers died, a hurricane killed 400 in the Florida Keys, Bonnie & Clyde were gunned down in a police ambush in Texas, John Dillinger was killed outside a Chicago Theater, Bruno Hauptmann was arrested for the Lindbergh kidnapping, the REA was passed bringing electricity to rural areas...but still the depression held folks captive....)

THE ROCK SPLASHED into the sparkling clear water, creating expanding rings that grew and grew in an ever-widening circle. Barclay watched intently, perched upon a smooth granite stone above the murmuring creek that gently flowed in front of St. Paul's mission. Paul David and two other boys competed in making the grandest splash before their obvious female audience. Barclay, already a thinker at the tender age of three, sat quietly observing his surroundings, with the early afternoon sun shining down upon his thick, dark hair.

"Here, Barclay, throw one," Paul David urged.

Taking the large rock in his small hand, he examined it carefully and then tossed it into the flowing water. *SPLASH!* The sudden impact caused him to jump, and the older boys cackled. He frowned at first, and then began to laugh, also.

The Sunday morning service had just concluded, and the gently flowing creek welcomed the younger parishioners, from toddler to teenager. They were drawn as if by a giant magnet to its familiar waters.

"Barclay, don't fall in! Paul David, get ya' brother an' y'all come on here now. We best be gettin' on home," Poky called from the church stoop. Reluctantly, the boys obeyed. On their way home, Paul David asked anxiously, "Miss Poky, is mama gonna get well?"

"We certainly hope so, Paul David. We certainly hope so."

"Seems to me she's gettin' on worse, stays in bed more an' looks awful poorly."

"Th'doctor been lookin' in on'er?"

"Don't think that doctor's doin'er any good, Miss Poky. Don't you have one'a your herbs that will pick'er up?"

"Done tried most'uv'em, Paul David. 'Course I can try some more."

"Try some more, Poky."

"Yeah, try some more, Poky," Barclay repeated.

Poky chuckled. "I'll do that, Mr. Barclay...I'll do that."

They found Mrs. Branham alone. Zeke and the older boys had gone over to the orchard to discuss plans for the upcoming week. The peaches were ready, and they would begin picking on Monday. Mrs. Branham was asleep. After checking on her, Poky set about fixing dinner for the boys, and she had it on the table by the time they showed up.

"Why Miss Poky, that's mighty kindly'uv ya' to stay an' put dinner on," Zeke Branham uttered gratefully.

"You folks gotta eat. Sit down there now an' enjoy this mess'uv cabbage I cooked up."

"Cabbage and cornbread!" John Jacob exclaimed with an echo.

"You gonna be pickin' at th'orchard?"

"Yes, ma'am, have work for awhile now. Things lookin' up some. 'Course don't make much...'bout ten cents an hour. Only get a dollar for ten hard hours'uv work," Zeke Branham complained.

"Leastways...it's work."

"Yes, ma'am, it is that."

Zeke and the boys began to grab for the food.

"Hold on there now, boys. We gotta say grace," Poky admonished, "...gotta thank th'one responsible for this'ere food...an' for your work at th'orchard, too."

"Yes, ma'am, Miss Poky," Zeke quickly acknowledged with a bowed head. The boys followed.

"Thank you, Lord," Poky began, "for this'ere good food an' for all your blessin's...for we know all good things come from you. Thank you, too, for th'orchard work...an' Lord, please be with th'Mrs....in th'name'uv th'Lord. Amen."

"Amen," Zeke Branham gustily repeated while reaching for the bowl of cabbage.

"Mr. Branham, ya' think maybe you can get Paul David's an' Barclay's hair cut before church next week?"

He looked up at their shaggy heads and nodded, "Yes, ma'am, we'll do that."

"I offered to do't myself, but Paul David has his mind set on gettin' his'n store cut like th'others." The three older boys smiled proudly.

"Got their'n cut for free downtown Lynchburg last week...when we helped Mr. Otterman take'is first load'uv peaches in. He's got a friend who's got a barber shop. Did us a favor, too, for Mr. Otterman."

"That sho was nice'uv him. Mr. Otterman...I hear tell he's a Jew."

"That's a fact, Miss Poky. Told me so hisself...nicer man you don't wanna meet."

"Glad t'hear it. Did y'all stay overnight?"

"Drove two T-model trucks, loaded down with peaches. Mr. Otterman drove one an' I drove th'other. We slept in th'warehouse'uv a Wednesday night. Hotter than...." He looked up suddenly at Poky. "Well, ma'am, it sho was hot, but that warehouse bein' so close down by th'river cooled off right nicely in th'night. Won't bad a'tall. Was it boys?"

They all shook their bent heads, obviously more interested in eating than talking.

"Y'all had somethin' to eat...besides peaches I hope?"

"Yes, ma'am. They treated us real nice like, let us eat at th'restaurant...Farmers Restaurant they call it, right there on Main Street."

"Well, they *ought* to!" Poky was well aware that most people didn't allow these folk to eat in their restaurants.

"Goin' back soon?"

"Soon as we get th'next pickin' done, yes ma'am, we'll be goin' back, th'boys an'me."

"Can I go, too, Pa?" Paul David begged, wiping his mouth on his sleeve.

"Naw, you need t'stay here an' help your ma an' watch out for lil' Barclay here."

He hung his head disappointedly.

"Mr. Branham, s'pose ya' let me know when y'all fixin' t'go...an' I'd be glad t'come over an' be with th'Mrs. an' Barclay." She looked down the table at Paul David's bowed head.

"I'd be obliged to ya', ma'am. Paul David will be more help for sure." The young boy's head shot upward, his eyes sparkled, and he looked gratefully at Poky.

The following Tuesday, Zeke Branham reluctantly handed Paul David the money for the haircuts, and they set out down the mountain and across the hollow to the nearest barber shop, Butch Hollaway's shop. Though the mountain temperature was a few degrees cooler than down in the valley, it was still hot. July had been a scorcher thus far, and the boys were sweating, their shaggy heads wet with perspiration when they arrived at the small shop, sitting adjacent to the neat two story house. Paul David knocked firmly at the screen door, while Barclay stared up at the beautiful candy striped barber's pole. No one answered. He knocked again. Still no answer. Paul David pulled open the screen door and walked in with Barclay following. Three men stood frowning at them, two older men, portly with greying hair and one younger, tall and robust.

"Can we get a haircut, mister?" Paul David addressed the portly man in the center.

The man swung toward him swearing. "If it ain't them durn Issues...now get on out'a here! Don't want none'uv your kind in here!"

Paul David stumbled backwards, pulling Barclay with him. The screen door slammed behind them. Tears welled up in Paul David's eyes as he hurriedly retraced their steps. Struggling not to cry, he kept repeating silently, 'big boys don't cry'. They crossed the hollow and started back up the mountain.

"Paul David, why can't we get no haircut?" Barclay asked while trying to keep up with his big brother's long strides.

"Just can't, that's why, just can't," Paul David answered angrily. "Don't want no haircut anyhow...that's just Poky wantin' us to look all nice like for church. We don't really need no haircut, do we?"

"Nope, don't need no haircut."

"Might just go fishin' instead. How 'bout that?"

"Yeah...go fishin'."

Not realizing how fast he'd been pulling little Barclay along, he suddenly noticed him panting and slowed his pace.

"Paul David, what's a *Issue*?"

Paul David stopped dead in his tracks. "Don't say that word! It's a bad word...an' don't ever let me catch ya' saying it again!"

Barclay hung his head. "I won't...it's a bad word."

The summer was waning. August was almost gone, and the heat had finally let up. Now the days were comfortably warm with the evenings getting cool. Poky stretched out on a large rock that jutted out from a lonely ridge. It was warm from the sun's rays. She lay back, letting the rays penetrate her clothing, looked up at a clear blue sky, and watched a few clouds far above slide lazily by. It was a comforting and peaceful setting, the surroundings embraced her, and she partially drifted off into a dreamy state of mind. Suddenly, she jumped. An eerie sound was heard throughout the forest...the sound of a woman crying. Poky sat up and rubbed her eyes. "You ol' screech owl! Gonna be another hard winter for sho," she said aloud, recalling the mountain forecast that a hard winter's coming when the screech owl sounds like a woman crying. The shadows were now falling, evening was coming, and she could feel the cool updraft. She rose to go home.

A three-quarter moon appeared and began its slow ascent as Poky reached her porch and sat down listening to what sounded like a solid wall of cicadas. She could hardly pick one out individually. A whole choir was lending itself to the otherwise quiet night. It was the end of summer all right, and the cicadas cast a spell of sadness about the darkened forest.

THE VARIED ROOFTOPS that scaled the hillside of Lynchburg were washed in the moon's silver glow, also. Lauralee walked out of the Isis Theater, and adjusted her eyes to the twilight. Soon it would be totally dark except for the moon's glow. She stretched her legs and quickly headed down Main Street. Three times she'd sat through the movie...something she often did. But she must hurry now or she'd be late for sure. Mama was getting off work, and she'd promised to meet her and walk her home. She turned up Sixth and passed by the car barn on the corner. The strong smell of hot electric motors wafted out to her. The trolleys had just been put up for the night, and after being run all day, they sent forth a distinct burning odor, a smell she never liked. She reached Church, and started up Monument Terrace steps. Quickly, she climbed the many steps, hurrying all the while. Turning down Court Street until she came to Twelfth, she saw The Lynchburg Steam Bakery up ahead and could see her mother standing out front waiting for her. Other employees were passing her on their way home.

"Mama!" she called out.

Hallie waved and walked toward her.

"Lauralee, dear, what took you so long?"

"I'm sorry, Mama. Guess the time slipped up on me. I practically ran all the way from the Isis."

"The Isis? You mean you were still there? But I thought you were going earlier...."

"I did...I mean...."

"How many times, Lauralee?"

She looked at her mother with a grin. "Three."

"Lauralee, you *sat* through that movie three times? I don't know how you do it."

"It was real good, Mama."

"Apparently so," she smiled, "but I thought you didn't like the Isis."

"It's all right, I guess. I just don't like the way the seats go up instead of down. Seems sort of backwards to me. The only one I really don't like, though, is the Gayety. It has *rats*."

"Rats! I should hope not."

"Yes it does, Mama. I saw them!"

"Really. You know, I've never known anyone who loves the picture show as much as you." Lauralee giggled as they headed home.

"How about some ice cream tonight?"

"Oh, Mama, I hoped you'd say that!"

On rare occasions, when Hallie felt it necessary to invest in a little more happiness, she'd stop on the way home from work and buy a quart of ice cream. Tonight was one of those nights. She felt unusually tired. These long hours were getting to her. Starting at 9:00 AM and getting off at 8:00 PM was just a bit too much, and she didn't know how much longer she could take it. But she was afraid to quit with times like they were. Jon Junior was a blessing, still sending money from the CCC's. He no longer was just an enrollee, but had been elevated to a leader, serving as storekeeper. She missed him being gone, but was thankful that he was able to get home a little more frequently. Jamey had just turned sixteen and would begin his last year of school in the fall. He, too, was talking about joining the CCC's when he finished school.

Then she would only have Lauralee. But still she must provide for Lauralee and herself. The road seemed long and hard yet, but she wouldn't think about that now. She'd just take one day at a time. Poky said that's what God advises...*to take one day at a time.* He knows we can't handle more than that. And on this day, she'd buy a quart of ice cream and enjoy it with her family.

The vanilla ice cream was cold and refreshing as they sat out on the second story porch of the once-upon-a-time store building. Darkness prevailed, but the glow of the three-quarter moon enabled them to dimly see all around. The view was magnificent at any time, but particularly on a moonlit night, such as tonight, allowing them to see almost down to the river itself.

"I love summertime, don't you, Mama?"

"It's nice, except for the heat sometimes."

"But the nights are especially nice, aren't they?"

"Yes, dear, they are."

"When's Jon Junior coming home?"

"Not before Thanksgiving, I don't believe. But he's planning on a nice long visit when he does come."

"Good," Jamey joined in, "he's supposed to bring me some information on the CCC's when he comes."

"You still thinking about joining?"

"Yes, ma'am, I am."

"Well, it's certainly been good for Jon Junior. I suppose it will be for you, too."

"Mama?"

"Yes, Lauralee?"

"A good movie's showing at the Isis Saturday. Think we can go?"

Hallie laughed.

"All she thinks about is movies," Jamey teased. She frowned back at him.

"I take that back. Little sister is growing up. You seen her do the *Charleston* lately? She's pretty good."

"Mama, make him quit picking on me, would you, please?"

"Jamey, that's enough. And we'll see, Lauralee, about the movie. Now look yonder how the moon keeps disappearing behind those clouds."

The three continued to sit on the top porch as the moon climbed higher.

CHAPTER EIGHT

1941

THE GREAT DEPRESSION came to an end, but a greater tragedy was looming that pushed it into the background. As we trace the pages of history, that eternal enemy called *war* fills the pockets of some, while claiming the lives of others. And it was raging...spreading all over the globe...Germany, Poland, Denmark, Luxembourg, the Netherlands, Belgium, Norway, France, Great Britain, Italy, Greece, Africa, the Soviet Union, Japan. Though aiding the Allies against the Axis, the United States still hoped to stay out of this massive war.

Folks on Oak Mountain, in Lynchburg, in Virginia and throughout most of America did not sense the ultimate climatic danger. Life went on much as before, except for daily newspapers and radio broadcasts that pushed the unwanted enemy into their otherwise passive lives.

Lauralee walked out of the Craddock-Terry offices and down the steps, inhaling the crisp autumn air, her favorite time of year. She turned right and headed for downtown, thankful her bossman had allowed her to get off a little early. Tomorrow was her mother's birthday, and she must get her something special. D. Moses was having a sale, and she wanted to surprise her with a beautiful fall dress. Her mother never bought anything for herself. But now that *she* was working, it was going to be different. Briskly, she walked up and down the familiar hills until she began her final descent to Main Street. "Oh my goodness!" she exclaimed aloud, noticing the large crowd of people lining Main Street. She'd forgotten. A large convoy of several thousand soldiers was due to pass through Lynchburg, actually right down Main Street, on their way to maneuver grounds in North Carolina. She hoped the store wouldn't be too crowded! As she pushed through the crowd, an old woman caught hold of her elbow.

"Young lady, you're just in time...I hear there'll be over four thousand soldiers here directly. Pretty as you are, you better stand up front!" The toothless old woman grinned mischievously. Lauralee pulled away and headed to D. Moses, thinking...the nerve of that little old lady!

After making her purchase and having it wrapped, she rejoined the excited throng outside, feeling the electricity in the air. Then she heard it, the sound of numerous engines up ahead. War time was suddenly brought close to home as a dusty field artillery convoy of forty-three hundred men and six hundred and sixty-seven vehicles pushed through the tiny town.

"They'll be camping here tonight, I understand. Out at Montview Farm...imagine that!" She turned to the elderly man informing her and nodded.

"They're late now, you know. Almost two hours, been standing here for over two hours myself. They came from up north, Pennsylvania, but they didn't count on our *mountains.*" He laughed.

"I see."

Lauralee stood somberly wondering what lay ahead for all of them.

OCTOBER WITH ALL its beauty began to wane, and the rich red, gold and russet leaves dropped beneath heavy autumn rains. Those that obstinately clung on were torn away by fierce November winds. These winds were blowing as Barclay and Poky steadily marched back and forth to the woodshed, carrying armfuls of dried wood to the porch.

"Winter's comin', Poky. It's gonna be so-o-o cold."

"That's right, son. But we got a good hot stove that'll run

us right out'a there. We don't need t'worry none. Smell'at wood smoke now. I can't think'uv nothin' I like better'n smellin' wood smoke'uv a cold winter day." She glanced up at the old chimney with its blue curling smoke.

"But what about th'animals, Poky...an' th'birds?" What're they gonna do?"

"Oh, th'good Lord takes care'uv'em, son. He figured it all out. Some'uv'em take off t'warmer places. Call it migratin'. Like th'beautiful monarch butterfly, for instance...they go away t'them warmer places. But they always come back, ya' know. A lotta birds do th'same."

"Where do they go, Poky?"

"Lots'uv places like down t'Florida an' all. I hear tell th'monarch goes clear t'Mexico sometimes. Ain't that somethin'?"

"Wow!"

"An' then again, some animals just plain find'em a hole undergroun' or somewheres where it's warm an' go t'sleep."

"...like bears...like Smokey th'bear."

"That's right. Not only bears, though. A lot'uv other lil' creatures do jest th'same. Th'chipmunk. They make'em a snug lil' den an' sleep all winter jest as sound as you please. Ground hogs do, too."

"This 'nough wood, Poky?" The little fellow asked with circles of warm air escaping his chapped lips.

"Think that'll be jest fine an' dandy, son. Why don't we take us a break an' fix up some hot tea?"

Barclay was spending more and more time with Poky, much to her delight. He loved roaming around the mountainside even with the cold winter winds whipping at his coattail. It was on such a day, after several nights of freezing weather, that he'd come upon a sad sight. He'd sat down for a bit underneath a large old oak. As he leisurely picked at the wet leafy moss with a stick, his eyes grew larger. It was a tiny tree frog lying partly beneath the leaves. It was blue. It was dead. Tenderly, he picked up the cold, stiff creature and carried it back to the cabin. Without telling Poky, he put it in a matchbox, and figured he'd bury it later when the ground thawed.

"Come on in'ere, son," Poky called to him, "let's sit down here a spell an' do a lil' readin'." She loved to have Barclay read to her. After reading the sixth chapter of Matthew aloud, he paused, "Poky, what does it mean when it says '*your heart is where your treasure is*'?"

"Go back an' read them verses, son."

He read slowly and deliberately, trying to fathom the words of wisdom, '*Lay not up for yourselves treasures upon earth, where moth and rust doth corrupt, and where thieves break through and steal; but lay up for yourselves treasures in heaven, where neither moth nor rust doth corrupt, and where thieves do not break through nor steal. For where your treasure is, there will your heart be also.*'

"Thank you, son. Now lemme see. God don't want us jest thinkin' 'bout gettin' things down'ere on earth. He's tryin' t'tell us they ain't that important. Instead'uv, He wants us t'fix our minds on things in heaven 'cause He knows we gonna be thinkin' 'bout an' carin' 'bout where our treasure is, ya' see. Whether it be down here or up in heaven. We gotta watch out for things, son. Always remember...*th'more things you have...th'more things have you.*"

Barclay pondered these deep thoughts.

"What ya' say we fix up a batch'uv peanut butter candy?"

"Whoopee!" He jumped to his feet.

As Poky rolled out the creamy white dough on the kitchen table, Barclay sprinkled it with flour, turning the lever and watching the powdery white flour sift through, falling lightly over the dough. Poky pulled down the large jar of peanut butter from her pantry shelf and handed Barclay a dull knife to spread it with. He happily proceeded to smooth the creamy peanut butter over the dough, covering the entire surface. Then Poky rolled up the dough in a long roll stretching across the table. She began slicing it, and small peanut butter pinwheels rolled away from the sharpened knife. The only thing better than helping Poky make peanut butter candy, Barclay thought, was helping her eat it.

A couple of days later, Poky was soaking her feet in a basin of water on the floor. Her corns had been giving her a fit. She was bent over in the straight back chair with her dress hiked up to her knees, immensely enjoying the soothing effects of the hot water, when suddenly something pounced and splashed into her water! Just as suddenly, it splashed out.

"WHAT IN TARNATION!"

A tiny frog leapt across the floor and sat under the kitchen table looking at her.

"BARCLAY!"

He slid into the kitchen. "Yes, ma'am?"

She just pointed to the frog.

"He's alive!" he shouted.

Poky stared at him quizzically.

"I found him, Poky, up on th'mountain th'other day when I went out walking, remember? But he was dead! An' I was gonna bury him...but he done come back to life...just like Lazarus from th'Bible!"

"Now hold on, son. I don't quite think so. Lazarus was dead all right...an' he come back t'life, all right...but that was 'cause Jesus raised him from th'dead. But this'ere lil' tree frog ain't never been dead! He was just froze up, I reckon. Remember I told ya' 'bout how animals survive these cold winters, 'bout th'monarch an' th'chipmunks an' all...well, I forgot to tell ya' 'bout th'frogs. Some'uv'em jest freeze up solid, stay frozen all winter an' thaw out in th'spring. But you done brought this lil' feller in next t'my wood stove an' he thinks it's spring already!"

"Can I keep him, Poky, please?"

She began to shift in her chair, creating a pull and twist on the worn cane bottom, while trying not to knock over the basin of water. "Well, lemme think on it awhile."

JAMEY SILENTLY WATCHED progress in place at the Lynchburg Iron and Metal Company where he'd worked for the past two years. He felt a lump in his throat as men from the Lynchburg Transit Company loaded two of its trolley cars onto flat cars to be shipped off to Norfolk. Unfortunately, all of the now considered 'outmoded vehicles' would be gone in a few days. A number of spectators had stopped to watch also, some just out of curiosity, others with glum appearances. Jamey remembered all during his childhood hearing the familiar clang of the trolley cars as they rolled past his house. It wouldn't be the same. But life was changing, everything was changing, and he didn't know whether or not he liked it. And the war...what was going to happen?

"Jamey, can ya' give me a hand with this'ere load of scrap metal?" Mr. Jones called out.

"Yes, sir." Reluctantly, he turned away from the scene and joined his supervisor. While hoisting the heavy metal up and over the side of the large container, Mr. Jones remarked sarcastically, "Funny we gettin' so high class, we don't need these old trolleys no more...got fancy new buses, but the big city of Norfolk's gonna take'em!"

"That's because Norfolk's booming...due to the war."

"I know...I know. Don't wanna hear nothin' more 'bout the war. Can't read nothin' in the papers but war. Tired of hearing 'bout it." The greying, middle-aged man threw his load over the side and strode off.

That evening as Jamey walked home, he thought about Mr. Jones's words... 'Tired of hearing about it.' That seemed strange to him, and he wondered why he wasn't tired of it also...but he wasn't! In fact, he couldn't wait each day to read the news or listen to the radio. He wouldn't tell anyone, even felt guilty about it, but somehow it was all very exciting! Of course, he didn't like to think about the killing...but the guns, the planes, the navy, the military strategy...it was all so exciting, certainly compared to his boring life in the little town of Lynchburg. He wondered if

Jon Junior felt this way. No, probably not. They were so different. Jon Junior seemed content with life, not at all like himself. He felt a restlessness, an unsettling spirit within. He thought of his dad and wondered again if maybe...just maybe he had felt the same. He wished he could have known him better.

Some nights later, Jamey and Jon Junior were jammed into the Municipal Stadium along with five thousand other Lynchburgers anxious to see the action close up. The unusual action was a simulated aerial 'attack' against Lynchburg's important railroad center carried out by a Coast Artillery antiaircraft regiment from Camp Pendleton. Jamey, so caught up in the drama being staged, a realistic defense with searchlights stabbing the darkened sky, didn't even notice Jon Junior slip away. His eyes were riveted to the targeted plane overhead, highlighted by the piercing searchlights. It was at the end of the impressive demonstration as all searchlights beamed skyward, waving around madly and resembling the opening night of a world's fair, that he noticed him missing. Searching through the heavy crowd, he was about to give up and go home alone when he spotted him standing closely to a young woman. Moving toward them with interest, he saw that it was Mrs. Browning, Lauralee's last English teacher. He remembered her from the PTA meeting he'd attended with his mother, the one she'd dragged him to because Lauralee was singing in the preliminary part with the high-school choir. But why was Jon Junior with her...and standing so close? He stopped before approaching them, feeling as if he was intruding upon something intimate. But he couldn't help but watch as they stood there staring into one another's eyes. Suddenly she turned and was lost in the crowd. Jon Junior stood looking after her.

"Jon Junior..." he called out abruptly. His brother turned slowly and joined him. He was quiet on the way home as Jamey rambled on about the demonstration, purposely avoiding any mention of what he'd seen. It wasn't hard for him to do, still caught up in the aftermath of all the excitement...but the scene he'd witnessed mysteriously hung over him as they parted and went to bed that night.

Early the next morning, the unit of eleven hundred men and fifty officers and over two hundred vehicles left Lynchburg, leaving the small town still trembling from its dramatic demonstration.

Jamey was already seated at the table when Jon Junior joined him for breakfast. Hallie placed the hot biscuits on the table and sat down with them.

"Well, how was it? The much talked about demonstration, I mean," Lauralee inquired, while quickly buttering a biscuit.

"Fantastic, just fantastic, never seen anything like it!" Jamey eagerly responded. "You should've gone with us."

"No, thank you. We could see it from here, most of it...certainly all I cared to see."

"They left this morning, I understand," Hallie said.

"Headed for Big Meadows to camp overnight," Jon Junior added, "to tackle its next problem — the defense of Swift Run Gap on the Skyline Drive. Like to be there myself."

Jamey watched his brother who seemed unusually despondent.

"What do you mean, Jon Junior?" Hallie questioned. "Aren't you happy to be home instead of away so long, the way you were with the CCC's?"

"Yes, Mother. Of course I'm happy to be home. You know I am. I just meant I enjoyed my time at Big Meadows. I'll always have fond memories of it, and it's been a long time since I've seen those wide open meadows."

Hallie looked from him to Jamey.

Jamey changed the subject. "Could y'all see the plane from here?"

"We sure did, but it gave me cold chills." Hallie shook her head, not wanting to think of war.

"I don't see why they came at all. Why can't they just leave us alone. Lynchburg's just a little town anyhow," Lauralee added, "...certainly not important enough to have all this soldier stuff intruding. First, they're marching right down Main Street, then drawing crowds to the stadium. What next?"

They all looked at each other, absorbing the profoundness of the question.

"Well, Lauralee, if war comes to us, it would certainly be a good thing if we're prepared, don't you think?"

"Jamey, if war comes, I don't think they'll be concerned about Lynchburg."

"You've got a point, for sure, except for the railroad. But it's still smart to be prepared."

She shook her head impatiently. "Let's change the subject. Let's talk about Thanksgiving. It's November, you know."

Jamey grinned at her, "...and you're baking the turkey this year, I understand."

"That's right," giving him a look that dared him to tease.

Putting up his hands, he joked, "I didn't say a thing!"

CHAPTER NINE

IT WAS DECEMBER 7, 1941, 7:55 AM when the first bombs fell! Eighteen ships anchored in Pearl Harbor sank or were severely damaged, nearly two hundred planes were destroyed and approximately thirty-seven hundred casualties. More than one thousand soldiers were permanently entombed aboard the battleship *Arizona*. And for the next several years *'Remember Pearl Harbor'* was the battle cry of the United States as the country became part of World War II.

That infamous day of December 7th found Poky quietly listening to her cherished radio as she did every day at certain times. She'd just finished her second cup of tea along with rereading Hallie's letter about Lauralee's new job as a stenographer at the Craddock-Terry Shoe Company. She was thinking about her visit years ago...and going to that picture show with her. Now here she was all growed up and working! But the good thing about all of it was that Hallie, poor tired Hallie, could finally rest from her labors. With all the children grown and working, it wasn't necessary for her to work so hard anymore. Both Jon Junior and Jamey had spent time in the CCC's and returned all the better for it, holding responsible jobs and certainly blessing Hallie. Then her thoughts turned to Barclay, and how fast he was growing up, too, already shining in school as she knew he would. And how he loved to learn, that boy! Suddenly, her program was interrupted with those dreaded words...***'Pearl Harbor has been bombed! At 7:55 this morning...a great fleet of Japanese bombers bombed our ships in Pearl Harbor, and bombed all of our airfields...The casualties are ex-***

tremely heavy....' The voice on the other end kept on talking, describing the aftermath, but Poky's mind had taken over. IT WAS HERE! WAR! IT WAS HERE! Her heart beat faster. She stood up and walked to the window, absently staring out at the starkness of Oak Mountain. Row after row of tall, naked trees swayed in the brisk winter breeze as they marched up the cold barren ridge. WAR! What would it mean? She grabbed her black cape and went outside, instantly meeting the sharpness of the cold mountain air. She walked out to the ridge, fulfilling her need to bond closer to her mountain. What did the future hold for Americans now? She thought of all the young and maybe not so young men that she knew...those on Oak Mountain, including the Branham boys...all but Barclay, thank goodness! She thought of Hallie's boys...Jon Junior and Jamey. Oh no! This would be too much for Hallie, just when life was beginning to ease a little for her.

She *must* talk to someone. She went back to the cabin, hurriedly packed a few items into a basket, and set out for the Branhams. How would they be taking this news? Suppose Paul David had to go! Who would look after Barclay? Ever since their mother passed away last June, Paul David had taken upon himself this new role, this new responsibility. Zeke Branham's health was ailing, too, and he was gone most of the time, working as much as possible. But even when he was home, he really wasn't home. He'd seemed to drift away from everything after Mrs. Branham's premature death. Poor Mrs. Branham just never strengthened after Barclay's birth, just seemed to waste away. But Paul David was holding the household together the best he could. She'd managed to get over fairly often, cleaning up and fixing a decent meal every now and then, although Paul David had surprised her with his knowledge of cooking. She pulled her cape closely about her against the biting winter chill. "War!" she said aloud as she trudged along. "Seems like everybody's fightin' ever since that Hitler took over an' began invadin' all them other countries." She'd been listening to it all on the radio..."Poland, Denmark, Norway, France an' th'others...now everybody's fightin'...China, Italy, Great Britain, th'Soviet Union...an' now us, too. Oh my! What's this world comin' to?" The Branham house was a welcomed sight with its smoke rising upward from the rock chimney.

"Poky, Poky..." Barclay exclaimed, pulling her in out of the cold.

"My gracious, boy, calm down. Act like you ain't seen me in a month'uv Sundays!" Since the loss of his mother, he'd looked forward to each and every one of her visits with great anticipation. He eyed the basket now. In a household of men focused on work and survival, Poky was a ray of sunshine in his young life.

"What ya' got in th'basket, Poky?"

"Young man, do ya' think there's somethin' in this'ere basket for you?"

He grinned excitedly as Poky pulled out the left-over apple pie.

"Apple pie!"

"That's right, now be sure t'share it." His happiness almost caused her to forget her purpose. She looked up at Zeke Branham.

"You heard, Miss Poky?"

Nodding, she sat down on the wobbly, cane bottom chair across from him. "Heard it on th'radio. Where are th'boys?"

"Gone down to th'store t'see what ever'body else thinks."

"I knew it was comin'...sooner or later...."

"Yes, ma'am. But I'll be doggoned if I 'spected th'*Japanese* t'do it!"

"Can't figure how they slipped up on'us...ya' know...able to attack an'all...can't figure that one out...."

"Know what ya' mean. Never thought it'd happen this'a way!"

"How th'boys takin' it?"

"No sooner they heard it on th'radio, they up an' took off. Seemed all fidgety like. Miss Poky, if they take my boys...."

She looked up at him, a man really not old, but old for his years. She was used to this. Most mountain men aged before their time, but Zeke Branham had aged even more in the last year.

"I mean, you know, after..." He glanced down at Barclay busy shooting marbles on the bare floor. "...I hate to see my boys go off to war...."

"Know 'xactly what ya' mean, Mr. Branham. I'll be prayin' for'em, I will. But first we gotta see what's gonna happen."

"I know what's gonna happen."

She stared at him, knowing too.

The associated press described the aftermath... *'like a momentarily stunned giant, the nation awakened to the grim fact of war'*. Though stunned, however, the young nation took the news calmly and prepared for the long months ahead while congressmen, cabinet members and supreme court justices crowded galleries looking to the president as he asked for war against Japan. *"With confidence in our armed forces, with the unbounding determination of our people, we will gain the inevitable triumph, so help us God."* Thus the president stated before them all, and before the uneasy nation. And amid the hurried recall of all its military resources, people gathered in small, silent groups to watch the news bulletins and buy extra newspapers and most of all to listen to their radios.

At quarter to ten two nights later, Hallie, Lauralee, Jon Junior and Jamey sat anxiously before the radio awaiting the national broadcast by the president. Hallie glanced at the clock on the wall. "He'll be on soon. Lauralee, would you hand me that afghan, please. It feels a little cool in here."

Jon Junior got up and stoked the stove. "Still hard to believe I actually saw him...the president, I mean."

"That was an honor for sure, son."

"He's certainly had his hands full, first the depression and now the war. I wouldn't want to be in his shoes," Jamey remarked.

"Now, that's hard to believe."

"No, it isn't, Lauralee. I wouldn't want that job...all that responsibility. No way. I'd much rather be where the action is myself."

Hallie quickly lifted her head from her pillow, but Jamey never noticed. "Here it comes...listen everybody." He moved his chair closer.

The president's voice came across the airways strong and somber..."*The sudden criminal attacks perpetrated by the Japanese in the Pacific provide the climax of a decade of international immorality. Powerful and resourceful gangsters have banded together to make war upon the whole human race. Their challenge has now been flung at the United States of America....*"

Lauralee turned from one to the other trying to read their thoughts. Hallie's tired face was strained, Jon Junior's was thoughtful and Jamey's held an aura of excitement. The detailed message held all of America's rapt attention from the Atlantic to the Pacific.

"*We are now in this war. We are all in it— all the way. Every single man, woman and child is a partner in the most tremendous undertaking of our American history.*"

Those grave words penetrated the Blue Ridge, as well. Barclay looked up at his older brothers and then to his father, trying to discern it all as the cold winter winds brushed naked oak branches against the cabin.

"*We must share together the bad news and the good news, the defeats and the victories— the changing fortunes of war....*"

"He's right about that for sure, he's right," Jack Jacob spoke up authoritatively.

"Sh-h-h-h," his brothers responded in unison. Zeke Branham spit tobacco juice into a rusted soup can, and set it down beside his chair.

"*...On the road ahead there lies hard work— grueling work — day and night, every hour and every minute. I was about to* *add that ahead there lies sacrifices for all of us. But it is not correct to use that word. The United States does not consider it a sacrifice to do all one can, to give one's best to our nation, when the nation is fighting for its existence and its future life. It is not a sacrifice for any man, old or young, to be in the Army or the Navy of the United States. Rather it is a privilege...."*

Barclay watched his brothers nod their heads, one by one. Zeke Branham watched also.

"*...It is not a sacrifice for the industrialist or the wage-earner, the farmer or the shopkeeper, the trainman or the doctor, to pay more taxes, to buy more bonds, to forego extra profits, to work longer or harder at the task for which he is best fitted. Rather it is a privilege. It is not a sacrifice to do without many things to which we are accustomed if the national defense calls for doing without....*"

Her mother's clock struck the hour, and Hallie felt a tinge of fright. She had done without through all those years, and now dreaded the thought of such a future. She looked at her children surrounding her, and they'd gone without, as well. Now, when they finally had a chance to get ahead, to prosper, the war came! She choked back a sob as the president continued.

"*...I am sure that the people in every part of the nation are prepared in their individual living to win this war...I am sure they will cheerfully give up those material things they are asked to give up...I am sure that they will retain all those great spiritual things without which we cannot win....*"

Hallie lifted her head with hope. Of course! He would see them through. God would be with them. She reached over and clasped Lauralee's hand. Lauralee reached for Jon Junior's, and Jon Junior grabbed Jamey's.

"*...but we must face the fact that modern warfare as conducted in the Nazi manner is a dirty business. We don't like it — but we are in it and we're going to fight it with everything we've got.*"

Jamey's face glowed.

The president's message finally concluded... *"and in the dark hours of this day — and through dark days that may be yet to come — we will know that the vast majority of the members of the human race are on our side. Many of them are fighting with us. For, in representing our cause, we represent theirs as well — our hope and their hope for liberty under God."*

Poky switched off the radio, slowly walked to her bedroom, undressed and pulled her large flannel nightgown over her head. She turned off the light, again thanking God for the miracle of electricity — what a blessing. The moonlight fell into the darkened room, and she paused before getting into bed, and crossed over to the window to look up into its full face. But what caught her attention instead was the old chestnut stump that stood out beneath its silver rays. It was a sad day when that dreaded enemy, the blight, struck and killed all the chestnuts. It will be a sadder day still now that this Nazi enemy has struck...how many young lives will it take? Kneeling beside her bed, she prayed aloud..."Lord, Lord, have mercy upon us!"

A few days later, Adolph Hitler declared war against the United States, announcing that Germany, Italy and Japan were pledged in a new alliance to fight it together to a finish.

THERE WAS A KNOCK at Hallie's door. She laid aside her mending to answer. It was Mr. Jenkins, her elderly neighbor who had moved in beside her a couple of years ago after his wife passed away. He held out the newspaper to her, pointing to the headlines... *'U.S. to Register all Men 18 to 64....'*

Hallie looked up at him.

"Imagine that, Mrs. Frederick. Me, an old man gonna be sixty-four on my next birthday, gotta go and get registered...imagine that!"

"I'm sorry, Mr. Jenkins, I'm truly sorry." Her heart went out to the decrepit old man, leaning on a cane.

"Oh, no ma'am, don't be sorry. I'm right proud that the United States still considers me worthy of something." He laughed, and Hallie laughed with him.

"Please do come in for a cup of coffee, Mr. Jenkins."

"Don't mind if I do." He followed her into the kitchen, "Paper says they're gonna register forty million men. That's a whole lot of men. Guess I'll get lost in the crowd." Hallie noticed how he rocked back and forth nervously on his feet. She pulled out a chair at the table and placed a cup and saucer before him.

"Have a seat, Mr. Jenkins."

"Thank you kindly, Mrs. Frederick."

"Of course all those won't be in the military, I'm sure."

"Oh, no ma'am. It says for possible military or non-military service. I sure would do my part if they called on me, though. Missed my chance in the first world war. Maybe I'll be the right age this time." Again he chuckled.

Hallie poured the hot coffee. "I heard the Draft Act was passed, and I expected it, of course. But I hadn't heard about the total registration. All those from nineteen to forty-four will be liable for military service. Maybe I'm being selfish...and yes, I admit I am...but I'm really concerned for Jamey and Jon Junior. There was an appeal for young soldiers of enthusiasm and stamina. They won't find one with more enthusiasm and stamina than my Jamey."

"He talking about joining up?"

"No. He's not talking. That's what troubles me, but I can tell there's something going on within."

"What about Jon Junior?"

"Jon Junior says he will do what he feels he must do. He's always been the responsible one. When duty calls, he will answer, I'm sure."

"I know it makes for a lot of worry for you, Mrs. Frederick. But if it's any consolation, I'm sure there are thousands of mothers in your shoes right now. Winston Churchill said, '*We are all in this.*' He's right, too. Really made me feel good to see his determination to stand by us. Thank God for Great Britain."

"That's right."

"Did you see the headlines yesterday? About the war darkening the Capitol?"

She nodded. "And the lights won't be turned back on the dome until peace returns. That could be a long time."

"Yes, ma'am. It could."

Hallie sat down in front of him and slowly sipped her coffee. She enjoyed the old man's company. He'd been a postal worker all his life until he'd slipped on ice, breaking his leg in two places. Unable to deliver mail anymore, he'd retired early. Now he was a lonely old man since his wife had died. Whenever he stopped by, she always took time for him. In fact, she enjoyed their conversations as he was definitely a very bright person, particularly interested in history.

"You still gonna move out in the country, Mrs. Frederick?"

"No. I don't think so," she answered rather subdued, "probably just a dream anyway. I always thought that once the children were grown and doing fine, I'd get a little house with a small yard and flowers and maybe a picket fence with rambling roses growing up on it, and my grandchildren could visit me. You know, I've had that picture in my mind for so many years, but I think it was just a ray of hope during those dark times." She looked around her at the familiar kitchen. "But I've been here so long now, I don't know if I'd feel at home anywhere else and, of course, I've never known anything but life here in the heart of town. I wouldn't know what to do with wide open spaces anyhow, probably feel lost." She smiled wistfully.

He returned her smile rather sadly and sought to change the subject, "Well, understand your church is getting a new organ. Be real nice for Christmas, I suppose."

"Oh yes, we're looking forward to it. I was up there the other day...saw it installed...the pipes, I mean...very large pipes...quite impressive. It'll be used for the first time at the Christmas service on Sunday. You should come, Mr. Jenkins."

"Might just do that. Been away from church for awhile...since the wife passed on, that is, but times like these...war and all...makes one draw nearer to...to the church...and to God, you know."

"I know."

CHRISTMAS PASSED ALMOST unnoticed as the nation, Lynchburg and even Oak Mountain centered their attentions on the business of war. December 30th found Lynchburgers lined up at City Hall registering for defense programs, including Mr. Jenkins. The New Year was ushered in by rain in Lynchburg. All day, a dreary incessant rain that started at sun-up pelted the small town, and shadows of war hung over its hills. Two days later, the United States, Great Britain, Russia and China formally agreed with twenty-two other nations to use their full military and economic might against the Axis. They pledged not to make a separate peace with the enemy, as well. The full fledged world war was on, and thus the new year of 1942 began.

Daily the papers were headlined with war victories on both sides. Hallie read each and every word with concern, for Jamey was gone now, one of the first to volunteer. She was not surprised.

"Mama," Lauralee called into the kitchen as she returned from work. "Did you hear the news...about the plane crash...and Carol Lombard?"

Hallie appeared at the door, drying her hands on her apron. "Carol Lombard?"

"Yes, she was on a plane with some others that crashed on a mountain in Nevada. Clark Gable must be going crazy!"

"For sure, he must...."

"It was on the radio. We heard it at work." Lauralee pulled off her coat and gloves. "Boy, it's cold out there. I figured you would've heard it, too."

"Today, I just didn't feel like listening...hearing all about the war...."

"You all right, Mama?"

"Yes, I'm all right. Wonder what Clark Gable will do now?"

"Who knows? They seemed to have such a wonderful romance and marriage."

"It's certainly good to have both. You don't want one without the other."

"Oh, I don't know, Mama. I hope to have romances, lots of them, but I'm certainly not thinking about any marriage. Jon Junior home yet?"

"No, he's late. Don't know where he is. That's sure terrible about Miss Lombard though and the others, of course."

"The broadcast said Mr. Gable flew out to Nevada right away, and paced a hotel room for hours waiting for news. Then he set off with the sheriff to the scene that was really almost inaccessible. But before he reached it, they met him and told him they'd found the bodies, including Miss Lombard. They said he's extremely distraught."

"Well, I'm sure. What a shame!"

"It said the scene is so mountainous that they'll have to bring the bodies out by horseback. That's got to be terrible."

Hallie shook her head. "Let's change the subject to something pleasant. There's so much trouble and pain in the world, we don't need to think on it too much. It's good for us to think on nice things. In fact, Poky just wrote me the other day about that." She reached over to the secretary for the open letter, "Listen to this, *'whatsoever things are true, whatsoever things are honest, whatsoever things are just, whatsoever things are pure, whatsoever things are lovely, whatsoever things are of good report, if there be any virtue, and if there be any praise, think on these things.'* I especially like the part *'whatsoever things are lovely'*."

"That's from the Bible, Mama. I remember that. It's beautiful."

"And so true. We really need to think about pure and lovely things these days and in the days to come, I fear."

Lauralee was quiet for a moment and then spoke softly, "Mama, I think Jon Junior's going to join, too."

Hallie just looked at her.

"He asked me yesterday...if I would feel comfortable with it being just you and me...."

She sighed, "I see."

"It's hard enough with Jamey over there, Mama. I can't bear to think of Jon Junior going, too."

"He must do what he feels he must do, Lauralee. It's a man's duty. Jon Junior and Jamey are men now."

"I could understand Jamey going. He's so caught up with the military, guns and all, the pure excitement of it. You know how Jamey is...but Jon Junior's not like that, Mama. He loves home."

"Jon Junior seems to be carrying a sadness within him these days. I don't know whether it's the war...or because he's growing older and still single. You know, he's twenty-seven now. However, he never says anything about such things."

"I know."

JANUARY WAS PASSING, and with every day the war was becoming more and more real to the folk on Oak Mountain and in Lynchburg, and the country as a whole, as they watched with trepidation the young men wave good-bye and board trains and buses to answer their call. It was also moving closer to home each day with rationing and defense talk everywhere.

Lauralee came through the door loaded down with a large brown package one Saturday afternoon. "Mama?"

"Oh, you're back already. My goodness! What's in that package?"

"Just wait till you see." She began excitedly unwrapping the large parcel and pulling out what looked like window shades and held one up for her mother.

"A black shade?"

"That's right. They're *Blackout Shades*...the first in Lynchburg, and Snyder & Berman just got them in. Everybody's buying them. Don't worry, Mama...they were only eighty-nine cents each. And this way, when we have the blackouts, we can carry on with what we're doing without cutting off every single light. As soon as we hear the alarm, all we have to do is pull them down...and when the alarm is over, we just let them back up. And they'll fit right over the regular shades. Aren't they clever?"

"Yes, very clever. Don't know what they'll think of next. There are so many strange things to do with a war, takes a lot of getting used to. In fact, I was reading earlier in the paper about Mrs. Roosevelt admonishing those who are hoarding things. You know, I never thought about hoarding anything, but apparently there are people who are doing it. She said anyone who's hoarding things like soap, sugar, silk stockings or auto tires is just kidding himself...that it's not going to be possible to hoard enough to last through this war. She said sooner or later the hoarder's going to have to face the shortage. In fact, Mrs. Roosevelt is setting the example herself by wearing black cotton stockings."

Lauralee glanced down at her own silk stockings somewhat embarrassed. "I always hated those old black stockings!"

Hallie laughed. "I remember."

"Where's the paper anyway?" She laid the shades aside for later.

"There on the table."

Lauralee scanned the headlined war news, then sat down to read the rest of the paper. She was quiet for a bit and then called out, "Mama, did you read about this *Doorkey Baby Problem?*"

"No, I didn't. Go ahead and read it aloud while I peel these potatoes."

"Well, it says here...this is in New York, of course... *'Billy can almost, but not quite, turn the key in the lock of the house where he lives. In about six months, when he's a little taller, and his fingers are a little stronger, he'll be able to do it. He'll be five years old in six months. Meanwhile, he's one more of America's growing group of 'doorkey babies'. Each morning, when his mother leaves for work in a nearby defense factory, she ties a doorkey around his neck. On the key there's a tag reading 'this child belongs at (his address). Please let him in if he wants something.' His mother ties a double knot in the string, kisses him good-bye, says 'be a good boy' and leaves him standing on the doorstep outside his home.'* Can you imagine such a thing?"

"No, I can't. That's scary."

She continued to read...*'There's a vacant lot around the corner filled with interesting piles of junk— old automobile parts, tin cans, broken glass. Billy will play there and on the street all morning. When he gets hungry, he'll ask some older child, or maybe a policeman, to take the key from around his neck and open the door to his home. He'll find lunch inside, there on the kitchen table where his mother put it before she left. Through the long afternoon, it'll be up to Billy to find occupation until night falls and his mother comes home again.'*

"That's terrible!"

"It is that."

"But it goes on to say they're talking about Day Nurseries that would solve these situations, and they're trying to open them in these areas."

"Good. The little ones need to be home with their mamas, but certainly things are not always that simple. I was blessed to be able to be with you all when you were little, and didn't have to work until you were older. I hated leaving you even then."

"But we did fine, Mama. You made sure of that, and of course, we had each other." Lauralee looked up thoughtfully. "When does Jon Junior leave?"

"Ten days from tomorrow."

"It's going to be awfully quiet around here with just you and me."

Hallie smiled sadly. "You're right." Unable to contain her news any longer, she blurted out, "How would you like to go to a *ball?*"

"You mean the Grand Charity Ball?"

"That's exactly what I mean, in honor of Rebecca Yancey Williams. Jon Junior could escort you, and you would have the opportunity of possibly meeting Mrs. Williams, plus all those celebrities that'll be there. What do you think?"

Lauralee's face was flushed with excitement already. "Mama, would you go, too?"

"I don't think so. I'd much rather see you and Jon Junior go and really enjoy a special night before...before he leaves. I have a little money saved, and I want you to get a new dress for the occasion."

"Oh, Mother!" Lauralee hugged her around the neck. "But suppose Jon Junior won't go. You know he doesn't like a lot of hullabaloo, as he calls it."

"He'll go. I know he will."

"What will he wear?"

"His Sunday suit will be fine. He looks very nice in it."

Midst all the woes of war, Lynchburg glowed with glamour and excitement as the World Premiere of *The Vanishing Virginian* was about to take place. Metro-Goldwyn-Mayer had produced a movie based on Lynchburg's Rebecca Yancey Williams' novel about her father, Captain Bob Yancey, and now it was to premiere right in Lynchburg. It was a welcomed interlude during the dark days of war, and much ado was being made over each and every detail to follow during the next two days of spectacular events. It was January 22, and Rebecca Yancey Williams and Ruth Hussey, the MGM star who was among the honored guests, were due to arrive by train in the afternoon. Miss Hussey was to arrive at the Kemper Street Station at 12:50 PM, and Mrs. Williams at the Union Station at

3:20 PM. Metro-Goldwyn-Mayer's advance staff would be holding a reception at 4:00 PM for the visiting press, who would also be arriving on Miss Hussey's train. A dinner would follow, and then the Grand Charity Ball at the city armory. The next day numerous distinguished guests and newspaper representatives would be arriving, including Mrs. Woodrow Wilson, Governor Darden, Senator and Mrs. Carter Glass, Senator and Mrs. Harry F. Byrd and many other governors, senators, Virginia delegates and members of the president's staff. Never before had Lynchburg, perched upon its seven hills, witnessed such a gathering of celebrities. It would be a time well to remember. The conclusion, of course, would be the World Premiere of *The Vanishing Virginian* at the Paramount Theatre at 8:30 PM, which was causing quite a stir.

Lauralee rushed into the house, throwing her bags down and frantically pulling off her scarf and gloves. "Mama, I'm home early. Did you get the dress mended?"

"Yes, dear, calm down. You've plenty of time. See, it's all done." She held up the simple black and white gown they'd purchased on discount due to a rip in the side. Hallie's nimble fingers had taken care of it, and it was good as new.

"What time will Jon Junior get here? Is he getting off early, you suppose?"

"I don't think so, but that isn't necessary either. Jon Junior won't take nearly as much time to dress as you, dear." She smiled up at her lovely daughter.

"Oh, Mama, I'm so nervous. Just think! A real *ball!* I never thought I'd get to go to a real ball, never in a hundred years! And with all those celebrities, too. I hope I get to see them all, but especially Rebecca Yancey Williams. I do want to meet her or at least see her."

"Oh-h, I thought it would be Miss Hussey you'd be all excited about. You've always been so caught up with the stars."

"I'm excited about seeing her, too. But to be an author

and then see your book come alive on the big screen...what a thrilling thing that must be! I can't even imagine it! Oh, I've got to wash my hair and put it up. Could you please help me, Mama."

"Of course, dear."

That evening was truly to be an evening long remembered by many, especially Lauralee. Escorted by Jon Junior, quite dashing in his neatly pressed grey suit, she practically walked on air as they entered the armory. The large converted ballroom literally shouted patriotism, decorated in red, white and blue, with American flags proudly hanging from the walls and windows. A huge crystal ball was suspended from the ceiling, reflecting many colored lights over the dance floor. At one end, a replica of the courthouse had been erected and stood stately overlooking all. At the far end of the floor, an orchestra was already playing. The place was packed, and Lauralee felt goose bumps on her arms, noticing all the exquisite gowns and stylish dress surrounding her. She was in another world! But Jon Junior stood somberly, his attention held by the many flags above him. Suddenly he felt very uncomfortable among the frivolity of it all.

"Have we forgotten we're in the midst of a war!" he said aloud.

"Sh-h-h!" Lauralee grabbed his arm, "Jon Junior, what's wrong with you? This is a charity ball, you know, and the funds go to very worthy causes."

He looked down at his little sister all dressed up, seeing her really for the first time. She literally glowed beneath the colorful lights. He *must* show her a good time. "I'm sorry, Lauralee, I don't know what got into me. Just got to thinking about the war, that's all. Let's enjoy this ball." With that he led her onto the floor, and the two young people were certainly a match for anybody there. Before it was over, Jon Junior was enjoying it as much as anyone, especially when the *Virginia Reel* was played, and a group of Captain Bob

Yancey's old friends joined together to dance. Lauralee got her wish, as well, meeting Rebecca Yancey Williams, even though quite briefly. Hallie was waiting up for them to hear all the details when they arrived home, both quite exhausted from such a gallant evening.

"Oh, Mama, I wish this evening could last forever." She twirled around in her lovely gown, reluctant to change.

"Not me. I'm hitting the sack." Jon Junior laughed.

"Jon Junior?"

"Yes?" He turned to Lauralee.

"Thank you."

"You're most welcome, and I bid you ladies goodnight." He bowed to them and left the room.

Lauralee smiled at Hallie. "Mama, I wish you could've been there."

"I feel like I was, Lauralee...through your eyes. And tomorrow evening, I'll get to see the celebrities, too, at the premiere."

"I can't wait to see the movie now."

Main Street transformed into Hollywood Boulevard on the evening of January 23, 1942, as throngs of people swarmed around the Paramount to catch a glimpse of the celebrities. It was the biggest thing to happen in Lynchburg since the Battle of Lynchburg in the Civil War. Even before supper-time, a large portion of Lynchburg had begun jamming into the Main Street block between Fifth and Sixth. People pushed and jostled behind a chain of state and city police to get a better view of the stream of national celebrities that began arriving about 8:00 PM. It was a most colorful scene with the Paramount's dazzling front, the large marquee illuminating *WORLD PREMIERE OF MGM'S "THE VANISHING VIRGINIAN,"* and its art deco lobby bathed in light from dozens of spotlights, movie cameras and photographers. The glorious theater, spaciously built on the grand scale of the early 1930s showplaces, on that particular night was ablaze with light and excitement. The gold entrance was gleaming even more amid the dazzling lights as they bounced off the gold-encrusted box office, gold railings and gold framed coming attractions. A large crystal chandelier, gracing the entrance, radiated the flashing lights, and the deep red velvet decor cast an aura of elegance truly signifying it was such a night. Gold designs embellishing the deep red carpet literally lit up from all the illumination. When the Paramount opened its doors, there was a double line waiting all the way to Fifth Street and further.

Finally, Hallie and Lauralee were seated in their seats, anxiously waiting. Lauralee looked up at the decorative ceiling plaster overhead and around at the magnificent murals and theater boxes that adorned the walls. She loved this theater. It was her favorite and had been ever since she was a child. They were seated toward the back, and she kept leaning forward to see who was entering.

"They'll have a formal announcement of everyone before the film begins, Lauralee."

"Of course." She sat back, a little embarrassed.

"You know, Mrs. Turbin said that MGM wanted to film Captain Bob Yancey's summer home in Bedford County, but they didn't."

"Why not?"

"She said when they arrived, before they even unpacked their gear, they discovered that Mrs. Russell, the elderly lady living there, had just passed away...a Mrs. Virginia Tate Russell, I believe she said. You know Mrs. Turbin seems to know everyone in Bedford County. It was certainly nice of them to respect the family now owning the place, however, it's a shame they couldn't film the real summer home."

"Where did they film it?"

"I'm not quite sure. Mrs. Turbin said she thinks maybe they went on to Charlottesville and filmed a similar home."

Guests for the premiere kept arriving in automobiles that halted at the curb in front of the theater, discharged their passengers and then moved on for others. Each celebrity was introduced over a public address system as they entered the theater.

*"Mrs. Kermit Roosevelt of Oyster Bay, N.Y., president of Young America...General Edwin A. Watson, aide to the president...the Secretary of State and Mrs. Cordell Hull...Governor Darden...former Governor Price...Representative Otis Bland of Newport News...Representative Howard Smith of Alexandria...Colonel Edwin Halsey, Secretary of the United States Senate and a former citizen of Lynchburg...Mrs. Woodrow Wilson...Colonel and Mrs. William Starling of Washington..."*on and on the stream of celebrities were announced.

"Daddy, who're all *those* people?" an impatient young lad asked his father.

"Celebrities, son."

The crowd outside, which had waited so patiently, was rewarded shortly after 8:30 PM when Miss Hussey and Bill Dudley, her all-American football escort from the University of Virginia, arrived and posed for five minutes in the glare of flashing bulbs. Miss Hussey wore a low-cut black gown and looked as fresh as the morning dew, certainly not like she'd just dashed all the way across the continent and been through a two day whirl of activities. She smiled prettily and waved.

Suddenly a Negro musician, clad in overalls and a tattered shirt, climbed on top of a bale of cotton beside the ticket booth, tuned his banjo and burst forth with...*Oh Susanna.* Percy Brown, his name was, kept up a string of southern melodies to the delight of his large audience.

Finally, the preliminaries were over and all the important people were in their seats in the darkened theater. Lauralee squeezed her mother's hand. "I just can't believe it. This is so-o-o...sensational!" Then the national anthem reverberated from wall to wall, as the white and gold-encrusted Wurlitzer organ rose from the darkened pit beneath the screen, sending forth its mighty rolling tones, filling the movie house specially designed for sound. The spotlight was on Ann

Melodie, the Paramount's lovely organist, as she regally rose with it, and the sounds of patriotism filled the magnificent theater, adding to the thrills of that special night. On the platform was a boy scout at attention, facing the flag of the United States several feet away. Then the Master of Ceremonies pushed through the curtains and began introducing the long list of celebrities. The spotlight played on each one from the projection room as they stood and were applauded.

"Mrs. Woodrow Wilson!" the master of ceremonies announced. Everyone arose and applauded. The clapping seemed to continue forever. Lauralee looked at her mother and smiled. It was all so exciting.

The master of ceremonies spoke again, "I hope we'll do after this war what President Wilson wanted to do after the last one."

Lauralee wondered what he wanted to do.

The impressive organ descended back into its pit, and long, heavy curtains gracefully parted in the center, disclosing the grand screen, and for the first time the audience saw the simple story of *Cap'n Bob Yancey* come alive.

The following day, the celebrities left for more exciting parts of the country and Lynchburg returned to its former sleepy state. Again the cloud of gloom rose from the horizon from a war they could not escape, and settled over the hills...with just a mere memory of those two glorious days and all its fanfare.

CHAPTER TEN

SPRINGTIME OF 1942 arrived, and dogwoods were blooming all over Oak Mountain, spreading a network of white lace intertwining throughout the dark forest as frozen ridges thawed out, sending forth numerous springs of ice-cold water.

It was late evening, and Poky sat in her porch rocker, listening to the early signs of spring. The tiny tree frogs, those little characters called spring peepers that you never see, were serenading with their clear shrill peeps. The newly formed maple leaves rustled in the evening updrafts, and a new moon, large and yellow, began its familiar ascent up the darkened sky. She continued watching for over an hour, as it climbed higher and higher, decreasing in size before her eyes. Tomorrow, she thought, she'd carry those pinto beans an' fatback over t'Barclay an' Mr. Branham. Most likely they'd be lookin' for her, especially Barclay. She'd carry him a hoecake, too. How he loved her hoecakes! She knew he was lonely, missin' his brothers, but particularly missin' Paul David. All four were gone somewhere in th'Pacific now. Seemed they couldn't wait to go, all joinin' up th'first chance they got, except, that is, for Paul David, who was drafted right off. He didn't waste any time respondin' either. Oh well, Poky reasoned, couldn't fault'em none for that...certainly can't fault patriotism. Leastways, Barclay has school, keeps'im busy some'uv th'time. But she didn't know what he'd do come summer.

A slow moving cloud momentarily covered the climbing moon, casting darkness over the forest. But then it was gone, and the silver rays fell upon the sleepy forest once again. Poky's thoughts turned to Hallie, as they often did. Her boys were gone, too, joinin' just as quickly as th'Branham boys. Hallie an' Lauralee were all alone now. She closed her eyes, shutting out the glowing moon and prayed for Jon Junior, Jamey, Paul David and his brothers, and for all those young men fighting all over the world. What a mess we've gotten ourselves into! "Lord," she prayed aloud, "have mercy upon us an' protect our boys."

HALLIE, TOO, SAT beneath the silver rays of the moon with Lauralee atop the porch in Lynchburg. Her thoughts were far away with her sons.

"Thinking of Jon Junior and Jamey, Mama?"

"Yes, Lauralee, I am."

"They'll be all right, Mama. I know they will."

Hallie smiled at her young daughter, now grown up so lovely and fair. "I know, Lauralee, I know."

"You heard from Poky lately?"

"Oh yes, a few days ago, a matter of fact."

"She doing all right?"

"Yes. Her letters are always such a blessing to me. She's busy helping out with that little boy, Barclay. All his brothers are in the war, too."

"All of them? Doesn't he have several?"

"Four to be exact. Poky said they all wanted to go...just like Jamey and Jon Junior."

Lauralee changed the subject, "I've been thinking, Mama, about you and me taking a little trip."

Hallie turned to her in surprise. "A trip?"

"I'd like to visit Poky...at Oak Mountain. I know she lives way up there in the mountains in sort of a primitive way, but still I'd like to visit her. I thought you might, also."

Hallie's thoughts began to race backwards to that visit so many years ago. "Well, I'd certainly love to go, of course. But how would we get there? And you have to work...."

"I have it all figured out. I can get off from work. I have some time coming to me for vacation the first of June."

"How will we get there?"

"You remember me mentioning a friend at the shop named Joy Bell Harris? Her elderly great aunt lives in the valley below Oak Mountain, and she's planning a trip to see her in June. She's already agreed to carry us along."

"Well, my goodness, looks like you've thought of everything." She stood up suddenly. "I need to write Poky...and tell her. She'll certainly be delighted, I'm sure." She paused at the door. "And how long would we be staying?"

"Only a few days. That's how long Joy Bell is staying."

"Poky is going to be so happy."

Easter of 1942 was different for its underlying tone of fear and thus a stronger need to unite on this Resurrection day, and different, too, for its record-breaking temperature in Lynchburg. The mercury hit ninety-one degrees in the shade. But the sweltering heat was not a deterrent in keeping people from donning their Easter frocks and heading to the many churches.

Hallie and Lauralee pushed up the hill toward First Baptist. "I can't believe it's this hot already!" Lauralee exclaimed, fanning herself with her church fan.

"It's going to be a scorcher all right, but what a beautiful Easter morning, Lauralee."

They welcomed the coolness of the large stone edifice as they entered the sanctuary, greeting those already seated. The deep resonant sounds of the new Kimball pipe organ filled the sanctuary and overflowed into the corridors. The processional hymn, *The Day of Resurrection*, followed, then the call to worship, and *The Lord's Prayer*. As the scripture was read from John, Lauralee settled back to its comforting words, and gazed up at the beautiful stained glass picture of Christ behind the pulpit. At first, she didn't like the idea of the refurbishment of the old church, particularly removing the choir from its lofty height. But now she was glad as she reveled in the exquisite beauty of the rendition of Holman

Hunt's painting that had taken its place. Christ knocking on the door, symbolic of the door to our hearts, was the center of the painting. Upon His head the crown of thorns, and in His hand a lit lantern, with angels on either side of Him. The inscription read...*'I am the light of the world'....*

"Even a world that is at war," she whispered.

The pastor concluded his scripture reading...*'And Jesus saith unto him, Thomas, because thou hast seen me, thou hast believed: blessed are they that have not seen, and yet have believed.'* He prayed, and they all rose to sing...*Christ, The Lord is Risen Today.* The Easter service continued and lifted the hearts of a weary people. Afterwards, the congregation lingered in the cool sanctuary, a haven from the heat and from the present chaotic world.

"Hallie, I can't believe this is little Lauralee. It simply does not seem possible. Why, it just seems like yesterday she was skipping around these pews."

"I know what you mean, Mr. White."

"Did you see where we had thirty-three men leave here this week for induction in the Army? They keep on leaving. Of course, it takes a lot of men from everywhere to make up that nine million draft. You hear from your boys, Hallie?"

"Yes, some."

"Hello, Hallie, Lauralee, Mr. White," said Mrs. Rickets as she walked up. "We sure need to be praying much. Y'all read where those three U.S. warships were bombed and sunk by the Japs, more than 700 men lost? Lord have mercy on us for sure."

"Come, Mother, we must be getting home." Lauralee pulled her by the arm. "See you all next week."

As they parted, Hallie whispered, "Thanks, dear." The heat was warm and sultry as they descended Eleventh Street. When they reached Main, the colorful crowds were out there, gayly clad and staging their all-day Easter parade. However, the Army khaki and Navy blue conspicuously stood out in the throngs.

"You want to stroll down Main Street, Mama?"

"Not this year, dear." Once home, they changed into their coolest clothes and began dinner.

"How about some iced tea, Lauralee?"

"Sounds wonderful. I'll get the glasses. What's this on the cupboard door?" A large newspaper clipping of Christ in the sky with soldiers in fox holes gazing up at Him. The caption read... *'In the world ye shall have tribulation; but be of good cheer: I have overcome the world.' John 16:33.*

"I cut it out of the paper yesterday. Makes me feel good when I look at it."

April passed into May, and Lynchburgers found themselves experiencing their first all out "blackout," although it was for only twenty-six minutes. When the sirens began to wail at 9:34 PM, lights started to go off and in little more than three minutes, downtown Lynchburg was in darkness.

"We certainly appreciate you joining us, Mr. Jenkins. We womenfolk don't particularly care to be alone during this blackout."

"Mrs. Frederick, it's my pleasure. I'm not too fond of being alone in it myself, reminds me of when I was a boy and scared of the dark." One of his comforting short laughs followed.

"See, Mama, I told you these blackout shades would be nice." The three sat huddled together in the living room with one small lamp burning.

"You sure this light can't be seen?"

"I'm sure. Remember I tested the shades when I bought them."

"That's right. Well, it's certainly better than sitting in the dark."

"But if it *were* the real thing, I'd cut that lamp out for sure."

"So would I, Mr. Jenkins. Would you care for some more coffee?"

"Just a little, ma'am. No more sugar, though. Gotta watch that sugar. How're you folks doing with the rationing?"

"We're fine. Could stand to cut back some anyhow. Now, if the boys were here, it'd be different. They loved their sweets." She became quiet, and the darkness seemed to close in around them. Lauralee quickly changed the subject.

"Did you march in the Patriotic Parade Friday night, Mr. Jenkins?"

"Sure did. Proud of myself, too. Didn't know I had it in me. Kept right up with the rest of them. Y'all didn't make it?"

"No, we were planning on it, but I came down with a twenty-four hour stomach sickness, and mama stayed home with me. I told her to go ahead, but she wouldn't leave. We read where there were over four-thousand that marched. Must have been something."

"Oh, it was all right. A sight to see with all those men dressed up in their distinctive uniforms, the Virginia Protective Force and the Virginia Flying Corps, and World War I veterans and even some Spanish American War veterans...plus the scouts, of course."

"And you were with your group?"

"Yes, ma'am, the Lynchburg Civilian Defense Organization...made up mostly of volunteers like myself...but there's a lot of us."

"Aren't y'all the ones responsible for the air raid sirens?"

"That's right. We man the warning centers around the clock. Those things will blow the top of your head right off." He laughed. "Would've been interesting to be on duty tonight. But don't get me wrong ladies, I'd much rather have the honor of keeping you company."

"And we feel so much the better for it, too."

"Thank you, Mrs. Frederick. By the way, did you ladies get out to Riverside Park to see the flowering cherry trees?"

"We missed it this year. I've seen them before though, and they are simply beautiful. But we did get to see the tulips at Miller Park, didn't we, Lauralee? And it was a lovely day."

"Mama and I walked around the park several times...I just

love springtime! Why couldn't every day be like that...instead of like this with war hanging over our heads?"

"Lauralee, I've wondered that myself a few times. Guess man has been wondering that since the beginning of time. Wars have always been and will always be...at least while we're down here on earth. There's just too much greed in a lot of people, and greed starts lots of wars, people wanting more land, more money, more of this or that...it's a shame, for sure."

THE 1938 PACKARD chugged up the rugged mountainside, and, skillfully, Lauralee juggled their baggage on her lap. It was all she could do to keep from spilling everything over with each and every bump and jostle. Balancing her wares, she quickly wiped her forehead. It was hot! Joy Bell sat beside her, oblivious to her surroundings, enraptured with a copy of *The Scarlet Letter.* Joy Bell read all the time. The worn copy jerked up and down and sideways as the car wheels attempted to follow the already imprinted deep ruts in the curving mountain road, and her eyes squinted narrowly. Suddenly Joy Bell's *Scarlet Letter* flew to the floorboard, and the startled passengers tossed back and forth. The deep, uneven ruts caused the Packard to swing sideways, straddling the slick, red clay bank. Just as quickly, it uprighted and continued on its upward course. Hallie pushed her straw hat back up on her head as she nervously regained her composure. "Now, Mr. Harris, you don't have to take us all the way. We can get there I'm sure...please don't go out of your way. This seems such an inconvenience for you...."

"Don't mind a'tall, Mrs. Frederick. I expect you'd be surprised how hard it might be to find a way up here, though."

Hallie hesitated, realizing he was most likely quite right. "Still we hate to put you out."

"Think nothing of it. If we make it up this mountain, won't

be any problem at all."

"I'm sorry it's so bad. It's been a long time, and I'd forgotten just how it was."

"Things don't change much up in these mountains, Mrs. Frederick. But I'm used to driving these kind of roads. Got'em down in the valley where Aunt Molly lives, too. I used to think it was a barrel of fun when I was the age of the girls here." Joy Bell looked up amusedly, and Lauralee continued balancing their bags. Higher and higher they climbed. As the car struggled up the mountainside, the slightly cooler temperatures were unanimously welcomed. Suddenly, steam poured from the hood with a loud hissing sound.

"Uh-oh...looks like she's heatin' up." Mr. Harris switched off the ignition and climbed out. Carefully he lifted the hood and a sudden rush of steam shot upward.

"Oh my!"

"Don't worry, Mrs. Frederick. It's just the radiator overheating. Been waiting for it to happen. Knew the Packard couldn't take it...not like my old Ford."

"It always happens, Mrs. Frederick," Joy Bell reassured her without looking up from her book.

Hallie glanced back at her questioningly.

"It'll probably take awhile to cool down, too." This time she looked up and smiled.

"Oh," Hallie responded and gazed about her, feeling totally cut off from all civilization. The narrow, rutted road was closely flanked on both sides with tall, straight trees and underbrush, creating a lushness of greenery. The steep mountain road climbed upward in front of them, disappearing in a curve. She leaned out the window and looked up to where the tall pines, poplars, hickories and oaks left off. Only a small patch of clear blue sky could be seen.

"You can get out and stretch your legs, ladies, if you like," Mr. Harris offered while looking for a rag in the back of the car to remove the radiator cap. "Might be awhile."

Quickly, Lauralee hopped out and opened the door wide

for her mother. Joy Bell remained, obviously enjoying the stillness of the car, and continued reading.

"Watch your step, ladies. These ruts will cause you to fall."

Heeding his instruction, Hallie carefully got out, welcoming the fresh earthy, mountain scents and looked all about her. Cautiously, she stepped into the deep ruts. Suddenly, they heard a racket...another vehicle chugging up the mountainside.

"Better clear out of the road, ladies."

Both Hallie and Lauralee retreated to the damp, red clay bank, and watched as an old beat-up pick-up rattled by and then stopped. "Gotta problem, mister?"

"Heated up on me. Will take her awhile to cool down."

Zeke Branham leaned out the window, silently staring at the three ladies in their rare city frocks.

"We were headed up to Miss Poky Fitzgerald's place. These ladies here are friends of hers and going to visit awhile. I'm Leroy Harris from over in Lynchburg, and this is my daughter." He pointed to Joy Bell in the car, who was staring awkwardly out at the old man.

"Name's Branham...Zeke Branham...and this'ere's my boy, Barclay." He continued to give the city folk a long once over, and then said authoritatively, "Any friends'uv Poky's is friends'uv mine. Be goin' by'er place shortly. Glad to give ya' a hitch. Hop in th'back, Barclay." The young fellow got out and obediently jumped up into the back of the truck and happily situated himself atop a pile of chopped wood.

A short while later, the old pick-up rattled up to the humble cabin and shut off. Zeke Branham got out, walked around the truck and opened the door for Hallie and Lauralee. Barclay struggled down from the back, dragging their luggage with him.

"Oh, what a helpful young man...but isn't that too heavy for you?" Hallie asked.

"No, ma'am," he answered proudly.

They walked up to the cabin only to find it empty.

"Probably in th'woods not far. You can wait here if'n you like." Zeke Branham waved to the porch.

"Oh, thank you, Mr. Branham. This will be fine and a welcomed rest," Hallie responded gratefully. "What do we owe you?"

A frown crossed his brow. "We don't pay folk for helpin' folk in trouble up here, ma'am."

"Certainly, of course not, and we're very grateful."

Zeke Branham tipped his hat, and turned back to his truck. Barclay followed, tipping his cap as well.

Lauralee looked at her mother with amusement, and Hallie sat down in the waiting rocker. "Well, guess we'll just wait...."

As Zeke said, Poky was walking in the woods, hunting specific herbs and deeply enjoying the solitude of being alone with God's creation. She'd learned that herbs gathered on a hot sunny day like today would have a stronger flavor, and thus she was taking advantage of the weather to replenish her stock. Farther and farther into the dense forest she rambled, while softly humming a tune, until she spied something glittering in the sun...a sign. She shook her head as she stooped to pick up the top...a Mason jar top, and continued walking. Then she spotted a thin curl of blue smoke rising from a thick undergrowth of brush. She advanced more quickly.

"Jes, you better come on out!"

Slowly, the thick laurel foliage parted, and an old man, who looked to be about sixty, rose up from a stooped position. "Aw, Miss Poky, you done gone an' got my back out'a shape again."

She walked up to him holding the jar top in her outstretched hand. "You dropped somethin'."

The wiry, weather-beaten man looked down at it and then back to her with a frown, silently reaching for it.

"This ain't none'uv my business, Jes, but you gonna get

caught as sure as th'sun's gonna set today."

"That's right, Miss Poky...it ain't none'uv your business, an' if'n I do, then he's a better man than me...an' I'll be obliged t'pay th'fine."

Poky watched as the old man went about his business. "It's like I said before, it ain't none'uv my business, but ya' know I don't like it...."

He kept quiet.

"It don't do no good, no good a'tall."

"Feeds my ol' woman an' fam'ly."

His words struck a note of reality. Poky well knew the plight of some of the mountain folk, no skills, no work, no hope. Some of them relied almost totally on their stills to make a living as their fathers before them, and a bare one at that. But still she believed there had to be a better way.

"I know that, Jes...but th'stuff makes folks crazy...like Otis Applebee th'other week a'beatin' up on his wife an' she ailin' an' all. You know Otis Applebee wouldn't beat up on his wife if he didn't have a belly full'uv th'likes'uv this...."

"Now, Miss Poky, you gonna go an' make me feel bad. I don't want ol' Otis t'beat up on'is wife...but I gotta think'uv my own. You know that!"

She started to leave. "Jes, you best be careful." Just before she disappeared into the woods, Jes whistled real low like. She turned to see him waving with his big toothless smile. She shook her head and waved back.

Poky came in sight of the cabin about a half an hour later, and squinted her eyes, looked like somebody sittin' in her rocker! Sho 'nough, somebody was! Two folks on'er porch...all dressed up. They wouldn't be Oak Mountain folk nor valley folk. Couldn't be! But something told her it was...*Hallie* and *Lauralee!* They both stood and waved. Poky dropped her herbs and rushed up to the porch.

"Miss Hallie an' Miss Lauralee...all growed up!" The three

embraced there on the porch. "How'd you get here?"

"Lauralee's friend brought us most of the way, and then a friend of yours, a Mr. Zeke Branham."

"That'a fact? Zeke brought you, huh. That's Barclay's daddy...you know my little Barclay."

"We met Barclay, too. A fine young man."

Poky grinned widely. "He is that! Well'sa, I'm so happy I could dance a jig. Got ya' letter for sure, but I didn't really think...well, bless my bones! An' lemme see this'ere gal, turn around for me, Miss Lauralee...."

Lauralee spun around on the uneven porch, almost losing her balance.

"My, she looks fit t'kill! Y'all come on in here an' make yourself at home." She led the way into the small cabin. "Gotta mess'uv squash an' turnip greens all cooked up...I know y'all must be hungry."

That evening the three of them sat out on the porch basking in each other's company and the cooling summer twilight that embraced them.

"Poky, that was a delicious meal."

"Why, thank you, Miss Hallie. So nice t'have company...'specially you folk. I don't have no fine picture show or big fancy church t'show ya'...but I can fix you up some good vittles...." She chuckled.

"And you *grow* everything you cook?"

"Just about, Lauralee, just about."

"Do you go to the store...or need to?"

"Once in awhile...get my sugar, salt, feed an' sech. Don't need much."

Lauralee looked around on all sides at the rich dark forest. "It looks so...so cut off...do you ever get lonely?"

Poky smiled. "Naw, I don't get lonely. Got too much t'do...an' I got my chickens an' ol' Bedford County...."

"Who?"

Poky laughed. "Well, I call'er that. She's my favorite hen,

can lay more eggs than you can shake a stick at...neighbor'uv mine gave'er t'me. He got'er from his friend over in Bedford County...so I named'er Bedford County."

"Have you ever been to Bedford County, Miss Poky?"

"Shucks, child...never been out'a these'ere mountains, 'cept for visitin' you folks over in Lynchburg, never had a mind to neither."

"Well, it's a beautiful place with picturesque mountains just like here."

"If its got mountains, it must be all right."

Suddenly the three fell quiet, and only the squeak of Hallie's rocking could be heard. "It's so peaceful here," she commented.

Poky nodded.

"How can it be so peaceful here when there's a raging war taking place right now?"

They both turned to look at Hallie in the waning light. Her question was not directed to either of them, but instead to the vast, dark mountains.

"You said you heard from your boys, an' they're both all right. You gotta keep faith, Miss Hallie."

"I know, Poky. It's just hard...not knowing what's going on with them any given minute. But I'm proud of them, for sure. Proud my boys are patriotic...I taught them to be. Just the other day on Flag Day, I was walking downtown and the flags were flying just all over the place...."

"That must've been somethin' to see."

"It was, and my heart filled with pride knowing my boys are over there fighting for freedom, fighting for our country...." She began to wipe her eyes.

Lauralee rose to get her purse. "I want to read something to you...something I cut out of the paper on Flag Day."

"Reckon we better go inside. Can't read a thing in this'ere dark, child."

Hallie and Poky followed Lauralee inside and sat down to listen. She pulled a folded piece of paper out of her purse, unfolded it and began to slowly read...*Just a piece of cloth, that's all it is — just a piece of cloth. You can count the threads in it and it's no different from any other piece of cloth. But then a little breeze comes along, and it stirs and sort of comes to life and flutters and snaps into the wind, all red and white and blue. And then you realize that no other piece of cloth could be like it. It has your whole life wrapped up in it. The meals you're going to eat. The time you're going to spend with your wife. The kind of things your boy will learn at school. Those strange and wonderful thoughts you get inside a church on Sunday. Just a piece of cloth, that's all it is — until you put your soul into it, and all your soul stands for and wants and aspires to be.'*

"How beautiful," Poky's voiced cracked with emotion.

"That's what I mean," Hallie added, "that's just how I felt walking downtown the other day...felt like I was going to burst with pride in my boys and in my country."

"I bet it would've been something to be in New York on Flag Day," Lauralee added, "they had fifty-thousand people parading, the paper said, and over two million spectators lined Fifth Avenue, even though they had broiling heat. Of course, it would be something to see New York anyhow."

"No thank ya', child. Don't won't no part'uv New Yawk. Too many killin's an' sech. 'Nough'uv killin' goin' on in th'war, don't need no more."

"They won't be drafting married men this year, according to the news," Hallie interjected, "not before next year, they say."

"That's good, Miss Hallie, an' maybe th'war will be over by then."

"Maybe."

"Miss Poky, how did you fare during the blackout last week?"

"No problem, Lauralee. Jest went on t'bed early an' slept through it. Figured nobody'd check on us anyhow up in these'ere mountains."

"Well, I don't know. They say it was quite successful and

especially being the first one for the state...and all night, too."

"It wasn't just Virginia, Mama. Lights were out from Maryland to North Carolina."

"I know they were. I just can't imagine what it must be like for the British. They've been having blackouts night after night for months and months. We're certainly blessed compared to so many countries."

"That Mr. Churchill is sho somethin'."

"He sure is, Poky. But why do you think he flew over to meet with the president again? Everybody's wondering that, and he came secretly, too, you know, to meet with President Roosevelt."

"They're discussing a second fighting front in Europe, Mama, to crush the Axis."

"Well, I know, Lauralee, that's what's speculated. I just wondered what thoughts Poky had on it."

"Don't have no thoughts on that, Miss Hallie. But I'm sure glad to have sech folks as Mr. Churchill on our side, an' so many able-bodied men protectin' us, too...an' they keep on addin' men. We don't have a lot more young men left in these'ere mountains. Fact is, only one left I know'uv is Otis Applebee's boy...an' Otis says he's gonna register come June 30 over in Madison Heights. 'Course Otis is glad he's gonna do it. Th'boy don't have a lot'uv get up an' go in'im, an' it'll be one less mouth for Otis t'feed. Th'fella is so skinny, don't know if he could fight'is way out'uv a paper bag, though."

"Well, it's good he wants to do his part. We all need to do our part."

"That's a fact, Miss Hallie." With that, she rose and fetched a jar from the kitchen cupboard and pulled something out of it. "Look'ere what I got...." Proudly displaying a United States Savings Bond Stamp Book, she grinned from ear to ear.

"Why, Miss Poky, where do you get stamps?"

"Mr. an' Mrs. Moore, who run th'store down in th'valley, make a trip into Lynchburg 'bout twice a month for supplies. They buy'em then, an' I send by them. 'Course it'll take a long time t'fill it up, but slowly it's gettin' there."

"Mama has one, too, and I'm helping her fill hers up. But, Miss Poky, you amaze me...and I thought you were way up here cut off from the real world...and you know as much about what's going on as anybody."

"Thank you, Lauralee. But ya' got one thing wrong. I ain't cut off from th'real world...I'm in th'real world." She smiled broadly.

The following morning, after delighting in an early sumptuous breakfast that Hallie said was fit for a king, the three set out walking across the field and into the woods. The day, already proving to be one of those days you heartily experience and then return to through hidden avenues of memory, was laid out before them as an intriguing map.

Poky lost no time in sharing her world on Oak Mountain, chatting away excitedly as they drew further into the dense summer foliage. Surely it was summertime in the Blue Ridge as the warm oozing sun shone brightly into the forest, creating patchworks of art on its leaf-strewn floor. A clear sky could be seen above the towering trees except for a few spotted clouds here and there. The mountain stream that followed beside their path flowed gently, offering a tranquil background of murmuring music, that only hours before was alive with croaking frogs. Tiny unseen creatures scampered off at the sound of footsteps invading their otherwise peaceful habitat, and disappeared beneath last winter's leaves and the cushioned pine needled forest floor.

"What was that?" Lauralee jumped at the rustling leaves beside her.

"See yonder, just a little ol' chipmunk. Scary little creatures, scared'uv everything."

Lauralee marveled at the little fellow sitting there like a statue, blending in with its surroundings so that one would hardly notice. She smiled at Poky. "The people here on Oak Mountain...are they all...like you? I mean, are they all so independent and resourceful?"

"These folk, Lauralee, are a hearty people, mainly 'cause'uv our Scotch-Irish ancestry. We come from strong stock, as we say 'round here." She chuckled.

"Oh my!" Lauralee was struck by the sudden impact of thick masses of jungle-like rhododendrons obstructing their path and bulging with huge purple flowers.

"Thought you'd like'em."

"They're absolutely gorgeous!"

"...an' there's their sister." Poky pointed to the delicate pink-white mountain laurel, bravely growing beside it, daring to compete with such a dramatic peer.

Ambling on into the friendly summer forest with Poky exhibiting her special treasures one by one, the morning sun rose higher, casting its warm rays down through the lush green canopy of gently swaying leaves. Pokeberries held them up for awhile as Poky demonstrated their rare capability of ready-made paint. "...painted ourselves up with it when we were young'uns...painted our faces...couldn't hardly get it off neither...had it on my hands for days...."

"Can you eat them?"

"No child, even causes trouble for th'birds...makes'em drunk."

"Really?"

"That's what they say...'course I ain't never seen a drunk bird myself...."

Further into the inviting mountain forest they hiked, coming to a narrow stream cascading down the mountainside, cutting its way before them. They crossed it, straddling a fallen, rotting gum as the clear, gurgling water deepened beneath them. Once across, Lauralee exclaimed again, "Mama, look!"

She was kneeling beside a lovely patch of vivid purple violets. "They're so pretty...so delicately pretty...." Hallie joined her.

"Well, bless my bones." Poky bent over. "Thought they

were all 'bout gone. Mostly bloom in th'spring an' early summer...called th'glory of th'spring wild garden, they are."

"I'd like to pick some and take them back...but it almost seems irreverent to do so...."

"Know what ya' mean, Lauralee. Leave'em there for other folk as they pass by...an' if'n nobody happens by...why then th'creatures will enjoy'em."

"She's right, Lauralee. Mama always said *'flowers are food for the soul'."*

Halfway through the week, Poky decided to take her guests a callin'...on Barclay and his daddy, setting out right after an early dinner. Briskly, they hiked down the mountainside, over the valley and back up to High Peak. Happily, Poky talked away, unaware of her city friends lagging behind and beginning to pant.

"Wait up, Poky...please...," Hallie called out.

Turning, she laughed. "My goodness, you two look like ya' been drug t'China an' back...." With damp hair framing their flushed red faces, they caught up and enjoyed the hike in spite of its strenuous challenge. Soon they were in sight of the Branham cabin with its sagging front porch and crumbling chimney. The screen door slammed, Barclay jumped off the porch and raced toward them. Hallie and Lauralee watched the two embrace while the man who'd given them a ride appeared sullenly in the doorway.

"Howdy, Mr. Branham, we've come a callin'. You remember Miss Hallie here an' her daughter, Lauralee."

Zeke Branham nodded silently while Barclay pulled Poky toward the porch, with Hallie and Lauralee close behind. After the cordial but awkward introductions, Mr. Branham excused himself and disappeared out behind the lean-to.

"Barclay, Poky certainly speaks highly of you," Hallie began. "I understand you want to be a fireman when you grow up."

"Yes, ma'am."

"Why's that? Why do you want to be a fireman?" Hallie welcomed the front porch to rest, wiping her forehead with the hem of her dress while staring up at the young fellow. Not normally quiet, these city ladies had evoked in him a shyness he was unaware of and looked to Poky for help.

"Why, Barclay loves th'forest an' th'mountains jest like me...an' he figures on protectin' them by bein' a fireman...ain't that right, Barclay?"

Nodding enthusiastically, he quickly added, "A fireman came to our school...an' he told us all about it...an' gave us one'uv these...." He reached into his two sizes too large pants and pulled out a folded piece of yellow paper which he unfolded to show a picture of *Smokey the Bear.*

"I see." Lauralee and the young boy exchanged smiles.

"Barclay, run get them drawin's...gotta show'em how you can make a picture like them artists in th'books." As he jumped up to get them, Poky bragged, "Jest you wait an' see his drawin's. Gonna be like them famous artists...ya' know...Michelangelo an' sech."

He returned with a long, slick yellowish piece of meat wrapping paper. Both Hallie and Lauralee stretched their necks to see. He turned it over and displayed a whole collage of sketches, a mixture of trees, plants, people standing, walking, running and splashing in water.

"That's Falling Rock Creek...an' me." He shyly pointed to a boy splashing in the water.

"What talent!" Lauralee exclaimed.

"Told ya' so." Poky beamed.

"And that's the best use of butcher paper I've ever seen...better than wrapping bologna," Hallie added, looking over their shoulders.

"I get it for'im down at th'store. Trade'em herbs for it. Sometimes we get real long pieces, don't we, son?"

He nodded.

As they rose to leave, Zeke Branham appeared again, and

seeing the long paper sprawled out on the porch, he admonished, "Barclay, come on here an' help with th'wood-choppin'."

Retracing their steps on their departure, they discussed Barclay and his talent and dreams.

"I gather Mr. Branham doesn't share your enthusiasm for Barclay's artistic ability?"

"Miss Hallie, you gotta understan' th'men'uv these'ere mountains. They don't cotton t'menfolk drawin' an' sech...think it's sissy, not manlike. They don't mean no harm, jest th'way they are. Now I'm gonna show y'all a real special place on the way back, take us awhile to get there, though. Y'all up to more hiking?"

"Sure," Lauralee answered a little too quickly, then looked questioningly at her mother.

"I am if you two are."

After hiking down the mountainside, over dried creek beds, and up and down slippery leaf covered hills, she finally led them to a wooded hollow...to the *mission*.

The ever-present sense of serenity encompassed them as they walked up, and sat down under the tall, shady trees. Falling Rock Creek lent a calmness with its soothing murmurs as it flowed between the tree-lined banks. The small white chapel, though the epitome of humbleness, dominated the tranquil picture, and they were drawn to it as if by an unseen hand. After resting a bit, they got up and moved toward it. Poky gently and reverently pushed open the door, exposing its cool, inviting interior. They quietly stepped in and sat down on the back pew, looking up and around them as a peace flooded their souls.

This particular day was no different as the afternoon sun bathed the chapel in its warm glow, while towering trees cast semi-shaded patterns along the creek banks. Nothing stirred but the murmuring creek outside, gently flowing over its rocky obstacles. As prisms of light fell through the windows and danced over the pews, Lauralee spoke hardly above a whisper, "Is this your church, Poky?"

"Belongs t'th'folk here in th'settlement...an' I'm one'uv them...in a way."

"You keep referring to the settlement...why is it a settlement...why is it set apart?"

"That's a long story, Lauralee. But th'settlement is like an *island*...set apart an' alone from th'rest'uv th'world, you might say."

Back outside in the sunlight, Poky smiled. "Well, y'all showed me your fine church in Lynchburg. So, I figured I'd show y'all mine."

"They're so different...but both beautiful and both houses of the Lord...."

"That's right, Hallie. But, ya' know, th'Lord don't live in neither one'uv'em. Th'scripture says... *'th'most High dwelleth not in temples made with hands...Heaven is my throne, an' earth is my footstool; what house will ye build me? Saith the Lord...'* Course he lives in our hearts. The scripture also says, *'know ye not that ye are the temple of God, an' that th'Spirit of God dwelleth in you.'* That's in Corinthians...First Corinthians, I think. I love Corinthians."

Lauralee stood silently looking up at the inspiring little chapel.

"What are those buildings?" Hallie pointed to the simply constructed buildings adjacent to the chapel.

"That's part'uv th'mission...where Barclay goes t'school."

"Barclay goes to school *here*?" Lauralee asked with surprise.

"That's right."

"But why?" she questioned with a frown.

"This'ere's all they have...it's th'school for th'settlement children. They can't go to th'white schools, an' they don't go to th'Colored schools neither...they're just caught in th'middle somehow...this'ere's all they have."

"I don't understand."

"There's a whole lot we don't understan' as we get older, Miss Lauralee. But th'school ain't all bad. Fact is, it's pretty good. They got Miss Isobel...an' she makes sure they learn their books, too! 'Course it only goes t'th'seventh grade...but that's better'n nothin'."

"Only goes to the seventh grade! Then they can't finish school...can't graduate...." She looked with astonishment at her mother.

"That's right, but most all'uv'em are needed at home anyhows by th'time they get that old...t'help out an' take care'uv th'younger ones at home, an' t'help in th'orchards an' sech. 'Course Barclay now, he's gotta get *his* education somehow. How else is he gonna be one'uv them famous artists?"

"But why can't they go to the public schools?" Lauralee persisted.

"'Cause th'gover'ment says so, says they're Colored, not Indian, an' have t'go t'th'Colored schools. They don't like that...bein' told they're somethin' they ain't, an' they don't go then. They prefer it here where they can be what they are, ya' see."

"But why did the government do this?" Lauralee questioned, still confused.

"Don't know...some say Virginia must not want any Indians, so calls'em Colored on th'census."

"That's crazy."

"I know, Lauralee, but that's th'way it is. Sometimes things don't make no sense in this old world."

The day after Hallie and Lauralee left, Barclay came visiting. He knew Poky would be alone again.

"Well, son, glad ya' come t'see me. You like my friends?"

"Yes, ma'am."

"You was kind'a quiet like."

"Yes, ma'am."

"That's all right, son. Ain't nothin' wrong in bein' quiet like."

They were sitting out on the porch, and the summer sun was blazing through the tree tops. Its brilliant array literally illuminated the mountainside, casting shimmering streamers of light everywhere.

"I want ya' t'look yonder...see that there beauty, son...th'sun in all its glory."

Barclay looked.

"...'bout hurts your eyes, don't it?"

He nodded.

"God's like that...I mean...His glory is s'bright...s'radiant, ain't nobody ever been able t'look at Him."

"Nobody?"

"Nobody. Onliest one ever got close was Moses. Wait a minute." She got up and went into the cabin, came right back out hugging her big black Bible to her bosom. Barclay waited. She flopped back in her cane bottom chair. "Right'ere in Exodus it is...Moses wanted to see God! Wanted t'see His Glory...an' God said...listen to this...*'thou canst not see my face: for there shall no man see me, an' live.'*"

"Why Poky?" He looked puzzled.

"I don't rightly know, son. Figure it's 'cause God is so holy...full'uv light like th'sun...an' ya' know we can't look right at th'sun. Let me finish readin'...*'an' th'Lord said, Behold there is a place by me, an' thou shalt stand upon a rock: An' it shall come to pass, while my glory passeth by, that I will put thee in a clift of th' rock, an' will cover thee with my hand while I pass by: An' I will take away mine hand, an' thou shalt see my back parts: but my face shall not be seen.'*"

"Gosh, Poky!"

She smiled.

"You think He's bright as that there sun?"

"Brighter, child. He made th'light, an' He is th'light. Th' glory'uv God...that's it. We ought'a be lookin', son, an' seekin' th'glory'uv God."

The small boy was quiet, pondering Poky's words of wisdom. Then he spoke, "He was on a mountain, too...when He talked to Moses, won't He, Poky?"

"He sho was. I figure He likes th'mountains, jest like us...else He wouldn't have made s'many."

Barclay looked around at the mountain ridges now lit up with the bright shining sun. "I'm glad He made this one."

"Me, too, Barclay, me, too."

CHAPTER ELEVEN

WORLD WAR II escalated with increased production of all war related items, therefore increasing rationing throughout America and, of course, fatalities tallied in the headlines. Boys quickly turned into soldiers and returned home men...if they returned at all. The Branham brothers returned, but the Branham household would never be the same. Paul David had been injured, but it wasn't his missing eye and missing leg that shook the family so...it was his missing spirit. Paul David was not Paul David anymore, nor would he ever be again. Barclay simply could not accept this or understand it. What had happened to his favorite brother? It was a trying time for all of them, along with scores of others, as soldiers returned scarred, broken, injured in body and spirit, burdened with memories they would carry to their graves.

Jon Junior came back even more sober than he left...*but Jamey did not return.* He would forever be one of those seventeen million vital statistics of the cruel, fatal world war.

It was the twilight zone for Hallie as she moved about her once familiar home. Suddenly objects reached out to her that previously had gone totally unnoticed. Everything bore Jamey's imprint from the time he was but a little boy, and her wounded, sensitive inner self recoiled from their grasp. NO! NO! NO! It couldn't be true! Surely he would return, making her laugh once again at his antics and smile at his loving gestures. The cruel war couldn't take her *Jamey*, even though it had taken thousands of mothers' sons...it couldn't take *her* son! Lauralee and Jon Junior followed her around in a daze, too worried about her to fully grieve themselves.

"...but I'll never know his surprise...." were her first words uttered after the two officers delivered the dreadful telegram. Jamey had written a letter just weeks before his death, telling her he had a wonderful surprise, but he didn't tell her what. Over and over, she reread the letter, repeating his words...'I must wait until I can tell you in person.' Jon Junior and Lauralee spoke in hushed tones of the mystery. What was he talking about?

That February of 1943 came to a close. March arrived and disappeared almost unnoticed...the first signs of spring appeared, and Hallie began to slowly recover. She planted some of Poky's seeds out beside the porch steps and remembered her mother's words...*flowers are food for the soul*...and her soul was empty.

POKY LAID THE letter aside, muttering to herself and letting the screen door slam behind her..."She done planted my seeds...God bless'er...will do'er good, too...does a body good t'watch new life push up out'uv th'ground...'specially after tastin' death..." She continued muttering as she picked up her hoe and went to working out the weeds in her herb garden. She was hoeing fierce and hard, trying to relieve her own sadness, when she heard a ruckus in the distance. She turned to see Willis Moore from down at the store yelling at her, "Miss Poky, it's down at th'Taylor place...Mrs. Taylor's 'bout t'give birth...she needs ya' t'come quick like."

She nodded and waved him off. "She's early, won't s'posed t'be till 'bout June," she said aloud and hurried back to the cabin, laying the hoe beside the porch. Grabbing her shawl and bag, she headed to the Taylor place, seeing Barclay coming toward her.

"Where ya' goin'?"

"Got business over at th'Taylor place. Mrs. Taylor's havin' her baby early. Gotta hurry...wanna come along?"

He quickly fell in step with her and reached out for the

bag. It wasn't the first time he'd accompanied her. It was exciting for the young fellow to experience new life, and he always felt mighty grown-up sitting outside on the porch with the menfolk while they spit their tobacco or snuffed their snuff, each trying to outdo the other with their tall tales until the first cry of life was heard. But he knew Mr. Taylor was gone overseas to the war, and Mrs. Taylor was all alone. This would be different, he figured. Poky was thinking her thoughts as well as the two hurried through the woods and down the worn path to the valley. "While death is raging overseas, life goes on here...," she muttered. Barclay looked up at her but didn't question. He was used to her muttering at times and respected her privacy. She wondered why Mr. Taylor had gone anyway with his wife being pregnant and all. And now she was all alone to face this! Barclay was swinging the bag and whistling as they descended the mountain. Every now and then, he'd smile up at her, warming her heart. He was happiest when he was with her. Since Paul David had returned and preferred to be alone, he was spending more time with her than ever. His other brothers stayed gone most of the time, drifting back and forth between the settlement and more enticing places. There was talk among them of moving away to some place in Maryland. Barclay didn't understand a lot of their talk at night as they debated the issue with their father, but he knew his father didn't really approve.

"Poky," he asked breathlessly. "What's it mean to be *os-tra-cized?*"

She quickly looked down at him. "Now where on earth did ya' learn such a fancy word?"

"That's what Jack Jacob an' George Lewis said we are when they were fussin' last night."

"Fussin'?"

"Yeah, they wanna leave, go to Maryland, Glen Burnie...where they got a lot of friends. Our cousin, Zack Hall Johns, already gone there. Said they don't os-tra-cize you there...but daddy...he gets mad when they talk about it."

"What about Herman Ray?"

"He can't make up his mind. Say's he wants to go, but don't wanna leave daddy, Paul David and me. What does it mean, Poky?"

"Well, it means...it means...shucks! Barclay, we gotta hurry. We'll talk 'bout this later. Mrs. Taylor needs us...an' we're jest 'bout there. Look yonder. See'er smoke comin' up from th'chimney now." Even though it was late April, and the dogwoods were blooming, there was a chill in the air. The thin curl of blue grey smoke rose steadily up from the small clapboard house that sat oddly alone in the valley without any of the lush foliage that enveloped Poky's cabin.

She shooed the chickens off the narrow porch stoop and knocked on the screen door before pushing it open. The little house was quiet and dark with drawn shades. Poky walked across the bare wooden floor of the meager living room that held only a worn sofa and a broken rocking chair. Following close behind, Barclay thought it odd to see a rocking chair without rockers. The adjoining room boasted of only an iron bed and one straight back chair plus some boxes stacked in one corner. Mrs. Taylor lay waiting, barely distinguishable beneath the light blanket in the darkened room.

"Oh, Miss Poky...," she breathed a sigh of relief. "I'm s'glad...."

"Mind if I let up this'ere shade, Mrs. Taylor?"

The young, frail woman, with straight brown hair, nodded her approval.

"Need some light in'ere." She gave the shade a quick jerk, causing it to fly upward, spinning around its rod a few times, and the afternoon sun was allowed full course to illuminate the small bedroom. Barclay stood uncertainly, and Mrs. Taylor's eyes fell questioningly on him.

"Brought my lil' helper. He's gonna stand guard out on th'porch 'case I need'im. Right, Barclay?"

"Yes, ma'am." With that he gladly hurried out.

"One'uv th'kids from th'settlement?"

"Yes, ma'am...an' a fine one, too." Poky commenced to straightening the bed covers. "How fast your pains comin', dear?"

"Right fast, Poky...shouldn't be long...but it's early...not supposed to be here for 'nother month or so...."

"Some'uv'em have a mind'uv their own...jest gonna come when they see fit...no matter...." Her words were interrupted with a shriek as Mrs. Taylor grabbed hold of the narrow iron slats above her head.

"Hold on, Mrs. Taylor, like you're doin'...you're gonna be fine...I'll boil some water now an' get everything ready." Barclay heard the shriek out on the porch stoop and sat with his hands over his ears. This was the part he didn't like...couldn't bear to hear the mamas holler and scream. The next yell was muffled as he jabbed his fingers down his ears and began whistling the tune to *Little Brown Jug*. Poky had taught it to him just recently along with several others. Often she played the guitar, and he hummed or whistled along with her. Now he whistled particularly loud to drown out the eerie sound of birth, but to no avail. He jumped off the porch to chase the chickens, certain this idea would cure his predicament. The chickens were hopping around, flapping their wings excitedly when Poky appeared in the doorway. "Barclay, this one's got problems! Gonna need th'doc...need'im right away...run as quick as your lil' legs will carry you an' fetch'im...." Before she got the last words out, all she could see was his hindparts. Mrs. Taylor let out another blood-curdling scream, and Poky was at her side. The baby was trying to come out the wrong way...breech...and she felt helpless. The last one like this didn't make it. The little Anthony baby...poor lil' thing all black an' blue when it came out...she didn't want this one t'die, too.

"What's wrong?" Mrs. Taylor cried out, fear seizing her.

"Everything's gonna be all right, Mrs. Taylor...everything's gonna be all right. Jest a lil' stubborn one...that's all...done sent for th'doc...he'll be here directly...you jest hold on...." It seemed like hours before Barclay returned. Without the doctor. He'd gone over to Charlottesville for the evening. Poky braced herself.

"Barclay, I'm gonna need ya' help!"

His already large, dark eyes widened, and Mrs. Taylor, though on the verge of passing out, weakly shook her head in protest. Poky ignored her and began instructing Barclay, "Hold onto her hands when she grabs out...she's gonna need us both, while I help'er get this little one born. Once it starts, we gotta get'im out quick like." Mrs. Taylor moaned and groaned and pushed and struggled for the life of her child. Simultaneously, the unborn was struggling silently. The afternoon passed into evening. Poky's face was taut, and Barclay's little hands ached as Mrs. Taylor squeezed them with all her might, a lifeline thrown out to her in drowning waters. He sat at her head, keeping his eyes riveted to her distorted face, afraid of what he might see on the other end where Poky kept her vigil. Soon the pitter-patter of a spring shower danced upon the tin roof, a soothing sound contrasting with the screams of birth...and Poky silently called out for help.

Constantly, she wiped Mrs. Taylor's beaded forehead with a damp cloth that Barclay kept cool by dipping in a basin of cool water as he ran back and forth to the kitchen. Mrs. Taylor seemed to be drifting off.

"Mrs. Taylor, hold on...you gotta hold on...we gonna have us'a baby here directly...you jest hold on...."

Barely able to focus her eyes, she tried to smile but didn't have the energy...and then another gripping contraction seized her body, followed by another and another. Poky's face lit up. "She's comin'...she's comin'! That'a girl...come on...." A strong new cry of life came forth, filling the small house and drowning out the spring shower as Mrs. Taylor fell back limply.

"A lil' girl, Mrs. Taylor...you got a lil' girl...look'ere Barclay...ain't she pretty?" The tired young lad smiled, thinking she was anything but pretty. But already Mrs. Taylor was sleeping, purely exhausted, unable to appreciate her words.

"She all right?" Barclay asked as he stared in wonder at the tiny bundle of wrinkled pink flesh that had stopped crying almost as suddenly as she'd started.

"She's all right. 'Course she's all right. Counted all'er toes an' fingers...got'em all."

The young lad smiled proudly.

Poky decided to stay on at the Taylor household for awhile. Who else was gonna help poor Mrs. Taylor till she got on her feet? She sent Barclay home with a list of things to pick up at her place. "You come back tomorrow an'stop by my place on th'way for these'ere things. I'll be lookin' for ya'...an' don't forget t'feed my chickens, too," she called after him as he scampered off into the woods, happy to share his news, but his news wasn't as well received at home.

"You did what!"

"Me an' Poky, we birthed Mrs. Taylor's baby...she had'a real hard time, too...but we did it...she's got a little girl...."

"Pa, you gotta do somethin' 'bout this boy...he's gonna turn into a sissy for sure. Drawin' pictures all th'time...an' now birthin' babies...Pa, you gotta do somethin'!"

"Aw, let'im alone. Leastways he's happy here on th'mountain...more'n I can say 'bout th'rest'uv ya'."

George Lewis shook his head and stormed out the door.

The next day when Barclay returned to the Taylor household with Poky's things, he had a surprise awaiting him. Mrs. Taylor was sitting upright in bed, holding the tiny infant and smiling at him. He looked around at Poky, and she was smiling, too.

"Barclay, it's because'uv you an' Miss Poky here that this little girl lives. It's only right that you two name'er."

Poky added, "I already got my part. What 'bout you, Barclay? What do you think she ought'a be called?"

Realizing this was serious business, the ten-year old studied for a moment before speaking and then his face lit up. "I know. I like Addie...there was a girl in my reader named Addie. Not skeered'uv nothin'. I like Addie."

Mrs. Taylor nodded, "Well, I like it, too...it's a nice name. Poky?"

"How 'bout Addie Jane? Named after my dear mama. She'd be proud."

"*Addie Jane*...it has a nice ring to it."

A few days later, just as the sun was setting over Oak Mountain, Poky and Barclay climbed its steep ridges toward home. Mrs. Taylor was up on her feet and doing better.

"Well, Mr. Barclay, there's a part'uv me an' a part'uv you down'ere in this valley now...lil' Addie Jane."

The small boy picked up his stride with pride.

SCHOOL WAS ALMOST out. It was the end of May, and Barclay rose that Saturday morning, hurrying to Poky's with a small box concealed under his arm. She was out in the garden, staking her tomato plants, which were already about two feet high.

"Look at these'ere 'mato plants, Barclay. Are we gonna have 'matos this year!"

Barclay knelt beside her and carefully lifted the lid from his box. "Look what I got, Poky." She stared down at the large red-eyed insect with thin wings folded over itself.

"A locust!"

"No, ma'am, it ain't no locust. It's a cicada. I read about them in my *Weekly Reader*."

"That so. What did ya' read?"

"This kind of cicada only comes every seventeen years...an' they're comin' now! I watched this one come up out of its hole an' climb up on th'lean-to. You know what it did then?"

"What?"

"It come right out of its skin...an' left it hangin' on th'side of th'lean-to. Then he climbed back down an' up th'big oak tree next to our house. That's when I got it."

"What ya' gonna do with it?"

"Don't know." He shrugged his shoulders. "Figure I'd show it around some, keep it awhile, maybe let it go...."

"Think you ought'a let it go."

"I know. The *Weekly Reader* said they only live a few weeks."

"H-m-m-p-h." She leaned way over her tomato plants again and glanced into the box. "Poor lil' feller, don't get much chance, does he?"

"Oh, but it's been livin' for seventeen years already, Poky...under th'ground!"

"That a fact?"

"Yes, ma'am...an' after they come up out of th'ground, they only live for three or four weeks."

"Well, shucks. What a life! Poor lil' feller stuck down there in that dark, damp place for seventeen years, an' jest when it begins t'enjoy this beautiful world an' th'sunshine an' all, it up an'dies...my, my...."

The next morning, Poky awoke to the eerie sound that saturated the forest around her...the drone of the cicadas...countless thousands competing in their mating calls. It resembled a tremendous orchestra blended together and off key. She rose and shut the window. "What on earth..." she mumbled while getting dressed. "Don't recall'em makin' this much fuss before...an' Barclay says this is their mating call...h-m-m-p-h...guess everything needs somethin' or somebody...." Suddenly she felt all alone, wondering what she'd missed, never knowing the bond of a man and a woman. Oh well, she had her friends, th'babies she'd birthed...an' Barclay...an' her mountain. She looked out at the rising ridges encircled with the early grey morning mist. She was content...God was good to her.

WORLD WAR II ENDED! In the summer of 1945, as actions came to a climax with allied forces capturing Okinawa, the

United States, Britain and China issued a statement threatening Japan unless it surrendered unconditionally. In spite of this warning, Japan kept on fighting.

A German-born scientist, Albert Einstein, had informed President Roosevelt at the onset of the war of the possibility of creating a superbomb. It would produce an extremely powerful explosion by splitting an atom. Einstein feared that Germany would develop it first. The United States set up a top-secret program to develop an atomic bomb, and did. This first bomb was dropped on Hiroshima, killing one hundred and eighty-nine thousand people. A second bomb was dropped on Nagasaki. Japan then agreed to surrender unconditionally.

The long war was over. President Roosevelt didn't live to see it, however. He had died of a cerebral hemorrhage in April that same year. The human suffering caused by World War II was certainly enormous, with countless cities in ruin and millions of homeless people resettling; but none would bear the scars as much as the families of the six million Jews, who had died horrible deaths under Hitler's vicious rule.

A new year came, 1946, the first year in awhile that didn't bear the burdensome baggage of war. People began to relax and forget or try to forget its ravages, focusing on a brighter future. The month literally flew by as Americans and people all over the world picked up the pieces and busily sought to make new lives for themselves. February disappeared, leaving Poky another year older and Barclay thirteen, a teenager and feeling quite grown-up.

"What do ya' say we call on th'Taylors an' lil' Addie Jane?" Poky suggested on the first warm day of spring. "Been awhile since you've been."

"All right," he agreed, though not too enthusiastically.

"I still can't believe she's three already," Poky commented while pulling on her sweater.

They headed down the mountainside, as warm springs of water oozed out of thawing ridges, and tiny, budding shoots barely poked through the wet, leafy ground.

"You know they're havin' them trials now...the Nazi trials, Poky, in a place called *Nuremberg* in Germany. You think they'll get convicted?"

"Don't know, been readin' 'bout it in th'papers, though. All I know is if they don't...they still gonna have t'stand before th'real judge one day."

"I hope they'll be convicted...an' hanged!"

Poky looked around at the serious young man he was becoming, and decided to change the subject. "Look yonder at th'mountains today...how clear they are...you can see th'ridges stretched clear all th'way t'th'sea most likely."

Barclay laughed. "They don't go all the way to the sea, Poky. There's many miles of flat land an' desert plus mountains much, much bigger than these before the land reaches the sea."

"You learnin' a lot these days, son. I know I ain't never been out'a these'ere mountains. Don't mind admittin' it. Don't know what them flat lands an' desert look like...but I know there can't be any mountains on God's earth prettier than these."

"I ain't seen them either, Poky...just seen pictures and read about them. Hope to see'em one day, though. I want to see a lot of things. You happy livin' here, Poky?"

She thought that a strange question coming from him, but answered anyhow, "'Course I like livin' here, wouldn't live no place else. I feel protected here, close t'God when I'm here in th'shadow'uv these ancient an' magnificent mountains." She looked at him strangely. "Somethin' on your mind, son?"

"You know I'm finishin' th'seventh grade this year...in a couple of weeks."

"I know, an' I'd hoped by now somethin' was gonna get better...an' you'd be able t'go t'th'public schools or somethin'...."

"They don't want us, Poky," he uttered sadly, and her heart broke.

"Don't you pay'em no mind, son...no mind a'tall, ya' hear. You know who you are...an' God knows!"

"Poky, I'm goin' away."

She held her breath.

"...to Maryland...to live with Jack Jacob an' his wife...so I can keep going to school."

There was a long silence between them as they continued down the mountainside with loose stones falling away beneath their steps. The melancholy whistling call of a whippoorwill could be heard in the distance.

"I see," she finally responded. "That's good, Barclay...that's good. You know I always wanted t'see ya' graduate...." Her words trailed off.

"You don't mind then?"

" 'Course not. I'm gonna miss you for sure...but you'll be comin' back, won't you?"

"Sure, I'll be back every summer to be with pa. He ain't too happy 'bout me goin'. Figures I don't need no more schoolin'."

Poky chuckled. "He'll be proud as punch when you become one'uv them famous artists."

"You gonna be all right, Poky?"

"'Course I'll be all right. You know your Poky's use'ta bein' alone...been alone all my life...'cept for you. But I'll make out...I'll miss you somethin' fierce. Might have t'call on lil' Addie Jane more." The familiar clapboard house came into sight, and they could see the small girl playing outside by the porch stoop, the sun's rays highlighting her shiny auburn hair. She looked up and saw them approaching. Poky waved, and she waved back reticently.

"Where's your mama, Addie Jane?"

She glanced toward the house, and Mrs. Taylor came to the door. "Well, my goodness, Miss Poky an' Barclay. S'glad to see ya'. Come on in an' sit a spell."

Poky reached down for Addie Jane, but the small child just stood there with a solemn look on her face.

"She's right independent-like, Miss Poky. Come on in. She'll follow."

Poky went in. So did Barclay, and Addie Jane followed, standing in the doorway watching them. A lovely little petite girl with a way of aptly observing all around her and silently analyzing it. Her dark green eyes missed nothing. Mrs. Taylor offered them some lunch, but Poky quickly declined, knowing her cupboards were not that plentiful. Mr. Taylor hadn't been able to find a decent job since the war.

"Barclay, you're sure growin' up."

He nodded with a smile.

"Barclay's goin' away t'school next year, gonna get a full education, gonna graduate."

"Oh my. Now ain't you somethin'."

Somewhat embarrassed, he hung his head and noticed Addie Jane staring up at him from the floor where she'd taken a seat.

They visited about an hour, and Addie Jane kept sidling up closer and closer to Barclay all the while. He found this rather amusing. Poky noticed Mrs. Taylor alternately glancing at the clock on the wall. She rose to go. "Well, we best be gettin' on."

"Don't hurry." But Poky couldn't help but see the quick look of relief on her face. Even though Barclay was certainly as instrumental as she in Addie Jane's birth, Mr. Taylor still resented him, couldn't bring himself to accept who he was.

That summer Poky and Barclay spent more time together than ever before, hiking their beloved mountains, fishing in the streams, and putting up herbs and vegetables from her plentiful gardens. They visited their neighbors, too, particularly little Addie Jane whenever her father wasn't home.

But fall came, and Barclay left, leaving a vacant spot in Poky's world. Seeking solace from her beloved mountains, she climbed their familiar ridges, always remembering his little footsteps behind her. Sitting down on a ledge in early

October, she breathed in the invigorating autumn air, and marveled at the exquisite colors of the Blue Ridge. Surely there was no place on God's earth as lovely. The bright yellow and gold of poplars, maples, hickories and locusts, the bright red and crimson of maples, dogwoods, sumac and gum contrasted with the dark green pines and cedars. The vivid drama was presented by each and every tree in the forest as they competed in this annual show of all shows. She smiled. Even the paradise — the little *tree of heaven* growing out from the ledge where she sat, was now clothed in its deepest red...scrawny little thing that it was. But persistent...persevering...struggling against all odds for its place...as if it knew from the start that its life might be short-lived, it grew faster than all the rest and reached for the stars.

The months rolled by, and Poky looked for his letters, sometimes frequent and other times not so. One of his first letters related the Nuremberg Trial, convictions of nineteen Nazi defendants, with twelve receiving death sentences, and how ten were hanged. 'May justice be done!' he concluded. Poky didn't miss the passion between the lines. Barclay felt things very deeply, especially injustice.

The void Barclay left was never completely filled, but sure enough Poky's involvement with little Addie Jane and watching her grow filled some of this emptiness of heart. Mrs. Taylor was glad for her visits now that she was expecting her second child. Once in awhile, she even took the little girl up on the mountain with her, and the child delighted in it all. On such a day, in the heat of July, little Addie Jane was visiting and watching Poky make hoecakes. Poky was cooking outside, as she'd done for years whenever it got too hot in the cabin, just as Sister Jane had done. Addie Jane loved watching the open flame in the center of the dugout, encircled by rocks.

"Don't get too close now, child."

She stepped back. "Time, Miss Poky...it's time...."

Poky quickly grabbed the large fork to turn the hoecake. She flipped the large cake over a little too quickly, and it fell with a thud into the blackened ashes!

"Uh-oh!" Addie Jane exclaimed.

"Never mind, child. It'll be all right." She fished it out of the ashes and placed it back on the hoe, brushing off the loose ashes with her fork, and grinned at Addie Jane who grinned back.

"Why you cook on a hoe, Miss Poky?"

"Jest for hoecakes, lil' Miss. Don't use it for nothin' else. That's why they're called *hoecakes*, ya' know. Back in th'old days when folks were workin' in th'fields, they'd use an old hoe they done broke for fixin' their cornmeal cakes, an' they'd call'em hoecakes. Sister Jane taught me this. Always liked watchin' Sister Jane do it, an' now I do it. Been usin' this old hoe for a mighty long time, too, ever since th'handle broke one day while I was a'hoe'n my garden. Made me mad an' I said right then, "Old hoe, you only good for hoecakes now!" She laughed her hearty laugh, and Addie Jane laughed with her.

"This one's gonna be good. I put in an egg, always makes it taste better. Sister Jane use'ta just use cornmeal an' water, but I always like'a egg in my hoecake." She scooped the large hoecake up, placed it on a plate and handed it to Addie Jane. The child broke off a small piece of the hot bread, stuck it in her mouth and smiled affectionately at her friend. Then she went to poking in the ashes with the hoe, stirring up the smoke. She began to cough. Suddenly she was coughing uncontrollably. Poky recognized that cough with horror. The attack was a short one, but not too short for Poky, who took her back home and questioned her mother. She was saddened to find out that the child was suffering with asthma. On the way back to her cabin, Poky's thoughts returned to her own childhood and Sister Jane's asthma attacks. How strange that she would be so close to two on earth that shared that dreaded enemy.

AWHILE AFTER BARCLAY left, Poky had received a letter from Hallie...a letter full of praise and happiness as she shared wonderful news with her. It happened the second week of December, during the first snow of winter, said Hallie. She was hemming a dress for Lauralee and quietly enjoying the soft sounds of snow blanketing Lynchburg when she heard a light knock at the door. She rose and opened it to a handsome young man in his twenties, leaning on a cane.

"Ma'am, my name is Luther Geiser from Brainerd, Minnesota. I have a message for you...from your son, Jamey Frederick."

Hallie caught her breath and turned white.

"Ma'am, I know Jamey's dead...but he sent a message to you before he died. I'm just late delivering it."

She slowly moved aside. "Please come in...."

The young man limped in on the cane toward the couch.

"Please...please have a seat...."

He sat down with one leg stretched straight out, took off his warm cap, gloves and shawl and loosened his coat. Hallie, still in a daze, forgot to ask for his wraps.

He came quickly to the point..."Jamey and I were buddies, you see. We both arrived in Okinawa the same day, both scared out of our wits. Oh, I know you probably thought Jamey was not one to be scared. He told me as much, wanted everybody to think he was really cool, not afraid, you know. But, ma'am, Jamey was scared...just like the rest of us...scared to death! Yes, ma'am, we were both filled with fear night and day. In fact, I think we were the two most scared soldiers in camp...but we tried not to let anybody know. We just told each other. We didn't want to die, ma'am...that's why we were so scared. But then something happened. Only a short while before we were attacked, and Jamey was killed...he started acting different...won't scared anymore...was happy all the time. I asked him what had gotten into him...what had happened? That's when he told me...."

Hallie was sitting on the edge of her chair.

"Told me he'd trusted in the Lord...gave his life to Him...and he won't worrying anymore...that he knew his life was in God's hands. Said if it was God's will for him to die, so be it. He said he was ready to die. And, ma'am, I know he was...because his life was different. He had a glow about him, and he spent his time cheering us up...trying to lead us to the Lord. I laughed him off...told him I didn't want none of that religion stuff. You see, I claimed to be an atheist back then. That bothered Jamey a whole lot...and he spent some time telling me about God and His great love for us. I made fun of him...not because I didn't like him. No, ma'am...I really liked Jamey...who wouldn't? But I was running from reality and truth." He began to loosen his coat more, obviously getting warmer in the cozy living room.

"Please forgive me, Mr. Geiser...let me take your coat...."

"I'll just lay it here, ma'am, and call me Luther. Jamey called me Luther...."

"Please go on, Luther."

"Well...I was with him, ma'am...when he died." The young man wiped his eyes. "That's why I'm here. If it wasn't for Jamey, I wouldn't be here. We were both in the same foxhole when the explosion hit us...and Jamey fell on me...not by accident, ma'am. He saved my life. I lost a leg...this here's my fake one...." He tapped his stiffened leg. "And the scar here...," he pointed to a large disfigured scar over his right eye, "is from surgeries...in fact two surgeries. I almost lost my eye, too. I have a steel plate inside, also. That's why I'm so long delivering your message, ma'am. I've been laid up in hospitals for over two years...had six operations altogether. But it wasn't the physical injuries that kept me down so long...I'd given up...didn't care after I'd seen what happened during the war...and lost friends like Jamey. But back to the message, ma'am. Just before he died, Jamey asked me to tell you...*he'd meet you in heaven...not to worry...that was his surprise – he'd made peace with God.*"

Tears flowed down Hallie's cheeks, and she rose to get a tissue and handed one to Luther.

"Thank you, ma'am."

They sat in silence for awhile.

"Would you like some coffee, Luther?"

"That would be real nice, ma'am."

She walked into the kitchen, feeling all warm inside and as she reached for a cup from the cupboard, she saw the fine snow falling in the darkness by the street light. Jamey was all right...he was waiting for her...and one day...she'd see him again. Just before Luther Geiser left, he told Hallie that he, too, had given his life to the Lord only a few months earlier...and all because of Jamey.

Hallie couldn't wait to share her news with Lauralee and Jon Junior, who were as happy as she to finally find out his surprise. She shared it with any and all she came in contact with, too. In fact, Hallie seemed to take on a new purpose in life...Jamey's purpose...to share his secret. Poky rejoiced in the news after reading the letter...and thanked God. Shortly afterwards, Hallie announced that she wanted to move. Downtown Lynchburg was changing, and they now could afford something better anyway. Deep down, she knew she hadn't been able to bring herself to leave the home Jamey had grown up in, but now she could. Jamey *was* at home.

The Frederick family moved. They bought a nice home in Rivermont, not so big like some that graced the wide avenue, but a nice comfortable home with lots of shrubs and trees and flowers, and even a rose arbor with tiny, delicate pastel pink roses climbing all over it. Hallie spent hours pampering the gardens and flowers. Lauralee and Jon Junior were pleased to see her so happy. Lauralee was happy herself, in love finally. She was tired of being called an old maid. She would soon be twenty-five, and it was time. Jon Junior still went about his steady, dependable way, but always alone.

CHAPTER TWELVE

EACH SUMMER BARCLAY returned home to his pa and Poky, and each time, she marveled at his growth and maturity. Her little boy was fast growing into a strong, handsome man with coal black hair and dark penetrating eyes, almost six feet tall, straight and broad shouldered. As he grew older, she didn't see as much of him. He was too busy working or studying, but she cherished the times he did come by. Four years quickly passed, and Barclay graduated from high school in 1950. He was seventeen years old. He joined the United States Air Force immediately and left for training. He thought the years in Maryland had been interesting, opening up a whole new world for him, with different kinds of people accepting him just as he was. But the next four years presented horizons he'd never dreamed he'd see or experience. He remembered the long days at the mission school when he'd read those *Weekly Readers* and *Current Events*...especially those *Current Events*. He'd saved them and reread them time and time again, allowing his mind to travel thousands of miles across the sea to exotic lands and war-torn places. He'd followed World War II through those *Current Events*...and now?

Three weeks after he'd graduated from high school, the Korean War began. It was June 25, 1950, and the country had hardly had enough time to get used to peace again before it was facing another challenge. It wasn't exactly coincidental that Barclay Branham found himself following in his brothers' footsteps. Instead, it was something he felt he must do, something he had to prove to himself, if not to everyone else. Perhaps it was because he was different, or thought to be different. Maybe it was simply that he needed to prove that he wasn't a sissy. Whatever the reason, for the next three years, Barclay was a part of it, stationed first in Okinawa and then in South Korea. As he flew over North Korea in Sabre jets, a part of the dogfights with the Soviet-built MIG-15's, he didn't expect to return. Though he didn't really want to die, he'd decided early on that that was better than returning like Paul David. But he would give it his best, what he was doing was important. It was his job to man the guns. Poky spent a lot of time on her knees. She was especially concerned when he was in Okinawa...where Jamey had died. Although she'd always been keen on keeping up with the news, she refused to read the papers or listen to her radio. She couldn't bear to think of Barclay in the midst of all that fighting! Instead, she focused more and more on Addie Jane, who was now seven years old and had taken to her the same as Barclay. Mrs. Taylor had given birth to two more children, both boys, and was pregnant again. Poky felt sorry for Addie Jane, who always seemed sad. She didn't quite know why.

"Hold your neck up, Addie Jane."

The small girl tilted her chin upward in the air while still trying to see her hands.

"No...no..." Poky laughed aloud. "I don't mean *your* neck, child. I mean th'guitar's neck...you gotta hold it up when ya' play."

Addie Jane looked confused.

"Here, lemme show you." Poky took the guitar, sat down and began to demonstrate the proper position.

"Play me *Down in the Valley*, Poky...I want to learn that one."

Poky began to softly strum the melody, and Addie Jane hummed along with her...

Down in the Valley
Valley so low
Hang your head over
Hear the wind blow

"It's kind'a sad like, child. You like it, do ya'?"

"Yes, ma'am. I like that one. Makes me think of th'wind blowing like it does sometimes. I like to hear th'wind blowing."

"I see."

They finished practicing, and Poky brought out the quilting materials. "Time for us t'work on your quilt, Addie Jane." Quickly, she jumped up, ready to help. Poky had been collecting material for sometime for this quilt...Addie Jane's quilt...to go in her hope chest. Addie Jane kept her hope chest at Poky's where she said it would be safe from the children at home. The hope chest was a small, worn metal trunk that Poky had had for years, and one day decided it would serve the purpose quite nicely. Its top was rounded, and it was covered with a thick canvas material with an interesting design in it. Addie Jane loved it, and often sat running her small fingers through the curves in the design.

"Every young lady s'posed t'have a *hope chest.*"

"Why, Poky?"

"Why? 'Cause one day you gonna get married, an' you'll have all kinds'uv things saved up for your first home. That's why."

"Did you have a hope chest, Poky?"

"Naw, child, an' ya' see what happened...I didn't get married!" She chuckled.

"I wanna be like you, Poky. I won't get married neither."

"Oh now, you jest wait an' see. Th'good Lord might have other plans for you. Ya' know He has a *plan* for all'uv us. Mine was t'be alone so's I could have lots'uv folk like you in my life...but your'n will probably be different. Some dashin' young feller might come along one day an' sweep you right off ya' feet."

"Like *Snow White?*"

"That's right...like Snow White."

"...but when you get married, you have babies...."

"So? What's wrong with that?"

"Babies cost money, pa says so...mama says so, too."

"They're right, child."

"But we don't got no money...an' mama's gonna have another baby...."

"Th'good Lord will provide, child. Don't you worry." But Poky noticed the frown on the little one's forehead. A forehead too small for a frown.

After awhile, Poky spoke up, "Addie Jane, you best be gettin' on home now. You gotta get your bath, tomorrow's Sunday." Together, they put away the prized material. The Taylors weren't church-going people. Poky had started taking Addie Jane with her to St. Paul's a couple of years prior, and she looked forward to it each week. Mr. Taylor wasn't aware of where she was going, just knew she was with Poky, and that was all right with him.

THE KOREAN WAR ended on July 27, 1953 with the United Nations and North Korea signing an armistice agreement, ending one of the bloodiest wars in history. About a million South Korean civilians were killed, approximately 580,000 UN and South Korean troops and about 1,600,000 communists. Again, the boys came home.

Barclay still had one more year in the Air Force and was reassigned to the states at Kelly Air Force Base in San Antonio. Although glad to be back in the states, he yearned for the mountains as he discovered the plains of Texas. Poky was happy to know that! She read his letter to Addie Jane... *'I thought the country in Korea different...now I wonder if I'm truly back home...no mountain ridges for comfort...just wide open plains...and hot...too hot...and no tall oaks for shade...no mountain streams to wade in...no shadows to walk in during the cool of the evening...I miss Virginia...I miss the Blue Ridge....'*

"Our boy'll be home soon, Addie Jane...I think he will."

Poky was right. Barclay couldn't wait to return to the mountains as soon as he got a chance. But it was the dead of winter before he got that chance. He arrived the end of February during one of the worst ice storms recorded.

The rains fell, downpours, gushing over the mountainsides with magnificent force...all day long...the rains fell...all night long...the rains fell...mountain streams overflowed and cascaded down the mountainside without a path...water several inches deep stood in the valleys...and then the temperature dropped!

Early morning was cold...cold...and grey with ice everywhere. Power was down over the valley. It was down on Oak Mountain and High Peak, as well. There was an eerie stillness that had settled over part of the Blue Ridge except for an occasional POP! Tree limbs cracking, splitting, trees toppling under the weight of ice. Poky wiped the fogged up window with her dishrag and looked out at the grey day, the grey sky, the icy grey trees with every single twig and branch covered with layers of grey ice. She jumped each time she heard a POP! Another tree down. All day, she watched as the temperature hovered at ten degrees. Her cabin was warm with pine logs crackling in the stove, and steam from the pot of pinto beans warmed it even more. She hoped her neighbors were as warm and cozy as she, but there was no way she could check now. Evening came, and then dusk fell and with it a heavy fog, lying low. The trees appeared deformed, twisted, burdened with the heavy grey ice. She lit her oil lamp, and its single light threw shadows about the cabin. She continued to stare out the window, feeling drawn to it somehow. The stillness was oppressing. POP! Her hands flew to her ears. "My...my...gotta do somethin'...." She muttered as she pulled her guitar off the wall, sat down by the flickering lantern and strummed a tune... *'I come to th'garden alone...while th'dew is still on th'roses...An' th'voice I hear...fallin' on my ear...th'Son of God...discloses...An' He walks with me...an' He talks with me...an' He tells me I am His own...An' th'joy we share as we tarry there...none other has ever known....'*

As always, those words comforted her. She knew He was right there with her even in the midst of this scary ice storm. And though she couldn't enjoy her garden now, she knew it was there, too, lying dormant under nature's icy blanket. An' when spring comes, she thought, those lil' shoots will appear, an' all th'earth will sing with me... *'an' th'joy we share as we tarry there...none other has ever known....'*

She blew out the oil lantern and went to bed. The ice covered mountain slept.

Early in the morning, someone pounded on her door, just about rattling the cabin itself. "My goodness...hold on...," she called out, while trying to pull her clothes over her head in the stark coldness. The fire had gone out in the night. The pounding grew louder! She opened the door and, to her surprise, there stood Barclay.

"Oh my! Barclay...come on in...you gonna catch your death out in this'ere ice storm!" He followed her into the semi-dark cabin, bringing with him the frigid air. "Lemme get some wood in this'ere stove first...."

"I'll do that, Poky." He took the wood out of her arms and started the fire. Once it was roaring up the chimney, they pulled chairs up close and began checking each other out.

"You're a sight bigger than I thought...an' handsomer, too...."

He blushed. "You're looking right good yourself, Poky. You doing all right?"

"Fair t'middlin', I guess." She chuckled. "Why on earth did ya' come out on such a morning?"

"Just got in yesterday...and I was worried about you...with this storm...."

"I see. You know you don't have t'worry 'bout your Poky."

"I know." He smiled his winning smile. "You got enough wood?"

"Didn't ya' see that pile'uv wood stacked up on th'porch yonder?"

"Guess I didn't. Too cold and too excited about seeing you."

"Barclay?"

"Yes, ma'am?"

"You out'a that Air Force for good now?"

He was silent a moment.

"You are..ain't you?"

"Poky, I re-enlisted for another four years...."

She looked at him with surprise. "Why on earth, son?"

"It's not all bad, Poky. And I'm going to school...college...and the military's paying for it."

"I see."

"You always wanted me to get an education."

"I did...I did...but I didn't figure on ya' keepin' on...college an' all...oh, don't get me wrong...I'm proud, Barclay...mighty proud. I guess I was just countin' on ya' comin' back, ya' know, to th'Mountain. I guess I was hopin' it could be like it used t'be...." She looked down at her cracked hands. "...but I guess I'm just a foolish old woman now. How can it be like it used t'be? You done gone an' growed up on me! All tall, broad shouldered an' handsome...." She kept looking at her hands, not wanting him to see her tear-filled eyes.

"I brought you something, Poky." He stood up and began rummaging in his pockets. She quickly wiped her eyes while he pulled out a small envelope. "Brought you some Bluebonnet seeds all the way from Texas. They're the state flower of Texas, you know. Figured with your green thumb, you might be able to grow them here in Virginia."

She smiled up at him. "I'll do my best." She turned the packet over and looked at the picture of the delicate blue flowers. "Mighty pretty lil' things...an' all th'way from Texas, too...you had your breakfast yet?"

"'Course not. I was coming to see you." He grinned.

"An' you figured your Poky might jest fry you up some bacon an' eggs with cheese in'em, with a hoecake or two to go along. Well, you jest sit yourself down an' tell me all about Texas while I whip you up a breakfast like you ain't had for a long time, I 'spect."

"You're right about that."

Barclay spent the day with Poky as the temperature began to slowly climb...all the way up to twenty-four degrees, but not enough to melt the ice, not enough to relieve the burden of the mountain trees as they groaned, prisoners of ice, still succumbing to its overpowering weight, and POPPING! Trees continued to fall throughout the forest all through the day and into the second night. The next morning, Poky was again awakened with a banging on her door. Puzzled, but hoping it to be Barclay again, she hastily dressed and hurried to the door. Instead, Addie Jane stood there, chattering from the cold. "Miss Poky, come quick, mama's gonna have'er baby! I gotta get back now." And she was gone like a flash through the icy forest. Poky got ready as quickly as she could, dreading the long walk to the Taylors through the cold and ice. Why on earth did babies always pick this kind'uv weather to be born? As she braved the cold, bundled up in her cape, she used a large stick to steady herself on the ice and made it without any trouble. Just before reaching the valley, however, she saw a tall figure approaching. It was Barclay!

"Poky, what're you doing?" he questioned with a frown.

"Gotta get to th'Taylors...Mrs. Taylor's havin' another baby."

He stepped up beside her, grabbing her bag. "Just like old times, huh?" he kidded. "Who said we couldn't go back?"

Circles of smoke escaped her grin as she looked into his laughing eyes. They reached the Taylor home just as Mrs. Taylor began hard labor.

"Where's Addie Jane?" she gasped between pains.

"Ain't she here?"

Mrs. Taylor shook her head.

"Where's Mr. Taylor?"

"Gone over to his pa's t'check on'im. Left 'bout a hour ago."

Poky wondered why he always seemed to be gone at these times. But dismissed it, too worried about Addie Jane, realizing she should've been back long ago.

"I'll go look for her." Barclay started back out the door.

"Be careful, Barclay. Them woods are dangerous with this'ere ice."

As he plowed up the crusty, ice-covered mountain, he was reminded of her words just after missing a falling branch. Now, he was beginning to get somewhat frantic. Where was little Addie Jane? Why on earth did her mama let her come out in this stuff? He called out...*Addie Jane...Addie Jane*...and listened to the ice tremble overhead, wondering if it would all come tumbling down on him. Knowing the woods like the backside of his hand was an advantage. He kept to the common path between the valley and Oak Mountain, carefully picking his way up along the icy ridges.

But Addie Jane was not on the common path. Having delivered her urgent message to Poky and filled with concern for her mother, she'd taken a shortcut, which unfortunately had led to a wrong turn in the woods. Normally, this would be next to impossible with Addie Jane. She, too, knew these woods inside and out...but the ice had skillfully and cunningly transformed the forest...causing it to become incognito and deceptive. Now she wandered about in a confused state, and the damp cold was biting at her. She was scared as overhead tree branches popped and came crashing down around her. She struggled to find her way. SWOOSH! A young, slender poplar suddenly fell just in front of her. She cried out! Running in the opposite direction, she slipped and fell on the cold, hard ice, and its splintered fragments flew into her face. She closed her eyes, but the sounds of popping trees were all around her, as the sleet begin to fall again. Crawling over to a sturdy looking oak, she held on...but even it fell prey to the ice, sending forth a heavy branch...downward it came...pinning Addie Jane to the tree trunk. She thought the whole mountain had caved in on her as she struggled to get free, but could not budge the branch. She peered through its icy fingers and felt a searing pain in her left side. She was dizzy and cold...so cold. Fear seized her, and she sobbed, afraid another branch or tree would fall, afraid she would freeze. She called out...HELP! HELP! HELP! Her call reverberated off the icy forest, sending forth crusty ice showering from above...she fell silent, afraid to call out again, and lay there for what seemed like hours. She listened to the eerie sounds of the forest she loved, but now was her captor by this ominous grey cloud of ice. Her mind raced backwards...she remembered her prayers for the past few months...prayers that she would not have any more brothers or sisters...there were too many in the family now...not enough money...not enough food...not enough to wear...she didn't want her mother to have another baby! She'd prayed that she wouldn't have this baby! She'd prayed it all during her mother's pregnancy...and now...was this her punishment? Or maybe, her punishment would be that the baby would be born dead...was God punishing her for this sin? She now realized it was foolish and selfish for her to pray those prayers...but at the time...all she could think of was too many...too many children and she didn't want to be poor. She shivered uncontrollably. Was she going to die...freeze to death? She'd read about such people dying this way, freezing to death, and how they didn't feel it. She didn't want to freeze...she didn't want to die! But it was so...cold...so cold...."

Then she saw it! Only a few yards from her and staring straight at her. She froze! Stealthily it moved toward her, its pointed ears arched forward, looking like a big reddish-brown house cat with dark spots, except for its eyes. And those keen eyes were riveted on her in a peculiar sort of way. Addie Jane didn't move, remembering what Poky had told her long ago, but she felt sick to her stomach. A few more steps and the bobcat was only feet away. SWOOSH! A tree fell!

The bobcat ran off, and Barclay rushed to her side. He'd witnessed the last moments, and just as he'd started toward them, the tree had fallen.

Quickly, he lifted the large branch, throwing it aside. He pulled off his coat and wrapping it around the small child, he gently picked her up and started back down the mountainside. Her dark green eyes, filled with tears, looked lovingly up at him before they closed.

The next day the sun came out and the icy mountain glistened...then it began to melt...millions of fragments of ice began falling from the tree tops...a shattering was heard throughout Oak Mountain and echoed all around...a shattering...a crackling...a crinkling...tinkling sound...little bells...little chimes over the mountain, creating a song as the ice turned loose its victims and fell to the ground...striking the many tree branches on its descent and shattering as glass...before its final crash to the ice encrusted ground. The forest awoke to a spectacular drama, this tinkling multiplied a thousand times over throughout the mountainside, creating a unique sensation for all...birds began singing...deer stopped in their tracks and listened...mountain folk came out of their cozy cabins and discovered a new earth...a brilliant sparkling earth...with millions of ice fragments shimmering in the bright sunlight while spiraling through the air...all was well...the ice was melting.

But Addie Jane hovered close to death. She had pneumonia. Barclay had taken her to Poky's when he found her, but her tiny body had suffered too much from the extreme cold. There she stayed as Poky and Barclay tended her. The doctor ordered hospitalization, and thus she was taken to the General Hospital in Lynchburg where her condition was deemed serious. Her mother came with the new baby, her little brothers came and stood silently, Mr. Taylor paced the corridors, Poky and Barclay kept a vigilant watch.

"We've done all we can," the doctor said, "now all we can do is hope."

"No, sir," said Poky, "No, sir, doctor...in all due respect, sir...there's more we can do. We can pray." She knelt beside Addie Jane's bed and called on the Lord for help.

That night was a long night as the family stayed, the little ones fell asleep one by one, including the new baby. Mrs. Taylor and Poky didn't close their eyes...neither did Barclay.

"Where's Mr. Taylor?" asked Poky.

"Walking the corridors...he can't sit still," Mrs. Taylor responded.

"I understand."

"Poky, you're like a doctor. Do ya' think...do ya' think Addie Jane's gonna...."

"Mrs. Taylor, I ain't no doctor, but th'good Lord is...let's jest call on Him. He knows best."

Barclay looked from one to the other, and back to the small form under the oxygen tent, and followed Poky's advice.

The next morning Addie Jane opened her eyes. She looked up and around...and smiled at Barclay. She was going to be all right!

Addie Jane recovered and discovered she had a fourth brother...and Barclay left again for another four years.

CHAPTER THIRTEEN

FOUR YEARS LATER. "Mama, you home? Mama...." Lauralee called out, but the house was silent. She wheeled the stroller around and started out the door. "Probably at the park, Frankie." Backing it down the steps, she headed toward Riverside Park. It was late May, and the day was warm and sunny, perfect for a stroll in the park. A slight breeze stirred the abundant new leaves overhead, and the old trees, lining the sidewalk, provided a shady path. Being a week-day, the park was quiet, only an occasional car could be seen leisurely cruising along the narrow, curving road that wound around and through the park, up and down its hills. Lauralee inhaled the sweet pungency of the honeysuckle that had intertwined itself through the thicket of shrubs along the road. Frankie, her youngest, a pixy little girl, sat upright in the stroller watching the movement of the trees overhead. Ever since they'd moved from downtown to Rivermont, her mother had fallen in love with Riverside Park and its inviting rolling hills, tall shady trees, dramatic view of the James lazily flowing beneath its bluffs and the "*boat*." The boat was actually just a portion of the hull of a boat that sat in the park for those who were interested...and Hallie was interested. Hallie had always been interested in history, and this boat or hull was history. It had been the packet boat called Marshall and had traveled primarily from Richmond to Lynchburg three times a week. But what caused its notoriety and its remains to lie in state indefinitely at the small park was the fact that it had carried General Stonewall Jackson's body to Lexington for burial. Hallie never came to the park that she didn't stop and linger a bit to view the boat. Lauralee followed the winding, narrow road through the small park, approaching its one steep hill, and literally held on with both hands as the stroller rolled down it, picking up speed. Frankie squealed with delight, throwing her little hands into the air. Lauralee laughed at her young daughter, so full of life. Such joy she'd brought her already. She felt most blessed, the mother of a wonderful little son, now a beautiful daughter..she felt contentment...yes, that's what it was...contentment. She looked around her at the tall summer trees throwing shade over the park. She felt good!

"We've got to find grandma. We'll come back again." She pushed the stroller up the curving hill and finally reached its crest. Panting hard, she strained to see if she saw her mother. Stonewall's boat was just ahead. And sure enough, there she was, leaning against a tree staring down at the decaying hull. Suddenly she turned.

"Lauralee...Frankie...I was just thinking about you."

"Oh yeah, well, we were thinking about you, too...and decided to visit."

"Good. What time is it? William still at school?"

"It's just quarter to two. I don't pick him up till three. It's a gorgeous day, isn't it?"

"Perfect." She grabbed Frankie out of the stroller, anxious to get her hands on her. "How's grandma's girl?" The little girl, almost one, hung her head shyly. "Now, don't act shy with me, I know better."

She straddled her on her hip as they began walking, but then put her back in the stroller. "Can't do that for long. She's getting heavy, for sure."

"How's Jon Junior?"

"Working hard as usual. You know, Lauralee, I worry about him. Wish he'd find some nice girl and get married."

"You'd be all alone if he did."

"I know, and I'd really miss him, too...just like I've missed you. Of course, since it's his house, he might not move anyway. But I don't want to hold onto him. He needs his own life just like you. It's way past time for him to be making a life for himself. He's forty-two, and he's given too much of his life to me and to the rest of us, you know that."

"I know, Mama. Did you hear about Mrs. Browning?"

"What about her?"

"She's been very ill...had to stop teaching. I even heard rumors that she may have cancer."

"That's terrible...I certainly hope not."

"Jon Junior said anything about it?"

"No, why?"

"...just that I saw him talking with her a couple of weeks ago. Thought maybe he'd know something." Lauralee didn't add that they were actually eating lunch together...which was very odd.

"Maybe I'll ask him. That is a shame...and she's such a dear, too."

"You know, Mama, it's really nice that you're living here so close to the park and all this beauty." She changed the subject as she handed over the stroller pushing to her mother.

"I know...I rode out here to the park on the trolley years ago when you were small, you wouldn't remember. It used to come out here. I never thought one day I'd be living so close that I could walk. You wouldn't think I'd miss the old place with all this...but I do. I miss the bustle of downtown, being able to look out over the rooftops on a clear day, a feeling of being right in the middle of everything. I guess I liked that more than I thought, at least I had gotten used to it after all those years. But it's much quieter here and like you say...so pretty."

"And it's nice being so close to the library. How many steps did I ever make walking back and forth from downtown to Jones Memorial, checking out all those books?" She laughed.

"I used to wonder if you'd ruin your eyes from reading so many books and looking at all those picture shows, but they kept you busy and happy while I was working."

They exited the park entrance, turned left and headed down Rivermont Avenue. Mrs. Alberta Fredonia, taking her daily stroll, approached them on their right. Mrs. Fredonia was one of Hallie's neighbors, one that made it her business to obtain, record and analyze any and all neighborhood activities. She considered it her duty to advise all residents on matters of concern, particularly national matters.

"Good day, Mrs. Fredonia."

"Good day to you, Mrs. Frederick. This, I presume, is your lovely daughter."

"We've met once before. I'm Lauralee."

"Yes, yes, you're right, of course. Who are you voting for, Lauralee?"

"Ma'am?" Lauralee looked up, surprised.

"Who are you voting for come election day?"

"Well...I...."

"Never mind, dear." The stern, thin lady pushed her bifocals back up on her nose and reached into her brown sweater pocket, pulling out a large round pin, a duplicate of the one she was sporting. It was about the size of a nice tangerine and flickered in the bright sunlight with Ike's smiling face appearing and disappearing, alternating with the bold words that had taken hold of the country...*I like Ike.*

"Here take one...and vote for Ike!"

Lauralee gracefully accepted the large pin thrust out to her. "Thank you."

"My pleasure...ladies, have a good day." With that, she turned and briskly walked away. Lauralee stared down at the pin and back at her mother with a grin. "Well, he does have a nice smile, and I'm sure he's gonna win anyhow!"

"Most likely. Oh, did you notice my peonies?" Hallie bent over the lush pink and white blooms as they arrived back home.

"Sure did. They're lovely, really full, seems like more than last year."

"Well, I don't know, but they surely have outdone themselves this year. Probably be peaking for the weekend, that is if it doesn't rain...rain beats them down, you know. Come on up on the porch and sit awhile. Let Frankie sleep there in the stroller...she'll be all right."

They climbed the steps. Lauralee chose the porch swing and sat down, pushing it back and forth listening to its rhythmic squeak. "Heard from Poky lately?"

"Not for awhile. Her last letter was full of news about Addie Jane. Seems she's replaced Barclay in a way. In fact, Poky says Addie Jane's in love with Barclay! Ever since he saved her life during that ice storm a few years ago. Of course, it's just puppy love, but she hasn't gotten over him."

"How old is Addie Jane?"

"Oh, I don't know...twelve or more, I guess."

"Well, that's about the age you have your first love...puppy love or whatever you call it."

"She'll certainly be crushed if he up and marries one of those British girls."

"Isn't that the truth, but it could happen."

IN FACT, THOSE were the exact thoughts troubling the young girl's mind and causing a thin furrow in her otherwise smooth brow as she sat at Poky's kitchen table.

"You don't eat enough t'keep a bird alive, child. Finish them 'tatoes."

Addie Jane absently pushed the fried potatoes back and forth on her plate as they grew colder and colder, sticking to her fork. "Poky, what was it Barclay said in his last letter about London?"

"Said it's a bustlin' place, excitin', with buses painted fire engine red runnin' all over th'place, an' they even have'a upstairs on'em. Can you 'magine such a thing? Said they got lots'uv little black cabs that folks get around in an' they'll run right up on th'curb if'n they have to. An' they drive on th'wrong side'uv th'road an' jest as soon run over you as not. Sounds like a place I'd rather stay clear'uv myself. Oh yeah, said somethin' 'bout Buckingham Palace...sounds like'a mighty fancy place with a whole lot'uv dressed up guards that have t'take their turns guardin' th'place...."

"I mean the part about how the young ladies look?"

"Oh, that part." Poky pretended not to know her thoughts. "Said th'young ladies are right nice lookin'...pretty as any picture...'ristocratic like...he said...an' he's sketchin' one even...."

"Which one?"

"Didn't say. But ya' know how Barclay likes his drawin'. Bet that picture'll be as pretty as th'girl, too."

Addie Jane pushed her cold potatoes away. "I can't eat anymore, Poky. I'm just not hungry."

"How you gonna put any meat on them bones, child?"

She shrugged her shoulders.

"You goin' t'th'Girl Scout Camp?"

"Guess so."

"Your pa get th'money?"

"Nope."

Poky looked up questioningly.

"They gonna let me go free."

Poky detected a sarcastic tone. The child just had too much pride to be poor. "Well now, that's real nice, Addie Jane. You get t'go t'camp...what's th'name'uv that camp?"

"Camp Sacajawea."

"That's right. Indian name, you said. Gonna sleep in a tent?"

"Yes, ma'am. When's Barclay comin' in on leave?"

"Shucks, child. I don't know. He don't tell me half th'time...just shows up."

"Like last time."

"That's right. What'd you say that Girl Scout motto is...somethin' 'bout bein' ready?"

"*Be prepared.*"

"Good advice, too."

Addie Jane stared out the kitchen window. Poky began clearing the table, wondering how the child could be so smitten and just thirteen years old. The next day at school, Addie Jane was daydreaming in English class when Miss Hopetell abruptly called on her. She looked up blankly.

"Addie Jane, you best come back and join us."

"Yes, ma'am." Her face flushed a crimson red as the class giggled. Shifting uncomfortably in her seat, she thought to herself while opening her textbook...they were all just a bunch of immature kids...not really knowing what life was all about. Again her thoughts returned to Barclay, already grown and serving his country, dressed in his smart military uniform, more handsome than any fellow she'd ever laid eyes on...the bell rang, interrupting her thoughts, and she picked up her books and left the classroom, hurrying down the corridor, not to be late.

"*She's got on my dress...*" the cruel, insensitive words pierced her heart like a sharpened sword. Addie Jane kept walking as if she hadn't heard, but she could see and hear the group of girls snickering as she walked past with her face flushed red and burning already. Her ever-ready tears were fighting her pride. Suddenly the soft see-through pastel print dress, that billowed out gracefully with its rustling crinoline, felt dirty. Only hours earlier she'd been so happy as she pulled it down over her head, proud to have something so pretty, so delicate...but now she couldn't wait to get home and take it off. She wished Mrs. Bolling had never given those dresses to her mother. *She'd never wear them again!* The tears were about to come as she boarded the school bus already brimming with anxious students in a hurry to get home. She claimed an empty seat near the back, and slid over to the window, grateful to have somewhere to look without the other kids noticing her. The old bus chugged out of the parking lot, gears roughly jerking, and started down the driveway. She blinked the determined tears back and hardened her heart against future attacks. Knowing someone had sat down beside her, she finally looked around to see who. Jean Lee Smith smiled at her, and she smiled back. Jean Lee lived out a ways, not in the valley, but her daddy owned the hardware store in the valley and treated folk fair and square, she'd heard. Jean Lee was an only child, something Addie Jane thought novel and simply heavenly, and she lived in a nicely painted white, two-story house up on a hillside, covered with ivy and surrounded by big oak trees with hostas encircling them. The hosta was one of the first things to turn green again after winter, and Addie Jane looked for it each year. In the summer, there were tall, bright orange tiger lilies growing atop the hillside. Addie Jane enjoyed just looking at the lovely place whenever she passed by.

"You going to camp?"

Addie Jane quickly looked at her, trying to discern her motive. Not able to detect any, she nodded.

"Good, so am I." Jean Lee settled back and opened her library book to read. Suddenly, Addie Jane felt much better.

The week at camp proved to be overall a happy time for Addie Jane, but it only reinforced her otherwise determined goal...one day she'd be different...not poor...she'd see to that. As their gear was carefully laid out, painfully her meager belongings stood out, labeling her as the *poor girl*...an identification she loathed. But her friendship with Jean Lee grew that week as the two drew closer, discovering each other's private secrets while sharing the small tent. All too soon the week was over, and Addie Jane found herself back home with the same dull routine of a big family struggling to get by in the valley. At least the family was finally complete with four little brothers, all clamoring for attention all hours of the day and night. If one wasn't crying from a bruised knee, another was screaming because he'd been hit in the eye by his brother. Which brother? Who knew? The summer dragged by. Her mother allowed her to be excused as often as possible to visit Poky or just ramble in the woods, climbing Oak Mountain. It was always a cherished retreat as her fragile nature simply couldn't accommodate all the demands of her younger siblings. Addie Jane had been forced to assume the role of mother too soon.

One such morning, a late hot August morning, she set out across the valley, crossing over her father's last year's garden, now grown over with row after row of deep green clover. The rich clover beckoned her, its cool covering felt like carpet beneath her bare feet, and she walked and ran, curling her toes upward, enjoying its tingling sensation. Suddenly she plopped down upon its cushiony bed, laid down and stretched out, looking upward into the sweeping blue sky. Her thoughts turned to Barclay as usual. Did he have a girlfriend? When was he coming back? Was he ever coming back? What would he think of her? She was growing taller, maybe not a lot bigger, but taller. Like Poky said, maybe she did need to put a little meat on her bones. Jean Lee had already gotten breasts and was wearing a bra. She grimaced at her own flat chest and decided to eat more. Suddenly a large flock of blackbirds flew overhead, shrilly chattering in unison. She watched them fly into a nearby clump of trees at the foot of Oak Mountain, causing the fruitless trees to suddenly bear a bountiful crop of excited chattering fowl. What were they talking about? How could they understand each other when they all seemed to be talking at once? Maybe it was an important meeting, a business meeting like they have at school sometimes. Oh well. She looked back down at the clover and began to hum the familiar tune... *'I'm looking over a four leaf clover....'* She daydreamed of her future...and always he was there.

Jumping up, she headed up the mountainside toward Poky's. Enjoying each foot of the way, she watched for deer and squirrels and chipmunks and any other resident of Oak Mountain. About half way there, she came upon a doe staring silently at her as she passed within a couple of yards, then it ran off, but not with the usual grace and elegance of the whitetail deer of the Blue Ridge. Instead it limped off slowly through a thicket of rhododendrons. "The lame one..." she uttered. She'd been spotting this doe for about two years. The first time was in Poky's front yard. She watched its white tail disappear now through the woods.

Poky was in her garden picking the last of the summer tomatoes. The August sun beat down upon her bent figure. Addie Jane joined her and began picking the ripe tomatoes and feeling their warmth from the sun, as well. She welcomed the strong acid scent ever present in the late summer garden. One couldn't help but be enticed! She wiped the smooth, firm specimen off on her dress and bit into it, squirting tangy juice and seeds out on all sides and savoring the warm tomato to the last bite.

"Nothin' like a hot tomato right out'a th'garden," Poky commented without looking up. "But ya' shouldn't ought'a wipe'em on your nice dress, Addie Jane."

"It's just a sack dress, Poky."

"No matter, sack dress or no sack dress. It's still a pretty dress...an' I admire your mama for usin' them pretty print sacks, too."

"Nobody wears sack dresses anymore, Poky." She gently touched the delicate funnel-shaped morning-glory that brushed her arm. Its vine wrapped itself up and around the tall staked tomato plant, and its many blue and white bugle blooms seemed to shout — "*tomatoes...tomatoes...last of the summer....*"

"Somethin' botherin' you, Addie Jane?"

"Nope. You know I love morning-glories."

"Me, too. My favorite flower. 'Spect it's 'cause they like a garden 'bout as well as I do." Poky gathered the last of the half ripe tomatoes into her apron, planning on putting them up later. She glanced at Addie Jane still caressing the morning-glories.

"You sho' there ain't somethin' botherin' you?"

"Not anything special like...just wish we won't so poor...that's all."

"Poor? Ain't nothin' wrong with that! Th'good Lord hisself never had anything'uv his own on this'ere earth...didn't even own a buryin' place."

"I know...but He *really* owned everything."

"Well, that's right. But th'good book says...'*to set your affection on things above, not on things on th'earth....*'"

Addie Jane nodded, knowing full well she couldn't win with Poky or the Bible. She continued to sit on the vine covered garden floor staring at the opened morning-glories.

"I know it ain't easy, child...but it's more important what we got on th'inside than on th'outside...."

"I know...God looks on the heart," Addie Jane added.

"That's right."

"...but people don't."

Poky knew she'd touched a sensitive chord. "You're right, Addie Jane. I ain't gonna lie t'you. Most folk don't look on nothin' but th'outside. But what we gotta remember is it's more important what God thinks...than what people think."

Addie Jane knew she was right, but for a thirteen year old seeking her own identity, but held captive by poverty, it was a major struggle. School reopened. Still Barclay did not return. Even Poky began to resign herself to the fact that her boy was gone, maybe gone for good.

CHAPTER FOURTEEN

TWO MORE YEARS passed. 1958 it was. Spring, summer, fall. Eisenhower was still in office, reelected in 1956. Oak Mountain was washed in its annual array of color, a glowing intensity of iridescent guise, a brilliant spectrum of red, orange, yellow, gold and many variations of each. The mountain folk marveled at its zest as if it were the first such fall they'd seen, when in fact they'd been privileged to witness many such falls. But each time it peaked, they bragged... *"best one ever, never seen such color."*

Addie Jane sat alone on a fallen poplar in the forest about half way up the mountain, with Poky's guitar resting on her right knee. A gentle autumn breeze teased the emblazoned trees and caused the brilliant rainbow of leaves to tremble, creating dancing patterns on the leaf strewn forest floor as the late morning sun streamed through the colorful canopy above. All that could be heard was the occasional creaking of tall slender pines as they gently swayed beneath the breeze and a soft strumming... *'down in the valley, valley so low...hang your head over, hear the wind blow....'*

Lost in the old ballad Poky had taught her, Addie Jane didn't hear the rustle of the crisp leaves nor did she see the tall handsome soldier standing behind her, quietly listening to her soft strumming.

Barclay had walked up on this angelic scene quite unexpectedly. Smitten by the loveliness of the blossoming maiden, he stood transfixed, unable to move. The warm autumn sun highlighted her thick auburn hair while the subtle breeze playfully swept loosened strands toward her pixy face that resembled a china doll with its deeply set dimple in each cheek. Her slim graceful figure swayed to the melody. Although he could only see her profile from his vantage point, he was immediately captured by her beauty...a quiet beauty...such as he had not seen before in all the wide open spaces of America, nor in the bustling cities of Europe or its picturesque quaint villages. Must he find such loveliness *here* on Oak Mountain? Addie Jane was now fifteen. Though still slim, she had acquired the soft curves of womanhood, plus the grace and poise of a lady in waiting. Barclay did not recognize the mysterious, mythical maiden as the little girl he'd saved in the ice storm years ago. Nor did he have any idea she was the babe he'd helped birth and name. Though he knew at that moment he stood solidly on Oak Mountain, he couldn't connect this lovely creature to the mountain. She seemed to have just appeared, an ethereal image, perhaps dropped from some celestial body. His heart was pounding.

She turned around. Though startled by his presence, she instantly gained control and looked straight into his dark eyes with a melting smile while she continued to play softly. Barclay sat down adjacent to her, never taking his eyes from hers. The melody continued to serenade the still forest as the two spirits joined together and formed a union that would forever remain.

Finally the melody ceased. Barclay stood up awkwardly, breaking the magic spell. "That was beautiful."

Addie Jane continued smiling, her dimples deepening, lending a cherub countenance. A whippoorwill could be heard in the distance, and the tall pines swayed and creaked.

"My name is Barclay Branham...I don't think I've had the honor of meeting you...."

"I think so...."

He looked puzzled. "You live on Oak Mountain?"

"...in the valley."

Still he looked puzzled.

"I'm Addie Jane...."

Apparent disbelief registered on his handsome face. "You've got to be kidding...little Addie Jane?"

"...from the ice storm...."

"Yes, yes, of course...but you've...you've grown up...."

She stood up, a full head shorter than him. "Not as much as you."

"Enough...."

She blushed, conscious of his appraising look. Hardly able to contain her happiness and speaking without thinking, she blurted out, "I guess I better be getting home...." Immediately she wished she hadn't said *that!* The last thing she wanted to do was go home and leave him.

"Please let me walk you home."

"Thank you."

They started back down the mountain, and he reached for her guitar.

"This old guitar looks familiar...."

"It's Poky's."

"I should've known. She teach you to play?" he asked, while rubbing the old guitar, and she nodded.

"She wanted me to learn once...a long time ago...but I was more interested in playing in Falling Rock Creek."

Addie Jane smiled to herself and seemed to glide down the rough terrain. He was intrigued by her youthful charm and wanted to know more...to fill in the gaps...all the years.

"So...you still live in the same place?"

Again she blushed, and he realized it was not the right question. "...I remember...I still remember going with Poky...the night you were born...."

"You do?" She looked up with interest.

"Sure. You were right stubborn in the beginning...didn't want to enter this old world...."

"My folks say I'm still stubborn."

"That so?"

"It's okay though. Better to be stubborn than to just give up and accept whatever hits you...."

He liked her spirit. "A little philosophical, I see." They were part way down the mountain. "You see Poky often?"

"As much as possible."

"I'll be staying with her awhile."

She waited.

"Maybe I'll see you there...sometimes."

She smiled. "I'll go on from here."

They parted, and Addie Jane had to restrain herself from jumping and running and shouting to the mountaintops that Barclay had come home...and Barclay had noticed her!

That evening, he and Poky sat out on the porch, reminiscing about the past. "Poky, little Addie Jane...what's she like now that she's almost grown?"

"Addie Jane? Oh, she's a sweet child...a little full'uv herself maybe. She's gonna be one t'challenge life...she ain't always satisfied with th'way things are...like bein' poor...has a hard time with it."

"I can understand that. I ran into her today when I went walking."

"Addie Jane? How about that! She see ya'?"

"Yes, ma'am. She's grown up to be quite a lovely young lady."

"That she has." Poky was amused, knowing how Addie Jane almost idolized him. She must be on a cloud just about now.

That night Addie Jane pulled the cover up close to her chin and prayed, "Dear God, please make him love me...please make *Barclay Branham* love me the way I love him!" This youthful prayer came straight from her tender heart, and she fell soundly asleep.

It was several days later, and Addie Jane couldn't wait any longer. She set out for Poky's place with the worn copy of *Pilgrim's Progress* under her arm. Poky had insisted she read it and laboriously she'd stuck with the arduous task until she was almost finished, but had laid it aside months ago. Anxious for a valid reason to call, she'd hurriedly completed it during the past few days. And finish it, she must, for Poky would most assuredly quiz her. Traipsing up the mountainside, she enjoyed as always the sound of acorns falling from the tall oaks, hitting the crisp leaves as they descended. The acorn sounds, the fairyland of color and the sharpness of autumn air was almost intoxicating as she nearly ran up the mountain path...or was it the thought of *him*? His presence had not left her since the day of the ice storm. It had conveniently lodged itself within her child's inner being...within her sensitive soul. It had grown with her. And now! Since the treasured reunion a few days ago, this presence had clothed her as the winter snows clothe Oak Mountain, as the breathtaking color clothed it now. She lived to see him again, but her intuition told her to disguise her emotions...for a later time maybe...not to reveal these precious feelings. Perhaps it was fear. Fear that once she did, he would vanish as the morning mist over the Blue Ridge. These thoughts raced through her mind as she neared the cabin. He was waiting on the porch, sitting on a step staring down the path. He stood up.

"Addie Jane."

She waved to him.

"What brings such a fine princess to this humble abode?"

Her heart raced as she heard his smooth voice.

"Not a fine princess, Barclay," Poky stepped out on the porch drying her soapy hands, "she's th'queen bee."

Addie Jane blushed, wishing Poky had stayed inside.

"Queen bee?"

"Tell'im Addie Jane...you remember."

Shrugging her small shoulders, she turned crimson. "It's nothing, just child's talk."

Barclay smiled and noticed how much prettier she was when she blushed.

"She always wanted t'be th'queen bee when she helped me gather honey."

"I see."

"'Course, I don't have but a couple'uv hives left now, not like before, when she used t'help me. What ya' got there, Addie Jane?"

"Your book...*Pilgrim's Progress*...I finally finished it...."

"You don't say. Remember this, Barclay?" She held up the tattered book.

"Sure do. We read it together. You'd read a page, then you'd make me read the next."

"That's right. Just makin' sure you didn't forget all these years while ya' been out seein' th'world an' all...been everywhere, Addie Jane...all th'way t'London...seen Big Ben, them crown jewels, London Bridge an'everything, tell'er, Barclay."

"I don't want to bore her with my history, Poky."

"Oh no, you won't bore me. It must've been great, I mean seeing all those famous things and all...."

Barclay looked straight into her thoughtful green eyes. "It was, but nothing I've seen is any better...certainly not any prettier than these misty blue mountains...and the ladies don't hold a candle...."

She shifted uncomfortably, and Poky witnessed the chemistry between the two. She experienced mixed feelings, certainly happy the two were drawn together, but reluctant to think of what it would be like if things ever went bad between them. Could she bear to see them both hurt?

Barclay stood up. "Think I'll take a walk through this fairyland. Its compelling charm is drawing me like a magnet. Care to join me, Addie Jane?" He grinned.

Poky marveled at Barclay's refined way of talking now. He hardly seemed like the same little Barclay she once knew. She watched the two disappear through the autumn forest, the vibrant colors encircling them as they were caught up in its magic. It was one of those days in mid-October that graces the Blue Ridge with warmth and color, subtly mixing with elusive gentle winds and creating an enchanting atmosphere.

"I wish every day was like this, every day of the year!"

Barclay smiled at her. "It would be nice."

They walked side by side midst the falling rainbow of leaves, feeling a keen awareness of beauty, beauty of the forest, beauty of autumn, beauty of life itself.

"Is it true what you said about nothing anywhere being any prettier than this?"

"Absolutely!"

"How about the people...the people in other places...like England for instance? Are they very much like us?"

"For the most part, I guess. However, some are a bit uppity...seem to think they're more sophisticated, more well-bred maybe than us Americans. In fact, I think some of them think we're still rustling cattle and washing our clothes out in the creeks."

She laughed. "Guess there are people everywhere like that. People who think they're better than others."

Barclay looked at her. "More than enough."

"Does it bother you?"

"What?"

"What people think?"

"Of course not," he answered a little too quickly and then fell silent. He realized as soon as he'd spoken the words they weren't true. Yes, it bothered him! It was his *thorn in the flesh*. Ironically, this very thing, his roots on the mountain, brought him much happiness. It is what drew him back again and again, no matter how far he roamed. Why should it bother him? But he couldn't erase all those years, the pain, the hurt that had been inflicted upon him during those impressionable years and etched into his memory forever.

"I've been attending St. Paul's for some time now with Poky."

"That so...and what does your father say about that?"

"He doesn't mind me being with Poky."

"I see."

They walked up to a ridge and stared off in the distance at other ridges layered with gold, russet and crimson.

"Listen," Addie Jane whispered.

He was silent.

"The wind...it's blowing up from the valley...."

He reached over and took her by the hand.

The next day, Addie Jane was preparing for her bath, a ritual not easily accomplished in the small crowded bungalow. First, she had to draw water from the well, heat it on the kitchen stove, pour it into a small basin and carry it to her bedroom, which she shared with the two oldest of her sibling brothers. Getting them outside so she could have privacy was another challenge. Having succeeded thus far, she was in the middle of her bath when she heard voices outside. "Someone's here!" she whispered. Quickly, she dressed, and just in time. The boys threw open the door, and Jean Lee and her cousin, Diane, stood there smiling. Addie Jane blushed as she noticed Diane looking behind her at the basin of soapy water.

"Just thought we'd stop by...see if you'd like to go for a ride. Diane's brother's driving now. He's waiting outside."

Shifting nervously before them, she quickly answered, "I can't. My mother's not well. She's lying down. Thank you for asking, though."

"Sure, maybe another time." Jean Lee started to leave. "See you at school." She glanced back at her, somewhat confused.

Addie Jane watched the car drive off, and tears welled up in her eyes, so embarrassed, knowing that both Jean Lee and Diane had bathrooms. What must they think? She looked out the window to the back of the house at the outdoor toilet standing conspicuously, dominating the otherwise flat yard as it leaned to one side with age. She hated it!

Autumn peaked. Addie Jane and Barclay took more walks as the colors began to wane. They watched the trees become partially clothed and hiked through their discarded remnants. Holding hands, they became friends and more than friends.

At the end of October as the last vibrant leaves hung on, they climbed upward to the summit of Oak Mountain. Though Addie Jane was as sure-footed as any mountain goat, she allowed Barclay to hold her hand protectively, enjoying immensely this new feeling of dependency. Her heart literally soared with the blackbirds overhead. The whole world seemed to sing with them, the rainbow of trees was magnified, the scarlet Virginia creeper covering the rocky crevices created extraordinary works of art, and Addie Jane marveled at it all. Surely she'd seen it all before, but not like this! Could it be this particular autumn was different? Or maybe because she was fifteen, going on sixteen? Or was it him? Did he actually make the whole mountain come vividly alive? Did he possess such power? Or was the power just over her? She took two steps to each one of his long agile strides as she watched and admired his strength as they ascended Oak Mountain, nearing its summit. They sat down to rest on a rocky ledge. Silence followed.

Then he spoke, "I used to come here when I was a boy."

She looked at him.

"One of my favorite places...."

"I can see why."

He stared out into the distance. "I came here mostly when I was hurting...."

"Was that often?"

Again there was silence. She waited.

"Too often. Too often for all of us."

"Us?"

He looked at her pointedly. "Me and my people." Suddenly changing the subject, he asked, "Have you been to the top?"

"A couple of times with Poky, but it's been a good while."

"Come on."

They were heaving and panting with their last steps, but there it was! The summit of Oak Mountain, rounded and enticing. Seating themselves on a massive grey boulder encrusted with greyish white moss and lichen, they quietly surveyed the forested mountainside they'd just ascended plus those of its sister peaks.

"Awesome!" His description was sincere and heartfelt.

"Anything like this in England?"

"If so, I didn't see it."

She smiled. They could see for miles and miles, row after row of mountains, the Tobacco Row plateau. The nearest ridges boasted of the fall foliage, those in the distance just appeared dark, those beyond blue and after that, the blueness faded, each one lighter than the other until they finally blended with the cloudless sky. "They seem to just go on and on...never ending."

"But they do end, Addie Jane...and the flat land begins. They have to end just as everything ends."

"Everything?" She didn't want to think of this moment ever ending.

"Everything," he answered somberly.

The autumn spent itself, exhausted with its own magnificent drama, collapsing withered and lifeless at the feet of the folk on Oak Mountain. Barclay stared out Poky's kitchen window and watched the beginning of winter, colorless and cold. He felt a chill. He missed Addie Jane. She hadn't come in several days. He was tempted to call on her, but remembered the last time. Her father's words still cut into his sensitive wounds, wounds of a lifetime...'My daughter, Addie Jane, she can't be seein' you. She's gotta court her own kind, you see. Sorry boy, but you 'kin understan'.' Of course, he understood! Hadn't he always understood?

"You all right, Barclay?"

"Yes, ma'am, I'm all right."

Addie Jane sat on her porch stoop, shivering and listening to her mother's despondent cries, wishing there was some way she could block out the depressing sounds. Lately, she'd become worse, and Addie Jane didn't know what was wrong. She watched the boys playing on the makeshift seesaw, a rough plank laid across a sawhorse her father had brought home from his last construction job. Bang! The wooden plank hit the hardened ground each time it went down, causing Jimmy to rise several inches off as he reveled in the air. Walter laughed, trying hard to knock his brother off the seesaw. Winfred clamored at their side, anxious for his turn. Only Christopher, the baby, now almost one, sat quietly in the middle of a barren dusty spot and delighted in putting as much of the red dirt on his chubby little body as possible. Addie Jane knew she should get up and intervene, take him inside and wash him off, but still she sat, unable to bring herself to move, not wanting to enter the tomb-like house. She felt helpless. She'd tried so many times before, but still her mother cried. At least the boys were happy outside, away from her cries. She guarded the doorway like a sentry. It was her job to protect her siblings from the sadness, from their own mother.

November blew in with a gust of chilled air...still Barclay and Addie Jane walked the brown forest and watched the north winds come. They shared the first snow flakes that gracefully descended from a grey sky overhead and gently lighted upon waiting pine boughs, upon the forest floor and upon each other.

Just before Thanksgiving, in science class, Jean Lee asked, "Want to spend Thanksgiving at my house, Addie Jane?"

"Thanks, Jean Lee, but I'll be helping Poky prepare dinner. Barclay and his brother, Paul David, are coming for dinner."

Jean Lee leaned over closer and whispered, "Addie Jane, don't you think you're getting a little too friendly with him?"

She turned away and pretended to read her science book. She really liked Jean Lee...she was her best friend, in fact. But still she smarted when she recalled their talk a couple of weeks ago concerning Barclay. Obviously, Jean Lee didn't approve of him because of who he was...from the High Peak settlement. But *why* did she feel that way? She didn't see any difference in the folk from the settlement. They were good people, like most other people.

Thanksgiving arrived, a grey wintry day just as a Thanksgiving should be, and Poky's little cabin was filled with aromas of baked hen just out of the oven, homemade yeast bread ready to go in, and corn pudding already cooling on top of the old wood stove, not to mention the sweet potatoes and string beans nor the custard pies waiting on the window sills. Barclay and Paul David arrived early.

Addie Jane was torn as to whether to go or not. Her mother was in bed and had been for several days now, crying and withdrawn from them all. As was his habit on Thanksgiving, her father had gone hunting and taken the three older boys. For sometime, Addie Jane had been living for this day, yearning for it to come. She wanted to cook for Barclay, to spend this special day with him. She wanted to meet his brother, Paul David, and, of course, spend another Thanksgiving at Poky's. She'd never forgotten that other Thanksgiving spent with her some years ago and cherished its fond memories. However, her mother had taken to bed. It wasn't the first time. In fact, her spells were becoming more and more frequent. Addie Jane had pleaded with her father to take her to a doctor, but he didn't believe she was sick, just *tuckered out,* he explained. But she knew differently, and she'd researched at the school library when no one was looking. It was *depression.* She was acting just like the books said, staying in bed, crying all the time, soft muted sobs mostly, but occasionally a tirade of yelling, accusations and hurting words thrown out into the air about her unfortunate plight. A prisoner held captive by the *valley.* This morning was no different. After her father and the older boys left, she occupied Christopher and began washing up the dishes from breakfast. She soon finished and not knowing whether or not she'd be able to go, she decided to get ready anyway, unwilling to accept the idea of not going. She bathed, washed and brushed her hair until it shined, and went quietly into the kitchen to touch up her lips at the small mirror over the sink. She smoothed the soft pink lipstick on that Jean Lee had given her as a friendship gift. She smacked her lips together, evenly spreading the sweet tasting lipstick, and looked admiringly into the dull, cracked mirror at the green eyed girl with ivory skin. Her lips were too small, she thought, and remembering what Jean Lee had said, she rubbed them together to help make them look fuller. The mirror clouded over as her mother's visage suddenly appeared.

"Going someplace...are you?" A quizzical look spread over her mother's red bloated face.

"I don't know...." Reluctant to tell her, she struggled for the right words, "...Poky wanted me to come...help her with her cooking. Remember, I told you about it a couple of weeks ago?"

"No...I don't remember...I don't remember anything...." Her mother dropped into the nearest chair dejectedly and began to weep again. Addie Jane, weary from days of the same, felt like running out the door and straight up Oak Mountain, but instead she stood there.

"...I won't go, Mama...I'll stay...."

Her mother wept louder.

"Daddy said he's gonna bring back a deer...and we'll have venison tonight if he does. You like venison, Mama. Please stop crying."

Her mother grabbed the dishtowel hanging on the wall and wiped her eyes. "No, no, you go on to Poky's. Go on an' go. I know you don't want to be here with me...I know you like Poky better...an' I don't blame you...go ahead...I'll be all right."

Addie Jane felt like crying, too, but hardened her heart. It wouldn't do any good. "I said I'm not going, Mama."

"No, no, I want you to go. You understand, I want you to go! Poky'll think hard of me if you don't. She invited you.

Everybody thinks hard of me anyway. I know they do. I don't care. I can't help it. Life's too hard...too hard...it's not worth th'effort...but no matter...I probably won't be here much longer...they told me so...told me again last night when they came...all at once in th'still of th'night...they came, all talking together...talking in that strange musical way, they did...."

Addie Jane felt scared again. She wished her mother wouldn't talk this way...crazy like...about creatures in the night telling her things. This was the second time she'd mentioned it, the last time being a couple of weeks ago when they were alone. She'd told her daddy, again he'd brushed it off, saying to pay no attention to it, that she was just tired, that's all.

"Go on, Addie Jane, go on to Poky's...I'm gonna lie down." She pushed herself slowly up from the table and ambled back toward the bedroom. Christopher began to fuss. She stopped and picked him up, taking him to the bedroom with her.

"I can watch Christopher, Mama."

"No. You go, I say!" She picked up the young lad, and the bedroom door slammed shut. Addie Jane hated to see young Christopher exposed to his mother's cries and fits of depression, but he seemed to want to be with her regardless, and she wanted him with her, as well.

Addie Jane opened the cupboard, and pulled down the half loaf of bread, opened up the ice box and took out the bologna to make sandwiches for the boys for their lunch. Then she left for Poky's. The temperature was dropping, and she vainly attempted to pull her coat sleeves down further. It was already too small; she'd hoped it would last another year, but she was growing taller. At least, she was glad of that. As she climbed higher, she felt something brush her cheek and looked up, smiling. The grey sky was filled with millions of feathery flakes descending upon the still forest, and suddenly she felt lighthearted and happy. *It was snowing!* The clouds of her life vanished, and she twirled around trying to catch the elusive lacy flakes that disappeared in her hand. The mountainside was transforming into a winter fairyland, and a unique silence ensued as intricate flakes continued falling more thickly now, clinging stubbornly to each and every twig, each and every pine needle, each and every crumpled leaf beneath her feet. It was Thanksgiving, and it was snowing! An idealist at heart, she yearned to enter the pages of the many books she'd read and live out a Thanksgiving such as they narrated, one with family and love and warmth for all, where the whole family gathered around a plentiful table, holding hands to share its blessings. One day...one day...she would have such a Thanksgiving. One day when she had a family of her own! And it would snow then, too. Thanksgivings should have warmth and snow.

She reached the cabin, and entered the humble abode. Suddenly, the contrast was vividly too much — the gloom she'd left behind and this warm, happy environment. Her countenance fell. Barclay moved toward her. "Everything okay, Addie Jane?"

She nodded. Poky, determined to share her happiness with those she loved, began thrusting forth instructions, "Addie Jane, get them rolls in th'oven there. Been holdin'em out for you. Barclay, fetch that other chair yonder by th'door...Paul David, sit yourself down at th'head'uv th'table an' make yourself comfortable, you bein' th'special guest an' all...." Soon the upsetting morning was forgotten, swallowed up by the love and happiness among that small odd gathering as they sat down to a feast fit for a king there on Oak Mountain. Outside, the warm blue smoke curled up and around the old chimney as the fine light snow kept falling.

THE WINTER OF 1958-1959 wore on, snows came and went on the mountain. Alaska, the last frontier, was being admitted to the union as the largest state ever, almost a fifth as large as all the rest of the United States, more than twice the size of Texas. Ike was warning against wage and price increases. Explorer I, first U.S. satellite, was launched from Cape

Canaveral, Castro-led rebels seized the provincial capital in Cuba, the last troops left Arkansas, and on and on and on...but things on Oak Mountain didn't change much. Barclay and Addie Jane saw quite a bit of one another, and Poky watched with interest.

By the time spring arrived, however, life had become almost unbearable for Mrs. Taylor and for Addie Jane, as well. The depression had deepened, tears were almost ceaseless; but worse still was her mental state, that of hostility toward those she loved, particularly Addie Jane. Her father continued to suppress it, rejecting reality. It was late May, and the tangled honeysuckle began to send forth its sweet scent as it wrapped itself up and around the lone cedar at the left corner of the Taylor place. Addie Jane inhaled its pungent sweetness as she quickly dressed for school. Hurriedly, she pulled up the covers on her bed, went to the kitchen to fix their lunches and hasten the boys with their dressing. The bus would be coming around the curve up the dusty country road in about ten minutes. Jimmy and Walter were arguing. "Nope, get it yourself!" Walter quarreled.

"Jimmy, gimme my belt, you had it last!"

"Want me t'hit you with it?"

"Just try!"

"Boys! Sh-h-h. You'll wake mama!" The last thing she wanted was to awaken her, but it was too late. The torrent of sobs came forth from the closed bedroom. With her father already gone to work, it was up to her to keep control. She felt herself getting nervous, but pushed the boys out of the house one by one. "Pick up your lunch pail, Winfred." The small boy obeyed and followed his older brothers down the rickety steps and out toward the bus stop. Addie Jane hurriedly gathered up her books and turned to leave. But her mother, looking deranged, stood before her, blocking the doorway.

"Mama, it's time for the bus! I gotta go!"

"You don't need no more education, Miss high an' mighty...who do you think you are? You just gonna get married an' have a flock of kids an' die here in this God forsaken valley! Don't you know what's gonna happen? DON'T YOU KNOW?" she screamed, her words cold and hopeless.

Addie Jane skirted around her, reached down for her sweater, but suddenly felt a blow as the child's rocker hit her shoulder, and then crashed to the floor. Shaken, she looked at her mother's wild and glazed eyes. But she must get to school! Fighting back the stinging tears, she walked out the door. Her mother yelled, "I told you, Miss high an' mighty, you don't need no education!"

The fresh morning air met her, and she wiped her eyes. The yellow bus was coming around the curve.

Saturday arrived. After cleaning the house, Addie Jane checked on her mother, who was sleeping. Christopher was also napping. Her father was out back with the other boys. She set out for Poky's and found her alone in her garden.

"Barclay's not here, Addie Jane. Said he was goin' into town."

She sat down on a large rock at the edge of the garden.

"You mighty quiet today. Everything all right?"

She shook her head while poking the rich black soil with the end of a stick.

"Wanna tell ol' Poky 'bout it?"

The words began to fall out like water from an overflowing bucket. Midst tears, Addie Jane told Poky about the little rocking chair her mother had hurled at her in anger, about her father refusing to believe she was ill, about the crying, about the dilemma she found herself in, and then all was quiet. Poky laid down her hoe and reached out for her hand. "Come with me, child...I wanna show ya' somethin'."

Trembling, Addie Jane stood up, holding onto Poky's hand. The two walked on up the mountainside until they came to a very large oak tree. Poky stopped and stared up at the mighty oak. "Addie Jane, you see this'ere old oak?"

She nodded while wiping her eyes.

"Well'sa, you know life is like this oak. You see its strong trunk all gnarled from age, its broad limbs a'reachin' out, an' its new little green leaves even. You see all that?"

Again, Addie Jane nodded.

"You see all'uv th'tree?"

Addie Jane looked puzzled.

"No, ma'am, you *don't* see all'uv th'tree. You jest see this'ere good side, th'new leaves a'blowin' in this'ere nice breeze, th'limbs a'soakin' up th'warm sun and all. But you don't see th'*other side!* It's got two sides, ya' know...a light side an' a dark side." She raked her foot in the rich black soil. "Down under, under th'ground, that's where its roots are. They're growin' an' reachin' out jest like its limbs are up here. But them roots, they're strugglin', fightin' for nourishment, for survival for this big old oak. You see, Addie Jane, it's down in th'dark side where we grow! Th'strugglin' them roots been doin' all these years is what's made this big old oak what it is today. You understan' what I'm sayin', child?"

The young girl listened silently.

"When life gets real hard like it does sometimes, Addie Jane, remember th'oak."

She turned to go. "I will, Miss Poky, I will." She walked back down the mountainside, and Poky watched her until she was out of sight. Then she knelt beneath the old oak. Only whispers could be heard in the gentle breeze.

CHAPTER FIFTEEN

IT WAS APRIL, and it was Addie Jane's sixteenth birthday! Gloomily, she walked out to the mailbox in the misty rain, wondering if it was an omen. First her mother had another bad day, and now the rain. Of course, she usually loved the rain, but today being her birthday, she'd really wished for a bright sunny day. She'd hoped to get over to Poky's, maybe see Barclay, maybe take a hike in the mountains, but no chance now. Her father had gone, and the boys needed her. She sighed and pulled open the old mailbox, its rusty hinges creaking with resistance. A letter was inside! Immediately she recognized the handwriting and grabbed it up. Thrusting it in her pocket, she walked back to the house to her room and closed the door. Suddenly there was a warm feeling deep down inside as she peeled it open and began to read.

Dearest Addie Jane,

I wish I had a medieval castle, an ocean cottage or a whole mountain to give you. You deserve even more. Maybe one day! But I do have something I want to give you. Poky told me she only gave you the first stanza of your favorite song, 'Down in the Valley'. It was all she had. But I found more at the library recently. Although this was written years ago by a stranger to a stranger, I feel it was really written for us. And now I send it to you...from my heart to yours...pick up your guitar when you receive this and play it softly...

Writing this letter, containing three lines
Answer my question, will you be mine?
Will you be mine dear, Will you be mine?
Answer this question, Will you be mine?

Roses love sunshine, violets love dew
Angels in heaven know I love you,
Know I love you dear, know I love you
Angels in heaven know I love you...

Barclay

Tears welled up in her eyes as she picked up the old guitar and played the melody softly. Her heart cried out...yes, my love...*Angels in heaven know I love you....*

That night on her sixteenth birthday, after all was quiet in the house, she stood looking out the window of her bedroom that she shared with Winfred, since Jimmy had taken to sleeping on the sofa. Winfred was already sound asleep. It had stopped raining, and there was a soft wind blowing. She gazed at the mountains rising sharply up from the valley. Where was he? Did he hear the wind blowing up from the valley? She crawled into bed, pulled the cover up around her and fell into a deep sleep. His strong arms held her close. She felt his strength, looked into his dark penetrating eyes. They were sitting atop a mountain, their mountain, and all the world was happy beneath them. The sky was a clear, clear blue, and the sun was shining brightly through the new spring leaves. There was a lovely little house in a grove of oak trees. Laughter...children's laughter came from within. The children were their children with happy faces all smiling at them, at her and Barclay. She was warm, safe and happy.

A few days later, Jean Lee approached her as the last school bell rang. "Addie Jane, guess what?"

"What?"

"I got my permit, my driver's permit, and daddy's letting

me drive his car this evening to the drive-in. Want to come with me and the girls? Please come. It's my first time out alone! Isn't it exciting?"

"Which drive-in?"

"The Amherst. Please come."

"Yes...yes, I'll try," she replied before she had time to think it over. But she was tired of staying home all the time taking care of everything and everybody. Fortunately, it all worked out, and she was able to go. Her mother was having a good day, and her father was home, as well. Jean Lee blew her horn excitedly, and Addie Jane ran out to meet them. Carefully, Jean Lee drove the large black Buick while the others sat in awe, anxiously anticipating their turn one day. They arrived at the packed drive-in, paid the man in the small ticket booth, pulled into a vacant spot, attached the speaker to the window and began to giggle.

"Who do you see?"

"Can't see anybody, too dark!"

"Gosh, you're right."

"Let's walk down toward the playground and on the way check out who might be parked with whom."

Clumsily holding onto each other in the dark, the four lively school girls traipsed over rows of asphalt humps resembling a giant washboard, giggling and looking sideways into the darkened cars they passed. A small playground was directly beneath the mammoth drive-in screen where gigantic movie stars were pacing to and fro across its illuminated path, throwing off varying degrees of light. The moving shadows fell upon young kids riding a rusted merry-go-round and swinging high in old swings that creaked incessantly.

"Did you see him?"

"See who?" Diane asked.

"Ainsley Anderson...in the last car on the sixth row...did you see him?" Jean Lee persisted.

"Ainsley Anderson! No!"

"Well, it's him all right! Sitting right there in that fifty-five black Chevrolet of his...with a girl!"

"Who?" Gloria demanded.

"How do I know? Couldn't see her good enough. Bet it's Katherine Markam though...betcha."

"Addie Jane, are you listening?"

"I heard you."

"Well, what do you think? We know he's sweet on *you.* Even asked me if you had a steady the other day...I told him no."

She looked at her. "Why did you say that?"

"You don't, do you?"

She didn't answer. The girls kept chattering away. She knew Ainsley Anderson, of course, and she was aware that he'd been noticing her. She was aware of his smiles in science class. It was a cute smile, too. In fact, she'd felt a little stirring the other day when their eyes locked, but nothing like the overpowering passion she felt for Barclay.

"Addie Jane, what's wrong with you?" Diane questioned. "Why don't you set your cap for Ainsley Anderson? I wish he were interested in me. Why, I wouldn't waste any time for sure."

"Me neither," Jean Lee added.

"Uh-oh."

"What?"

Gloria leaned over and whispered, "It's them!"

"Who?" Addie Jane glanced over at a group of young people in the dark, between the ages of about ten and fourteen, that were playing on the merry-go-round.

"Don't look at them! Mama said to ignore them!"

"Ignore them!" Gloria repeated. "Why should we? Who do they think they are...coming here acting like anybody else...this is our drive-in! Just watch!" She moved closer to the group and hollered back, "Come on over girls, there's *nobody* here!" Several boys across from them picked up on what was going on, and noticing the young people from the settlement, they moved in also to mock them.

"What're y'all doin' down here. You better be gettin' back up in the mountains where you belong. This here place is not for the likes of you!"

One young fellow stepped out from the rest of the group and replied, "You gonna make us?"

Just what the restless boys were waiting for. They each grabbed up a handful of gravel and began hurling it at them, others nearby joined in. Too much for the small group to take on the whole playground, they quickly dispersed and disappeared. Addie Jane watched silently, afraid to say anything.

"Come on, girls. Let's get back to the car," Jean Lee said while staring at Addie Jane.

It was the following week-end, and Addie Jane finally got the chance to visit Poky. Barclay was there, obviously waiting for her. It was the first time she'd seen him since the letter. Hardly able to contain her feelings of happiness, she smiled at him. He smiled back, but not his usual smile. She was puzzled. Poky sensed something was wrong. "Think I'll feed th'chickens. Why don't you two jest sit out on th'porch a spell an' enjoy this'ere nice spring." She idled off. The two sat in silence for a moment, then Barclay spoke.

"Were you at the Amherst Drive-In this week?"

Noticing the unusual tone of voice, she tried to look into his eyes, but he avoided her. "Yes, I went with Jean Lee, Gloria and Diane."

He looked troubled. "I see."

"Why do you ask?"

"...because...because I heard about what happened. I was hoping you weren't with them."

"Them?"

Suddenly his handsome face twisted in anger. "Yes, *them*...the yellow faced bunch of high class nobodies...that...that think they're placed on earth as judges of mankind! Never having been out of Virginia, they don't have sense enough to come in out of the rain...much less know how to judge people! The bloody...." His acquired British slang halted.

Addie Jane was bewildered. "Go ahead and say it! Don't mind me. You don't seem to mind calling my friends names!" Her face was flushed.

"...I thought you were different...."

She stared at him in disbelief.

"...I guess I was wrong," he concluded and stood up.

Her mind was all confused. How could he blame her? She didn't do anything!

"I'm sorry, Addie Jane. I need to go." He looked at her sadly and walked away. Speechless, she stared after him. He disappeared into the forest, and she burst into tears. Poky came around the corner of the house.

"What's a matter with you, child? Where's Barclay?"

She kept crying. Poky hugged her trembling shoulders. "Did Barclay make you cry?" Between sobs, she related what had just happened.

"My, my. What'a mess. I think I see what happened."

"Why, Poky...why did he blame *me?* I didn't do anything! I was just there."

"I know, child. I know. But that's all it took, you jest bein' there. It's a real sensitive thing with Barclay. You see, he's got a wound that ain't never healed. I don't know if it'll ever heal. Oh sure, you can forgive an' maybe forget a little, but them scars, they just don't go away. Seem t'stay with ya' for life as a reminder'uv where ya' been an' where ya' come from. You know, sometimes I think th'good Lord lets us keep them scars t'keep us humble. Folks have a way'uv gettin' big heads, ya' know. We need somethin' t'keep us humble."

"I don't know, Poky. Why do people treat them differently? I don't understand any of it...the settlement...my friends...."

Poky sat back thoughtfully. "Well, lemme see. Th'settlement

is jest a place like any other place...'cept folks 'round here have a mind t'think it's different. It really ain't no different from anything else. Good folk there same as us, livin' an' dyin', tryin' t'make a'livin', tryin' t'raise their young'uns same as everybody else. Most of 'em believin' in th'good Lord, go t'church on Sundays, worship th'Lord, sing their hymns an' pray, you know that. I don't know why folks don't accept'em, Addie Jane. Jest 'cause they look a lil' different an' maybe act a lil' different...." She laughed. "'Course I look an' act different, too."

"That's right, Poky."

"But I'm proud'uv all my ancestry just th'same. Even though my old daddy run off when I was born an' left me, still th'same he come from good stock. Irish folk. Can't find no better folk than Irish folk, ya' know. They tell me his folk come all th'way over here from Ireland, lookin' for a place t'live like they wanted to. Wish I could see that place...*Ireland*...hear it's mighty pretty...all green an' all. 'Course, my real mama, God bless'er soul, who died givin' birth t'me, was Indian...Cherokee...an' I took after her. That's why I look like I do. But Sister Jane, who raised me like I was'er own, was a Colored lady...fine lady, I might add. Now, some folk might say I'm all mixed up, an' I reckon I am...but I'm proud'uv it...proud'uv all my ancestry. Took'em all t'make me!" She laughed her hearty laugh.

Addie Jane smiled at her, already feeling better.

"Now th'folk from th'settlement, they tell me they're Indian, don't exactly know what kind. Makes us sort'uv kin, I reckon."

"I just wish people wouldn't treat them so badly. Even my friends."

Poky looked at her. "Maybe you ought'a tell'em so, Addie Jane."

"...I tried...a little...but seems like then they want to treat me the same."

"I see."

"But Barclay should know different. He should know I wouldn't be unkind to his people! Of all people, *he* should know."

"Like I said, child. Barclay's been hurt...an' 'cause'uv folk like them at th'drive-in, he's still bein' hurt...him an' th'others. I don't know when it'll ever stop...."

"But what should I do, Poky...about Barclay?"

"Give'im a little time, child. He'll come 'round. I know that boy, an' I know how much he thinks'uv you, too. He'll come 'round sooner or later."

Addie Jane rose to go. "I hope it's sooner...."

It wasn't sooner. Barclay left Oak Mountain and went to Maryland to think things through, to get a clearer idea of his life, his plans. Poky had to relay this to Addie Jane, who stubbornly refused to cry this time. Instead, she set her face toward the valley and hardened her heart. She couldn't let this hurt her. She wouldn't. She struggled to push him out of her mind, only in vain. Whether at home, in school or walking in the woods, his handsome face, his penetrating eyes followed her.

It was the last day of school, and she was getting her books together when she felt a presence very close behind her.

"Could I help?"

It was Ainsley Anderson.

"No, I'm okay," she replied uncomfortably.

He leaned against the wall in his charming way. "A bunch of us are getting together tonight to celebrate school being out. Just driving over to Lynchburg, check out the *Southerner*, see what's going on, you know. You been to the Southerner Drive-In Restaurant?"

"No, I haven't."

"It's cool. Everybody just driving around over and over, doing nothing, just seeing who's there. 'Course they have good food, too. Can order right from your car, and they bring it out to you. I'm driving my car. Would you care to go with me, ride with me, that is?"

She didn't know what to say, realizing this was an opportunity that all her friends would die for, and realizing her father would be extremely pleased...he was an Anderson. Recalling the two story brick home he lived in with his successful father, she couldn't say no. Even with the small voice yelling *no* inside, she heard herself saying, "Yes, I'd love to."

The night turned out to be lots of fun. Many of the kids from school were there, riding around the small drive-in restaurant. It was a time to laugh and feel light-hearted, feeling young and knowing school was out for another year. Addie Jane fit right in, laughing at all the jokes Ainsley was able to come up with. It was the first time she really felt a part of the class, one of them, and she reveled in this new feeling of acceptance. The night flew by, and all too soon it was over. It was a dark night, no moon, and Addie Jane giggled at Ainsley as he tripped over a rock in her yard walking her to the door. She was glad there was no moon, making it difficult to see anything. She waved good-bye to them as they drove off and stood outside the door, hating to go in, to end such a fun-filled night. Suddenly, she saw a figure, barely visible, but coming toward her. She gasped and was about to run in when she recognized that step...*Barclay*.

"MAMA, YOU HEARD the news?" Lauralee called out.

"I'm out on the back porch, dear. Come on out...what news?" It was a hot, humid day in late August, and Hallie had escaped to her cool back porch, screened in and protected from flies and other unwanted guests.

"We have a new state...*Hawaii...our fiftieth!* How about that? Just came over the news."

"Well, goodness. First Alaska, now Hawaii. Wonder what will be next? Where's Frankie?"

"Bill has her. He has the day off and is giving me some time off, as well. Thought you might like to go downtown, do a little shopping maybe. You need to get out of this house."

"Oh, Lauralee, you know I love this house. I don't get tired of being here."

"I know that, but a little change of scenery will do you good. Why don't you get dressed?"

"Well, that would be delightful. I don't know when the last time was I was downtown. We could eat at Woolworth's for lunch, too. You know how I love their toasted ham salad sandwiches."

"My mouth's watering already. I'll wait out here on the porch and enjoy its coolness while you get dressed."

"Thanks, dear. Pour yourself some lemonade, too. It's on the top shelf in the refrigerator." Hallie hastened off to get ready.

As they approached downtown, Lauralee complained, "My, this one-way traffic sure confuses things. Don't know why they couldn't just leave things the way they were."

"Times are changing, dear...times are changing."

She pulled over, and parked on the corner of Eleventh and Main Street. They got out, and Lauralee deposited change in the meter and started up the street.

"Wait just a minute, Lauralee. I need to run in Patterson's here, got to pick up some Alka-Seltzer, won't be long." Lauralee followed her into the drug store, watching her carry on easy conversation with the clerk just like she'd done when she was small. Some things didn't change. They left and proceeded on with their shopping, Leggett's, Baldwin's, Miller & Rhoads, Guggenheimer's, taking time out for lunch at the counter at Woolworth's. Perched atop the old stools, Lauralee had to restrain herself from twirling around the way she'd done as a child. She peered into the mirror facing her above the grill that was grilling her toast for her ham salad sandwich. The lady staring back at her looked mature, somewhat stylish, even rather pretty. She was proud of her image, but felt it really was deceiving...that she hadn't changed within! She was still that little girl of yesterday, but concealed behind a fabrication of forced adulthood. Sitting there with her mother, waiting for her sandwich, she felt sad. Why did one have to grow up?

"We might run into Jon Junior. He said something about coming down to Bailey Spencer's during lunch. Needs some nails he said, working on the back steps, you know."

"How's he doing, Mama? Still working himself to death?"

"Oh, I don't know. Jon Junior wouldn't be happy if he wasn't working hard."

"Do you think he's happy?"

"What do you mean?"

"I mean...do you think Jon Junior's *really* happy? He's never seemed that happy to me, especially since we've grown up...and his life seems so...so empty. Never marrying, no children. It's hard for me to think about life without children now."

The waitress shoved their plates in front of them, the warm ham salad sandwiches met their expectations again, the delicious aroma attesting to the fact before the fact. Both mother and daughter bowed their heads briefly, and the hurried waitress respectfully waited to set their drinks down.

"Thank you." Hallie smiled up at the middle-aged woman and suddenly realized that Jon Junior was middle-aged, too. "You know, it's hard for me to think of Jon Junior being in his forties, it's hard for me to think of you being in your thirties. You're both just children to me, and I guess you always will be."

Lauralee smiled. "I'm glad, Mama." She sipped the cold Dr. Pepper that was more ice than drink, just the way she liked it.

"I do need to go by the shoe shop, Lauralee. I almost forgot. I've been needing heels on these shoes for some time. Do you mind?"

"Of course not. We'll go right after we eat."

As they leisurely walked up Main Street toward the Paramount Shoe Shop, Hallie spoke suddenly, "Lauralee, isn't that Mrs. Browning coming toward us, your old school teacher?"

She stared at the attractive lady approaching them in a somewhat hurried state. "Yes...yes, it is. Although, I must say, she doesn't look old."

"Well, she isn't, of course. She wasn't a whole lot older than you back then." She looked up with a smile. "Hello, Mrs. Browning."

"Why, Mrs. Frederick...and Lauralee...my, look at you. How time flies!"

"Well, you haven't changed a bit, Mrs. Browning, haven't even aged. You still look the same as you did when you taught me."

"Thank you, Lauralee. That's very kind of you. Are you all doing some serious shopping today?" The smartly dressed lady ran her fingers up and down her shoulder bag strap unconsciously, obviously she was somewhat hurried.

"No, not really. Just spending some time together, picking up a few odds and ends. We did just enjoy a delightful sandwich at Woolworth's, however."

"That's where I'm headed now. You can't beat their sandwiches, can you?"

"Absolutely not. Well, we won't detain you any longer. Enjoy your lunch," Hallie added, "it was nice seeing you."

"Same here." With that, she continued briskly down the street.

"Mama, remember how there was talk about her having cancer years ago?"

"Matter of fact, I do remember now. I'd just about forgotten. Apparently, she's fine now. Certainly looks fine."

"I did hear that it had gone into remission. She must be healed completely."

They approached the door of the shoe shop, went in, and Hallie took off her shoes for repair. "Looks like I need some heels."

The second generation of skilled cobblers replied, "That you do. If you'll just have a seat, I'll have them ready for you in a few minutes."

Hallie sat down on the bench barefooted, and Lauralee sat beside her. "You know, Mama, I always felt kind of sorry for Mrs. Browning. I don't exactly know why, except for the fact that she seemed sort of sad to me, I guess."

"I know. Not that I spent that much time around her, but I think I know what you mean. One never knows what another is going through, what is on their heart."

Lauralee nodded as an older gent walked in and up to the counter. "Come to pick up my shoes, Mr. Hawkins." He looked their way and tipped his hat. "How y'all ladies doin' today?"

"Fine, thank you," Hallie replied.

"Y'all ready for Khrushchev?"

"Sir?"

"Khrushchev...Nikita Khrushchev...he's comin', ya' know, next month. Don't know why on earth the president wants *him* over here...winin' and dinin' him too...now, if it was me goin' to the White House, I'm doggone sure they wouldn't be winin' and dinin' me...and me bein' a tax-payin' bona-fide citizen of the United States, too...sure not any communist!" He grabbed his shoes off the counter, nodded to Hallie and Lauralee and left.

"Well, I expect a lot of people feel that way about Khrushchev's visit next month," Hallie commented in hushed tones.

"Eisenhower said he hopes it will melt a little of the ice of the cold war. I think it sounds like a good idea myself."

"Certainly I'm for peace, but I don't know that I trust them...the communists."

"I agree. Well, he's bringing his family over, too. Guess maybe Eisenhower will take Mamie when he goes over there."

"Maybe so. However, the president has another trip coming up first...Britain...you know. He's going to visit the queen."

"Now that's where I'd like to go...to England to meet Queen Elizabeth. Why, we're about the same age. Well, I'm a few years older." She smiled at her mother. "She's thirty-three, you know. I wonder if she, being the queen and all, is really getting into this pregnancy...I mean like we did when we were expecting."

Hallie crossed her legs uncomfortably, trying to hide her barefeet. "I imagine so. She's a woman and a mother first, I'm sure, and this *is* her third child. I was just reading in the paper the other day where she was knitting and sewing baby clothes and discussing nursery furniture with Prince Phillip."

"Really. That's neat."

"It also said she's laid aside all appearances of state until after the baby is born. Now, I admire that...this is the first baby to be born to a reigning British monarch in more than a century."

"Ma'am, your shoes are ready. That'll be fifty cents."

As they left the shoe shop and headed back downtown, Hallie remarked, "They feel funny, like I'm walking real straight-like. Didn't know I was walking so crooked."

They passed in front of the Paramount Theater and looked at the marquee... *'blue denim'* was coming in five days. "Mama, we need to go to a movie! Let's do this again soon and next time, take in a movie, too. I haven't been in ages."

"...and how you loved them when you were a youngster, never knew anyone so taken with the picture show."

Lauralee laughed. "Remember that night during the war...that special night when *The Vanishing Virginian* premiered here. What a night!"

"It was that. The other day, I came across a copy of *Carry Me Back*...Rebecca Yancey Williams' other book. I'd read it years ago, forgot about it actually, just finished it again. A delightful little book. I'll give it to you when we get home. Tells all about life here in Lynchburg years ago. Things certainly have changed, just like these stores downtown. If one can't find what they're looking for now, he must be awfully choosey."

As they passed by Woolworth's again, Mrs. Browning sat on a bar stool at the end of the counter. She ate slowly, obviously in deep thought. She looked toward the open doors to the street, noticing the drone of the ceiling fan just overhead as it rotated slowly round and round, stirring up the warm air and helping to circulate it through the store. Hallie and Lauralee glanced in as they walked by, but didn't notice Mrs. Browning. Nor did she see them. There was a furrow in her brow, and little did she know it would deepen in days to come.

CHAPTER SIXTEEN

JORDAN LAWRENCE MCKENZIE sat alone on the shore of the Back Bay of the Chesapeake. It was the last days of summer fun at the popular Virginia Beach area, and scores of people, young and old, had flocked to its sunny beaches, packed with suntan lotion, more books than they'd read, and hopes for one last relaxation before the grind of school and work began again. But Jordan avoided the hurried tourists and found solace in his own private spot, one that most would not seek out. He sat watching the winds of the nor'easter blow the shallow bay waters in, causing its depth to increase considerably, and creating micro waves that rippled its otherwise placid waters. How he loved the ever changing waters of coastal Virginia that flowed into the sounds of North Carolina. In fact, from where he sat, the North Carolina waters were only about fifteen miles south. Jordan, not too long ordained a Presbyterian minister, was prone to sit quietly by the bay and meditate on deep philosophical questions of the universe. It was not uncommon for him to do this for hours at a time. But today, an imminent crossroad faced him, one that required much wisdom, and he being just a young man, now sought answers from the familiar waters and from their maker. Should he risk his comfortable place in life, possibly throw a rock into its placid waters? After years of study, and seeking God's direction, he was now fairly secure within his small parish, enjoying the fruits of his labor. With a modest income, all that the small congregation could afford, he was somewhat comfortable, at least as comfortable as one would expect an humble servant of God to be. Why risk hurt and humiliation? Part of him chose to remain in his safe cocoon, while the other half struggled for answers, for identity. Ever since his dad's death three years ago this November he'd faced this impasse. A young seagull momentarily swooped down in front of him, bracing itself against the nor'easter winds, and just as quickly swooped up again and off toward the adjacent marshlands. He watched its articulate navigation, listened to its shrill cries and again felt a kinship to the bay and all its family. What if fate had handed him a different plate? He would not have grown up in this rich, natural environment, abundant marshlands reeling with wildlife, snow white egrets, greyish-blue herons, classic mallards, a Back Bay filled with delicacies, plentiful blue crab, catfish, bass, perch, flounder, spots, croaker and on and on, sunny blue skies with heavenly creatures galore, including the red-winged blackbirds, shiny black fish crows and, of course, his favorite, the graceful seagulls. He would not have had the opportunity to love and appreciate it all, to taste the salt in the air, to hear the breaking of the waves in the stillness of night. Suddenly, he felt a presence, looked around to see Sarah standing behind him.

"Well?" she asked softly.

"I have decided."

"And...."

"I must take the risk...."

She put her arms around him in support, and he needed it. He needed this strong but sensitive lady...oh how he needed her. But yet he wasn't ready to make that commitment. He wasn't willing to marry and father children until he knew himself and his own history, but Sarah was getting a little impatient. He knew that. Not that she'd nagged him or given him an ultimatum or anything like that. But he knew. He knew Sarah. The two young people sat there facing the water as the nor'easter continued to blow, both caught up in their own thoughts.

Two weeks later, now into September but still feeling like August, Jordan was acting on his decision. Driving west, every mile registered on the odometer was putting him further and further away from his beloved bay. He no longer smelled the salty air or felt the cool ocean breezes. Instead, the sultry, still, inland air encompassed him. Passing by Suffolk, his mind was sorting through all sorts of outcomes. What if? What if? Too quickly, he came up behind a tractor trailer loaded down with crates stacked one upon another, chicken crates they were and crammed with chickens. All he could see, however, were white feathers poking out of open slats and blowing hard in the truck's wind. It was moving on, and he followed behind, counting the crates. Nine to ten high they were, with white feathers blowing out of them, blowing into the hot air, across the highway, across his windshield. Now he could see the poor chickens packed together like sardines as they flew up Route 460, smoke billowing up from the tractor's exhaust up front. He decided to pass, pulled out and around the large truck, now he was side by side the chickens. He looked up and saw one of the fragile victims peering out at him between the slats. Its beady eye beneath its red comb stared at him. The poor wretched thing! What a plight! But mercy was on her side, she didn't know her plight. Victims of their birth. "Fate!" he said aloud, gratefully zooming past the burdened truck and breathing a sigh of relief.

Suppose he'd been born otherwise? He thought of his mother back in Chesapeake. What would she think if she knew where he was headed? Of course, he couldn't tell her. Probably break her heart. To this day, she thought he believed her story. And he probably would have if it hadn't been for Grandmother McKenzie. He'd never forget that day. It was springtime, and he and Grandmother McKenzie were crabbing in the bay, catching a good mess for supper. The crab cage was already crawling with nice blue crabs, but Grandmother wanted more. She loved the very act of crabbing, called it an art for the wise. They waited patiently, enjoying one another's company, and watched a duck with its new ducklings swim by, all in a straight line. One, two, three, four babies. She swam up to the shore, jumped out of the water and up onto the bank, turned and looked back at her babies, waiting for them to follow. They stared up at her and continued swimming in circles. She jumped back in and tried again. The act was repeated several times. But never did the baby ducks even try to make that high jump. After awhile, she jumped back in and led them off and out of sight. Grandmother McKenzie chuckled. "Determined duck. That's the way mamas are, I guess."

Jordan pushed his wavy hair out of his eyes, and the sea breeze blew it right back. "Grandmother, have you noticed how reddish blond my hair's gotten lately? Did I get it from the McKenzie line or from mama's?"

Grandmother McKenzie laughed. "'Course you didn't get it from either one, how could you?" As soon as the words were out, she gasped and her hand flew to her mouth. Jordan, now wisely fourteen, knew instantly what she'd implied. Although she tried desperately to talk her way out of the blunder, it was to no avail. He persisted for days until he wore the old woman's resistance down, and she told him! She also told him that his mother, Elizabeth McKenzie, had so wanted a baby that when they finally resorted to adoption, she acted out a clever charade, to the point of wearing maternity clothes for several months. When she returned from a visit to her in-laws in Richmond, she brought with her the newborn son. Nobody knew the difference in the Chesapeake area. Elizabeth McKenzie had had her baby! Jordan would never have guessed. Just like Grandmother McKenzie said, he'd seen pictures of his mother when she was expecting, or at least he'd thought so. But Grandmother McKenzie made him promise, and all these years, he'd kept her secret. He planned to tell her what he'd done once he'd accomplished his mission, but not until.

Suddenly the chicken truck swerved back around him with feathers skimming his windshield. Again, he reluctantly followed his doomed feathered friends as the rig swayed back and forth. "If those feathers keep blowing off while you race up this highway causing tornado effects on the poor chickens, they won't need plucking when they reach their destination!" he voiced aloud. They hit a slight hill, and the truck began to lag. He quickly pulled out and passed again, this time without looking up. Enough is enough!

Virginia Diner....25 miles...the sign read, *Peanut Capital of the World.* Peanuts, he thought, that sounded pretty good. That must be what he'd been seeing in the fields, a low-lying dark green plant. He remembered they grew underground like potatoes. He tried to think about peanuts and how they grew, but his thoughts returned to his mission...to his fear of rejection. *Suppose she won't see me? Suppose she doesn't want to see me? Ever?* Apparently, she doesn't. She's never once tried to contact me! He drove on, his thoughts keeping him captive.

Virginia Diner...20 miles...'Ole Virginia ham.' Now that sounded really good. He could certainly stand some good ham biscuits. His mouth was already watering. *Wonder why she never tried?* Especially not having anymore children, wonder why? His mind sought for answers...answers he hoped to find. He wondered what she would be like? Did he look like her? Did she have the strawberry blond hair? Investigator Mangold wouldn't tell him anything, preferred to wait, he said, for the meeting.

The miles rolled on, and his anticipation increased with each one. *Virginia Diner...7 miles.* Thank goodness, he was definitely hungry. A cold iced tea sounded good, too.

Soon he arrived in a small place called Wakefield, one of the many tiny hamlets along Route 460, and saw the little diner on the left sitting practically on the highway. True enough, it was an authentic diner that appeared to have been added onto as the needs arose. In actuality, it had begun in 1929 just a diner car. As extra dining rooms were needed, they had been added over the years, giving it just that appearance, too. He walked in, noticed the antique peanut vendor roasters and buckets of free peanuts, and grabbed a handful as a matronly, Colored waitress in a crisp white uniform appeared. She graciously led him to a table in keeping with the setting, painted white with a red and white checkered tablecloth. He pulled out a white bentwood chair and contentedly sat down.

The waitress reappeared with a glass of cold water. "Good evening, sir." She whipped out her pad. "Our special today is *fried chicken....*"

"That's all right, ma'am." Jordan held up his hand. "Think I'll pass. Actually I was thinking more along the line of ham biscuits and potato salad." He ordered while munching peanuts. "And by the way, these peanuts are delicious."

She smiled a big smile, displaying a mouthful of pearly white teeth. "Thank you, sir. In th'beginning, we used to serve our peanuts fresh from th'fields right here."

"Well, these taste like it. Why's this place called the peanut capital?"

"'Cause we grow a ton of'em here,...an' th'first crop was grown just up th'road here way back in 1842, I believe...by a Dr. Harris."

"Sure sounds like you know your history. How long have you worked here?"

She smiled again. "Oh, a real long time, mister."

The ham biscuits were definitely the right choice, simply delicious, and he even asked for more. When he received his ticket, the waitress asked, "You a preacher, sir?"

"Why, yes, I am. Why do you ask?"

"'Cause I saw you bow your head before you ate. Figured you must be prayin'...an' somehow you kind'a look like a preacher...a young one...but a preacher still."

He laughed. "Well, you're right."

He left a better than usual tip and felt good as the doors closed behind him. However, back under the wheel, his thoughts returned to his impending situation, and he studied what he would say...if he got the chance. He looked at his watch. Investigator Mangold was supposed to meet him at 5:00 PM in front of the courthouse on Court Street. He had his map of the city, figured he could find it with no trouble even though he'd never been to Lynchburg. The closest he'd come was to Charlottesville when he'd visited Monticello with his folks some years ago. The memory of that day flooded back, a day he wished he could block out of his memory along with many others. His dad, successful, strong and exacting, never allowed for mistakes...an impossible environment for a sensitive lad to grow up in and survive without scars...particularly a lad prone to clumsiness and forgetfulness. Yes, William Andrew McKenzie II had been a tall act to follow, one in which Jordan did not succeed, much to his father's chagrin. Having pulled two stints in the Navy, his father revered strength and quick decisive actions, none of this deep thinking. Jordan had known from a very early age that he and his father were cut out of different molds, that they would never see eye to eye. After his accidental discovery from Grandmother McKenzie, at least he knew why, and it was easier to accept these differences. As a result of this barrier between them, he'd drawn closer to his mother from the start, another irritant to his father, who considered this "sissy" and humiliated him more than once in front of his friends. His mother tried to shield him through those formative years from his father's explosive behavior, but Jordan determined in his heart as a small boy that he would never be like his father. He had no call to worry, nothing could have been further from reality.

His odometer racked off the miles, and his back began to feel sore. Turning on the radio, the car suddenly reverberated with *Jailhouse Rock*. The voice of Elvis was clear and commanding as always, just like he was next door and not thousands of miles away in Germany. He'd felt sorry for him ever since his mother died. He couldn't imagine being without his own mother. Again memories of his past returned, and he recalled the day he'd decided to tell his folks about his decision to become a pastor. It was on that day at Monticello, after touring the grand home of the third president and enjoying its extensive gardens. The three of them were sitting on the expansive green lawn, facing the mansion and reflecting on Jefferson's unique architectural ability as the autumn breeze blew through his mother's greying hair. The warm sun caressed their relaxed bodies as they listened to the rustle of crisp colored leaves. But as soon as he'd voiced his plan, there followed a deafening silence, and then his father exploded, "YOU'RE GONNA DO WHAT? A *PREACHER!* A MAN THAT WEARS *DRESSES!* HAVE YOU COMPLETELY LOST YOUR MIND?"

Nearby tourists eyed them strangely through the corners of their eyes, though pretending not to hear. "William...William...s-h-h-h. People are listening...," his poor mother pleaded.

"I DON'T GIVE A DANG WHO'S LISTENING!" Quickly the curious tourists turned their heads. "WHAT'S HE TALKING ABOUT, ELIZABETH? PRAY TELL ME WHAT'S THIS FOOL-HARDY BOY TALKING ABOUT? I FOR SURE DIDN'T RAISE ANY SISSY-BRITCHES PREACHER!"

At that, Jordan vividly remembered, he'd stood up defiantly. "Dad, we'll finish this later."

"NO...GALL-DURNIT...WE'LL FINISH IT RIGHT HERE! WHO IN TARNATION PUT SUCH CRAP IN YOUR MIND?"

"Father, I wish you wouldn't...."

It was at that moment his father turned around to everyone nearby and throwing his massive arms up into the air, exclaimed, "I RELINQUISH MY RIGHTS AS A FATHER, I GIVE UP!" And he strode off, kicking up dust from the smooth brown gravel. Even after all this time, it still pained Jordan to remember that day. "Monticello, your great image will forever be marred because of one William Andrew McKenzie II, my illustrious father!"

When did he discover his father did not love him? Did not even like him. As a lad sitting on his knee when he spilled coffee down his favorite trousers? When he missed the ball repeatedly during little league games? When he began to write of his deeper feelings in verse in high school? This really irritated him, and he seemed to enjoy ridiculing him in front of his then sweetheart. It didn't matter anymore. He'd come to accept it as one of those cruel tests in life that people often encounter and are called upon to overcome somehow. But his mother had made the difference, and, of course, his Grandmother McKenzie. He smiled just thinking of his grandmother and her little place on the Back Bay. How he loved the Back Bay. Though newcomers had finally found this hidden secret and begun to build their expansive and lovely sea cottages along it, the old McKenzie place remained the same. Each year it blended more with its surroundings, the brackish water, the greying marshes, the twisted scrub pines that enfolded it, camouflaging it from the eye of the tourist. It had not changed in all his years, and he hoped it never would.

JORDAN SAT IN THE back seat of Investigator Mangold's plush Lincoln, with its black tinted windows, as they drove along the narrow streets of Lynchburg. It was nearing five-thirty, and the sun was waning as he stared out at the quaint town with its tree-lined streets and Victorian style houses and classic architecture. Every now and then a leaf fell and somersaulted to the wide, cracked sidewalk, a preview of what would dramatically occur later. The car came to a complete stop in front of one of those past era houses. It was of modest size, and boasted of one small rounded turret, painted white with green shutters and black wrought iron porch railing.

"This is it," the investigator announced, while opening the door. Jordan watched him walk around the car and up the narrow sidewalk, bordered with dwarf marigolds, to the front porch. He hesitated just a moment before knocking on the large oak door sandwiched by long slender ornamental glass panes. Then the door opened, and a small, dark-haired lady, who appeared to be in her forties, stood in the doorway. Jordan leaned forward, straining to see through the tinted windows, but the shade of the porch conveniently disguised her. He could see Investigator Mangold seriously talking, and suddenly she caught hold of the door. Investigator Mangold attempted to help her, but she pushed him away and stepped out onto the porch into the sunlight, letting the door close behind her. Now Jordan could see her dark brown hair as it shined in the sunlight, and her smooth fair skin, an attractive lady for sure. She was twisting a dishtowel in her hands. Her head dropped, and she wiped her eyes with the towel. Jordan could feel his heart pounding, chill bumps covered his body...*it was her*...he knew it...his mother!

She began to shake her head, and Jordan's heart fell. The ready tears were forming in his own eyes as Investigator Mangold continued to talk. Then he turned and began walking toward the car. She went back inside and closed the door.

Investigator Mangold explained to Jordan on their way back to the hotel that this was often the case, the shock was simply too much. She needed a little time. They would stay the night at the Virginian Hotel on Church Street, giving her the opportunity to call if she so decided. Jordan couldn't just sit by and wait in the hotel room. While Investigator Mangold took off his shoes to get comfortable, and sprawled out over his bed watching television, he decided to walk the streets of the small town, get a feel for the place where his mother and possibly his father had spent their lives. He hoped to rid himself of the knot in his stomach, as well. He walked up Church Street to Fifth, climbed the hill, and passed by Court and on up to Clay. There was no traffic on that quiet evening, so he walked in the middle of Clay Street over the uneven cobblestones, enjoying the solitude. He found himself standing atop one of the crests of Lynchburg, looking down at the rooftops and church steeples that silently climbed its many hills. A very large sun was hanging just over the skyline...a fiery, yellowish-red autumn sun. There was a haze that was cast out over the city as a result of the hot, humid day that was coming to its inevitable end. Varied shapes, spires and domes made an impressionable scene as the sensational sun cast its flaming glow. Jordan sat quietly on a curb wall and watched the ball of fire disappear beneath the skyline of the small town that had drawn him like a giant magnet. He continued to sit as dusk fell, thinking all the thoughts over again that had been plaguing him for years. Within an hour of the fiery sun's disappearance, it was dark...and lo and behold...there was another large, fiery reddish ball in the dark sky, looking quite the same. But alas, it couldn't be the sun. It was dark! Never had he seen the moon look so much like the sun. In all his years of imposing sunsets and stunning moons on the Back Bay, he'd never witnessed anything more awesome than these two majestic lights over this small, insignificant town. Was it an omen? Of course, he didn't believe in omens, but what awaited him here among these hills?

Jordan closed the door quietly behind him, noticing Investigator Mangold already asleep on top of the bed covers. He crossed the room, switched off the television, leaving only the sounds of his uneven snoring. He prepared for his shower. Stepping into the hot, steaming spray of water, feeling the soothing sensations massage his tired body, he proceeded to lather his entire body...and then the phone rang! He caught his breath and waited for Investigator Mangold to answer. It continued to ring. He jumped out of the shower, dripping wet, and ran to catch it, wondering what he would say.

"Hello."

There was a pause, then a soft feminine voice addressed him, "I am calling...Jordan McKenzie...."

Jordan was speechless, standing there naked and dripping wet. He looked toward Investigator Mangold for support, but saw that he was still sound asleep and now snoring softly. The moonlight was shining through the third story window, casting shadows about the small room. Jordan found his voice. "This is Jordan McKenzie...."

Another pause, and then the voice, now shaky, continued, "This is...your *mother*, Jordan...and...and I would very much like to see you...."

He felt his heart leap within.

"I was wondering...if it would be all right...if I came over now...to The Virginian?"

"Yes...yes...of course. We could pick you up...no...you might rather meet us...."

"I will come now." With that she hung up. Jordan's pulse was racing. He began to shake Investigator Mangold, who grudgingly awoke, and, with a grin, stared up at the naked, wet young preacher. Jordan looked down for the first time realizing his predicament. "I'm sorry, sir. Forgive me...but I'm a bit shaken."

"That's all right, Reverend. Just not used to seeing you without your collar." He laughed.

Jordan proceeded to tell him what had transpired as he dressed. Investigator Mangold got up and straightened his clothes. They went down to the lobby to await their expected visitor. The lobby was vacant, only the desk clerk was busy shuffling papers.

Then Mrs. Browning walked through the door of the hotel, looking rather uneasy, but anticipation was written all over her pretty face. She turned toward them.

Investigator Mangold jumped up and rushed to her, extending his hand. "Mrs. Browning, so glad you came." He led her toward Jordan, who was glued to the same spot, staring at this pretty woman whom he knew to be his real mother. She returned his stare, and both seemed to drink in the other's presence. Jordan awkwardly reached out to shake her hand.

It was then she smiled the familiar smile. It was his smile. Investigator Mangold found a secluded spot in the vacant lobby for the two of them to talk...and talk they did.

Finally, he approached the subject, "Do you...do you know...where my father is?"

She nodded.

CHAPTER SEVENTEEN

OAK MOUNTAIN SHIVERED in the first days of fall, and nights cast a foreboding chill over the hollows, ridges and the rugged cabins that tenaciously clung to its steep sides. Addie Jane welcomed her last year of school with no clue that it would prove to be a most trying year for her...a year full of decisions. She purposely avoided Ainsley Anderson, which wasn't easy, and much to her friends' disbelief. He seemed to appear on the other side of every door, around every nook and every corner. Totally unable to comprehend anyone giving him the cold shoulder, he kept resurfacing. She could feel his steady gaze now as she sat in government class.

"...and what's our three divisions of government?" Miss Donald asked.

Rosemary's hand flew up as usual. "The Executive, the Legislative and the Judicial..," she answered proudly.

"Thank you, Rosemary." The middle-aged and greying old maid teacher rattled on about the inner workings of the United States government, and the particular role of each of the said divisions. But her words drifted into oblivion as Addie Jane relived the night Barclay came back — the night she'd been out with Ainsley Anderson and the others, celebrating school being over. They'd dropped her off at home, and Ainsley had walked her to the door and left. There he was! Just remembering made her all warm inside. They'd stood there at first in the darkness, staring at each other even though they really couldn't see, but they didn't have to. They knew. It was as though an electric current surged from one to the other, spanning the darkness...spanning time...spanning eternity. He moved first. She followed. Their young bodies clung to each other in desperation, as if lost in a turbulent sea.

"I'm sorry," he blurted out. She put her hand over his lips, and he kissed it first, removed it and placed his eager lips to hers.

"Come with me." He pulled her toward Oak Mountain. Just as they began to climb, the thick clouds shifted, and a quarter moon appeared to light their path. They picked their way up the mountainside, giggling and laughing all the way until they came to a grove of oaks, very old oaks, a special place of Barclay's. The silver moonlight fell through the treetops, and on Addie Jane's face as she watched him take off his cardigan sweater and lay it gently beneath the largest oak. He sat down and reached up for her hand, pulling her down beside him. Their kiss was long and passionate. Addie Jane felt as if she were drowning in happiness, but suddenly he pulled away and sat up straight. "Let's talk, Addie Jane, we need to talk." Her heart was pounding, her thoughts tumbled and disoriented, but she nodded weakly.

He was staring hard and seriously at her in the darkness. He hesitated and then spoke purposely, "*Addie Jane, I want to marry you.*"

Her ivory face glowed in the moonlight.

"...but not yet..." he continued, "don't get me wrong, I'd marry you tonight if I could...but...well...we've got to wait until you finish school...and this will give me time to get a good job and get a place for us and everything. I need to be in a position to offer you more...."

"...but all I want is you...." She wrapped her arms around him.

Again they embraced, kissed long and hard, and again Barclay pulled away. "...and...Addie Jane...we've gotta be careful about this. I don't want anything to happen. I want to save that wonderful part for our wedding night."

She smiled up at him.

"I live for that day..." he continued, "...our wedding day. I want to spend the rest of my life with you...and have a family...lots of children."

"Lots?" She giggled.

"Yes." He laughed with her, "And I want them all to look just like you, to have your pretty auburn hair and your deep green eyes and your dimples...they must have your angelic dimples."

She hugged him again. "No, no, Barclay, not all of them. The boys must look like you...tall, dark and handsome. I want them to have your dark hair and beautiful dark eyes...and then one day, they'll sweep the girls off their feet just like you did me."

"You mean like this?" He grabbed her up with both arms, all one hundred pounds, and lifted her high into the darkened night and began to dance around beneath the tall, old oaks as the silver moon slid gracefully back under the clouds, darkening Oak Mountain in its absence. Still they danced in the darkness.

The shrill school bell rang out! Addie Jane jumped as she was suddenly thrust back into reality.

Christmas was fast approaching, and the winter chill penetrated through Addie Jane's lightweight coat. Even though it wasn't the warmest, still she loved it, a soft brown with a dark brown fur collar and matching fur cuffs. When she'd first pulled it out of the box, it was the most beautiful thing she'd ever seen, and Poky delighted in her happiness. The large gift box had been sent to Poky from her city friends over in Lynchburg. Addie Jane didn't even know these people, but apparently they did it for Poky. This Lauralee must be rich, she thought...such pretty clothes and almost like new. Besides the coat, there were three lovely dresses, each a different color and style, two cardigans and two skirts.

She opened the mailbox and slid in her letter, her thank

you to Lauralee, and pushed up the rusty flag. Wistfully, she looked up into the grey sky, hoping it would snow. Her brothers came running full speed out of the house as the school bus rounded the curve. Once on the bus, she looked back at her forlorn house, still sitting dejectedly at the foot of the mountain, still unpainted and in need of repair, an object of humiliation for her. Her mother would still be asleep. At least, times were better since she'd received the last treatment at the hospital. She shivered at the thought of an electric current running through her mother's brain, causing convulsions or seizures, even if it was for just a fraction of a second. But it had worked! Immediately, her mother seemed relaxed and happier. She still had her days, but nothing like before. When her father had first explained it to her, she'd doubted how in the world an electric current could change her mother's state of mind and bring her out of the severe depression she'd experienced for some years now. But she, too, was willing to try whatever, any glimmer of hope, especially since that last episode, her mother's suicidal attempt. She could still see the deranged look in her mother's eyes as she held the shotgun to her breast. She'd talked to her for over an hour before she was able to take the gun away. Her father was gone, working a third shift. The boys were asleep. It was 3:00 AM, and the wind was howling outside, thus muffling her mother's cries. The boys slept on, much to Addie Jane's relief. Each time she moved forward to try and retrieve the gun, her mother would quickly point it at her, threatening to kill her. She'd back off and continue talking to her, pleading with her to put the gun down. Finally, her mother dropped to the floor in exhaustion, and Addie Jane was able to grab the gun. At that point, her mother put up no resistance, her fight was spent for the time being.

The bus arrived at school, and Addie Jane's thoughts returned to the future instead of the past. The morning flew by, and she rushed to rehearsal for the Christmas play. Throwing her books on the floor, she grabbed the soft blue muslin material and draped it around her shoulders, letting it fall gracefully to the rough, wooden floor. Then she covered her auburn hair with a lighter shade of blue material. Pulling her compact out of her pocketbook, she stared at herself in the small round mirror, wondering if she looked anything at all like the holy Virgin Mary. The door opened and in walked Ainsley, likewise adorned in his Biblical attire.

"And how is my little Mary today...stunning, I must say for a simple peasant girl."

"Ainsley, you shouldn't be so flippant about the Holy Mother," she scolded and then blushed.

"Forgive me, my lady. You are absolutely right. But as Joseph of Nazareth fell in love with the lovely Mary, so too, I must confess my adoration for you, my lady." He fell on his knees before her.

"Get up, Ainsley, before someone comes in!"

"I have no pride, my lady. Just to be near you is enough," he kidded, "but don't you think it's interesting that out of the whole senior class, you and I were selected for this honorable part?"

"No, I don't. Miss Jennings said we just sort of...looked the part."

"Exactly, my lady...we look the part! It is destiny...you and me...don't you see? I have the keys to open a whole new beautiful world for you...think about it...."

Though Addie Jane never meant to think about those words again, they kept resurfacing and haunting her. All her life, she'd suffered from poverty in the valley, and her number one goal was escape...she must not end up like her mother!

Two weeks before Christmas, Barclay left, returning to Maryland to look into a promising job that a friend was holding for him. It was the beginning of his plan. They said their good-byes at the foot of Oak Mountain as a raw drizzle fell, slowly soaking their winter wraps. They shivered and anxiously held onto each other.

"It won't be long, Addie Jane. I'll be back in the spring...when the dogwoods are blooming...and I'll write every day...you must write back, too...every day...."

She cried softly, "...but the stamps...that will be a lot of stamps...."

"Don't you worry about that. I'll send them to you in my letters...just don't fail to write. I'll live for your letters." He kissed her forehead, her cold damp cheeks, her cold ears. "One day, my love...one day."

When he was gone, the whole valley and mountain seemed to echo an emptiness. Addie Jane sought solace in her visits to Poky, which she did as often as possible. Christmas passed slowly with *Elvis's 'Blue Christmas'* resounding through the airways as it filled the otherwise holiday cheer, and Addie Jane's loneliness was suffocating while school was out. She climbed the winter mountain, now able to view its many ridges with thousands of skeleton troops marching up the sharp slopes and yearned for spring...and *his* return. But school resumed, and soon her days were filled with excitement and the various events that crowded her senior year. The new year caught her up in its fever, as well, the anticipation of unknown futures at hand, and the buzz and talk of dreams and success. She found herself dreaming, too, of her escape from the valley. It was of no small consequence that Ainsley Anderson was skillfully pursuing her with a planned outcome. The Sweetheart Dance was at hand, and he begged her to accompany him. Jean Lee pressured her, also, even offering to lend one of her beautiful formal dresses, the deep green taffeta that matched her eyes. She'd tried it on once while visiting Jean Lee and never wanted to take it off. "Addie Jane, you've gotta go to the Sweetheart Dance with the rest of us. You're one of us!" Jean Lee had coaxed. "If you don't go, you'll live to regret it." Her folks encouraged her, as well. Torn between her love for Barclay and her desire to be one of them, to live as a normal teenager, she struggled for an answer. Leaving Poky's one cold evening, her attention was drawn to the vivid scene that faced her — the sudden dip of the winter sun. She walked out to the nearest ridge and stood looking at the dark mountain outline sharply edged against a fiery sky left by the flaming sun. The skeletal forest allowed a panoramic view as each and every tree was starkly contrasted in black, creating an antique-like silhouette picture. Winter winds blew steadily through this barren twilight forest, whistling eerily a melody that seemed to fill her being...a sad, pensive melody...a melody of loneliness and abandonment. She shivered. Almost a week passed with no letter from Barclay. Confused and saddened, she decided to go to the Sweetheart Dance.

February the fourteenth came. It was extremely cold, and Addie Jane wore her brown coat over the lovely green taffeta. The lustrous fabric rustled underneath, giving her a feeling of distinction. Proudly, she climbed into Ainsley's dad's new cream colored Dodge. Inhaling the rich, new leather scent, she was impressed with the luxury of the interior as she sank into its comfortable cushiony seat. She enjoyed the comfort and beauty surrounding her, making her feel important. The night was a wonderful light-hearted affair, full of laughter and fun as she danced to the upbeat rhythm of the *Beach Boys'* music. The slow numbers gave her a chance to breathe and gave Ainsley a chance to get close. Addie Jane relished the obvious distinction placed upon her because she was Ainsley Anderson's date. It was all very new to her...and she liked it. She liked it very much.

"You two make a handsome pair...a natural," Jean Lee whispered in passing.

Mr. Bradley, their math teacher, toasted them as they danced in front of his table. "...to the couple most likely to succeed," he called out.

Addie Jane's head was spinning when she exited the schoolhouse at 11:00 PM, arm in arm with Ainsley. Just before arriving home, he pulled the car over to the side of the country road.

"Ainsley?"

"Just to talk, my lady. I have something important to say." He pulled out a pack of Winstons, fished out a cigarette, stuck it between his thin, narrow lips, flicked his silver lighter and lit the cigarette, inhaling long and hard. "Addie Jane, I'll get right to the point. You know how I feel about you. Well, in a few months our school days will basically be behind us. We'll be facing this world as adults...and...well...I'd like to face it with you...."

Addie Jane looked at him surprised. "Ainsley Anderson, are you asking me to...."

"...to marry me! Yes, I am."

She was confused.

"You know I can...I mean...I can offer you a rather comfortable life."

"I thought you were going to college?"

"Maybe...maybe not. Mother has her heart set on it...but dad's okay with me starting in the business with him right away. He says he didn't need any college education to get where he is."

"I see."

"The business will be mine anyway one day."

"This is quite a shock, Ainsley. I...I need to think through it all." Even as the words rolled off her tongue, she silently chastised herself. How could she even think of such a thing? What about Barclay?

The weeks that followed found a troubled Addie Jane, grappling with the decision...whether to follow her heart or her mind. She knew she loved Barclay Branham. She had as far back as she could remember! But the glitter and glory of being an Anderson was so very tempting, and she found herself imagining all the luxuries it would provide. Never again to worry about money, to live in comfort the rest of her life! Probably in one of those big, brick two-story houses, with a maid even! She'd wear the best of clothes, no more hand-me-downs! She'd most likely drive a big, shiny car that smelled of leather, too. One night she fell into a troubled sleep, and found herself facing a crossroad. One way was literally shining with glitter and gold, the enticement was overwhelming. The other way was obscured with a heavy, low lying fog like that which hangs over the valley at times, preventing her from seeing what lay beyond. She struggled to know which way to go, so much so that her head was literally throbbing. She awoke early in the morning with a terrible headache. She thought and thought over the days until she was weary from thinking. She knew how fortunate she was that Ainsley Anderson was even interested in her, much less wanting to marry her! Turmoil raged within, what was she to do? She finally went to Poky for advice.

"Should a person follow their heart or their mind?" she asked.

Poky, realizing the seriousness of the question and its possible implications, pondered slowly her answer. "Well, child, th'way I see it, they both can lead ya' wrong. Th'good book says '*in all thy ways acknowledge Him, an' He shall direct thy paths.*' This comes out'uv th'book'uv Proverbs...whole lotta good sense in Proverbs!"

Addie Jane didn't appear too satisfied with Poky's answer, and after finishing her supper, headed back down the mountain. Poky thought about all that was said. Poor little Addie Jane, but so strong-willed. Poky feared she would have to learn a lot of her lessons the hard way. Though she'd spent the same time and instruction with both of them, Barclay's little heart had always been more like a sponge, soaking up and believing. He trusted God's direction. Even though he'd faced more obstacles and would face many more for sure, she knew he'd be okay. But Addie Jane, she just didn't know.

It was Barclay's next letter that did it, that sealed her answer. He spoke excitedly of his change in plans. He'd taken the liberty of contacting Mr. Mason, who owned the little house in the valley just over the hollow from her folks. He was willing to rent it to them for a nominal fee, something they could certainly afford. And even though it needed a lot of work, it was livable, and they could work on it a little at a time. Meanwhile, they'd be saving up to buy a piece of land on Oak Mountain one day. He'd decided he couldn't leave Oak Mountain. Addie Jane knew exactly which house he was speaking about. Suddenly she could see herself growing old and tired and depressed. The valley would consume her, too, like her poor mother, eating away at her a little at a time until all that was left was a shell of a person, defeated and lifeless. A fear welled up inside, growing into a monstrous creature, and she felt like running as fast and hard as she could. She must escape...she must escape from the poisonous venom of the valley!

ORGAN PIPES RESOUNDED throughout the United Methodist Church as the last guests arrived and squeezed in tightly on soft cushioned pews. The church was tastefully draped in white and a soft muted green, Addie Jane's choice of colors. The altar was backed by a lovely white latticed rose arbor entwined with delicate white roses and green leaves. Candelabras faintly flickered on either side of the arbor, and the scent of roses was omnipresent. The day was mild and sunny with radiant sun rays shining through brightly stained windows, creating prisms of gold and scarlet over the filled pews. It was June the first, a perfect time for a wedding most agreed as they awaited the wedding march, glancing over their shoulders to see who was there. The majority in attendance were family and friends of the Andersons, some very prominent personages, who sat tall and proud in their respective pews. Poky sat up tall and proud, as well, even though she was keenly aware her presence was not quite in keeping with the others. She knew she should be happy today, but she couldn't shake the ominous cloud hanging over her. Addie Jane's little brothers all sat beside her, scrubbed clean and smiling from ear to ear. They were glad to be getting more room at home, not realizing how much they would be missing her. The side door opened, and in walked the minister, followed by Ainsley and his father. They proceeded to the center of the altar and stood facing the congregation. Poky couldn't help but notice the proud look on Ainsley's face. She couldn't read the look on Mr. Anderson's face, and the Reverend appeared to have assumed this role too many times. Soon the wedding march began, and cold chills ran down Poky's spine. A smartly dressed usher led Ainsley's decrepit grandmother slowly down the aisle, assisted by her cane. Next followed Mrs. Anderson, marching proudly down, more than hinting of extravagance with her silk Vogue dress and matching accessories. Her hair done up in a sophisticated bun created a sternness about her. She looked neither to the right nor to the left, her eyes riveted on the esteemed son who was smiling directly at her. Next came Addie Jane's mother, clinging to the young usher's arm, obviously nervous about the whole affair, although her overall appearance safely disguised her turbulent past. The wedding party followed one after the other, all looking rather juvenile, but polished in their costly attire. Suddenly the music changed, and the traditional bride's march began. All eyes turned to the center aisle as Addie Jane appeared, holding onto her father's arm. She was lovely by all accounts, adorned in a pristine white wedding gown with tiny pearls stitched into the bodice and a vast flowing skirt, all of which was Mrs. Anderson's doing. The long train rustled down the aisle behind her. Her lovely face was shielded by the net veil, but not enough for Poky. The look she carried with her was one of determination and purpose, not of love and anticipation as is fitting for a new bride. The fear Poky was hiding now increased. All whispers ceased, and the ceremony began with Reverend Robert's monotone voice. The audience settled back with the familiar words. "*Dearly beloved, we're gathered together here in the sight of God to join together this man and this woman in holy matrimony, which is commended of Saint Paul to be honorable among all men, and therefore is not by any to be entered into inadvisably or lightly, but reverently, discreetly, advisably and in the fear of God. Into this holy estate, these two persons present come now to be joined. If any man can show just cause why they may not be lawfully joined together, let him now speak or else hereafter forever hold his peace."*

"I CAN!" a deep voice echoed throughout the church.

All heads turned to the very back where Barclay Branham stood defiantly in the open doorway. Addie Jane stared at him, and a strange look came over her face. Suddenly she bolted, and ran swiftly to the side entrance and out the door, with her white train trailing behind much faster than intended. The astonished guests fell into an uproar, both the preacher and the groom stood speechless! Barclay had vanished as well. Some of the guests followed after the fleeing bride and now stood crowded in the side doorway, watching a cloud of white silk and ruffles disappear through the lush green woods bordering the church. Another group knelt over Mrs. Anderson, who had immediately fainted, and fanned her profusely with paper fans. Still others mingled out front looking for the intruder. Poky struggled to suppress a smile. Surprised and confused, the guests began to disperse, their obvious comments left floating in the air, "...and one of *them,* too...can you imagine!"

It was a week before Addie Jane consented to see anyone. Immediately following the episode, she was thrown into an asthma attack from all the emotional stress, then she struggled for strength and peace of mind. The strength returned, but not the peace of mind. Mr. Anderson had called on her immediately, but she refused to see him. Ainsley himself followed the next day, still she refused. The pastor was even put off when he showed up the third day. By the end of the week, she began to realize she couldn't stay in hiding forever. She had to face the world. And when Jean Lee called, she consented to see her.

"Addie Jane...why?" she blurted out.

Addie Jane walked over to the window, sat down and stared out at the fine misty rain falling, soaking the ground, creating a muddy yard for the boys, that thick, red mud that would be tracked through the house for days. "I just couldn't do it, Jean Lee."

"...because of Barclay Branham?"

She looked around with tears in her eyes. Jean Lee paced the floor. "...but Addie Jane, have you really thought this through? You know who Barclay is. How can you throw your life away like this?"

Addie Jane turned back to the window.

"You know how people treat them. Is that what you want? What you want to subject your children to? And what can Barclay Branham possibly give you? A life like the Andersons?"

Jean Lee left, throwing up her hands in despair. Addie Jane smiled at her weakly. A few days later, her brother, Winfred, brought a letter in from the mailbox, and immediately she noticed the familiar handwriting. She closed her door, sat down on the creaking bed to read...

On Saturday at noon, I will be on Oak Mountain,
beneath the grove of oaks, remember?

Please come!
Barclay

Saturday morning, Addie Jane rose early. The morning's fog had not lifted. It hung like a wilted cloud over the valley. But once the sun had a chance to burn through it, she figured it would be a warm, sunny day now that the rains had ceased. She was glad. Quietly, she went about the silent house doing the chores, glad to be alone with her thoughts. She couldn't help but feel the elation, knowing that she'd see him at noon. But what on earth would he say? What could she say? Was he terribly angry? Of course, he must be! She'd jilted him, almost married another guy...what else could she expect? Would he ever forgive her? She wouldn't blame him if he didn't, but could she live with that, the fact that he'd never forgive her? The troubling thoughts tumbled about disjointedly in her mind until she heard her father stirring around in her folk's bedroom. Soon the small house would be alive with noise and confusion.

The morning dragged by with the boys fighting more than usual, her father leaving for work later than normal and her mother's curious questions. She'd never been really close to her mother and didn't feel the urge to confide in her now. All those years of trauma from her sickness had left their mark. Alone, she carried her problems and sought for answers. She would've liked to talk everything over with Poky, but somehow couldn't bring herself to do that either. What must Poky think of her now? She knew she'd let her down when she'd decided to marry Ainsley in the first place. The clock over the kitchen stove made her more anxious. It was almost eleven thirty. She casually informed her mother that she wished to take a walk, trying hard to conceal her true feelings. Her mother nodded indifferently.

Signs of early summer were everywhere as she climbed upward. The familiar path was scattered with anxious green shoots sprouting from underneath last year's wet leaves. She remembered Poky's words, 'Don't always be looking down, look up and see what you see.' The sky was a beautiful clear blue, at least the small part of it that she could see. The natural thick canopy of foliage blocked its vast breadth. A cardinal swooped down in front of her and lit on a thick outstretched oak branch. It was a female, lacking the rich red plumage of the male, but it didn't lack in song. Her heart sang along with the happy little creature as she literally raced up the mountainside. There it was. The grove of oaks. He was sitting beneath them...waiting. Her heart raced. She stopped, and Barclay stood up. For a second the two stood awkwardly, each watching the other...and then they were in each other's arms.

For over an hour they walked the mountainside, arms

entwined, pouring out their hearts to each other, reuniting their souls, recommitting their lives. Barclay bent over and gently picked a delicate purple violet growing out from a mossy ledge. He placed it in the button-hole of Addie Jane's wool cardigan. She bowed her head, touching her chin on its velvety surface.

"I love you," he whispered. Tears filled her eyes. "...and I love you."

"This little violet is special. I've always loved violets, even when I was a boy. Poky would pick them and bring them to me. You know what she said?"

"...that violets are the glory of the spring wild garden."

He smiled, "...told you, too, huh. I love them because they love the forest just like I do. They love the mountains. They don't need the wide open sunny places like so many other flowers. They can grow and outshine most of them right here tucked away in the shadows, thriving on the dewy forest."

Addie Jane wondered how she could ever have thought of living without him and his sensitive, loving soul.

The wedding was small, held at the Mission with only the closest of family and friends. Addie Jane carried a Bible given to her by Poky and a fresh bouquet of wild violets from Barclay. Everyone rejoiced with them in their obvious happiness, but no one more than Poky, who beamed from ear to ear.

CHAPTER EIGHTEEN

JORDAN LAWRENCE MCKENZIE tried to shake the nervous feeling that he now wore like an old coat. Would his life ever return to normal? He parked his car on Rivermont Avenue beneath a full size maple that comfortably shaded his already hot car. This June was rendering true to its character, hot and humid. He wiped his face with his handkerchief, inhaled and exhaled long zesty breaths in hopes of relaxing like the self-help books said he would. He stared at the two-story white frame house across the street with its wide veranda and neatly painted green shutters. It had character and class, but there was warmth about it, too. Suddenly though, he felt like leaving, changing his mind. Did he have what it took to go through this again? No, he'd come too far to turn back! He got out and walked up the wide sidewalk toward the house, climbed the front steps, stepped across the freshly mopped green porch and knocked on the door.

Hallie opened the door, mop in hand, and caught her breath.

"Mrs. Frederick?"

She nodded.

"Jordan Lawrence McKenzie, ma'am. I'm looking for Jon Frederick."

It was as if time had turned back, and Jon Junior stood before her! She was speechless as she stared at him.

"Does he live here?"

"Yes...yes...of course...," she stammered, "but he isn't home just now."

"What time do you expect him, ma'am?" Jordan asked,

struggling to hold his composure.

She glanced at her watch. "He should be here around four." Noticing his collar and realizing she was speaking to a man of the cloth, she asked, "Won't you come in, Reverend?"

"Thank you, ma'am. But I'll return at four."

Hallie watched the young preacher walk down the steps and down the sidewalk toward his car. He even walked like Jon Junior. Suddenly her knees felt weak, and she sat down in the over-stuffed chair near the door, with the mop handle across her lap. She was still sitting there when Jon Junior came whistling in the door an hour later. He'd seemed happier these past few weeks. She'd even begun to think that he'd finally resigned himself to his bachelor state and was content with it. He leaned down and kissed her on the forehead, noticing the mop.

"You feeling all right, Mother? Unusual to find you sitting down this time of day."

"Yes, dear. I'm fine...." She cleared her throat. "Jon Junior, there was a young preacher here to see you earlier...."

"Preacher?"

"...yes...he...well...he was rather young but wore a collar like the Presbyterians and Episcopalians. I don't know which he was...he might even be Catholic...could be a priest."

"Wonder what he wanted?" he responded, absently walking into the kitchen to pour himself a tall glass of lemonade. "Did he say?"

"No...but he said he'd be back at four." She looked down at her watch. "...and it's almost that now."

"Good. I need to go over to Jim Black's tonight around six. We're working on plans for the CCC reunion. You know, I find myself getting excited about that, seeing the guys again. I'm sure I won't even recognize most of them. We were just boys back then...and now...." He laughed.

"Well, I'm glad y'all are having a reunion. Think I'll begin supper now." She pushed herself out of the chair and joined him in the kitchen. There was a knock at the door.

"That must be him." Jon Junior went to answer the door. Hallie remained in the kitchen. She heard the door open with its annoying creak, and then there was simply silence. Her heart was pounding. She started to go into the living room, but decided not to. No, something told her to stay put...leave it to them!

The two men stood looking at each other. Finally, Jordan spoke, "Sir, my name is Jordan Lawrence McKenzie. I'd like to talk with you, if possible...privately." He figured Mrs. Frederick must be nearby.

Obviously rattled, Jon Junior responded quickly, "Yes, certainly...ah...I'll be right with you...we can take a walk." He turned back into the house. "Mother, I'll be back directly, gonna take a walk."

"All right, son," she answered without leaving the kitchen. As much as she wanted to see what was happening, she restrained herself and waited until the door shut. Then she hurried to the front window and peered out, seeing the two of them walking down the sidewalk beneath the shady green maples.

"There's a nice park, Riverside Park, just ahead. Why don't we go there. It's always such a pleasant walk...especially in the summer...lots of trees...big old oaks and plenty of maples, too...." He found himself rambling, desperately trying to fill the awkwardness between them. Jordan walked quietly beside him.

As they approached the park entrance, Jordan spoke, "Mr. Frederick, by the look on your face, I suspect you have many questions. That's why I'm here...to answer those questions...and to meet you...." They followed the narrow, curving lane in the park.

"There's a place we can sit...down yonder...." Jon Junior pointed to a small stone gazebo, quite inviting on such a hot day. They climbed its few steps, entered the stony interior and sat down on the circular rock wall. Jordan looked up at the pointed wooden roof that shaded them nicely from the hot sunny rays. Jon Junior watched him expectantly.

Jordan returned his gaze and spoke softly, "*Sir, I am your son.*"

The startling words evoked a suffocating feeling within him, and he shifted uncomfortably on the stone wall. His mouth was dry and for the life of him, he couldn't think of a word to say.

Jordan continued, "I've already met and spoken with my mother...she told me about you...how I could find you that is...."

Tears began to roll down Jon Junior's cheeks. He quickly wiped them with a trembling hand.

"It's okay, sir. I don't hold any grudges, no ill feelings at all. I just wanted to meet you...meet both of you...."

Jon Junior blinked through tears that were falling freely. He extended his shaking hand, and the two men awkwardly shook. A slight summer breeze began to blow through the park and through the gazebo, and tender green summer leaves surrounding the gazebo gracefully danced in its aftermath. The breezes increased as the two sought to know each other, alone there in the little stone shelter.

"...those were hard times...back then," Jon Junior spoke with difficulty, "...your mother...Beth...was such a sweet, obedient girl...always wanting to please her folks. She never wanted anything like that to happen. We were...so in love back then in high-school. She was a lovely girl. But her folks wouldn't hear of the two of us together. Perhaps, if things had been different, everything would have...oh well. You see, Beth came from a fairly well-fixed family, at least for our little town anyway. She was the only child and the single focus of her parents' love and dreams. They wanted only the best for her...and, unfortunately, that didn't in any way include me. And, of course, they were right. My life was as far from hers as the east from the west. My father had disappeared, leaving my poor mother destitute with the three of us kids. It was during the Great Depression. I was the oldest, and the burden fell hard on me. Of course, mother tried not to let it be so, but she needed help. In other words, we were on the other side of the tracks. So, our courtship was conducted in secret, stolen sweet moments. I saw there was only one thing for me to do...leave...go away and make something out of myself. The CCC's had just been established. It was an opportunity for many of us, a gleam of hope. Not only would I be able to send money back home to my family, but I could learn skills, get ahead."

"A noble thing to do," Jordan remarked softly, more like a reverend than a son. Jon Junior smiled at him.

"It was the only thing I could do. But the night before I left, Beth and I met, secretly, of course." He turned his head away momentarily. "...she was so distraught when I told her. I'd waited to the end to tell her...afraid she'd change my mind...and knowing full well I'd never be able to resist her. She cried and cried...I guess it was the crying...that did it. To make a long story short...it was that night we gave in to our feelings...feelings of young love and hopelessness...it was that night that...that you were conceived...."

Jordan reached out and laid his hand on Jon Junior's arm that was trembling.

"...when she found out...I was gone, of course. She was just a kid...and felt all alone. She told me this years later...at first she tried to keep it a secret, bear it all alone...but finally she had to go to her parents. As you can imagine, they were horrified. Sent her away...to Richmond...to have the...to have you...and adopted you out. All the while, I was busy getting ahead in the CCC's, still making plans to one day be suitable for Beth and Beth's parents."

Then he was quiet. Only the rustling of the leaves could be heard overhead.

"...she told me what happened then," Jordan added softly.

Jon Junior shook his head. "...that's what destroyed my dreams. Her parents persuaded her to marry a fellow from a *good family with means,* as they said. She was young, confused and as I've said, always tried to please her folks...."

"It was a noble thing for her to do, as well...."

"That's right. We both did the noble thing...and missed out on a lifetime of happiness. I guess she told you that she could never have any more children."

"She told me. It grieves my heart...to know all of this...the pain the two of you have felt."

Jon Junior looked up suddenly, seemingly seeing his son for the first time. "...but I never knew...I never knew about you...until it was too late," he stammered revealing how distraught he was.

Jordan longed to embrace him, but the two sat silently. Then he spoke softly, "It's okay. Don't be sorry. I've had a good life...a wonderful mother...a good upbringing for the most part. I really can't complain...except for...."

Jon Junior waited.

"...except for missing out on a father-son relationship...that I feel I would have had...with you...."

"I'm sorry...so sorry," Jon Junior's voice cracked with emotion, "...but what about your father, your adoptive father?"

"...he tried, I guess. But it just didn't work. I'll tell you about that another time."

Jon Junior smiled. "...we have a lot to catch up on. By golly...what about mom? My mother...I mean you have to meet your grandmother!"

"I think I already have."

"That's right. You have...but I mean officially...if it's okay with you?"

"I'd love to." The two got up and left the little gazebo.

That evening as the three of them sat down to supper, Hallie couldn't take her eyes off her newly revealed grandson. "...and to think all these years I've had such a fine young grandson...and didn't even know it! And a preacher, too!" she exclaimed with joy. Jordan laughed.

"Well, you know it now, Mother. We'll just have to make up for lost time!"

"You're right about that, son. Pass those potatoes to Jordan, Jon Junior. I know you'll like my mashed potatoes...take a big helping."

Between the two of them, they'd told Hallie the sequence of events as gently as possible. Shocked, she was, but true to her character, she rose to the occasion, putting the disappointment behind her and seeking to look to the present.

After Jordan had left with the promise to return in a week, Hallie and Jon Junior sat together on the front porch listening to the cicadas perform their nightly chorus and silently reviewing the day's shocking event. The cool night air was welcomed after the hot summer day.

"I still can't believe it!" Hallie broke the silence. "...I missed him as a baby...watching him learn to walk...his first day of school...seeing him graduate. I missed it all!" Suddenly she looked over at Jon Junior in the moonlight. "Oh son, I didn't mean to say all that. Here I am talking about myself...and you...dear...how you must feel! But we mustn't think of the past now...it's gone...water over the dam...we must think of now. A preacher. Imagine that! I always wanted a preacher in the family. Jon Junior! I was so baffled...I forgot to ask him what kind of preacher!"

He laughed. "A Presbyterian, Mother...he's a Presbyterian minister."

"Oh thank goodness. I always liked the Presbyterians. Had a wonderful Presbyterian neighbor years ago on Church Street. You remember Mrs. Knowles? No, you wouldn't. You were too young. I'm just glad he isn't Catholic...oh, not that I don't respect the Catholics...it's just that I don't know much about the Catholics...they always seemed so formal with their ways. Don't know how us Baptists would fit in." She laughed and Jon Junior loosened up.

"Uh-oh, Jon Junior, you forgot about your meeting with Jim Black!"

"You're right. I'll call him." He hesitated before getting up.

"I just feel so sorry for poor Beth," Hallie's voice trailed off.

Jon Junior hung his head. "So do I, Mother...if there was anything I could do...."

"Oh, I don't mean that, Jon Junior! Of course, there's nothing you can do. She's a married lady and has been for years."

"...but, she's not well, you know."

"I thought she was okay...had overcome that cancer years ago."

"Jordan says she's not well...."

"What did he say?"

"He didn't go into detail...just indicated on the way back here today that she isn't well, and he plans to spend as much time with her as possible...."

"I see."

The following Wednesday the rains came, a relief to most Lynchburgers who'd suffered from the long hot and humid spell. Dog days, some were calling it, though it was officially too early for them. First it came in small spatterings, hitting the dusty red clay, leaving minute indentations in the otherwise solid red surface, then in increased stinging drops, finally the sky seemed totally awash with floods of water as heavy clouds scudded across it and stormy torrents poured down. Townsfolk scurried across Main Street hovered under open umbrellas, jumping over large puddles, quickly seeking any available shelter. Jon Junior held firmly onto his big black umbrella as the winds increased. A Christmas gift from Lauralee, it had certainly come in handy more than once. He hurried toward The Virginian Restaurant, straining to see through the rain-covered windows. Was she there? She always ate lunch at The Virginian Restaurant on Wednesdays. Would she be there today?

She was there, sitting alone as usual, reading a book while she ate, one of her favorite pastimes. He folded his umbrella and stepped inside the small cafe, with its booth lined walls.

"Mind if I join you?" She looked up and smiled rather

timidly. He sat down slowly, hanging his dripping umbrella on the corner of the booth.

The waitress appeared. "Something for you, sir?"

"Yes, ma'am. Please bring me the same as the young lady here." She quickly scratched something on her pad and turned away. The two looked at each other as the rain pounded outside, lashing at the windows and creating a cozy atmosphere within the small restaurant.

"Yes...he came."

She nodded and lowered her head.

"It's okay, Beth. I'm glad you told him. In fact, he's all I've been able to think of since Saturday." He leaned toward her. "...we have a beautiful son...."

Her face brightened at once. "...yes, we do. He's a lovely person, too. His...other parents...they did a good job."

"Yes, they did."

There was an awkward silence.

"Beth...are you all right?"

She looked up. "What do you mean?" Her face was suddenly flushed.

"I mean...well...Jordan told me that you really aren't well...."

"I see."

"And?"

She sighed audibly and looked around. "Jon, it's important to me that you and Jordan develop a real solid relationship...a father-son relationship, you know...."

He waited.

She looked him in the eye. "It has come back, Jon...and this time, I don't know whether I can fight it...."

"...but you must!"

She smiled at him. "I wish I could, Jon. Believe me, I wish I could."

"What do the doctors say? What are they doing?" he asked urgently.

"They're doing all they can. In fact, I'll be leaving week after next, going to California...a last ditch effort, you might say."

Jon's face registered pain. "Who's going with you?"

"Katherine, Thomas's sister. You know, Thomas isn't well either."

"Has he ever been?"

"Jon...."

"I'm sorry. But you need someone to take care of you...to watch over you...I...."

"Jon...."

He put his head in his hands.

"Jon, please."

He looked up with anguish. "What can I do, Beth? What can I do?"

"The most important thing you can do for me, Jon...is just what I've said...bond with our son...build a strong relationship. He had a good mother, but he missed out on a real daddy. Be a daddy to Jordan, Jon."

The waitress placed his hot hamburger in front of him, and smoke rose up from the plate. He looked at hers. "You've hardly touched yours. Have I upset you?"

"No...no...I'm not hungry much these days...."

He tried eating his as she absently flipped through the record selections on the table jukebox between them. "Ah...remember this, Jon? It's an oldie." He read the title, *Stormy Weather*, and dropped a dime into the slot. The nostalgic melody filled the quaint cafe.

Don't know why...there's no sun up in the sky
Stormy weather
Since my man and I ain't together
Keeps rainin' all the time
Life is bare, gloom and mis'ry ev'rywhere
Stormy weather

Just can't get my poor self together
I'm weary all the time
So weary all the time

When he went away, the blues walked in and met me
If he stays away, old rockin' chair will get me
All I do is pray the Lord above will let me
Walk in the sun once more
Can't go on, everything I had is gone
Stormy weather
Since my man and I...ain't together
Keeps rainin' all the time
Keeps rainin' all the time

The song ended, and they were silent for a moment, taken back to another time...another place...but now they sat opposite one another just as their lives had always been — opposite one another.

"Well, the rocking chair sure didn't get you," Jon Junior remarked with just a hint of sarcasm.

"Jon, you know why...but it's all history now."

"I know."

She looked at him sadly. "You'll never know how much I listened to that old song back then, and felt every word of it. Ironically, it did seem to rain more after you left. Maybe it was just because I was so in tune to it." She gazed out at the pouring rains. "Yes, it was stormy weather for sure."

She stood up to go. Jon Junior continued to sit, thinking of Jordan's words... *'it was a noble thing to do'*. Yes, and he'd acted in a noble way all his life. Never getting any closer to the woman he loved than this...across a table. But always in his mind, he'd dreamed that possibly one day...possibly one day she'd be free, and they'd be together at last. But now! His heart ached.

Jordan returned a week later and had supper again with Jon Junior and Hallie. But most of the time he spent with his mother. Even though Jon Junior yearned to be with him, he was glad that Beth had this happiness, what little happiness she'd had in her lifetime. She flew to California, accompanied by her sister-in-law, but the miracle she'd counted on didn't happen. She returned to Lynchburg, worse than before, and went into seclusion basically, undergoing chemo and dealing with the wretched sickness and loss of her beautiful hair. Every weekend, Jordan left his beloved bay and headed for the mountains to spend as much time as possible with his fast ailing mother. Thomas Browning, never questioning, was glad to have the young Presbyterian minister so attentive to his wife, particularly since his entire heritage was steeped in the Presbyterian faith, as well. He himself simply couldn't deal with her sickness. It was all he could do to deal with his own. Somehow, he hadn't let himself really get involved; therefore he seemed not to grasp the seriousness of her illness, or either he chose to deny it. It was the end of September, and fall was definitely in the air. Mrs. Browning had lain upon her bed all morning, too weak to rise. She'd watched the young maple outside her open bedroom window, iridescent in the sunlight, and listened to its gentle stirring in the autumn breeze. Part of the tree was a brilliant yellow, and the other half a fiery red. She tried to fathom its unique beauty as an occasional leaf broke loose and parachuted to the ground. Jordan found her this way.

"You know," she practically whispered to him, "I've always loved the beauty of life, especially fall...I'm sure going to miss it."

Quietly Jordan reached inside his coat pocket, pulled out his small black Bible and knowingly flipped through the tissue paper pages. "You think this is pretty! The scriptures have something to say about that, you know." He began to read from lst Corinthians..."'*But as it is written, Eye hath not seen, nor ear heard, neither have entered into the heart of man, the things which God hath prepared for them that love Him.*'"

She smiled up at him. "Did you know that's in the Old Testament, too?"

He nodded and turned to Isaiah 64..." '*For since the beginning of the world, men have not heard, nor perceived by the ear, neither hath the eye seen, O God, beside thee, what He hath prepared for him that waiteth for him.*' "

"A Jewish friend of mine read that to me."

He smiled. "All this beauty here on earth, the lovely springs, the awesome falls...none of it can compare to what God has in store for us...those of us who wait on him and love him."

Mrs. Browning was quiet. She stared out the window.

Jordan cleared his throat. "Mother...I...I hope you don't mind me calling you that...."

"Mind?" She turned to him, tears filling her eyes. "All these years I've yearned to hear it...to be called Mother...you'll never know...."

He gently reached for her hand. "As a minister of the gospel, it is my duty to ask you this question...but more than a minister, I need to know for myself...." He hesitated. "Mother...are you ready...are you ready to meet Him?"

She shifted in the bed and a tear fell down her smooth cheek. "I'm really not sure, Jordan...I'm really not sure...but I want to be...."

Jordan turned to the book of Acts and read... "'*Believe on the Lord Jesus Christ, and thou shalt be saved...*' "

"It seems so long ago...when I was young, very young, I did believe...but somehow life...the disillusionment...all of it...I'm just not sure...."

He flipped to Romans..." '*For whosoever shall call upon the name of the Lord shall be saved.*' "

She looked at him with understanding.

"That *whosoever* is you, Mother...and me and all of us...any of us. If you're really not sure, you can be sure. You can pray and call upon Him right now."

"Help me, Jordan. I want to...."

"All you have to do is believe in Him, Mother, and call on Him.." They closed their eyes.

The room was quiet. All that could be heard was the rhythmic ticking of the round alarm clock on the bureau, and the soft rustling of maple leaves outside. Soon she looked up through teary eyes and smiled.

He read from the scripture... "*'and him that cometh to me, I will in no wise cast out.'* You can rest assured that you are in His protective arms now, forever, whether in life or death."

"And Reverend McKenzie," she half whispered, "I want you to know that I've asked God's forgiveness for my sins, all my sins, especially the one that caused all the pain for your father and me...and even you...I know He's forgiven me. I have a peace about that, probably because I've sought Him so much over it."

"I'm sure He has, Mother."

"...and I ask you to forgive me, too, son."

"There is no need, Mother. You never did anything to intentionally hurt me. You were a child yourself, a victim yourself in so many words. You have given me so much already...your love...and a father...a real father. I don't look back, Mother. I look forward...and I look forward to the day we will all be united in Heaven."

"I'll be waiting for you, son...in that beautiful place that eyes have not seen nor ears heard...that wonderful place God has prepared for us...."

He squeezed her hand.

"I would like to hear you preach, son. I really would."

"Well then, you just get your strength back, and I'll see that you do. I'll personally drive you to my beautiful bay area, to my little parish."

She smiled, and he saw contentment in her smile.

Beth Browning never got to hear her son preach. The weeks passed, and with each passing week, her life seemed to ebb away, to slowly drain out of her. October turned into November, and on a cold, windy day, she left the starkness of winter for that beautiful land that now her eyes could see. The funeral procession filed in through the gates of Spring Hill Cemetery and wound around narrow, curving lanes beneath old oaks with outstretched arms and crisp brown leaves. The slow moving line of cars passed by tall, massive and impressive tombstones of prominent Lynchburgers who had filled the popular resting place for decades. It stopped on a hillside, and family and friends stepped out with bowed heads, pulling their sweaters and coats tightly about them against the northern winds. They huddled together around the temporary tent-like shelter, listening to the preacher read from the scriptures. Thomas Browning sat up front, motionless and apparently in shock. His sister sat next to him, and the nieces and nephews and cousins of the Browning family filled in around them. At the back of the group stood a young minister, obviously so with his coat and collar. People glanced at him with no recognition. Perhaps had their glance prolonged, and they studied his likeness to the man beside him, there would have been cause to whisper, cause for raised eyebrows, but this didn't happen. Too much wind, too cold, with their heads downward, the young minister went unnoticed. But Hallie watched.

Jon Junior stared at the large spray of red and white roses atop her casket. A pain seized him again. He'd never been able to give her roses. He'd never had the right. He blinked back the tears.

The preacher began with a deep base voice sufficiently able to compete with the wind... " *'The Lord is my shepherd; I shall not want. He maketh me to lie down in green pastures: he leadeth me beside the still waters. He restoreth my soul: he leadeth me in the paths of righteousness for his name's sake. Yea, though I walk through the valley of the shadow of death, I will fear no evil: for thou art with me; thy rod and thy staff they comfort me. Thou preparest a table before me in the presence of mine enemies: thou anointest my head with oil: my cup runneth over. Surely goodness and mercy shall follow me all the days of my life: and I will dwell in the house of the Lord forever.'"*

The crowd wedged closer together to resist the biting sting of the cold wind, and the round, greying preacher coughed several times, then cleared his voice. "It is not by choice that we gather in this city of the dead, hallowed by the sacred memory of its inhabitants. The monuments, some of them quite elaborate, intricate and somewhat overwhelming, only serve as symbols of the affection of surviving friends. But the absence of the souls of these inhabitants is a monument to a loving and life-giving God. As we now offer the body of Beth Browning, we are reminded that there is life immortal that shall indeed survive this grave. We commit this one to the arms of a God who gives life that never ends."

Hallie watched Jordan put his arm around Jon Junior.

The preacher continued, "We cannot escape life's troubles, life's sadness, life's suffering. It mingles with the joys, the laughter and the happiness when we inherit life on this earth. There is only one way to escape these troubles, this sadness and this suffering, and that is the path that Beth Browning is now on as she enters new life. We all know that our sweet Beth endured much suffering...."

Jon Junior dropped his head.

"...but the scripture says in Revelation 21...'*God will wipe away every tear from their eyes; there shall be no more death.*' We can rest assured that Beth Browning is with her Lord as we speak, and He is wiping away those tears. Just before the end, I spoke with Beth. I spoke with her about her soul, and there was a quiet joy there. She told me she was ready, that she had made peace with God. And friends, it was obvious, even in death, there was a glow about her. Beth asked me to read this last scripture." Jon Junior looked up.

"Matthew 11, verses twenty-eight through thirty...'*Come to Me, all you who labor and are heavy laden, and I will give you rest. Take My yoke upon you and learn from Me, for I am gentle and lowly in heart, and you will find rest for your souls. For My yoke is easy and My burden is light.*'"

There was silence there on the hillside in the cemetery with only the moans of the ever present wind. Then the preacher prayed, "Lord, in the midst of grief and pain, your strength is sufficient. And as Beth Browning enters into her new life, give us left behind, her family and friends, your strength and your grace to carry on. We offer this prayer in our Lord's name. Amen."

Hours later, after the crowd was gone, the tent-shelter removed, the grave filled in with a mound of red dirt as a reminder, and flowers of every color covering it, Jon Junior returned alone to say his final good-bye. The sun was setting, and the wind was whistling through the oak trees. His lone figure was silhouetted against the melancholy background.

IT WAS NOVEMBER the fifteenth, and a balmy day for November. The sun shone warmly over the brown terrain as Jordan's car passed the flat, dormant fields on its way to the coast. Keeping one hand on the wheel, he turned his Coke upward, finishing it off while Jon Junior studied the outstretched map on his lap. "...about another two hours, you say?"

"That's right. Should arrive around dinner time."

"...and that's with your grandmother on your McKenzie side?"

"Correct. Grandmother McKenzie can hardly wait to meet you. I've told her all about you." He stuffed the Coke can in the litter bag hanging from the cigarette lighter.

"Seems rather odd that your grandmother, the mother of your dad, your adopted dad, would be anxious to meet me."

"Grandmother McKenzie is kind of odd, or rather I might say unique, one of a kind. And of all people, she knew the void in my life as a child...because of her son's inability to be a dad. Unfortunately, he didn't take after her. Grandmother just wants my happiness. That's all she's ever wanted."

"I see. Well, she sounds like a special lady, and I'm anxious to meet her." He folded up the map and placed it back in the glove compartment.

"And she's just as anxious to meet you. Hope you like broiled mackerel. That's her specialty, and she generally serves it to all first time guests."

"Sound's great. I like just about anything, especially fish, except that is for catfish out of the James."

"You should taste our catfish out of the bay, the way grandmother fries them. They're almost as good as her broiled mackerel. She'll probably have some New England chowder and home cooked rolls, too. Boy, my stomach's growling just talking about it."

Jon Junior laughed.

Sure enough, the broiled mackerel, lightly flavored with lemon, was placed in front of him, along with the steaming chowder and hot rolls plus homemade slaw. Grandmother McKenzie sat down with them as proud as a peacock. "Now, Jordan dear, would you say grace?" You'd think she was asking a child instead of a reverend. The prayer of thanksgiving was offered, simple and brief.

"Now, Mr. Frederick, do you mind me calling you Jon?"

"I'd be disappointed if you didn't, ma'am," he responded, while receiving the homemade yeast rolls passed to him.

"Actually, Grandmother, he goes by Jon Junior by everyone in Lynchburg."

"Why, then it's Jon Junior here on the bay, as well."

Jon Junior grinned, liking the genteel lady already.

"Jon Junior, I wish to formally and personally welcome you into our side of the family. You've already made my Jordan here very happy. I'm quite sure that his dear mother will welcome you, as well, when she returns home from her trip up north."

"Thank you very much, ma'am."

"I already explained..." Jordan looked at his grandmother, "...about mom spending some time in Boston with Aunt Estelle."

She smiled warmly at them both. "How's your chowder, Jon Junior?"

"Delicious, ma'am...it's delicious." He stirred the hot broth, thick with diced clams and potatoes.

She nodded a thank you. "And just what is it you two fellows plan to do tomorrow? I hear it's going to be a lovely day, in the high fifties, maybe even sixty, one of those sunny interludes that rejuvenates our spirits as winter takes over."

Jordan looked over at his dad and grinned. "Well, if that forecast is right, we're going boat riding."

Jon Junior looked up from his chowder and quickly wiped his chin with his cloth napkin, feeling the smooth broth seeping down. "We are?"

The next morning proved the forecast to be right on target, with a warm winter sun already burning away the coastal fog and beckoning the sea gulls out for excursions. Jon Junior peered out Grandmother McKenzie's upstairs dormer window that overlooked the beautiful expansive bay, glistening in the early sun. He gently pushed the white cape cod curtains to the side to see even further. What a view! Only a mild breeze was blowing, causing the brown marsh grasses, bordering the sloping yard, to barely sway to and fro. Several ducks were resting at the edge of the yard. One stood up, stretched and fluttered its wings and strutted off toward the water, jumped in and swam out of sight behind the marshes. He figured they must be the babies Grandmother McKenzie told him about last evening. Babies that a mother duck had abandoned last summer, and Grandmother McKenzie had put them in a small plastic pool she'd gotten from K-Mart and fed them every meal herself. Now they called this place home, as well, often going off, but always returning. An old wooden dock, in need of some repair, extended out from the sloping yard with pilings on each end. A lone sea gull was perched atop the tallest piling, quite statuesque. Everything seemed so tranquil, so peaceful. No wonder Jordan loved this place. A deep resonant sound rose from the scrub pines that bordered the house. He then saw the chimes hanging from one of the pines as they gently played their angelic music. It was almost hypnotizing, the total effect of it all, and he succumbed to its magic, resting on his elbows at the dormer window.

KNOCK! The loud knock broke the spell as Jordan called out, "Jon Junior...Dad, ready yet?"

"Yes, just about."

Grandmother McKenzie stood on the porch, waving her dishtowel as Jordan pulled the rope to the old Evinrude. It sputtered and cut off. He tried again, and it repeated itself. Jon Junior was too busy looking back at the little shingled house that seemed a part of the water, sky and marshland. He wanted to make a mental picture of it to tell his mother and Lauralee. The shingles were a sea-weathered grey now, and its steep roof added to its charming image, with two dormers jutting out over the porch roof. Gnarled and twisted scrub pines, hugging its sides, created an oriental appearance, and dormant flower gardens climbed the sloping yard, now with only weathered conch shells standing out among its brown aftermath.

The old motor caught, and Jordan cried, "Hallelujah."

The small green jon boat eased away from the marshes and out into the full bay waters, its motor purring. Jordan tossed Jon Junior a Coke, and he caught it in midair. "Don't think I have room for it after that sumptuous breakfast your grandmother fixed."

"She does know how to fix a breakfast fit for royalty, doesn't she?" They both looked back toward the house and saw her still waving the dishtowel.

"That's a fact." He noticed how young Jordan looked, dressed in a plaid flannel shirt without his collar. Not so much like a preacher, but like any other young man now. There was a look of contentment on his face as he maneuvered the small boat out into the fairly smooth waters. Obviously, it was something he'd done scores of times and was as natural to him as getting out of bed. The water was relatively calm, as it often is in early morning. Dark green cypress bordered the shoreline and mingled with maples, stripped for the winter. Crispy, brown leaves flanked the banks, and some limply floated out into the bay waters, hanging up around dark wet cypress stumps that conspicuously poked out of the waters, resembling weird trolls from Norwegian story books. The faded, green boat gained speed as it moved out into the wide waters, passing an obviously much used duckblind, with its wooden frame now exposed. Only a few dead pine limbs remained for its covering. Leaving it behind, a feeling of freedom and adventure from the vast openness overcame Jon Junior, and he inhaled and exhaled the pristine moist air, refreshing as it was. Moving faster against it, he found himself getting much cooler, wishing he'd taken Grandmother McKenzie's advice and brought along a coat. Even though he felt they were traveling rapidly over the rippled bay waters, Jordan informed him otherwise. They were actually only traveling about ten miles an hour. He suddenly understood why Jordan loved these waters.

They passed an expansive marsh area, brown with winter's coming, and cattails swaying in the gentle sea breeze.

"Look!" Jordan pointed toward the picturesque marshland.

Jon Junior looked and wondered what he was looking for.

"See it?"

He strained, searching the thickly overgrown marshland. "See what?"

Jordan pointed emphatically. "The egret...there to the left of the jutted edge."

Still Jon Junior saw nothing. He blinked in the fine spray of brackish water, tasting the salt, as it splashed back from the boat's bow piercing the shallow waters. Then he saw it and understood why it had proved so difficult. The elegant sea bird was poised, still and silent, with its brownish plumage camouflaged against the marshes, one leg lifted and crooked as if someone had photographed it while in action, capturing its unique position. But it was no picture. The egret purposely held its odd position, uncertain of its surroundings. Jon Junior watched it and the marshland grow smaller as the little boat continued on. Almost a half-hour passed with Jordan following the Deep Channel southward, the smooth, tranquil scene broken only with crab pot markers, an occasional boat in the distance and the soaring, swooping sea gulls with their raucous cries. It created a calming effect on Jon Junior, a cut-off from the rest of the world and its problems, a desire to remain in status-quo.

"Well, what do you think? Great, isn't it?" Jordan called out with a smile.

Jon Junior nodded in agreement.

As they approached a small, wooded island, Jordan instructed, "Keep your eyes on this island. As we get closer, you'll see a house...."

The small island, approximately five acres, now loomed larger, filled with pines, cedars, maples and cypress. Then Jon Junior saw a clearing in the center of the island, and a white frame bungalow sitting in the midst of it, a perfect setting. It was quiet now, a summer home for someone, most likely. Jordan let up on the gas, maneuvering the shallow water, and the jon boat idled up to the bank, coming to rest beside a path leading up to the empty house.

"My dream house." He laughed. "...guess it'll always be a dream...on a preacher's salary."

Jon Junior was quiet, taking in the utopian setting.

"Why don't we tie up here, stretch our legs and sit there on the path for awhile," Jordan suggested, while already actively carrying out the plan. At a closer look, the place already needed another mowing, obviously the result of fall growth.

A lone sea gull glided over the island as Jon Junior sat down on the smooth pathway leading up to the house. He looked up into the sky which was a striking clear blue. It was good to put his feet back on land even though he'd enjoyed the ride immensely. They were both quiet for awhile. The tranquil setting lent itself to intimacy.

"...you know, your mother's last wish...was for us to be together, get to know one another...."

"I know."

"...there's a lot of years to catch up on, guess we'll have to spend a lot of time together to do that."

"I want to know all I can about...all of you...you and my Grandmother Frederick and Aunt Lauralee and her family...."

Jon Junior's tone took on a subdued note, "I wish you could've known Jamey...your Uncle Jamey. You two would've hit it right off, for sure."

"Your brother who died in the war?"

"My little brother, my only brother. He was something, full of life, not like me. I was always the conservative one. Not Jamey. He was the adventurous one, always wanting to take chances, a zest for life. Too bad he had so little of it."

Jordan was quiet.

"But he was ready to go, that's for sure. We had a witness to that. A fellow came to the house sometime afterward and told mother all about how Jamey had gotten right with the Lord and had a real joy even in the midst of all the fighting and war."

"I'm glad to hear that. But it's always hard to lose someone so young, the cutting off of the rose before it has time to bloom."

"Yeah."

"And your sister, Lauralee? She seems like such a sweet lady."

"She is that. We were always close, Lauralee and me. But after Jamey's death, we drew even closer. I really don't know what I would've done all these years without her...and mother."

Jordan looked at his father, his age more prevalent in the bright morning sun. "Guess it's been lonely for you remaining a bachelor all these years?"

Jon Junior sighed. "More than you know. Seems I've been lonely most of my life. First growing up without a dad, wishing I had one like other guys I knew. Then losing Jamey, the only other male in my life. And Beth, sweet Beth...."

Jordan changed the subject. "I know something about loneliness, but not poverty. Mother told me about the hardships everyone endured during the Great Depression. I can't even imagine."

"You don't want to either. Those were dark days...dark days we hope to never see again."

The next day was Sunday, and Jon Junior and Jordan rose early for a walk on the beach at sunrise. The warmth of yesterday was only a memory. It was cold, windy and a grey semi-dark when they arrived and began slowly jogging on the wet, sandy beach with their heads down and hands stuffed in their pockets. Then the sun made its sudden appearance, just a smidgen, a sliver of sparkling gold barely visible, poking up from the massive, rolling waters. Slowly though, it ascended from the waters, casting dazzling golden streamers out over the restless ocean. Jon Junior watched reverently as they slowed to a walk. "What a sight!" he barely whispered, and Jordan nodded. Soon it hung radiantly above the water for all to see. Glaringly, brilliantly, it hung, suspended between the heavens and the sea.

" '*And God made two great lights; the greater light to rule the day, and the lesser light to rule the night...*' Genesis 1:16," Jordan quoted softly.

They continued to walk quietly, casually strolling the shoreline with its foaming, incoming waters that brought in tangled seaweed, broken shells and minute crabs that were cast unwillingly upon the cold beach. Just as quickly as the small creatures found themselves exposed, they scrambled up and hastily retreated sideways back to the water, or dug themselves into the wet sand. "Poor little fellows," Jordan commented, bending over to pick up a small channeled whelk shell and handed it to Jon Junior. "Take that back to Aunt Lauralee for me."

"I'll do it." He carefully tucked it away in his coat pocket. "You know, I certainly enjoyed our boat ride yesterday. The ride back was a lot more exciting with the boat bouncing up and down on the waves, but I think the peaceful ride down was my favorite."

"Know what you mean. That's why I like going out early in the morning. The water often gets rougher as the day wears on." They walked about a half mile further down the beach, turned and walked back. As they returned, they noticed up ahead a large number of sea gulls assembled in one place, sitting quite still on the beach, all facing the same direction, facing the wind. About forty or fifty of them, seemingly waiting on something.

"Looks like a service going on...."

"...and there's the preacher!" Jon Junior laughed.

A large sea gull, heavy with age and winter plumage, strutted up in front of the feathered congregation and stood facing them with the wind ruffling up its feathers.

"Must be Presbyterian...too quiet for Baptists," Jon Junior added with a grin.

"Amen," Jordan laughed. "Well, speaking of congregations, guess we'd better head back for breakfast before it's time for us to make an appearance." As they walked off, Jon Junior glanced back at the sea gulls still bracing themselves against the wind.

Jon Junior's heart swelled with pride even though he knew it shouldn't. As he watched the handsome young minister, clothed in a black robe standing behind the pulpit, it was hard to believe he was his son. He noticed the congregation's rapt attention. Obviously, they held considerable respect and love for him, and the small church was nearly full. Absorbed with watching the mirror of faces in the congregation, in the choir loft, and particularly Jordan's, he almost forgot he was in church until the big Bible was opened and Jordan began expounding the scriptures.

"Today, I'm going to talk about something that is quite ambiguous, very subtle, elusive, not even real in a sense...the shadow." He paused intentionally for effect and then calmly continued, "...recently, I attended a funeral of someone very dear...." Jon Junior, who was signing the visitor book that passed in front of him, suddenly jerked up his head, and Jordan steadily met his gaze.

"...and at this dear person's funeral, a well-known passage was read, one that I'm quite sure you're all familiar with, as well, found in the beloved Psalms. Yes, Psalm 23... *'Yea, though I walk through the valley of the shadow of death, I will fear no evil.'*

"Now, I've read that passage many times myself, used it at funerals, as well. But it was like the first time I'd ever heard it. Literally, it jumped out at me...and since then, I've given much thought and study to the word *shadow*. Shortly after that day, I flew up to New Hampshire to visit an old college buddy, and on the flight back, it was again brought to my attention. You know how sometimes we have to go round-robin to get to Virginia. Well, I had to connect in Charlotte. And flying in on the DC-9, I was staring out the window, as usual. The sun was shining brilliantly, reflecting off the plane's wings in an almost blinding way, and the autumn colors were peaking in Charlotte. I can see it now, looking down on the mirage of multi-colored tree tops, golds, crimsons, russets...and there it was! A dark, barely visible speck in the midst of all that color. At first it seemed to be stationary, and then I saw it was moving very slowly. A tiny shadow gliding over that fairyland of tree tops. My eyes followed it. As the heavy aircraft moved, the shadow moved. I watched it for some time, and then very slowly, it began to grow larger as the aircraft gradually began descending. I couldn't take my eyes from the shadow, watching it grow larger and larger. Now I could see its intricate shape, the aircraft's shape, that is. I pressed my head to the window, hypnotized by the moving shadow. We were just over the tree tops ourselves now, and the two were moving toward each other, merging, the shadow and the plane. As the wheels hit the runway with a bump, they joined.

"Again, I pondered the mystery of the shadow. Of course, I understand as you do the reasonable explanation of a shadow. And Mr. Webster tells us *'a shadow is the dark figure cast upon a surface by a body intercepting the rays from a source of light.'* Now, I understand that, but still a shadow lends mystery to the reality around it. Mr. Webster goes on to say that *'a shadow is an imitation of something; a copy.'*

" *'Yea, though I walk through the valley of the shadow of death...'* " he paused. "Not really death? Its shadow? Death as we know it is the end of something. But when we leave this earth, it is not the end. Our lives are eternal, the scriptures say. And, of course, it depends upon our relationship with God as to where we spend this eternity. Blessed be to God, the dear person I was referring to is now, as I speak, spending her eternity with Him because she trusted in Him before she left this earth.

"Still intrigued by the shadow, I went to the scriptures to see what else God had to say about it. And guess what? The word shadow is mentioned on numerous occasions in the Bible, specifically pertaining to two different subjects. One describes life and the other means protection. Listen to some of these...'My days are like a *shadow* that declineth: and I am withered like grass.' 'Man is like to vanity: his days are as a *shadow* that passeth away.' 'For who knoweth what is good for man in this life, all the days of his vain life which he spendeth as a *shadow?* For who can tell a man what shall be after him under the sun?'

"How true...how sobering such a message God delivers.

Our lives on earth are so elusive, so temporal, like a shadow. So we know the shadow is a copy, an imitation, not real, and we know it is temporary, as well. It doesn't last. Thus, when the Bible says we walk through the valley of the shadow of death, this is saying it is temporal. What is on the other side of the shadow?"

The congregation was quiet.

"The second meaning, however, I like to ponder. And it is used in this context most often...that of protection. From Psalm 91...'He that dwelleth in the secret place of the most High shall abide under the *shadow* of the Almighty.'

"In Isaiah 49...'And he hath made my mouth like a sharp sword; in the *shadow* of his hand hath he hid me, and made me a polished shaft; in his quiver hath he hid me.'

"Then in Isaiah 51...'And I have put my words in thy mouth, and I have covered thee in the *shadow* of mine hand, that I may plant the heavens, and lay the foundations of the earth, and say unto Zion, Thou art my people.'

"Lamentations 4...'under his *shadow* we shall live among the heathen.'

"Lastly today, we look in Hosea...my favorite...Hosea 14 ...'They that dwell under his *shadow* shall return; they shall revive as the corn, and grow as the vine: the scent thereof shall be as the wine of Lebanon.'

"You know, I think of that airplane and the shadow and how the two came together and joined in the end, bringing me to safety. Believers...today God Almighty is in Heaven, and we traverse this earth in His shadow, one day we too will make our final exit. And the protection of His shadow will unite us with Him...bringing us to glory."

Jon Junior drove back to Lynchburg alone, silently. A peace flooded over him. He smiled...*God's protective shadow.*

CHAPTER NINETEEN

AN ICY FROST covered the window panes, and the small house was cold as embers smoldered in the wood stove. But under the heavy quilts, Addie Jane and Barclay were content, warm and cozy as their bodies drew heat from each other. It was Saturday morning, the second week into a frigid December. Her head rested upon his bare chest, feeling it heave up and down. His strong arms surrounded her, the weight of them almost too heavy.

"I believe there's going to be another little Branham in about nine months," he said matter of factly.

"What do you mean?"

"Just what I said," he teased.

"How do you know?"

"Wait and see."

She looked up at him. "Oh, Barclay, I hope so!"

"What will we call him?"

"Him?" She giggled.

"Of course."

"How about Gray...spelled G-r-a-e."

"All right by me. But if it's a girl, I'll name her."

"Name her what?"

"Rose...like in your song," he answered softly while stroking her thick, tousled hair.

"Violets are in the song, too, and they're your favorite, you know."

"True, but for a little girl, I like the name Rose."

Christmas Eve on Oak Mountain fulfilled Addie Jane's dream. It was snowing! Large, white flakes floated downward from the greyish white sky, very slowly they descended as if to say, it's Christmas and we're here to celebrate. They fell gracefully, dancing through the cold pristine air, lighting gently on frozen pine boughs and bare skeletal oaks, poplars and maples. They slowly covered leathery green rhododendron leaves now hard and curled for winter. They covered the thick tangled underbrush beneath the tall forest trees, magnifying its maze of haphazard design. And if by chance they happened to miss all of them, they came to rest on the frozen sleeping earth, dusting it like confectionery sugar atop gingerbread. The feathery flakes continued, increasing in number, the mountainside was soon a solid brilliant white. Barclay and Addie Jane were spending the night with Poky.

"We might just get snowbound here," Barclay teased as he looked out the kitchen window at the falling snow.

"You know I'd like that," Poky responded. "We can jest have ourselves a fine Christmas. Don't reckon nobody'll be needin' me anyhow."

Barclay added, "Don't figure anybody will be coming out on an evening like this unless it's a real emergency."

"You're right about that. An' nobody's in th'family way right now."

"Well, I don't know about that now." Barclay grinned and Addie Jane giggled. Poky looked around at the two of them.

"What you two tryin' t'say?" she questioned, full of anticipation.

"Addie Jane's gonna have a baby!" Barclay blurted out while grabbing Poky and whisking her up into the air.

"Put me down, young man!" she laughed aloud. "You'll go breakin' your back."

He sat her down gently in the chair facing Addie Jane, who was smiling happily. Struggling to regain her composure, Poky straightened the combs in her long pinned up braids. "Well?" She examined Addie Jane's face. "Just what do you have t'say 'bout all this?" The posed question was her way of finding out exactly how Addie Jane felt about being in the family way.

Her face lit up. "We're not exactly sure yet, Poky. But Barclay's determined it's true."

"And if it is?"

"I've never been so happy! Can you believe it? We might be having a baby!"

"Yes, child, I can believe it. It's th'most natural thing on God's earth. Well, I reckon this calls for a celebration, an' bein' that it's Christmas an' all, we ought'a have us a real nice celebration. Think I'll fix you two a fine dinner, potatoes an' onions t'start with an' biscuits...now lemme see, where's my flour?"

Addie Jane jumped up. "I'll get it, Poky, and what about that ham Barclay brought you the other day?"

"Well, I was savin' it for tomorrow, but we'll bake it now! An' I'll fix some'uv them apples we put up, too." She was already digging into the cupboards, placing various things on the table.

"M-m-m-m and we need a special dessert. What do you think about a chocolate meringue pie?" Barclay suggested with a grin.

"Reckon we can do that, too, Mr. Branham...soon t'be papa." She laughed. "We got th'fixin's."

As they sat around the table feasting on the meal later, Poky spoke up, "Now children, I've been thinkin' 'bout somethin' for some time, an' I've decided t'do it now. I wanna give you a piece'uv land down yonder by th'spring...t'build yourselves a nice lil' house...."

"Now, Poky, we can't...."

"Hear me out, son. Gotta respect your elders, ya' know. I say I wanna do this. Don't try an' change my mind. It's made up. An' you can get plenty'uv timber off th'place t'build you a nice lil' house. Now that you got a family comin' an' all, you gonna need somewhere t'put down your roots, ya' know...."

"Poky, you know my roots are already here on the mountain, but I don't want to take...."

"You ain't takin', Barclay. It's a gift from me t'you an' Addie Jane. You know you're both like my own young'uns...an' I'm bein' kind'uv selfish, too. I'd like t'have ya' close by me...an' I'd sho like t'see that little'un grow up."

"Well, I don't know...."

"Well, I do...an' if it makes ya' feel any better, you can pay me a lil' here an' there...."

"That's more like it. I'll pay you for the land, Poky, a little at a time."

"All right then, it's a deal. Soon's th'weather breaks in th'spring we'll start cuttin' th'timber an' clearin' th'land an' sech."

Excitedly, they talked on about the plans for the house and the new baby. The snows continued to blanket Oak Mountain, creating a soft quietness outside as smoke rose up from Poky's chimney and then curled downward. After supper, the sweet aromas of ham, fried apples, potatoes and biscuits still permeated the cabin, and sounds of blended voices and an old guitar could be heard from within, where a fire flickered in the small fireplace, casting shadows on the rough log walls.

"Sure am glad you taught Addie Jane how to play, Poky. Makes for a real relaxing evening."

"Could've taught you, too, if you would've listened t'me. Ya' know, back when I was a girl, it won't proper for a young lady t'play a stringed instrument. But I learned anyhows. Guess that was th'onliest thing I got from my ol' pa who skipped out on us."

The night was late. The voices chimed in together...*Silent night...Holy night...all is calm*...and the snow continued to fall.

January 1961 quickly followed that joyous Christmas, bringing more snows to the cold Blue Ridge. February ensued with freezing temperatures hovering not much above zero. And March's blustery winds didn't give much relief to the mountain folk either, as howling sounds lulled them to sleep on cold nights, their hot stoves banked, with hopes the fires wouldn't go out. Not a wonder then that April brought smiles galore as ice began to melt beneath warm sun rays, and tiny, budding shoots sprang forth from a thawing earth. It was spring! Once again, dogwoods graced the dark Blue Ridge, creating their intricate pattern of lacework that only God could envision. Lovely redbuds accompanied them as always, and the Virginia mountains came to life once more.

Barclay's expression was intense as he sat alone on a Sunday evening, the forest encircling him, embracing him, reaching out to him. It was at such times he truly felt a part of the forest, a part of the mountain, a part of God's creation, and he struggled to convey this on canvas. Since he and Addie Jane had married, his desire to paint, to create, had increased significantly. Most likely, he figured, because he was at peace, and had found true happiness and contentment with his sweet wife, more than he'd ever hoped. Their spirits had united and bonded as glue. He thought of that verse the preacher had read at their wedding... *'For this cause shall a man leave his father and mother, and shall be joined unto his wife, and they two shall be one flesh.'* Truly, this was the case, and he felt all warm inside just thinking about it...one flesh.

A tiny chipmunk pounced from a fallen, rotting limb and scampered off. He smiled. Already he'd painted the redbuds, the dogwoods and the violets, the beautiful fragile violets. But today, he was on a mission, focused on his goal. What he hoped to capture was much more challenging. It was Oak Mountain's shadow. Briefly, it would cover the heavily forested mountain, its inhabitants, humans and creatures alike, as it threw a dark blanket over the valley that rested at its foot. When this occurred, Barclay must act quickly in order to capture the effect. He waited. It was almost time. The glowing sun was sliding gracefully down the evening sky. There it was! His brush moved swiftly and skillfully over the raw canvas as his trained eyes danced between the canvas and the shadow.

"What time do ya' s'pose Barclay will get here?" Poky asked as she stirred the steaming pot of pinto beans, vigorously shaking in more salt and pepper. There was a spray of black and white all around the pot, as well.

"Soon, I hope. You know, he sometimes loses all sense of time when he's painting."

"Tells me he's gonna sell'em, an' folks might pay as much as fifty dollars for jest one of'em."

Addie Jane nodded. "There's this art sale coming up in June over in Lynchburg, and he's gonna put some there to sell. I hate to see him sell any, but we can sure use the money on the house."

"Well'sa, we'll be ready t'start soon now that th'land's 'bout cleared."

"Thanks to you, too. But, you shouldn't be doing all that strenuous work at your age, you know." Addie Jane never looked up, but kept on stitching the tiny white dress.

"I beg ya' pardon, young lady...but I ain't *that* old!"

She laughed. "You know what I mean. Leave the work to us."

"...an' I s'pose you gonna do it! Better for me than you...bein' in th'family way an' all. Don't ya' go havin' no miscarriage."

"The baby's fine. Not due until the end of July, and I feel just great. A little work never hurt anybody in my condition."

"Keep that in mind...a little work. How ya' comin' 'long on that dress?" She leaned over Addie Jane's shoulder. "My, it looks real purty like!"

Addie Jane held up the little dress all finished except for the sleeves yet to be stitched in. "It is, isn't it?"

" 'Course, don't know how Barclay, Jr.'s gonna fit in it!"

"It's gonna be a girl, I told you, Poky. I can just feel it."

"Who ever heard'uv sech...feel it. Th'only thing you should be feelin' is that baby kickin'."

"Oh, I feel it kicking all right, especially at night. It decides to really carry on just when I lie down to sleep."

Poky chuckled. "Always th'way."

It was a good spring for building, not too much rain, and warm, balmy days with just enough breeze to cool off a sweaty brow. The foundation was dug, the frame went up and by the middle of June, the house was under roof with a living room, kitchen, two small bedrooms and a tiny room set aside for a bathroom just as soon as Barclay could scrape together enough money for a septic tank. Addie Jane was ecstatic, her own house, brand new. She was handing Barclay nails to nail down the flooring one Saturday when Poky popped in with a basket of dinner, fried chicken, potato salad and hot biscuits.

"That'll hit the spot!" Barclay laid down his hammer, and stretched his arms.

"Thought you young'uns might need a lil' dinner. This place is sho shapin' up. Gonna be a fine house." She looked all around her and back at Barclay, who was already digging in the basket. They sat down on the floor, and Poky said grace. As soon as they lifted their heads, Barclay grabbed a chicken leg. "Nobody fries chicken like you, Poky."

"Brought ya' some lemonade t'wash it down with." She pulled out a frosty milk jug of cold lemonade and poured it in three small jelly glasses, and then sat back to drink hers. "Ought t'put some shelves in that pantry for ya' cannin', Addie Jane."

"No, ma'am!" Barclay spoke up with a mouth full of chicken. "That's gonna be our bathroom."

"Oh, that's right. I plum' forgot."

"And when I get ours done, I'm gonna fix you one, too."

"An indoor john...now why on earth after all these years do I need sech? Spend your money on somethin' else for th'two'uv you...on th'baby...."

"Nope. I've made up my mind. If we have one, so will you. And, you're gonna love it once I finish it, too."

"Maybe so. Would be nice in th'cold an' th'snow not t'have t'go outside t'carry out th'pot. You kids gonna spoil your Poky."

Reluctantly, Addie Jane spoke up, "Poky, you know

everyone's...well just about everyone is going to the hospital to have their babies nowadays. Of course, I know you've got more experience than most of the doctors...but...well...Barclay and I've decided to have our baby in the hospital...over in Lynchburg...."

Poky looked up, surprised, and then her face registered hurt.

"It's not that we don't trust you. Of course, we do...but we talked it over and decided the hospital's safer...in case of any emergency or anything, you know. They've got all kinds of new equipment and things in case of any problems. And I know, most likely there won't be any problem, at least we certainly hope not, but just in case, we'd like to be on the safe side and, you know, be prepared." She ran out of words.

"I see," Poky responded.

"Addie Jane's right about all that new fangled equipment, Poky. Why, I saw some of it myself just the other day."

"I reckon you're right. Y'all ready for some cobbler?" It was obvious she wished to change the subject and set about spooning out the peach cobbler in three small saucers.

"But Poky, I want you there...of course...when the time comes...Barclay and you." She sought her eyes as she received her cobbler, but Poky kept them cast downward.

"You know I'll be there, child. Now, eat your cobbler." She quietly cleaned up the mess.

That night as Addie Jane snuggled up to Barclay, enjoying the cool night air coming through the open window in the bedroom, she whispered, "I think we hurt her feelings."

"I know." He stroked her thick hair.

"What can we do? I don't want to run the risk of having our baby here at Poky's or in our new home. I want to have it in a hospital!"

"And we will, honey, we will. Poky will be okay. She'll get over it. You know Poky's strong. She always bounces back."

"But she's been so good to us...the land...letting us stay here so we can work on the house more...all she's done for both of us all our lives...."

"I know, but Poky knows times are changing. She might be old fashioned, but she's nobody's fool. She knows."

"That doesn't mean she agrees with it."

"No, but she's too smart to stand in its way."

"Barclay, feel it...it's kicking again....kicking up a storm!"

She placed his hand gently on her bare stomach, and he felt the quick sudden thrusts from within. "Strong little feller."

"You really do want a boy, don't you? Then I hope it's a boy for you."

He kissed her soft lips. "I'm just kidding. I'll be happy either way, but I don't know how I'll withstand the charms of two sweet little gals."

It was nearing the end of June, a hot sticky Saturday, and the Sheetrock was almost up. Barclay was finishing it off with the help of his brother, Jack Jacob, who was in from Maryland for awhile. They had all the windows open, hoping for a mountain breeze, but the air was still and sultry.

Jack Jacob wiped his forehead with his sleeve. "Looks like you're the only one of us that's stayed here in the mountains...guess you'll never leave now that you've got this house and a wife and a baby on the way."

"Why should I?"

"Didn't say you should. Just talkin', that's all. 'Course I'm glad enough to be away from the place. Too many bad memories...and don't look like much has changed either. I saw the way folks looked at me when I stopped by the gas station on the way in...same ol' way. You don't get this?"

"Sometimes. Don't pay much attention to it. Too busy."

"H-m-m-p-h. Gets my dander up. Best I'm not here. But you always did love the mountains even when you was a kid."

Barclay nodded with a smile.

"But you know, I kind of envy you in a way. You seem so happy and all. You and Addie Jane have a good thing. Now that I'm divorced for the second time, don't know if I have the nerve to try it again, but it's right lonely this way sometimes."

"I reckon so, but you have pa with you."

"Ain't the same."

"You say he's feeling poorly."

"Yep. Real senile, too. Don't make a whole lot of sense most of the time. You better come on up and visit him soon."

"Planning on it after the baby's born."

Addie Jane and Poky were canning the last of the tomatoes. Thus Poky's kitchen was extremely hot, and Addie Jane constantly wiped her brow. It was then the first pain hit!

"Poky!"

Recognizing the alarm in her voice, she rushed to her side. "It's it, ain't it? We'll time th'pains, an' I'll go get Barclay." She struck off out the door.

"But Poky!" she called after with fear. "It's not time yet. It's too early!"

"If th'baby's comin', then it's time." She hustled down the hillside to the unfinished house in the distance.

Barclay excitedly dropped his hammer, more afraid than Addie Jane. Hurriedly, they packed a few things while Poky timed the pains at five minutes apart already. Leaving Jack Jacob standing in the driveway, soon the truck was bouncing down the mountainside, Barclay nervously driving, and Addie Jane seated in the middle between him and Poky.

"Everything's gonna be fine. Don't you worry none. I've birthed many a fine, healthy baby that's come earlier than this." No one responded. The trip to Lynchburg seemed to take forever. Barclay was quiet, concentrating on getting them there quickly as possible, while trying to block out his nagging fears for Addie Jane and the baby. Addie Jane's pains were increasing, along with her panic. She groaned openly now. Poky kept talking, trying to divert their anxieties. The truck sped down the mountainside, careening around curves on its way to Lynchburg.

"Better slow down, son...if we gonna get there a'tall."

They were almost there. The truck picked up speed descending Amherst hill toward the James River, passed quickly over Williams Viaduct and turned right onto Cabell Street. Addie Jane was crying loudly now, stretched out in the seat, her feet pushing hard against the floorboard. Poky was rattling on about the beautiful houses they were passing on Rivermont Avenue, and how her best friend, Hallie, lived in one of them, but she didn't know which one. The Virginia Baptist Hospital came into sight, and then the series of events rolled off like clockwork with the trained hospital staff taking over. Addie Jane was wheeled into a labor room immediately. Barclay followed but was asked to wait outside in the fathers' waiting room. He began pacing the newly waxed floor with Poky right beside him. A plain white clock faced them on the otherwise bare wall, across from the couch. Its large hands moved ever so slowly as they both anxiously watched. Thirty minutes...an hour...two hours....

"I thought the baby was coming! Why's it taking so long?" Barclay demanded, twisting his hands.

"Now Barclay, you done gone enough with me t'know birthin' takes its own time." She sat down on the uncomfortable couch. Her feet hurt, her head hurt, and she was more afraid than Barclay. After all, she'd witnessed too many close calls over the years. No matter what folks say, birthin' brought womenfolk to th'doors'uv death itself. She thought of her own dear mother.

What was going on in the delivery room behind those closed doors was going to be a nightmare for them all. Addie Jane was out from the anesthesia, and that was a blessing. The doctor and nurses struggled to bring the infant into the world, but there was a problem.

"Forceps again, Nurse Adamson!"

The tall, thin nurse quickly obeyed, and watched him try again to reach the baby. Finally the doctor pulled the lifeless little body out, a bluish purple, badly bruised from the forceps. He shook his head sadly as they went about the motions of trying to revive it. But the baby was dead. Addie Jane slept on, unaware that her tiny daughter, now separated from her womb, was also separated from her life.

Doctor Williams finished the routine procedures, removed his surgical gloves, washed his hands vigorously and went out to the fathers' waiting room. Barclay jumped to his feet, Poky beside him. The doctor hesitated and during that brief moment, revealed his dreaded news.

"Addie Jane! Doctor, is she...." Barclay burst forth.

"Yes, yes, the mother is fine...doing fine...but I'm sorry to report your daughter...was stillborn."

Barclay slumped to the couch with his head in his hands. Poky looked frantically from him to the doctor, obviously confused. "Stillborn!" She directed her words straight to the doctor, "But ya' have all this!" She lifted her hands into the air as if to encompass the vastness of the hospital. "...an' all that new fangled equipment...an' *you couldn't* birth'er alive?"

"Ma'am, I'm sorry...so sorry...we did all we could."

"Is Addie Jane awake?"

"No, ma'am. She'll be coming around in the next hour or so. There's a nurse with her now. It would be best if her husband would be there when she awakens. Are you her mother?"

"Her mother?" She started to shake her head no, but heard herself saying, "You might say so. I'll be there, too."

The doctor left with a promise to return shortly. Poky sat down beside Barclay, who was quietly suffering.

"You all right, son?" She put her arm around his broad shoulders.

"I'll be all right," he nodded, "...but why, Poky, why?" He looked up, his face twisted with pain. "I know we're not supposed to ask why...but I can't help it...why *our* little baby? We wanted her so badly...."

Poky patted his back gently. "I know, son, I know. It's all right t'feel that'a way. It's sho hard medicine t'swallow...all I can say is God don't make no mistakes. We can't always understan'. We jest gotta believe God don't make no mistakes. Th'scripture says... *'Trust in th'Lord with all thine heart an' lean not unto thine own understandin'*...that's all we can do, son."

"I know, Poky...but what about Addie Jane? How in the world is she gonna...."

"She'll cope. Addie Jane's strong. After th'shock, she'll get along."

It wasn't quite an hour before the anesthesia began to wear off. The nurse had just stepped out momentarily when Addie Jane's eyes opened to a blurred room. The ceiling finally focused and came into view dimly, then the plain grey walls. She squinted and blinked repeatedly, trying to clear the picture from its vague hazy film. She looked down at her stomach and rubbed it gently. Had she already had the baby? She wasn't really sure! It must be over, she thought. Noticing the plastic hospital bracelet on her arm, she struggled to read it to see what she'd had...a boy or girl! But the hazy film, still clouding her eyes, prevented her from deciphering it. *"I hope it's a girl,"* she whispered to the empty room. The door opened and in walked the nurse, followed by the doctor, Barclay and Poky.

Barclay wrapped her in his arms as the doctor proceeded to gently break the news. There was a stunned silence, and then a very weak voice whimpered, "My baby...our baby...."

"Honey...." Barclay tried to speak but couldn't.

Poky stood in the corner, visibly shaken to see the two she loved most grieving so.

"Was it a....?" She looked up at Barclay.

"A girl...a little girl...." Tears streamed down his face. But Addie Jane did not cry.

"*Rose,*" she whispered.

Barclay looked at her tenderly, and nodded.

The next day, Poky flipped through the phone book and

found Hallie's number. She dialed her and told her the news. Hallie, of course, was very saddened, but delighted to know her old friend, Poky, was just down the street from her. Within an hour, she'd walked to the hospital and met Poky in the foyer. They embraced, so glad to see one another.

"I just can't believe you're really here, Poky!"

"You know I don't leave Oak Mountain less it's somethin' powerful important...an' 'uv course, my Addie Jane's baby...." She wiped her eyes.

"I'm so sorry, so sorry for her, Poky." She reached into a little pink bag she was carrying. "I brought Addie Jane a gift."

"Come on up, an' I'll introduce you t'my children." She led the way to the elevator. But when they reached the room, the door was shut. Poky quietly pushed it ajar and found Addie Jane sleeping.

"Th'poor child's sound asleep, plum' wore out."

"Please, let's not wake her. I'll come back another time."

"Don't know where Barclay is, probably out walkin' somewheres."

The two old friends decided to do the same and catch up on all the happenings of each other's lives. The temperature had dropped a little, creating a comfortable summer day, accompanied by a mild breeze that caused the deep green leaves overhead to quiver ever so slightly. It was a day made for walking, and walking they did.

"Do you feel up to walking all the way to my house, Poky? And you think it'd be okay for you to leave for that long?"

"'Spect walkin' will do me a sight good, an' I'm sure th'children won't even miss me."

"Well, we'll do just that. I'll show you my new house. Of course, it isn't new anymore, but I still call it my new house. My, my, the last time you were here with me, we were downtown in the old house...seems so long ago."

"'Twas long ago."

"You're right. Time certainly doesn't stand still. Seems only yesterday Barclay was just a little boy, and now he's married with a young wife. I'm sure he's a fine young man, and I know you're really proud of him."

"Won't find no better."

"I'm so sorry for him and Addie Jane. I hope they'll be okay, you know, get over it and look to the future. They're young, and they can have more babies."

"I ain't so worried 'bout Barclay. He has a way'uv lookin' at things th'right way, don't get bitter. Oh, he used to." She chuckled. "He sho used to. But Barclay's handling things a lot better these days...a lot better. It's Addie Jane I'm troubled 'bout. Now that young lady's so stubborn an' independent, an' she has a coldness 'bout her, a hardness, Hallie. Oh, I can't hold it against her none. Th'poor child just learned it all them years she was growin' up. Had t'get hard an' tough t'survive, I s'pose. Ya' see, her mama was sick-like, her nerves it was. She couldn't help it, but it was mighty hard on Addie Jane. She used'ta come up t'my place an' tell me 'bout it. I felt so sorry for'er, but it won't nothin' I could do."

"That's sad. What happened, I mean to her mother?"

"Oh, Mrs. Taylor got better, she did. Had them 'lectric shock treatments. Did th'trick, they say."

"Really. I knew a lady up on Clay Street that had to have shock treatments, but they didn't do her a bit of good. How come her mother's not here now?"

"Mrs. Taylor's nerve problems got better, but then she commenced t'havin' a lot'uv migraine headaches. She don't hardly go out'uv th'house now."

"What a shame. But Addie Jane has you."

"Addie Jane's like my own...she an' Barclay. What 'bout yours?"

"Goodness, they're all fine, Poky, just fine."

"What 'bout this'ere new grandson'uv yours...Jordan...is it?"

Hallie's face lit up. "Jordan Lawrence McKenzie. But you know, Poky, he's changing his name to Frederick. Can you believe it? Said he'll be called Jordan Lawrence McKenzie Frederick. He'd keep McKenzie out of respect for his mother and grandmother, of course."

"Boy, that'll be a mouthful. I know you're mighty proud t'have a preacher in th'family!"

"I am, Poky. I certainly am, but I never dreamed I'd get one this way."

"Life's full'uv surprises, ain't it?"

They approached the nice two-story house of Hallie's. "Well, there it is, Poky." She nodded in its direction.

"My...my...Miss Hallie...ain't you done gone an' fancied yourself up with such a fine lookin' house."

"Well, it's because of Jon Junior, of course. But we really love it. I especially love those big maples all around it and the yard...a real yard to plant flowers and tend to."

"I understan', Miss Hallie. I used t'feel real sorry for you when you lived downtown in that old house, didn't have no yard a'tall. An' comin' from th'country, I plum' nelly got claustrophobia when I'd visit you."

Hallie laughed. "Poky, it's so good to see you again. Somehow, you always lift my spirits."

"Your spirits ain't down, are they?"

"No. But if they were, you'd certainly lift them up as you always have. You said Barclay and Addie Jane are building a new house down from yours?"

"A fine lil' house. Almost finished, too. Gonna have a indoor toilet later on when Barclay gets th'money. Shucks, Miss Hallie, he says he's gonna put one in my house, too." She chuckled.

"That's wonderful, Poky. You talking about feeling sorry for me without a yard. Why, it's always bothered me about you living way up there in the mountains without any conveniences."

"I've been happy, Hallie. I love my place."

"Come on in." Hallie led Poky through the house on a tour, and Poky marveled at all the nice furnishings.

"Lotta pretty things, Miss Hallie."

"You know, Poky, I guess I'm trying to copy what my home used to look like back when I was a child. Mama had everything so nice. Of course, after everything was lost practically, I used to take pleasure in remembering. Guess I'm trying to make my memory come alive now."

"Well, it's real nice, Miss Hallie."

"Thank you, Poky. Would you like some iced tea or lemonade?"

"Lemonade sounds good."

"I'll pour us a glass, and we'll sit out on the front porch for a little while. How about that?"

"Sounds mighty nice. An' how's Lauralee? You say she's busy with'er family an' all?"

"Oh yes. Her oldest, William, turned a teenager this year. Can you believe it? Frankie, her little girl, is taking swimming lessons at the YMCA and dancing lessons at Carole Riggs, and I don't know what all else. Kids are too busy these days."

"Lauralee happy?"

"Oh yes, she's happy enough."

"Well, that's what matters. They goin' t'church?"

"Every Sunday like clockwork. Lauralee teaches Sunday school, and she's doing a good job with raising those children. I'm very proud of her." She led the way back out to the porch. "Sit there in the swing, Poky. I know you'll like it."

"Always did like t'swing." She eased down in the wooden swing and pushed it way back, causing it to creak and groan as it flew forward with her legs sticking straight out. She sipped the cold lemonade. "This is sho nice, Hallie. I'm havin' sech a gran' time I almost forgot 'bout my poor children."

"I know. I'll walk back with you directly."

"Oh, but I'm s'glad I got t'visit with ya'. Things are changin' so fast an' time's jest a'flyin', ya' know. Everything's new, ain't like it used t'be. Even got a new young president...hard t'believe he's old enough t'lead this'ere big country."

"I know, but seems everybody's right happy with him. Did you hear his inaugural speech?"

"Sho did...*'ask not what your country can do for you — ask what you can do for your country....'*" Poky mimicked.

Hallie smiled. "Makes a lot of sense."

"Sho does. Folks need'ta think more 'bout givin' than gettin'."

"Especially the young ones."

"Yes, ma'am. Mr. Kennedy said 'a new generation'uv Americans has taken over.' Calls it a new frontier. Don't know 'bout all that."

"And now with this meeting with Khrushchev, I hope things'll be better. Their discussions on nuclear weapons bothers me, though."

"Don't bother me none, Miss Hallie. I don't know what th'future holds...but I know *who* holds th'future."

"You're right, of course."

"Well'sa, I do get a kick out'uv all th'hullabaloo they make out'uv th'president's wife though. Kind'uv fun t'keep up with it, an' all them pretty clothes she wears, an' them funny lil' hats."

Hallie laughed. "Pillbox hats, they're called. Lauralee's bought her one already. Seems everybody wants one."

"The first lady's got one t'match every one'uv them pretty suits."

"I think so."

" 'Course I don't care for them communists, but I saw Mr. Khrushchev's wife on th'television when she an' Mrs. Kennedy got together over there in Austria. An' I tell you what's a fact, I took t'her way'uv dressin' more, just plain like, no puttin' on airs, ya' know."

"I saw that, too. She just looked like somebody's grandmother, with her hair pulled back in that bun without a hat or anything. Well, I guess I have mixed feelings about Jacqueline's style. I don't agree with all the money she spends on clothes, but I do take pride in seeing how nice she looks when she goes about representing our country."

"You ain't th'only one, Miss Hallie. Papers said all them folk over there in Austria were just'a callin' *Jack-eee, Jack-eee, Jack-eee.* Seems she was a big hit with'em."

"Personally, my favorite is little Caroline. Now, there's a little doll, quite photogenic."

Poky nodded. "I'm thinkin' th'same thing. Well, Hallie, I reckon I best be gettin' on back."

"Before we go though, I'd like to show you my garden."

"Flower garden? I see ya' got all kinds'uv pretty flowers."

"Thank you. But, no, a vegetable garden. Not like yours, of course." She stood up. "Come around to the back, and I'll show you." Poky followed her around to the half shaded, half sunny back yard. In the sunny spot was a small, neatly kept garden, bordered on one side by a row of sun flowers about halfway up.

"Those are my English peas, and my strawberry patch is on the far end. I have tomatoes and cucumbers and even a few squash. What do you think?"

"You're becomin' a reg'lar gardener, I might say. Ought t'get into herbs next. I'll teach ya'."

"Oh, I don't know about that." She laughed.

Rose Marie Branham was buried in the small churchyard of the new Baptist Church at the foot of Oak Mountain, a space given them by the church. It was a relatively small funeral. The tiny casket was all but covered with the colorful assortment of roses, carnations, mums and baby's breath. Addie Jane and Barclay clung to each other, drawing strength as the preacher concluded his brief sermon... *"'The Lord gave, and the Lord has taken away; Blessed be the name of the Lord.'"* Job 1:21. Poky nodded in agreement, and then looked up quickly at Addie Jane and Barclay standing still and solemn. Everyone else had begun to gradually move away from the grave, fanning themselves with papers and such. The day was still and muggy, the temperature steadily rising since daybreak, and now it peaked at ninety-three degrees. It was even hot in the shade where the crowd unconsciously shifted. Still Addie Jane and Barclay stood over the small grave clinging to each other. Poky waited, and wiped the tears from her face.

CHAPTER TWENTY

A WEEK AFTER the funeral, Addie Jane moved about silently, a hardened image. Barclay was worried about her and sought Poky's advice.

"Folks grieve in their own way. Let'er grieve, Barclay. She'll come 'round sooner or later."

"I know. It just bothers me. I feel a bitterness in her, especially after we got the birth certificate."

Poky looked up at him. "You mean...."

"Yes...she's listed as...Negro."

Poky shook her head angrily. "Ain't nothin' wrong with bein' Negro, you know that. My sweet mama, Sister Jane, was...but ain't nobody got th'right to mess with somebody's rightful birth. Lil' Rose was part Indian an' part white, for sho. Anybody could see that!"

"Anybody but the ones making up those birth certificates, it seems." He smoothed the apple butter on the large hoecake she'd set before him. "It's got to change one day, Poky, it's got to!"

"I'm sure it will, son." But she couldn't help but remember his dear mother feeling the same way when he was born, and things still hadn't changed.

"But I can't think about that now. I've got to take care of Addie Jane."

"That's right, son, but give'er time. I'll talk to'er soon. Don't you worry none. You get back t'finishin' that house. Once she moves into that pretty lil' place, she's bound t'perk up."

"Guess you're right." He smiled at her.

It was clouding up to rain when Poky walked down to the new house a couple of weeks later. Barclay was down on his knees stirring paint in the living room.

She patted him on his head. "See ya' fixin' t'paint."

He nodded, and she passed on by and went into the kitchen where Addie Jane was cleaning the newly installed windows. "My, my, don't they look nice."

"Thank you." Addie Jane didn't look up, but kept right on wiping the clear glass panes. The room was empty and appeared larger as a result. She spanned it quickly, and noticed something in the window over the sink. She moved over to take a look. "What's that?"

Addie Jane glanced up and then at the object. She didn't answer at first, but Poky could see it was a beautiful glass dome with a deep red rose inside. "My, ain't that th'prettiest thing you ever did see!" she exclaimed.

Addie Jane smiled. "It is, isn't it. Look closely, and you'll see tiny drops of dew on it."

Poky leaned over. "Well, bless my bones, you're right. Looks like a real rose."

"Your friend, Mrs. Hallie Frederick, gave it to me."

"She did? So that's what she had in that box."

"I put it there in the window...reminds me of our little Rose. I'm going to keep it there always."

"I think that's a nice thing t'do, Addie Jane."

Suddenly Addie Jane's eyes filled with tears.

"Come here, honey child, let'em fall. They s'posed to, ya' know."

"It's so hard...." she cried, "...to understand."

Poky put her arms around her tiny shoulders. "Child, we don't have t'understan' life...only return to it."

And that's what she did. The beginning of August saw the house completed, and Barclay and Addie Jane took up residence. As if Hallie's gift had been a closure to her pain, or at least the beginning of hope again, she began fixing up the house with renewed interest, sewing curtains, painting old hand-me-down pieces of furniture and constantly working in the yard, determined to have a lovely home.

Fall arrived. The second week of October brought spectacular drama to the mountains, transforming them into an exquisite production about to unfold. Barclay couldn't wait to get going, intense with creative drive, he headed up the mountain, with Addie Jane at his side. While he struggled to paint the vibrant scene, she sat comfortably beneath a large, black oak, and watched him, while sipping a glass of iced tea.

"There's so much beauty here for you to paint."

"That's the challenge."

"What do you mean?"

He looked up at the radiant canopy of color above them. The deciduous woodlands and mountainsides surrounding them were now transformed into a brilliant array of color, illuminated by the piercing autumn sun. The entire mountainside seemed to shimmer, creating a fairyland atmosphere where one could easily escape reality. Addie Jane followed his gaze and soon understood as she took in the deep red maples, the golden hickories, yellow poplars and dark red dogwoods. She watched the large, crisp, yellow poplar leaves float gracefully through the air, brush against their peers still clinging on, and descend ever so gently to join the already leaf carpeted forest floor. She saw where the rich, red vine of Virginia creeper had climbed over large moss covered stones and intertwined itself up and around a brilliant yellow maple. The crisp autumn air added to the pristine beauty, causing one to feel an overwhelming urge to be a part of this magnetic scene, to run, to inhale, to laugh. Suddenly Addie Jane jumped up. "I know what you mean!"

Barclay smiled up at her. "You know, only God could paint this picture! Who am I to try to duplicate it?"

"But Barclay," she argued, "...wouldn't He want you to try...to try to paint something so beautiful for others to enjoy, too. Some people don't get to see this like us."

Suddenly he was struck by *her beauty.* He laid down his brush.

"Now, you'll never get it painted this way," she teased.

He took her in his arms and kissed her gently there in the midst of all God's glory.

"...but maybe there's something even more important...." he whispered.

"...maybe...."

Autumn faded into winter as the last stubborn leaves turned loose. Oak Mountain was left cold and bare with its sharp ridges now exposed. North winds whistled through the skeletal trees as Thanksgiving approached. The Branham household was a happy one, for once again there was hope. Addie Jane was pregnant, conceived, they were sure, on that beautiful autumn day. It was a happy Thanksgiving, a happy winter and an even happier Christmas. Barclay and Addie Jane decided their Christmas gift to Poky would be a visit to Lynchburg to see the Christmas lights, and of course, to see her friend, Hallie, again. Addie Jane wished to personally thank her for the thoughtful gift, as well. Every time the sunlight fell through her kitchen window, the small glass dome lit up, and the dew drops glistened in its warm rays. It had a soothing effect on her.

Needless to say, Poky was beside herself at the thought of seeing her dear friend again. Soon the day arrived. Two weeks before Christmas, the three of them drove to Lynchburg. Barclay and Addie Jane had dinner with Hallie and Jon Junior before leaving Poky for a week's visit. The next morning, Jon Junior drove Hallie and Poky to the First Baptist Church in his brand new Fairlane Ford Sedan.

"Ain't this a fine lookin' automobile, Hallie?"

"Jon Junior's certainly proud of it. First brand new car he ever bought, right Jon Junior?"

"Yes, ma'am. Took me a long time to decide to spend that kind of money."

"Betcha cost a mint."

Jon Junior laughed. "You betcha right."

"Almost two thousand dollars, Poky!" Hallie remarked before she thought. She quickly looked at Jon Junior who was focused on his driving.

Poky drew her booted feet together as if not to soil the floor. No wonder it was so fine an' dandy, she thought to herself. Jon Junior parked the shiny, black automobile on the downhill street across from the church, carefully turning the wheels to the curb. He got out and walked around the car to open the doors for the ladies.

"That's what I like...a gentleman!"

"Why thank you, Miss Poky." Holding onto her elbow, he helped her out. She stood on the sidewalk, looking up at the elegant old church, remembering her last visit. The three of them thoroughly enjoyed the special Christmas service that morning.

Monday was true to the weather forecast, a mild day that hovered around fifty degrees. Hallie and Poky caught the city bus downtown to do some Christmas shopping. They went to Snyder & Berman's and bought a Van Heusen dress shirt for Jordan for four dollars.

"It's expensive, but then Jordan deserves it. He can wear it when he's not wearing his collar," Hallie explained, proudly carrying the package under her arm.

"Is that th'drug store there?" Poky pointed toward the obvious store front with large letters overhead spelling Patterson's.

"Yes, you'll find what you need there, I'm sure."

"I jest need a bottle'uv Black Draught. Th'store back home's been out for a month or so."

"I'm surprised you need that stuff, Poky, with all your herbs and home remedies."

"Jest use it once in awhile when nothin' else helps. Keeps ya' real reg'lar, ya' know."

They entered the drug store. "I need some Little Boy Blue bluing, too. They usually stock it. Hello, Mr. Brown."

"Hello to you, Mrs. Frederick." The rather rotund and balding gentleman peered over his gold rimmed glasses at Poky as she moseyed down the aisle looking for the Black Draught. Dressed all in black herself, including her black army boots and black straw hat pulled down over her forehead, she presented a rather ominous picture. Mr. Brown leaned sideways, his beady eyes following her down the close packed aisle and practically jumped when Hallie addressed him.

"You move the Little Boy Blue bluing, Mr. Brown?"

"No, ma'am, should be right over the Clorox near where you're standing."

"For goodness sakes, there it is staring at me." She laughed.

They stopped in Kresge's after leaving Patterson's and picked up some stationery for Lauralee and some soft, yellow material for Poky to begin making a shawl for the baby.

"Sho would be nice t'eat at that counter where we ate th'last time we were here, Miss Hallie. They made some right fine sandwiches."

"Woolworth's. We're headed there now."

They ate their ham salad sandwiches with chips on the side, and drank the cold fountain sodas. Poky again watched with amusement all the hustle and bustle that went on behind the counter — busy waitresses slapping bread on grills, spewing drinks out of fountains, while scrambling to pass each other in the narrow work area. "These folk make me tired jest watchin'em," she half whispered to Hallie. "I think city folk jest hurry too much, ain't good for ya', ya' know."

"You're probably right, Poky." She looked at her friend in the mirror facing them, and smiled at her. Poky smiled back. Afterwards, they crossed the street with Poky holding onto Hallie's arm, still leery of all the traffic around them. They needed to go to Leggett's, and they would be finished. As they approached the department store in deep conversation, a large metal object came sailing through the air aimed directly at them. Just as they caught sight of it, they were roughly pushed aside. Hallie fell up against a brick building, and Poky found herself straddling a light pole. A young lad had swiftly jumped into the air and stopped the dark object with his baseball glove, although it was too heavy for him to catch. Hallie and Poky attempted to regain their equilibrium and stared in disbelief at the lad holding what appeared to be the obvious assailant meant for them. Hallie quickly began picking up her packages that were strewn all over the sidewalk. Poky pulled herself together, retrieved her straw hat that was spinning around on the sidewalk and noticed something black running over the curb and out onto the street. "My Black Draught!" she exclaimed, and looked sharply at the young lad. "What'd you do that for?"

He proudly held onto the rather large object. "Sorry, ma'am...but this here thing could've walloped you up side your head!"

The fact began to slowly register with Hallie. "I do believe you're right, young man. I guess we owe you a thank you."

He shrugged his thin shoulders. "It's all right, ma'am." He was busy examining his catch.

Poky was still shook up. "What in tarnation is that thing?"

He looked up at the old lady in black that was straightening the most awful looking straw hat he'd ever seen. "It's a spring, ma'am...a big spring."

"I can see that now...but where in th'world did it come from?"

The lad gazed up ahead at the large Santa and reindeer display perched atop the entrance to Leggett's Department Store. The usually moving reindeer were perfectly still.

"You mean...?"

He nodded. "Yes, ma'am. Ain't the first time neither. Mr. Hinks, my school teacher, nelly got knocked over with it last week when it flew off. I hoped I'd get a chance at it...been standing over there off and on for about a week now. Didn't think it'd happen again." The freckled faced, sandy haired lad of about ten smiled, "...but it did."

"What're you going to do with it now?" Hallie posed the obvious question.

"Take it back to the store. They need it for Santa and the reindeer to start back up."

"You're right, of course. Son, you better tell them that they need to fix that thing. It could really hurt somebody!"

"I will, ma'am." With that, he ran off lugging the heavy spring with him. They watched him disappear through the front doors of Leggett's.

"Don't know 'bout this'ere city life, Miss Hallie...."

Hallie laughed. "Can't blame you, Poky."

As they entered Leggett's, they caught a glimpse of a well dressed man patting the lad on his back as he retrieved the wayward spring.

Just before the end of Poky's visit, Jordan drove up from Chesapeake, and Poky was finally able to meet this grandson she'd heard so much about.

"Jordan McKenzie Frederick, ma'am." He extended his hand warmly to Poky while she checked out his appearance from head to toe.

"Glad to meet ya', Rev'rend." She glanced around at a beaming Hallie.

"The pleasure is all mine." Gently shaking Poky's hand, he noticed her unusual appearance.

"I've heard a lot about ya', Rev'rend. My friend, Hallie's, awful glad t'have a preacher for a grandson."

He smiled. "Likewise, I'm quite happy to have your friend, Hallie, as my grandmother."

Poky liked him immediately. "An' well you should, Rev'rend. Won't find a better lady in all'uv Lynchburg, or in Virginia for that matter."

"I'm sure you're right."

After supper, they all sat down in the spacious living room, and naturally, the reverend being present, the topic quickly led to spiritual matters. Jordan marveled at Poky's knowledge of the Bible, uneducated as she was, her simplistic but faithful outlook was rather refreshing. He'd never known any mountain people, certainly no one quite like her. They spent the better part of the evening discussing Biblical doctrine, and Hallie and Jon Junior sat with rapt attention enjoying it all, especially the topic of heaven. As Jordan read scripture referencing heaven, Jon Junior listened intently, and his thoughts turned to Beth.

"'*And I saw no temple therein: for the Lord God Almighty and the Lamb are the temple of it. And the city had no need of the sun, neither of the moon, to shine in it: for the glory of God did lighten it, and the Lamb is the light thereof. And the nations of them which are saved shall walk in the light of it: and the kings of the earth do bring their glory and honor into it. And the gates of it shall not be shut at all by day; for there shall be no night there....*'"

"You know I love th'sun an' th'moon, Rev'rend, but can ya' figure on how nice it's gonna be when th'glory'uv God lights up everything...hard t'imagine, ain't it?"

"You're right, Miss Poky. It's beyond our comprehension, for sure. Listen to this...'*And the building of the wall of it was of jasper: and the city was pure gold, like unto clear glass. And the foundations of the wall of the city were garnished with all manner of precious stones.*' And it says...'*the twelve gates were twelve pearls; every several gate was of one pearl: and the street of the city was pure gold, as it were transparent glass.*' Now that's hard to imagine."

"I've always loved pearls," Hallie interjected.

"I ain't never been too much on jewels an' gold an' sech. Read th'part, Rev'rend, 'bout no more tears an' no more pain. That's th'part I like."

The young minister relaxed in the overstuffed chair and continued to read from the book of Revelation...'*And I heard a great voice out of heaven saying, Behold, the tabernacle of God is with men, and He will dwell with them, and they shall be His people, and God Himself shall be with them, and be their God. And God shall wipe away all tears from their eyes; and there shall be no more death, neither sorrow, nor crying, neither shall there be any more pain: for the former things are passed away. And He that sat upon the throne said, Behold, I make all things new. And He said unto me, Write: for these words are true and faithful. And He said unto me, It is done. I am Alpha and Omega, the beginning and the end....'"*

"Makes chills run up my spine, Rev'rend."

He smiled at her. "I know what you mean, ma'am."

"I didn't know there was so much scripture on heaven," Jon Junior added.

"There's lots more," Jordan responded. "The last verse I'd like to read is...*'And there shall in no wise enter into it any thing that defileth, neither whatsoever worketh abomination, or maketh a lie: but they which are written in the Lamb's book of life.'"*

"Only folks whose names are found in *that* book gonna be there," Poky added.

"That's right, only those who've believed in Him and His finished work on the cross."

"Well, I feel like I've been to church," Hallie sighed.

"Now all we need is a little music," Jon Junior concluded. "Jordan, you should've brought your guitar along."

"Guitar? Rev'rend, you play?"

"Well, Miss Poky, let's say I play at it."

"Poky plays, too," Hallie remarked proudly.

"Is that so?"

Poky blushed. "Been playin' since I was a youngster, Rev'rend. You play in your church?"

"Well, no. I haven't been able to do that yet."

"How come?"

"Somehow, I guess I've always felt that the piano is the proper instrument for church."

"Now Rev'rend, I thought you knew th'scriptures! *'Upon an instrument'uv ten strings'* th'Bible says. If ten strings is all right with th'Lord, why then I figure six ought'a be jest fine. Mind handin' me your Bible, Rev'rend?"

Jordan passed his small black Bible over to her, and she flipped through the pages to the Psalms and handed it back to him. "Would ya' mind readin' Psalm 92, Rev'rend?"

He smiled at her. "Certainly...*'It is a good thing to give thanks unto the Lord, and to sing praises unto thy name, O most High: To shew forth thy loving kindness in the morning, and thy faithfulness every night, Upon an instrument of ten strings, and upon the psaltery; upon the harp with a solemn sound. For thou, Lord, hast made me glad through thy work: I will triumph in the works of thy hands. O Lord, how great are thy works!'*" He looked up at Poky. "You have a point, Miss Poky."

"Reckon ya' might wanna have a little talk with th'Lord 'bout that guitar playin' in church, Rev'rend."

"I reckon you're right, Miss Poky." He grinned.

"An' I'd be mighty proud if you was t'visit Oak Mountain sometime, Rev'rend."

"I'd like that." He turned to Jon Junior. "Maybe sometime in the future." Jon Junior nodded.

1962 ARRIVED AND moved along quickly. March winds blew in and out as if pushing time along with it. Spring created quite a stir, an unusual splendor but swiftly passed into summer. Ironically, Addie Jane's baby was due in July, just as little Rose had been. Therefore, when June came, her anxieties increased. Would she make it this time? This was her first thought in the morning, and she went to bed each night with it weighing heavily on her mind. But soon it was July, firecrackers shot upward, spraying the spacious skies in celebration of the nation's 186th birthday, from the Tidewater lowlands to the Blue Ridge Mountains, across the windswept plains on out to the magnificent Rockies and finally to the wide Pacific. Hallie and Lauralee took William and Frankie to Harvey's Drive-In to enjoy the fireworks, and Frankie squealed with delight, sitting on the hood of the car while William sat discreetly within, hoping none of his friends spotted him. But things on Oak Mountain were still and quiet, seemingly unaware of the nation's birthday. The only sound on the hot, sultry night was that of cicadas creating a solid wall of the shrill but comforting shouts. Addie Jane sat out on their small porch, enjoying the last of the homemade peach ice cream that Poky had made earlier in the day. A slight refreshing mountain breeze cut through the sultriness, gently caressing her soft, wavy locks of hair.

"Only three more weeks," she whispered.

Barclay admired her in the silvery light of the three-quarter moon, always marveling at his extreme good fortune of having won such a lovely wife, and now with the glow of motherhood, she was even more so. He reached out and clasped her hand tightly. "I know."

Further up the mountain, Poky turned off her light. She'd been feeling particularly tired lately and decided to turn in early. She knelt at her bedside and talked to the Lord, thanking him for her blessings and laying her requests before him..."Lord, if you see fit, please give Barclay an' Addie Jane a child that's live an' well, a child that'll be a blessin' to'em." This same prayer she'd prayed for over a year now, ever since little Rose's stillbirth.

God answered her prayers, and on July 27, 1962, a son was born to Barclay and Addie Jane...Grae Barclay Branham...alive and well. There was rejoicing on Oak Mountain for sure. Little Grae, seven pounds, seven ounces and twenty-two inches long, was immediately predicted by Poky to be a tall, handsome man. She proudly showed him off to all interested and to some who weren't. She stated to everyone that if she never birthed another baby, she was happy and content now. Yes, Addie Jane had decided to have Poky bring this baby into the world, and was gloriously happy she did. Barclay was ecstatic, especially as all acknowledged the little fellow looked just like him, with dark hair and dark eyes, that were sure to turn even darker, and smooth olive skin. Addie Jane was happy for this, too. Motherhood came naturally to her, and she basked in its warm cozy feeling. The year following was one of the happiest ever for all of them, watching the miraculous transformation from infancy to toddler, seeing him smile for the first time, watching him reach out for the first time to touch, seeing him crawl and then take his first steps, listening to his first words. It all captivated them, bringing gladness to their hearts. Before they knew it, he was approaching his first birthday, and a big party was planned. Verbal invitations went out to the whole family and close friends. Barclay had bought a portable grill and decided to fix hotdogs and hamburgers, and Poky was making her peach ice cream for dessert. Addie Jane baked a three-layer chocolate birthday cake with a big number one in the middle. The day turned out clear and hot even in the mountains, but the heat didn't hamper the excitement and joy. Both her mother and father arrived, much to her surprise, and all but one of her brothers showed up. The youngest, Christopher, was happily away at camp. Barclay's father came along with two of his brothers, Jack Jacob and Paul David. George Lewis and his family were there, also, having moved back to the area recently. Only Herman Ray and his family did not make the trip. All of the surrounding neighbors attended. Little Grae wallowed in the attention, being passed from one to the other and encouraged to show off his latest accomplishment, that of walking. Paul David limped along behind him, his camera flashing at every antic. Poky grabbed the old guitar and led the crowd in *'Happy Birthday to little Grae.'* The party proved to be a great success for everyone, particularly the Branham family.

"You know, Barclay, we're so blessed," Addie Jane whispered that night as they both looked down upon a very tired and sleeping little boy. He nodded.

Summer ended, and that fall was to be a fall of events that would make indelible impressions upon many for years to come. School began, and for the first time ever, the children of the settlement were allowed to attend public schools. On June 25, 1963, the State Pupil Placement Board, meeting in Richmond, approved twenty-four admissions to public school from the settlement, and a month later, additional applications were approved. This determined the end of the 'mission school.' Excited but fearful, the mission children prepared to go to the big schools, the schools where everyone else went, the schools that held only the unknown for them...and they very well knew they also held the children that up until then had only pointed at them, called them names or harassed them. Therefore, it was with no small amount of trepidation that they faced the first day of school. Barclay was glad little Grae wasn't old enough. His brother, George Lewis, had two to enter, eight year old Jerry and six year old Geraldine. Geraldine, in her childish innocence, was all excited to be going to the *big school,* but Jerry was reluctant. The whole family encouraged him, seeking to erase his fears. Finally the big day came, and the mission children joined the ranks of the mainstream, but the battle was not over. Even the teachers were confused as they were forced to label the children *Negroes* on their permanent record cards, though they looked Indian or white. The prejudice created an invisible but impenetrable wall that immediately rose up between the children from the mission and everyone else. And though they were physically a part of it all, they were more separated than ever. Geraldine came home crying soon after.

"Mama, they called me *Issue* again...why...Mama...why do they call me that?" Her tear stained face caused a knot to form in her mother's stomach, a hard painful knot as she groped for the right answer.

"Geraldine, dear, just don't you worry none about what they say. You know who you are and God knows who you are...and that's all that matters!" She stroked the child's dark, silky hair. Geraldine looked up at her mother and smiled weakly.

"Okay, Mama. I won't...but do I have to go back? Can't we go back to th'mission school?"

Shaking her head, she answered, "No, Geraldine. The mission school is gone now. You must make it in th'big school. You gotta have faith, Geraldine...and th'good Lord will help you."

"Okay, Mama." She turned to walk away but added, "Mama, they've got chocolate milk there in little bottles. I like chocolate milk."

Her mother's face relaxed and the knot eased somewhat. She decided not to tell George Lewis. He would get too angry and might not let the children go to school...and they had to go to school! How else would they ever have a chance?

Several weeks passed. A chilly autumn morning, saturated with a raw drizzle, met Barclay as he left his warm home to drive over early to see his brother, George Lewis. He couldn't wait to tell him the news. Paul David had met a lady, a nice lady, too. He was the only single one left, and due to his disability, they never figured he'd get married, or even get a girlfriend for that matter. Too long he'd wallowed in self pity, but now things were looking up. As Barclay carefully maneuvered the pick-up around the slick, curvy mountain road, he fell in behind a big yellow school bus that was climbing up the mountainside. Unable to pass, he sighed impatiently and resigned himself to follow slowly, stopping twice behind it as it picked up wet children that happily boarded the warm bus. He was almost there when he noticed the bus brake, slow down and then resume its speed, passing a small group of children huddled together in the misty rain. Instantly, Barclay saw they were children from the settlement, including his brother's kids. He braked suddenly and rolled down his window. The two younger children were crying.

"What's the matter?" he hollered.

"Th'bus passed us!" blurted out the eldest.

Angered by the predicament, Barclay struggled to stifle his own emotions that were flooding back. "Well, come on, get in. I'll take you to school." He grabbed the bag of dogfood beside him, slid it under the seat and motioned for them to climb in. All four squeezed in beside him, cold and shivering, Jerry and Geraldine and a boy and girl from up the road.

"This happen before?"

"Happen' last week one time," Jerry answered. Geraldine started crying again.

"Shut up cryin', Geraldine! No use actin' like a baby." Her brother scolded, and she cried harder. Barclay glanced over at the other two, who were sitting quietly staring out the window, but the youngest had tears rolling down her cheeks, too.

Later that evening, he was still fuming inwardly, and Addie Jane put her arms around him as he sat at the table. "What's bothering you, Barclay?"

"I really don't want to talk about it...just makes me madder!"

She moved around in front of him, fully seeing his expression. "Tell me what it is...please."

He looked at her, his eyes dark pools of anger. "Same old stuff, Addie Jane!"

She waited.

"It'll never stop! They'll never treat us right...."

"What happened?"

He pushed his chair back. "This morning, I went over to see George Lewis, you know...."

She nodded, afraid of what she was going to hear.

"...a school bus was in front of me, and it was raining. It stopped twice and picked up some kids waiting on it...."

"And?"

"...then it passed right on by *our* kids...and two of them were Jerry and Geraldine."

"No!"

"I took them to school, of course, and then...."

"And then what?" she asked reluctantly.

"I just paid a visit to the school...looked for that bus driver."

"Did you find him?" she asked quickly.

"No, but I will."

"Barclay, I know how you must feel, but...."

He swung around. "Do you, Addie Jane? Do you? How could you? You've never been called names you wouldn't call your dog! You've never been kicked out of places! You've never felt the pain of feeling you're not good enough! How could you know how I feel?" He spoke loudly and angrily. Little Grae began to cry in the other room. Tears rolled down Addie Jane's face.

"I'm sorry, honey...I'm so sorry." He knelt beside her. "I didn't mean to yell at you. I don't know what got into me."

She looked down at him and smiled through her tears. "It's all right...and it'll be all right one day. Things will be better, Barclay. We have to believe that."

He rose and walked slowly to the window. "I'm going for a walk...to clear my head. I'll be back before supper...." Addie Jane watched him disappear into the thick autumn forest. She was glad. The mountains always renewed his strength...his faith.

Poky knocked on the door. Addie Jane unloaded her concerns for Barclay while feeding Grae. "It helps to have someone to share all this with, Poky. But, I feel so bad for Barclay...."

"I know, dear, I know. An' Barclay's such a sensitive soul. They say all'uv them artist-like people are sensitive...take everything so hard, ya' know. By th'way, did he sell all'uv his pictures?"

Addie Jane nodded to the one lone painting standing upright in the corner. "All but one."

Poky studied the painting. "Barclay explained that one t'me...Th'Shadow...he calls it."

"Guess you gotta be a part of the mountain to understand it, though. Folks over in Lynchburg didn't seem to cotton to it much."

"That's all right, honey. It ought'a be here anyhow, don't ya' think?"

"Guess you're right."

"'Course I'm right...an' I think it's th'prettiest'uv them all anyhows."

Addie Jane smiled. "That's good, Poky, because he mentioned something about giving it to you."

"That a fact. Well, I'd be mighty proud."

Barclay pushed his anger aside, finding it hard to hold bitterness midst all the beauty of autumn on Oak Mountain. He took little Grae for walks, showing him the magic and mysteries of the mountains, and the three of them enjoyed picnics loaded down with Poky's leftovers. One day the little fellow traipsed over crisp, leaf covered paths, following his dad until he was tired and stumbling. Barclay picked him up and perched him atop his broad shoulders. "Now you've got the best seat in the house, son. You can see all around and the beauty of the trees God has given us."

"Twees...." Grae mimicked.

"That's right, son. Trees. You'll some day grow up to love them just like your dad, I hope."

"How could he do anything but?" Addie Jane laughed. "He's part of us...a part of the mountain."

October, nature's month of unequaled beauty, passed into November, stark, drab and cold. Barclay had been working unusually hard, trying to save up money for Christmas, and he was tired. It was Tuesday evening, and he carelessly tossed his coat on the chair as he entered the house.

"Addie Jane, honey, how would you like to go to a movie?"

She turned to him, surprise registering on her face and then a smile spread over it. "You know I would but...."

"No buts. We need a break. Get little Grae ready. We're going to the drive-in. Sounds like a good movie playing...*Spencer's Mountain* with Henry Fonda, and you know I like anything about a mountain!"

She laughed while already pulling things together. It turned out to be a lovely night. Grae fell asleep before the main feature hardly started, and they felt like they were courting again. Romance bloomed there in the cozy, warm truck as the motor ran off and on for warmth, but they really didn't need it after all. They were happy, life was good, Christmas was coming. Little did they know that three days later the world would be shocked and thrust into one of its worst nightmares.

PRESIDENT KENNEDY WAS KILLED!

CHAPTER TWENTY-ONE

ASSASSINATED! AMERICA'S HANDSOME young leader, full of charm and charisma, who'd won the hearts of so many in such a short time, lay in state in the nation's Capitol, now a sorrowing Capitol. The fatal shots, fired from a textbook warehouse overlooking the expressway down which the president's car was heading, had taken the life of husband, father, son and the thirty-fifth president of the Unites States of America. The horror was witnessed by Dallas crowds standing ten to twelve deep along the curbs as the motorcade passed by, but it was felt by millions as the startling news went out over the airwaves. People everywhere ceased what they were doing to listen.

Barclay laid down his pencil and looked away from his graphic design, his forehead a furrow, his eyes filled with sadness. Addie Jane, at home mixing up a meatloaf for supper, heard the same words and sat down in a chair, stunned.

Poky had just come in. "No!" she exclaimed.

"I can't believe it!" Addie Jane felt a queasy feeling in her stomach.

"God have mercy!" Poky paced the floor. "Mama used'ta tell me 'bout President McKinley gettin' shot. I don't recollect it much myself, but she remembered it...an' now...God have mercy! Poor Mr. Kennedy...an' he was Irish, too, jest like Mr. McKinley...both'uv'em."

"He was so young...and has little children...." Addie Jane looked over at Grae sitting on the floor playing with the pots and pans he'd pulled out of the cabinet. "The poor little things now without a father."

"They'll make it...they'll make it if they got a good mama jest like I did...an' you know what? They's Fitzgeralds, too! Their grandma was a Fitzgerald jest like me. I always felt like kin to th'president...me an' him both bein' Fitzgeralds, ya' know."

It was the same reaction throughout the nation as men, women and children heard the dreadful news...the president shot with Mrs. Kennedy right there beside him, cradling his head in her arms, blood and all. Radios and televisions flashed the news of the shooting to the shocked world.

Hallie and Jon Junior watched their new console television, sitting grimly side by side on the couch, shaking their heads.

"Must be a dream, can't be true!"

"Afraid it is, Mother." Jon Junior got up and went to the telephone in the hallway. "Gonna call Jordan." Hallie listened. The two stayed closely in touch, and she was glad. He hung up and returned to the couch, sitting down blankly. "Wasn't home."

"Oh my goodness!"

"What is it, Mother?"

She rose and rushed to the secretary, opened it and began rummaging through a stack of papers.

"What're you looking for, Mother?"

"Will show you in a minute...if I can find it." She kept tossing papers aside, obviously knowing what she was seeking.

"Here it is! Remember...I showed it to you when I cut it out of the paper...right before he was elected." She handed him a newspaper clipping neatly trimmed with pinking shears and folded. He opened it and began to read....

> '*New York (NEA)- If history repeats itself, the man who is elected to the White House this November may well die therein. Ever since 1840, the man chosen to be Chief Executive every 20 years has perished before he*

left the office. So far, according to the grim timetable, death has claimed six of our presidents, three times at the hands of assassins....'

Jon Junior stared at her with a funny expression. "This gives me chills." He read the date. "It was printed three years ago!"

"I know. Just before he was elected. Keep reading."

'The weird every 20-years jinx started with the man elected president in November 1840, William Henry Harrison. He was a strong man physically, renowned as an Indian fighter. Yet within one month after taking office, Harrison was dead of pneumonia. Twenty years passed. In November 1860, the United States elected Abraham Lincoln. In 1865, he became the first of our presidents to be murdered, a tragedy he seemed to have known would befall him the night he went to Ford's Theater. Then in November 1880, James A. Garfield became 'the last of the log cabin presidents.' He was a preacher, teacher and Civil War general. Less than four months after taking office, Garfield was shot at a Washington railroad station and died of his wound. With grim regularity, the curse continued....'

Jon Junior looked up and cleared his throat.

"Keep on," Hallie urged.

'In November 1900, William McKinley was reelected Chief Executive. Six months after his inauguration, he was shot to death by an anarchist named Leon Czolgosz. After another generation, the White House 'curse' loomed on the political horizon. Warren C. Harding was warned by political writers to beware. He laughed off the deaths, calling them coincidences. In November 1920, Harding was elected, and in 1923 he died suddenly while being treated for pneumonia. November 1940 brought the reelection of Franklin D.

Roosevelt. And just 15 years ago, he fulfilled the 'curse' by succumbing to a cerebral hemorrhage.'

"And now this!" Hallie added somberly. They sat in silence.

"Strange...very strange," Jon Junior said quietly.

A page of American and world history had turned abruptly with this dreadful drama, and the world mourned with the First Lady and young Caroline and John Jr. as John Fitzgerald Kennedy's funeral was held with full military honors. The picture of the young widow in black and two small children standing at attention would be indelibly stamped on memories everywhere and printed on pages down through the ages. Virginia reacted the same way as news of the assassination spread throughout its mountains and valleys. Lynchburgers mourned, as well, many recalling his visit to the hill city in 1957 as a United States Senator. They remembered his keen Irish wit, being a descendant on both sides from Irish immigrants of the mid-19th century. On Sunday, several Protestant churches and the Jewish synagogue conducted memorial services in his behalf, and on Monday, November 25, 1963, the city's many churches rang out their bells for fifteen minutes, asking residents to observe a few moments of prayerful silence. The bells ceased at 12:00 with the noon chime of the bells in the Old Courthouse, and just prior to the funeral services at noon in St. Matthews Roman Catholic Cathedral in Washington. The funeral was crowded with world dignitaries, the tiny three year old's salute to his father's casket was recorded for history, the eternal flame was lit and the world went back to what it was doing before. However, as families gathered throughout the land to celebrate Thanksgiving a few days later, a pall hung over the usual festivities.

It was an unusually warm Thanksgiving in Lynchburg, rising to the mid-sixties, but clouds had gathered, and a light rain was falling.

"Doesn't seem like Thanksgiving, ought to be cold," William complained as he paced the floor.

"Can I have some turkey, Grandma?" Frankie stood in the kitchen looking wistfully through the oven window at the big bird roasting to a golden brown, its enticing aroma permeating the whole house.

"Not yet, dear. Not ready yet, and we'll all have to sit down for Thanksgiving dinner together," Hallie responded cheerfully. It was her favorite time of the year. In spite of the recent tragedy, she was determined to make their holiday a happy one. Her whole family would be together, and her adrenaline was pumping as she jumped from one thing to another in the spacious kitchen, making sure it would all come together just right at the exact time. "Lauralee, could you please check the potatoes?"

She happily assisted, feeling the same as her mother. "Do you think this will be enough potatoes, Mother?"

"I think so, dear. Hand me that potholder, please."

"When's Cousin Jordan coming?" William asked, while slouching on the table, rubbing up against the bowl of creamy, yellow cake batter.

"I don't know, William...please get your elbows off the table, and why did you put *those* jeans on? Just look at the knees...they're full of holes!" Lauralee scolded. "What time do you think, Mother?"

"Should be anytime. Said he'd try to get here early as possible. Bringing Sarah, you know."

"His fiancée?" William joked. "Don't see why he's gonna mess up a good thing and go and get married."

"William, that's his decision," his mother explained, "...and the day will come when you, too, will be making such decisions."

"Don't think so...gonna be a bachelor...have a girl in every port. 'Course don't guess Cousin Jordan would want a girl in every port, being a preacher and all. Man, I wouldn't want to be a preacher for nothing."

Hallie looked at him and then at Lauralee before speaking, "And why not, son? That is the highest calling, you know."

"Awe, I know, Grandma...but seems so boring to me."

"He's a teenager, Mother. Everything seems boring to him."

Hallie sighed. "Hope he'll outgrow it. Life's too precious to spend it being bored."

"Can I lick the bowl, Grandma?"

"Sure, Frankie. Here, you can have the big spoon, too. See, I left a fair amount for you." Happily, she sat down with the large, white mixing bowl between her legs and began scraping it clean.

"Jordan's here!" Jon Junior called from the living room.

Finally it was ready, and they all sat down to the feast before them.

"Jordan, would you mind?" Hallie asked.

Jordan waited his usual few seconds of silence before he spoke, "Dear Father in heaven, we come before thee thanking you for this blessed event and all this wonderful food. You're so good to us, and we praise your holy name for it. Thank you for another year of protection and love. And though we come together with heavy hearts with the rest of the nation, we know that you are in control. We cannot understand it all, but we trust your almighty wisdom and goodness. Please be especially close to Mrs. Kennedy and the two precious children, lift them up and strengthen them, warm them with your overpowering love as the sun warms the earth, shower them with thy blessings as you send the rains to a thirsty earth, fill that vacancy with your holy self, and let this be a reminder to all of us that life is only temporal, but everlasting life lies beyond the grave. Lord, please be with *this* family today and the year before us, guide and protect us, and we pray that everything we do and say will be pleasing to you. Thank you, Father, in Jesus name. Amen."

Heads lifted reverently and glanced at Jordan. He smiled back. It was good to have a preacher in the family.

"Pass the salad, please." Hallie handed the large glass bowl of tossed salad to Jon Junior, and the sumptuous meal began.

"Everybody at school's saying we won't have another president like him," William remarked, while helping himself to a large portion of potatoes.

Jordan spoke softly, "A tree is best measured when it is down."

William looked up at his cousin. He said the strangest things.

But Lauralee readily agreed, "That's so true. We often take people for granted until they are gone and then...."

"...and then it's too late," Hallie finished.

There was silence as thoughts turned inward and backwards. Hallie remembered a time when there was another at the table. It had been so many years now. Jon Junior thought of Jamey, too, and then Beth, and he felt a lump in his throat as usual. Jordan was wishing he'd had more time with his mother. Lauralee looked around the table and asked quickly, "So, Cousin Jordan, when's the big date?"

He smiled at Sarah seated across the table beside Frankie. "Well...we think it will be this January."

"January! So soon? Oh my!" Lauralee exclaimed. "Will it be in Chesapeake?"

"Since that is Sarah's home and mine...and my church family, too, yes, it will be in Chesapeake. Of course, we're expecting all of you to be there."

"Of course," they answered in unison.

"Can you get it all together so soon, Sarah?" Lauralee skeptically questioned.

The lovely young lady smiled. Her composure was almost unsettling to Lauralee, who rose and fell with the waves of life. "I think so," she answered calmly.

"Well, if you need any help...."

"Actually, we would very much like Frankie to be our flower girl."

Frankie looked up questioningly. "Do I have to wear one of them big dresses?"

"You'll love it, dear." Lauralee was riding the wave now. "What day in January? My goodness, we'll have to go shopping right away. Mother, maybe we could go to Roanoke and shop. Oh my!"

"It's the end of January," Jordan answered the question left hanging. "The thirtieth actually, and don't worry, you have time. It's not going to be a big affair. We want to keep it simple."

"Simple, huh," Lauralee repeated, "...and your church? What about them?"

"Oh, the congregation's invited, of course. But they're all family to us."

"Aha. I see." Lauralee looked around the table in disbelief.

Hallie chuckled. It was going to be a busy new year.

And it was...locally and nationally. There was much unrest sparked by the heightened racial tension and violence that followed, and the Vietnam War was escalating. On the home front, Jordan's and Sarah's wedding went off like clockwork, much to Lauralee's amazement. Even Frankie enjoyed the occasion, all decked out in a striking white dress trimmed in yellow, with ruffles from head to toe. Exactly two months later, Jordan and Sarah were expectant parents, and by springtime, they knew the little bundle of joy would be two little bundles. The entire Frederick family was elated...twins! The end of school was hastening, and the boys and girls in the Lynchburg schools could hardly contain themselves. Already, the mercury climbed high enough on some days to cause the classrooms to become hot and stuffy. Teachers raised the heavy windows, which only tempted the already anxious boys to gravitate toward them. It was on such a day that Hallie's grandson, William, her first-born, that is with the exception of Jordan, who came on the scene late, found himself dangling from a two story window. His counterpart, Jes Jennings, stood with his back to the window, trying to look studious but whispering..."Jump...stupid...jump!"

But he couldn't *jump*! He was afraid of heights. How in the world did he get himself in such a mess?

Mrs. Karnegy peered over her horn rimmed glasses at Jes while holding a nub of chalk in midair. "Jes Jennings, is there something more interesting outside than in?"

"Oh...no, ma'am!"

"Then I suggest you take a seat with the rest of us." Her tone was not a suggestion, but a definite mandate. Jes glanced over the edge at William still dangling. "Sorry, buddy-roe," he whispered and deserted his post. William glanced to the left and to the right, trying to avoid looking down. "Doggonit!" He spit on the warm, red brick wall facing him. Why did he do such a dumb thing? His fingers were stinging, his arms were aching. He couldn't hold on much longer! Suddenly he felt a presence, and reluctantly looked down. Mr. Overby, the new principal, stood just below him with his short arms crossed over his protruding middle, and a satisfied smirk on his round, pudgy face.

"Well, Mr. William, I would say you've gotten yourself into a rather perilous predicament this time. It appears you have simply two alternatives, either jump or fall...and of the two, I do believe jumping would be less painful."

William agreed. "Oh well," he moaned, letting go of one hand while pushing off with the other and making an almost perfect jump, landing painfully on his hindparts and at the feet of a pleased Mr. Overby.

"Come along, son, to my office." He reached down to help him up, but William pushed himself up off the dusty ground.

Hallie was preparing porkchops for supper when Lauralee arrived. "Hello, dear, have a seat."

Lauralee slumped into the nearest chair. "Got another call from school today."

"What this time?"

"Seems he got caught hanging from a school window...."

"Oh my goodness!"

"Oh, he's okay...for now that is. He won't be once his father hears about it. I don't know what's gotten into that boy lately!"

"Well, dear, he's not a bad boy, just a little mischievous. He'll get over it...all too soon I'm sure."

"Not soon enough."

Hallie dragged the raw porkchops through the bowl of flour. "He reminds me of Jamey...."

"I know, Mother, you've said that before, and I agree. You know, I hate to say this, but it's hard for me to see Jamey's face clearly sometimes."

"It's been a long time, and time has a way of doing that...erasing one's picture or at least clouding its image. But he's in my heart, Lauralee...and his memory is very much alive."

Lauralee reached for the newspaper laying on the table, ready to change the subject. "Well, looks like Prince Edward schools might have to open up this fall. Says here the Supreme Court ordered them to open on an integrated basis. Gosh, it's been five years since they closed!"

"Been that long? They may as well quit fighting. It's inevitable."

"You need to go grocery shopping, Mother?"

"Yes. You going?"

"Thought I'd go before dinner. Need to get some seasoning and a few things. I'll pick up Frankie, and see that William is confined to his room...without his record player, and then I'll pick you up."

"I'll be ready."

Lauralee and Hallie pushed their heavy creaking carts down the long aisle of the Piggly Wiggly on Main Street. Mrs. Fredonia, their opinionated neighbor, had found them on aisle two and followed behind with her sparsely filled cart. "You folks must eat all the time from the looks of those carts!"

Lauralee winked at Hallie. "Just about, Mrs. Fredonia."

Hallie decided to give it back. "And from the looks of yours, Mrs. Fredonia, you're going to starve."

"Oh, no ma'am, I believe in eating light, vegetables, fruits and a few nuts. That's what keeps me in such good health, and I'm getting on up there, you know."

"That's good, Mrs. Fredonia, that's good," Hallie commented.

"You folks would be better off if you didn't eat so much of that red meat you got there."

"FIRE!" a loud voice yelled out.

Mrs. Fredonia's cart rolled off by itself as she grabbed hold of Hallie. "Law, Mrs. Frederick, what're we gonna do?" Already Lauralee was pulling her mother toward the front entrance. In succession, Hallie pulled Mrs. Fredonia along. Fortunately, there weren't too many shoppers in the store, being that it was Tuesday. The unfinished shoppers soon were all out front, across the street and watching as every fire truck in the city emerged upon the scene, enclosing the building. Smoke billowed from the rooftop.

"Mother, we'd better be getting home. I think there's enough firemen to take care of things. Come along, Mrs. Fredonia, we'll take you home, too," she suggested, her voice shaking. For once the old lady was speechless and only nodded yes. That evening at the supper table, William was relieved that his escapade was somewhat dimmed in light of the Piggly Wiggly fire. The subject was soon exhausted, and Jon Junior announced that Jordan and Sarah would be spending July the fourth with them in Lynchburg.

"Wonderful!" Lauralee exclaimed. "I can't wait to see how Sarah's doing with her pregnancy. She must be big now...with those twins."

POKY ROCKED BACK and forth in her rocking chair on the porch as she finished reading Hallie's letter... *'I'm deeply touched by the thought of two little ones, but, Poky, it makes me feel so old...'* She could understand her friend's words, her thoughts.

She suddenly felt old herself, even though she wasn't going to be a great grandmother. She got up and walked out to her tomato plants. Work is what she needed, work in the soil. Springtime on Oak Mountain had come subtly and gradually, but now quite visibly clothed itself in a green array of new life. The rhododendrons were budding with hints of purple splendor to come. Once again, the world was aquiver with life. The sleeping forest floor, no longer winter brown, was covering itself with a velvet green carpet of moss. The sweet, succulent honeysuckle scent drifted over the warm earth and hung like a perfumed cloud for all to inhale. Poky glanced up from her digging, and stared at the bright, red cardinal perched on a gnarled, apple tree branch. She smiled, and continued spading her herb garden. Then she heard a swiping sound nearby, and recognized it as the sound of a scythe cutting away. She looked up again and peered down the mountainside, but saw nothing. She returned to her spading. The swiping sound continued to draw nearer. Again, she glanced up and in its direction, this time to see the humped over figure of Lucas Morcom slinging his long sharp scythe back and forth. She waited till he got closer and yelled out, "Lucas Morcom, what ya' doin' way up here cuttin' them weeds?"

He looked up, surprised. "Oh, hello, Miss Poky. I been aimin' to stop this'ere danged kudzu, plum' nelly takin' over th'place. Ain't ya' seen it comin' up th'mountainside? First thing ya' know, we'll all be buried alive!"

She laughed aloud. "Now Lucas Morcom, ain't ya' got nothin' no better t'do than chase that ol' kudzu? You best be gettin' your pole beans in!"

"I aim to, Miss Poky, I aim to 'rectly after I finish this'ere job." He went back to agilely slinging the long, heavy scythe back and forth. "That there Japanese feller should'a never brought this stuff over here," he yelled back, "...an' them farmers that thought they could feed it to th'cows...why th'cows were smarter'n them!"

Poky chuckled as she continued her spading. Springtime's

a good time, she thought to herself. Folks're busy fixin' up things, th'birds done come back an' are singin' t'beat th'band, everything's a'growin', even th'kudzu! She grinned and commenced to whistling.

Summer eased in. Soon it was July 4, 1964, and Jordan and Sarah arrived to celebrate with their extended Lynchburg family, who welcomed them with open arms. They spent a week with Hallie and Jon Junior. Lauralee and her family were there just about every day, as well. After a fun-filled typical Fourth, cook-out, hamburgers, hotdogs, watermelon and the works, Jon Junior woke early to a still house. He lay thinking of the day before and all the joys of family life. Early morning sun rays fell across his bed, warming the sheets around him. It promised to be a splendid day, just as predicted. Was he up to it? He grinned to himself. Sure he was. Throwing his legs over the side of the bed and grabbing his trousers hanging on the chair, he headed to the bathroom. Just because he was going to be a grandpa didn't mean he couldn't climb a mountain.

Jordan and Sarah heard him whistling in the shower as they opened their eyes to the bright, sunny morning, and smiled at one another.

"I like your father," she yawned.

"So do I, dear."

"Are you really going to climb that mountain today?" she teased.

"I sure am and looking forward to it, too. I hate to admit it, but I've never climbed a mountain before."

"Uh-huh."

"Uh-huh what?"

"Nothing, just hope you'll feel like shopping tomorrow. Remember we're going to Roanoke to look at baby cribs."

"No problem. You seen my watch? Thought I laid it here on the dresser."

"I put it on the bathroom counter beside your billfolder."

"Can't get it now. Listen to him, honey." Jon Junior's whistling had turned into singing, with increased vocalization from the shower.

"Sounds like he's happy. Is William going, too?"

"Said he was. Hope so. Give us a chance to get to know one another better."

"Seems like a nice boy," Sarah remarked while pulling her pink chenille robe around her much expanded stomach, struggling to make it reach.

"Sure, he's a good kid, just going through those awkward years. You remember how it was."

It was still early morning when Jon Junior backed his black Fairlane out of the driveway and headed down Rivermont Avenue. Everything looked fresh and new, particularly Mr. Brizentine's side garden which was lined with dew coated morning glories, their fragile blue and white faces turned upward to the radiant sun. William was finishing his last biscuit, dripping with butter. "Nobody makes biscuits like grandma!" he bragged with a mouthful, realizing there was no one in the car to reprimand him. He wiped his mouth on his sleeve, feeling very masculine. "Uncle Jon, you think you can keep up with us today?" he challenged, losing a few crumbs in the process.

"You wait and see, young feller."

"Just how long is this hike up the mountain anyway?" Jordan queried.

"Not that long, just over a mile actually...but it's straight up...a bit taxing," Jon Junior replied casually.

"We could go up the goat trail...now that's really straight up!"

"Don't think so, William. The regular trail's challenging enough."

"We took the goat trail last fall, me and the guys...ran up it mostly...was cool."

"I'm sure it was. Glad you came with us today, Willy," Jon Junior expressed his true feelings.

"Didn't have nothing else to do."

"No girlfriends?" Jordan questioned jokingly.

"Not anymore. She ditched me."

"Oh well, we've all been there a time or two. You just get up and try again."

"Plan to. Going to a party tomorrow night, check out the girls, you know. Think I'll play the field awhile."

Jordan grinned at Jon Junior. They were headed west toward the small, picturesque town of Bedford, neatly nestled at the foot of Virginia's most famous mountains, The Peaks of Otter. The name could be deceiving as there certainly were no otters around.

Soon the distinct blue mountains rose before them, both Sharp Top and Flat Top, which comprised The Peaks. True to their names, Sharp Top pierced the clear blue sky with its artistic pointed peak while Flat Top only gently buffered with its stately rotund figure.

"There they be," Jon Junior stated matter of factly.

"Beautiful...simply beautiful," Jordan commented. Throughout their existence for hundreds of years, The Peaks actually seemed to draw people to them in some mysterious way, and thus it was on that day. They stood out from all other mountains, and gently beckoned the three of them.

"Gonna be standing on that *point* in a little while," William bragged.

"That one, huh?"

"Yes, siree, that's it, Cousin Jordan," William chuckled.

As they neared the lush, deep green mountains, their blue appearance was more of a bluish hue, and the large rock formations at the top became visibly apparent. Jon Junior's Fairlane pushed its way up the mountain, with its valves singing a little tune on the way. They arrived at the base of the mountain and climbed out.

"Sure feels good to stretch your legs."

"Oh, you gonna stretch your legs all right, Cousin Jordan."

He smiled at William, who was obviously enjoying the day so far.

Soon they stood below the mountain, looking up, and William read the sign aloud...*'Sharp Top elevation - 3,875 feet'*. They began hiking up the woodsy mountainside with William leading the way, of course. "Come on fellows, what's holding you up?" he yelled over his shoulder. Jordan glanced back at Jon Junior and grinned.

"We're taking our time, Willy, enjoying this wonderful natural atmosphere," Jon Junior called back while shifting his backpack containing their gatorade and snacks. He watched Jordan stepping cautiously over twisted, exposed roots and slippery rocks as he leaned into the leaf strewn upward path. Thickets of mountain laurel surrounded them, and large moss-covered ancient stones bordered the narrow path that wound around the mountain. The further they climbed, the more rocky the trail, often directly in their path causing them to step over and around them when possible, or sometimes barely squeeze through. After a short while, Jon Junior was breathing hard as old Sharp Top challenged him. He scouted around for a large rock and sat down to rest. Jordan looked back and followed his lead. "Take time to smell the roses," he remarked while catching his breath also. Almost out of sight, William glanced back and shook his head, but sat down to wait.

"You're right about that," Jon Junior responded after awhile.

"What's that?"

"*Take time to smell the roses.*"

Jordan nodded.

"Life goes fast...too fast...and first thing you know, you missed them...the roses...the trees...the mountains...the beauty of it all...you know, what really matters...."

Jordan was silent. They looked ahead. William was standing, waiting impatiently. Jon Junior eyed Jordan. "But when you're young, you don't see it." They rose and continued climbing. The higher they climbed, the cooler the temperature, leaving the July heat down below. And at the same time, the further they ascended, distancing themselves from the world below, the more they felt a kinship to nature, to the circle of life, to God the creator.

About three quarters of the way up, Jon Junior sat down again on a fallen tree to catch his breath, and Jordan joined him. This time, even William joined them without complaining. All that could be heard was the singing of birds, and the rustling of dried leaves as an occasional small creature scampered through the underbrush. Otherwise, there was a soothing blanket of silence that permeated their souls.

"'Be still and know that I am God,'" Jordan quoted the scriptures reverently.

"It's true, isn't it? When we're still like this, seems our thoughts turn upward. Guess that's what He means."

Jordan nodded.

William listened without comment. Finally they got up and proceeded upward. Just before they reached the summit, Jordan received a surprise. There was a small stone house atop the mountain, wedged in between the giant boulders. It had been there for years through many a mountain storm, but solidly anchored midst the boulders holding its spot. He ducked his head and went in. Jon Junior followed. William was already sitting within, enjoying the damp, cool air of the expansive open room. Except for the large fireplace, the place was empty. He looked up at the open rafters, and a wren flew out.

"Didn't think you'd find a house up here, did you?" William asked.

"No, I didn't."

"Let's go on up." Jon Junior was at the door anxious to show Jordan the summit. They stepped out into the bright sunshine and oddly found the wind blowing quite strongly. Jordan looked around.

"Wind usually blows up here on top," William explained.

"We're almost there then?"

"Just a few more steps."

The three headed up together, and Jon Junior watched

Jordan's face as they arrived on top of the mountain, surrounded by large residual boulders piled high upon each other, greenish grey from extreme weathering. He looked around in awe, taking in the massive granite rocks, the sheer feeling of height and the expansive 360 degree panoramic view all around him. He could see many other mountain ridges on out into the distance, blue green, dark blue, fading to a light blue, lighter and lighter, blending with the spacious sky. He whistled, "WOW!"

"You can see forever, as they say, up here."

"You can say that again, William." Jon Junior began to point out familiar objects down below, way down below, that appeared so minute. "There's the lake and the lodge. And if you look straight across, that's Flat Top over there. She's over four thousand feet, but due to some optical illusion, Sharp Top appears taller."

Jordan took it all in, enjoying every minute. "You ever climbed Flat Top?"

"I have," William boasted, "takes a lot longer. Not nearly as straight up, but much longer. About a four mile hike. We did it last winter, Ken and I."

"I haven't tackled it yet."

"Uncle Jon, it might just be too much for you," William teased.

"You might just be right," he joked back, partly serious. "You know, I remember the first time I ever climbed this mountain. Guess I was about your age, William. I brought Lauralee with me. She was just a wee thing, and it was summertime, hot, like today. Her shoes were hurting her feet, and she kept on complaining. Finally, she took them off and climbed the whole mountain barefooted. It was her first time, too, of course. Well, when we got to the top...." He began to chuckle.

"What's so funny?" William asked.

"Just remembering...I was in awe, of course, looking around at all this, and I kept on talking to Lauralee. She didn't answer. I looked around and didn't see her. I was about to panic when I looked down...and there she was crawling around on all fours. I said, "Get up, Lauralee, get up!" I was embarrassed, you see. There were a few other people up here, too. She answered, "I can't, Jon Junior!" I like to never got her up from there. Well, that's when we discovered she had a fear of heights, and she's never been too keen on coming back, either."

"I can understand," Jordan commented, "the poor thing."

After the magnitude of it all settled in, Jordan sat down contemplatively, while William and Jon Junior snapped pictures with William's Brownie camera. He looked down on the roof of the little stone house and thought about his call to the ministry and how compelling it was, and how rewarding it had been thus far. He wondered if he'd always feel this way. He recalled his father's words of discouragement and pushed them out of his mind. He determined in his heart to follow the Lord's guidance and to serve Him and mankind to the very best of his ability. He thought of his unborn children and felt a tinge of excitement. He would be there for them, the father he'd never had. A yellow jacket swarmed around the warm rocks, looking for somewhere to light. That seemed odd to him that a tiny bee would be way up there on top of the mountain. Then two more joined that one. He smiled to himself. They were part of God's creation, too, and they had a right to be on the mountain top, even if they didn't have to climb it to get there. *"On the mountain top,"* he whispered. Now there's a sermon! How good it felt to be up there on the mountain top. But he had to go down. He knew that. Life was like that, too. We have our mountain tops...becoming a minister, marrying Sarah, finding out they would be having twins...finding his real father! He heard him talking to William on the other side of the boulders. God had been so good to him, allowing him and his father to bond this way. And now, not only did he have his Grandmother McKenzie but his Grandmother Hallie, as well, and all this extended family.

Yes, he was on a mountain top, for sure, not only this mammoth granite one but a much more meaningful one. But, just as sure as the rains would come, the storms would come, too, and he would find himself in a valley. "'*Man that is born of a woman is of few days, and full of trouble,*'" he quoted. But he would enjoy the mountain top for now.

CHAPTER TWENTY-TWO

SUMMER PASSED, the fall, too. Soon the earth was blanketed with its first snow the beginning of November. It had been snowing all night, and the ground was covered, so was every tree, twig and leaf. A clinging wet snow that created majestic works of art surrounding the humble cabin, elevating it to new and unknown heights of beauty. Poky marveled at it all, not that she hadn't witnessed such beauty many times before. She loved the snow and how it softened the world it touched. Leaning against the window, she sighed with pleasure. Then she saw a dark hooded figure trudging through the deepening snow, head down. Immediately, she recognized Barclay's distinct proud walk, the way he carried himself, even in the snow. She quickly moved to the door, waiting for his step and flung it open before he could knock.

"Come on in, son. My, my, ain't it a surprise you callin' on your Poky on sech a day."

He pulled off his wet gloves. "Well, the shop didn't open up today. Thought I'd mosey up and see if you're doing all right."

"I sho am. Doin' jest fine, jest fine, enjoyin' all this'ere snow."

He struggled with his warm anti-freeze jacket that didn't want to come off. "Know what you mean." The wood stove was blazing, and he rubbed his cold, stiff hands together over it, cringing with the stinging sensation.

"Addie Jane...lil' Grae all right?"

"They're fine. She's mixing up a batch of oatmeal cookies right now."

"That a fact? Sounds mighty good. Want some hot chocolate t'warm your bones?"

"I wouldn't turn that down. You got enough wood in?"

"Sho 'nough. You know I stay ready."

"I figured as much, but just thought I'd make sure."

"Thank you, son. I 'preciate you askin'." She poured milk into the pan sitting on the wood stove, and it sizzled momentarily as it hit the hot pan.

They sat down together at the kitchen table to drink the steaming hot chocolate. Barclay slowly turned his cup around in his hands. "This old cup takes me back. How long you had these cups, Poky?"

"Shucks. Been here s'long I don't know when nor where they come from." She chuckled. "Better watch it though, might burn your tongue. It's hot all right."

"That's what I like about this place. Nothing ever changes."

"How's th'new job comin' along?"

"Getting better. At least, I feel like I know what I'm doing now."

"You drawin' a lot?"

"Yes, ma'am, but not pictures. Not like my paintings...but graphs and the like. Business stuff that goes into making our product."

"Uh-huh," she nodded, obviously not too interested in the business stuff. "Everybody...your boss an' all...nice folks?"

"Nice enough, I guess." Poky noticed his handsome face cloud over.

"What ya' mean you guess?"

"Well, you know. There's always gonna be some."

"Uh-huh."

"This here fellow by the name of Melvin, well actually he's my boss. But he really irks me."

"Givin' you trouble?"

"Not really...but...well...he grew up in the valley...and he's full of prejudice. A product of his family, I'm sure. Just yesterday, he said, 'You people....' I repeated, '*You people?*' He quickly responded, 'You know, y'all all stuck together up there in the mountains...probably the best thing, too.' I challenged him, 'Why's that, Melvin?' He evaded the question, changing the subject. But it was written all over him. His disdain for us, that is."

"Uh-huh." She sat thinking. Barclay rose and walked over to the window, staring out at the descending wet snow flakes falling heavily from the grey sky.

"You remember, Barclay, th'story'uv creation an' how God put Adam in th'garden?"

He turned and looked at her and wondered what that had to do with Melvin Mullins.

"Well," she continued, "th'scripture says...'*An' th'Lord God took th'man an' put'im into th'garden of Eden t'dress it an' t'keep it.*'"

Barclay nodded.

"Well'sa, God places us in *our gardens*, too...an' we s'posed t'dress it an' keep it. All th'folks 'round us, family an' friends an' folk we work with an' all...they're part'uv our garden. Another part is th'gifts an' talents God gives us an' what we do with'em...how we use'em...like you bein' an artist an' all. God 'spects us t'use th'gifts he gives us. Don't want us t'hide them, act like we don't have none. Th'good Lord gave everybody gifts. But th'most important thing in our gardens is th'people. God's mind is on people. Now, you know when you work in a garden, it ain't all easy. You got rocks an' stumps an' sech in a garden which causes you some trouble. You got storms which can cause a whole lotta trouble. In fact, some storms can jest about tear up your garden, destroy it completely. Then what're you gonna do? Onliest thing t'do is call on Him who sent th'storm! Yes, we got all kinds'uv things in our gardens, an' we jest gotta get up an' over an' around'em. An' one more thing. Gardens have weeds in'em, too." She chuckled. "An' sometimes you get ready t'pull that ol' weed right out'a th'garden...an' then ya' realize it ain't a weed a'tall, but a flower jest needin' a lil' cultivatin'...needin' a lil' love an' care. You see what I'm drivin' at, son? Folks is like that, too. Folks in our garden. An' this'ere Melvin, whatever his name is, sho seems like'a weed t'me...but ya' reckon...."

Barclay was smiling. "Poky, I declare. You never cease to amaze me. Now every time I look at ol' Melvin, I'm gonna think of him as a weed. I just hope I don't get to laughing."

She smiled back, glad to see him happy again. "Jest you remember, son, one day th'good Lord's gonna want t'know how we tended our gardens."

"I know, Poky, I know."

IT WAS DECEMBER, and Jordan's and Sarah's emotions were vacillating between excitement and fear. Fear of the unknown, the birth process, the prospect of being parents and responsibility for two helpless little people. The time came just three days after Christmas, and Hallie was there. Having volunteered to stay with them for a few weeks to help out, she'd gone down the day after Christmas. Jon Junior had taken her, but had to return to work afterwards. It was a beautiful event for Hallie to share, the birth of her first two great-grandchildren, Joshua and Caleb, both weighing just over five pounds each and healthy as could be. As soon as Sarah began labor, Hallie called Jon Junior, and he'd returned immediately, bringing Lauralee with him. They arrived just after the twins were born.

"That one looks like Jon Junior...his grandpa," Lauralee pointed out proudly.

"Yes," Hallie agreed, "...and that one, little Caleb there, looks like his Uncle Jamey." Both Jon Junior and Lauralee looked from her to the baby.

"He does, Mother?"

"Yes, Lauralee, he looks like Jamey when he was a baby."

"Well, how about that!" Jordan happily joined them.

"Jamey would be proud," Jon Junior commented softly.

"He would, son, he would."

The twins helped to bring in a happy New Year as 1965 arrived, and the Frederick family basked in its glow. Poky read again with delight Hallie's card announcing their birth.

"Now, don't that beat all! If'n one ain't enough, Miss Hallie done gone an' got herself two great gran'children. Joshua an' Caleb, straight out'a th'Bible, too. 'Course, you'd 'spect as much with their pa bein' a preacher."

"Sometimes I wish I'd named Grae a Bible name like that, but I liked his name so much."

"Addie Jane, it ain't th'name one gets when he's born that counts. It's th'name he leaves when he dies."

Addie Jane pondered those words as she watched little Grae playing outside in the snow with Barclay. He was a striking image of his father, already quite the handsome little fellow at two and a half years old. Even his actions and mannerisms duplicated Barclay, and she was glad for it. They were patting snow in place with their snow encrusted gloves in an effort to make an igloo. That's what Grae wanted, not a snowman, but an igloo. Barclay treasured the moments he could spend with his son, no matter how tired or how cold. The snow was still falling lightly, and Grae's little red stocking cap was a dusty white.

"Gonna catch their death if they don't come on in'ere. Call'em in, Addie Jane."

"Let them play, Poky. They're having such fun. That's all Grae's talked about for days...wanting to build an igloo when it snows."

"An igloo! Whoever heard'uv sech. Better add some water to them beans yonder before they burn." The pinto beans had cooked down to the bottom of the large pot. Addie Jane grabbed a glass, filled it to the brim with water from the spigot and poured it into the pot. They sizzled at first, then quieted to a subdued bubbling.

"Just in time," she remarked, "better start mixing up the cornbread."

"Want some help?"

"You sit there and rest, Poky. Today's your day."

"Child, I done had s'many birthdays, they jest like any other day t'me."

"Well, not this one. We're gonna celebrate. I made you a cake, and Barclay got some peach ice cream, your favorite."

"Can't argue with that. With them beans an' cornbread an' now your cake an' peach ice cream, y'all gonna spoil me for sure."

"When you reach sixty-seven years old, you ought to be spoiled, don't you think?"

"Don't feel like no sixty-seven. My mama was sixty-seven an' she seemed old t'me, but I don't feel old like that. Kind'a funny, ain't it?"

"You don't act old either."

Poky laughed. "I jest act like Poky, that's all." She moved over to the window. "Well, bless my bones, if that don't look like one'a them igloos, an' that lil' Grae is tryin' his best t'get in it, too." All you could see was his hindparts wiggling through the small doorway.

"If you had your wish, Poky, what would you want for your birthday?" Addie Jane asked while stirring the corn meal.

"I already have it, child. I'm right here with my fam'ly...you an' Barclay an' lil' Grae. Ain't nothin' could make me happier."

Addie Jane smiled to herself, hardly able to contain her secret. Barclay had called her dear friend, Hallie, from Lynchburg, and invited her up for Poky's sixty-seventh birthday. Jon Junior had assured them his mother would be there, but now with this snow, she wondered. She finished pouring the creamy yellow batter into the already heated pan, and popped it in the oven of her new Hotpoint range. Every time she used it, she felt good. And the window in the oven! Now, that was something. She could watch the batter rise and brown, knowing just when to take it out.

"Poky, this is what you need instead of that old wood stove."

"Naw, Addie Jane. I been cookin' on my wood stove all my life, no need t'change now. That indoor toilet's quite enough for you young folk t'give me."

"Bet you enjoy it."

"Now, you know I do."

Barclay and little Grae burst in, brushing the snow off all over the floor.

"Now, you fellers should'a done that out yonder," Poky scolded.

"But it's cold outside. We're freezing, aren't we, Grae?"

The little fellow was jumping up and down partly from the cold and partly from excitement. "Look't my igloo, Mama!" He ran pointing to the window.

"I already did, Grae. I've been watching you build it, and it looks real nice. Just like a real one."

"Gonna sleep in it...."

"Well, now...I don't know about that. You're not an Eskimo, son. Only Eskimos sleep in them."

"Me be a Eskimo."

"What ya' talkin' 'bout, son?" Poky quickly interjected. "You can't be no Eskimo. You're a Virginian, an' there ain't nothin' no better'n a Virginian!"

"What's that I hear?" Barclay looked out the window. Addie Jane and Poky followed.

"Looks like somebody's comin' up th'mountain...in all this'ere snow, too. Who ya' reckon it could be?"

"Don't know." Barclay glanced at Addie Jane over Poky's head and grinned. The four wheel drive vehicle pushed its way through the foot of snow and came to a stop at the end of the long driveway. Poky peered through the frosty window, puzzled at who it could be. Jon Junior climbed out all bundled up, not at all recognizable, and trudged around the truck to the other side and opened the door for Hallie. She, too, was all bundled up, but the old friend couldn't fool Poky.

"HALLIE!" she hollered out, running to the door and flinging it open. "My goodness, if you ain't a sight for sore eyes...comin' out in this'ere snow, too!"

Jon Junior helped Hallie through the snow and up on the porch. She was smiling and waving all the way.

"Sure didn't think you'd make it in this." Barclay ushered them in. "...but glad you did."

"Wild horses couldn't have kept mama back."

Hallie and Poky embraced there in the middle of the small living room, laughing and crying at the same time. "*Happy birthday, Poky.*"

"Awe shucks, Miss Hallie. You done come all this way t'tell me happy birthday?"

"I sure did."

"Won't much problem with my new pick-up," Jon Junior added proudly, rubbing his cold hands together.

"Y'all come over here by th'fire an' warm your bones. Addie Jane, y'mind addin' two more places to th'table?"

"Already doing it, Poky."

Poky caught the gleam in her eye. "Now, you young'uns didn't by any chance know anything 'bout this?"

Addie Jane kept on smiling while setting the places.

"I ought'a spank ya' bottoms, both'uv you. But it's a mighty fine surprise. Miss Hallie, you lookin' jest dandy. Betcha 'bout froze gettin' here, though."

"Not really. Jon Junior's new truck kept me warm and toasty as a summer day. Addie Jane, you have a real nice home here."

"Thank you, Miss Hallie. We're mighty proud of it. Hope you like pinto beans and corn bread. That's Poky's favorite meal." Addie Jane was adding the extra chairs, including a stool for herself.

"On a day like today, I can't think of anything better."

Little Grae, who'd been standing quietly in the shadows, slowly emerged. "And look how this little fellow's grown. I can't believe it." Hallie put her arms out to him, and he quickly retraced his steps.

"He's a bit shy at first. He'll get used to you after awhile. Y'all can come on to the table. Miss Hallie, why don't you sit there beside Poky, and Barclay, would you mind saying grace?" He honored her wishes with a short but meaningful prayer and then added, "Please pass the cornbread."

"Miss Poky," Jon Junior began, "since we made it to *your* birthday party, you've got to come to mother's in the fall when she turns seventy-four!"

"Oh my goodness, Jon Junior. There you go telling my age again!" Hallie cheerfully chided.

Barclay spoke up, "We'll see she gets there. But Miss Hallie, you don't look a day over fifty-five. You must've found the fountain of youth along your way."

She smiled. "Thank you, Barclay. That's very sweet of you. But I can assure you that if there was such a thing, I doubt I'd be standing in line. Youth has its ups, but it also has its downs. And I'm very content with the peace and tranquillity my life offers right now."

"A very profound statement, Miss Hallie."

"Of course, when you were young, Mother, there was the Depression and the war."

"You're right, Jon Junior. Speaking of the war, it's hard to believe Churchill just passed away. What a loss."

"A great loss for Britain...and a loss for us all," Barclay added.

"Leastways, he died gently. Th'news said he slipped into a deeper sleep. Sounds like th'way t'go," Poky remarked, "...an' he did live t'see ninety. Hope I can do th'same."

"The way you're going, Miss Poky, I'm sure you will," Jon Junior kidded. She laughed and shook her spoon at him.

"Well, I certainly feel sorry for his wife. His 'darling Clementine.' She's really going to miss him. I don't know what I'd do if I were in her shoes," Addie Jane said looking at Barclay. He smiled at her tenderly.

"You're right, Addie Jane. Well, I was glad to see the queen make sure he got a state funeral."

"Me too, Hallie. An' they only give'em to Britain's greatest heroes an' statesmen, they say."

"If anybody ever got one, Sir Winston certainly deserved one." Jon Junior reached for his second helping of beans.

"He did that," Barclay agreed, "...and America never had a greater friend."

"'Course he was half American hisself," Poky added.

"Changin' th'subject, but Miss Hallie, how is your grandson, th'Rev'rend an' them two fine lil' great-grandsons, Joshua an' Caleb...an' Jon Junior, how's it feel t'be a grandpa now?"

Hallie and Jon Junior exchanged grins, and Jon Junior waited for his mother to speak first. "He's doing fine. Both he and Sarah haven't come down out of the clouds yet. They're so happy with those two little fellows."

"And to answer your question, Miss Poky, I love the whole idea of being a grandpa. Can't wait until they're a little older though, so I can take them fishing."

"Well, I'm s'glad they named'em Joshua an' Caleb...from one'uv my favorite stories in th'Bible. When God told Moses t'send them spies into Canaan t'check out th'land...th'promised land, ya' know, twelve'uv'em from th'twelve tribes of Israel went...but them two stood out...Joshua and Caleb. When they all returned, they said surely it was th'land'uv milk an' honey, but it had lots'uv strong people an' big walled cities an' giants...yessiree...an' they were askeered'uv'em. 'Cept that is for Joshua an' Caleb. They won't skeered. Caleb spoke right up an' said, *'Let us go in t'overcome it.'* Ya' see, it all depends on how we see th'picture. All twelve'uv them spies saw th'same thing...but Joshua an' Caleb saw it with faith. Faith that they could overcome."

"And that's what we all need, Miss Poky...faith," Hallie added. "The scripture says more than once, *'without faith we cannot please God.'*"

"But it's one of the hardest things to have," Barclay acknowledged.

Grae began fussing, tired and ready for bed. Addie Jane picked him up, cradled him in her arms and sat down in the little rocker next to the stove. He was immediately content as she rocked.

"Well, you sure have to have faith in times like these. Otherwise, you could get rather discouraged."

"Ain't that th'truth, Jon Junior," Poky quickly agreed. "Don't know what's got into folks anyhow...fightin' over in Vietnam an' fightin' here back home, too."

"And it looks like Vietnam is a dead-end street for sure with no way out."

Barclay agreed, "Sure looks that way."

"But the violence here at home bothers me even more. War I can understand somewhat, but all these riots left and right, I don't know," Hallie added, "...and all this anti-war protesting. I saw where they were even having what they called anti-war musical shows. And all the sit-ins. Just a whole lot of unrest, a whole lot of problems."

"And drafting over five-thousand men a month!"

"You mean, boys, Jon Junior. They're only boys," Hallie corrected.

"And what about the flower children? They're multiplying by the thousands. And the drugs! God have mercy!" Barclay added.

"Bet you don't have any here...I mean flower children that is," Jon Junior kidded.

"On Oak Mountain...haven't seen any."

Addie Jane interrupted, "Well, changing the subject to something lighter, have any of you seen any little green men lately?"

Everyone laughed and loosened up, and little Grae flinched in his sleep. "Seems like every day now someone in Virginia sees one, even a minister over in Marion, Virginia."

"I saw that, too, Addie Jane," Poky responded, "said he saw a flyin' saucer right over downtown Marion. Now we ought'a be able t'believe our rev'rends."

"But what he saw and what he thinks he saw may not be the same, Poky."

"Maybe not, Barclay. But they been seein' them UFO's everywhere...Williamsburg, Waynesboro, Staunton, Harrisonburg, everywhere."

"After that reported saucer landing in Harrisonburg, one of the professors at the Eastern Mennonite College took a Geiger counter and checked the site, and reported a high radiation level," Jon Junior added. "That was before Christmas."

"Strange things happening." Hallie began clearing the table. "Keep your seat, Addie Jane, and keep rocking that sweet little boy. I want to do this."

"Well, thank you."

Addie Jane continued, "Did y'all see where that little green man with a glowing head was arrested in Salem last week?"

They all stared at her.

"...but he turned out to be a bunch of cardboard boxes of different shapes glued together to look like a three foot person with a plastic jug for a head."

Laughing, they began helping Hallie clear the table.

"Can ya' imagine? Now who in th'world would go to all that trouble to do that?"

"Who knows, Poky. Some people always get in on the act."

Later, all the peach ice cream was gone, and only a small portion of the four-layered chocolate cake leaned tentatively on the large plate. Barclay handed Poky her guitar, and soon they were singing all the old familiar ballads. Little Grae was fast asleep in Addie Jane's arms, and Hallie and Jon Junior stayed the night. The snow let up in the night, and they left for Lynchburg the next morning.

March blew in, and north winds whipped the barren hills as winds of strife whipped the already heated emotions. America groaned beneath the violence as its children rose up against one another, black and white against each other. Meanwhile, the never-ending war across the seas continued to rage, taking more and more young lives each and every day. Discord was everywhere. Dissidents flurried north to Canada refusing to fight. Americans questioned the long war, asking why? Tired and disillusioned soldiers returned to angry stares instead of patriotic welcomes. And everybody had a cause. Martin Luther King's cause was for equality for his people as he led them down the streets of America, nearly four-thousand in Selma, Alabama, with locked arms, three abreast marching through black and white neighborhoods;

five thousand in Montgomery, the one-time capital of the Confederacy, a fifty mile march to the state capital. Confused young people donned colorful flowers and rose up against the system, against the war, and against their parents as they sought answers. And much to America's disgrace, the volcanic drug scene erupted, sending forth its dreaded lava into the next generations. Cries of protests mixed with songs of peace wafted up through heavy clouds.

But soon springtime came again, and in the midst of all the discord, dogwoods bloomed, spreading their white lace throughout the forest, and redbuds burst forth alongside them. Trees, old and new, adorned themselves once more with tiny green buds. People sighed, happy for the interlude. It was April 9, 1965, and Jon Junior drove east out of Lynchburg, headed for Appomattox. He was looking forward to the day, not only the celebration itself, but spending it with Jordan. He recalled with sadness Beth's last wish for him to bond with their son. That had been the easiest thing he'd ever done, not only because it was what he wanted most, but because they had so much in common, like history, for instance. Jordan had jumped at the chance to come along today.

He came into the little town of Appomattox, and soon noticed the small motel on his left with its sign depicting Lee and his famed horse. *Traveler's Inn* it read. He pulled up in front, and Jordan came out smiling.

"So glad you could make it. Sarah didn't mind you leaving her with the twins so soon, I hope?" he asked as Jordan climbed in beside him.

"Matter of fact, I think she was actually glad. Gives her and her mother a reason to spend time together."

"That's good. I felt sort of guilty asking so soon after their birth, but I knew how much you like Civil War history...and...well...today is history, too." Lee's surrender was to be commemorated at the old Appomattox Courthouse recently restored, and already native southerners, full of pride and love for their heritage, crowded into the small historic park. They were fierce defenders of the century-dead Confederacy and ardent admirers of their late leader, the revered Robert E. Lee. Approximately fifteen to twenty-thousand people were expected to fill the little town.

"Sure am glad I made reservations. This place is popping at the seams."

"And I don't think they have but three motels."

"Had some northerners there, too."

"That so?"

"Civil War buffs mostly, but certainly sympathetic to our cause."

They drove as close as possible to the historic grounds, then got out and began walking toward it. Some men were in uniform, women and children donned civil war dress. Seeing the Confederate flag flying once again over the crowd caused chills to run up their spines.

"A hundred years...." Jordan commented.

"Yeah," Jon Junior responded reverently.

It was a grey, overcast day, and the crowds were exceptionally large. They kept bumping into people as they tried maneuvering around the grounds. Finally the ceremony began.

They watched as Robert E. Lee IV, Lee's great-grandson, and Major General Ulysses S. Grant III, Grant's grandson, cut the ribbon to the restored courthouse. They listened to the Pulitzer Prize-winning historian, Bruce Catton, speak to the crowd, telling what happened on that eventful day in April over a hundred years ago and why. *"If there hadn't been the surrender— if, as one of Lee's lieutenants wanted, the Army of Northern Virginia had dispersed to carry on guerrilla warfare— America would have been ruined forever...and for the Civil War to have ended that way— with a surrender, and the men returning home— was remarkable. The attitude of the veterans, much revered in the south today, was remarkable, too. Living the rest of their lives in the shadow of a lost cause, they were ready to meet the future. And it was Lee who caused them to do it; Lee who said farewell to his troops by commending them for unsurpassed courage and fortitude, for valor and deeds well done. The result — the legacy of the Appomattox surrender then was not indigestible hatred and bitterness, but a romantic legend of a great leader and his valiant followers. This legend helped put the country on its feet again and has helped everyone."*

Jon Junior was choked up and tried to clear his throat, "What a heritage we have, Jordan."

Jordan nodded quietly.

A little later, a few drops of rain fell as the governor spoke. But it stopped when the firing squad aimed their rifles. They exploded toward the sky, then the melancholy taps wafted over the crowd. Jon Junior placed his arm over Jordan's shoulder. The two were silent.

When they left the surrender grounds, Jordan thanked Jon Junior for inviting him, as he prepared for his long drive back home.

"My pleasure. Sharing such a memorable event with you made it all the more special."

"You know, being there today, walking on the same grounds as our ancestors did a hundred years ago makes you really meditate on life and time...and how you fit into the big picture."

"Know what you mean," Jon Junior replied.

LAURALEE PLACED THE small white replica of Michelangelo's Pieta on her mother's coffee table and stepped back to admire it. She moved forward and slid it slightly to the right and retreated again for another look. Yes, that was perfect. Frankie came running up behind her and reached for the Pieta.

"No, Frankie. Don't touch...just look please."

The rather gregarious child looked at her mother quizzically. "He's dead."

Lauralee knelt beside the coffee table. "Yes, Frankie. He *was* dead. You know He died for us, all of us."

"But why do you want to give that to grandma? He's not

dead anymore!" She skipped out of the room and out of the house, slamming the back screen door. Lauralee smiled and shook her head at the child's frankness and words of wisdom. She continued to sit on the floor in front of the coffee table while memories flooded back. Memories of another Pieta, not quite this nice, but still lovely. It was for sale at Guggenheimer's, and she'd so wanted to buy it for her mother for Christmas, but could never get quite enough money. So when she saw this yesterday, she just had to have it. Her mother would love it, she knew.

It was Good Friday and Hallie had been visiting Mrs. Stein, who was hospitalized with gallstones. As she walked home, her thoughts were on this holy time of year. Mrs. Stein, her Jewish neighbor and friend, had just finished telling her that she'd miss the Seder Passover observance at her home tonight. Passover started at sundown and continued for eight days in memory of the escape of the Israelites from Egypt more than two thousand years ago. She said she'd never missed a Seder, and was sad she would this year. Hallie felt sorry for Mrs. Stein, realizing how much this meant to her. Her thoughts turned to this most solemn day, Good Friday, and the sadness that accompanied it, but she knew it would be followed by the most joyous day, Easter. Her spirits lifted. All her family would be home, and they'd all attend church together like they did when they were but children, Lauralee and Bill, William and Frankie, Jon Junior and Jordan and Sarah and little Joshua and Caleb this year. It was supposed to be a pretty Easter, sunny and warm. Maybe they'd walk downtown and stroll Joshua and Caleb. She'd like that. There wouldn't be any Easter Parade, people didn't do that anymore, but maybe they'd walk down anyway, just the Frederick family. She could hardly wait.

CHAPTER TWENTY-THREE

AN APRIL THUNDERSTORM erupted suddenly over Oak Mountain in a fierce and overwhelming fury, coming out of nowhere and casting a shroud of darkness over the sunny afternoon as rains beat down and winds swept up ridges, bending young saplings to the ground. Lightning zigzagged across an ominously darkened sky as peals of thunder cracked with vibrating frenzy. Frightened forest creatures scattered, seeking shelter among its crevices and burrows.

Poky peered out her kitchen window through rain swept panes, knowing it was really spring now that the storms had come – those powerful Virginia storms. Though she didn't care for the storm, she heartily welcomed the rain. Too long it had been without rain. The earth was hard and dry, resisting the fragile budding life struggling to burst forth. It cried out with thirst. Suddenly she jumped as a bolt of lightning lit up the mountain, and thunder shook the cabin. She pressed against the wall beside the window, afraid to look out again, afraid she'd be struck herself. It had hit something!

Poky was right. Some miles away, a tall, aged oak split down the middle and one half fell lumberingly to the earth, leaving the gaping wounded other half still standing in the periodically illuminated forest. A flame leapt from the fallen half, racing down the length of it, igniting the crisp dry underbrush and masses of dry pine needles beneath it. Though the rains fell, they were no match for the hungry flames that eagerly lapped at the waiting dry forest.

The storm was short-lived, and Addie Jane opened her door wide to the damp air, fresh with a pungent pine scent.

She stepped out on the porch, inhaling the invigorating pure air. Oh, the rain was good. But....

"Barclay, come quick!"

Instantly, he was at her side witnessing the smoke in the distance. Rushing back in, he grabbed some blankets and reached for the broom in the corner as he stepped out again.

"Barclay...."

He looked down at her.

"...be careful."

He turned and ran toward the smoke that was now hanging as a cloud over treetops in the distance. As he disappeared, Poky came running down the hill. "Where's Barclay?" she called, out of breath.

"Already gone, took some blankets and my broom...."

Poky looked worriedly toward the smoke. As is often after a storm, the winds were picking up, but fortunately they were blowing in the other direction. She quickly assessed the situation, realizing that a fire, whipped by wind and hungrily feeding on the extreme dryness of the forest, could be a dangerous enemy. Coupled with the fact that the fire was down the mountain, she feared even more, knowing fire always travels faster uphill. Addie Jane anxiously watched her face.

"It'll be all right, won't it Poky?"

"'Course, child, 'course it will." She forced a smile. "Come on t'my place. Get lil' Grae an' come on up t'my place."

When Barclay reached the fire, the rolling black mass of smoke blocked the bright red-orange flames that were lapping behind it. Quickly, he ran toward it, shielding his eyes behind his sleeve and coughing within the heavy smoke. He faced the enemy head on, beating it fiercely with his blankets and broom. Soon he was joined by others, and they spread out seeking to encompass the flames and flail it out with brooms and brush and whatever they happened to have. Unfortunately, the harder they beat, the fire gained strength, growing rapidly out of control. The fact that there had been no rain for almost two months, except for the brief storm, contributed to the hazardous conditions, and the hungry flames fed on the dry crispness of the forest. The wind was abetting the crime, constantly changing its course, spreading flames in all directions as hot embers rode the strong winds.

Poky and Addie Jane took turns at the window keeping watch on the smoke. It was Poky's turn, and Addie Jane spread peanut butter on a slice of bread for Grae. She hummed a tune to calm her nerves.

"Listen...you hear it?" Poky interrupted, "...it's comin'...th'wind is blowin' up from th'valley...it's gonna blow that fire straight up th'mountain."

Addie Jane looked up quickly. "What're we gonna do?"

"Gotta get out'a here, that's what. Get down to th'valley. You get Grae. I'll grab a few'uv my belongin's, put'em in this'ere sack." She pulled out a burlap sack from behind the wood box. "We'll stop by your place on th'way down for a bit. Be thinkin' 'bout what you'll get. Can't take much. You can drive th'truck, can't ya'?"

"...yes, sure. But what about Barclay?" Her voice trembled.

"We can't wait on'im. He'll be all right, an' if I know Barclay, he'll be fightin' that fire till it's over. But we'll be safer in th'valley. Hurry now."

They threw the heavy sacks onto the back of the truck, lifted Grae in and took off down the mountain. Poky tried to conceal much of her own fear. She knew this fire was too big and too close. As the old truck rumbled down the loosely graveled mountain road, Poky looked back. A large, black umbrella of smoke was hanging over Oak Mountain, threateningly. Grae, standing up between them and holding onto the back of the seat with one hand, pointed to it questioningly.

"It's all right, honey child. It's all right." She was glad she'd gotten him and Addie Jane away. The sacks jostled in the back of the pick-up as it bounced down the mountainside.

"I reckon all the menfolk around must be fighting the fire," Addie Jane's voice cracked.

"I reckon so, child." Poky couldn't help but notice the smoke coming closer and closer as they descended. She was puzzled, didn't think it would've spread over this way, too. But, they'd soon be down off the mountain.

"Oh no-o-o-o!" Addie Jane exclaimed.

"What is it?"

The pick-up had stalled. Addie Jane frantically turned the key in the ignition and pumped the gas. It groaned as it attempted to start, but then died out. "It's been giving us trouble. Barclay was gonna get Mr. Davis to work on it next week...Oh no!"

"Try it again!"

Several more times, she turned the ignition and pumped the gas until finally it died completely. She looked around at the encroaching smoke. "Poky, it's coming this way!"

"It's doin' that all right. We're jest gonna have t'walk th'rest'uv th'way an' hurry. You take Grae. I'll grab th'sacks." She hauled the heavy sacks out of the truck and onto her back. They half walked and half ran down the mountainside. But the smoke followed them as a voluminous buzzard reaching its black puffy wings out to them. Addie Jane was coughing now, and Grae began to cry, "Mommy, my eyes hurt."

"I know, honey...we'll be down the...mountain soon, and they won't hurt anymore...just close...your eyes," she instructed between coughs and looked back at Poky, who was stumbling over the rocky road under the weight of the sacks.

"Poky, just leave them!"

"Don't have too far t'go now. Don't wanna leave'em." Stubbornly, she held on to the sacks, but she was more worried about Addie Jane's asthma getting stirred up. "You doin' all right, Addie Jane?"

"Yes, ma'am," she coughed.

Meanwhile, winds whipped the flames up and across Oak

Mountain. Animals ran blindly out of its path, seeking shelter, many dying in the process. Many more, still nesting, couldn't escape the flames. Those that the flames didn't grab, the smoke and lack of oxygen consumed. The fire's path now covered acres and acres of mountainous timberland, and as it grew, it created powerful winds. Numerous birds were helpless and plummeted to the fiery floor. White tail deer, usually so graceful, now stumbled about in the black smoke filled forest, confused and frightened. The sky above the umbrella of smoke was a glowing red as fiery sparks rained down from tall, aged oaks. The scorching fire proceeded to grow, not only from the increasing winds, but now it fed on its own superheated air. Barclay continued to beat the flames with all his strength, though it was ebbing away. His muscles ached unmercifully, and his eyes burned so that it was hard to keep them open. But he couldn't let this monster win! It must not burn up Oak Mountain! He struggled to see through the blinding smoke, to see if there were others nearby, and occasionally caught a glimpse of another human form bent over in the distance flailing the flames. There was no way to hear anyone with the deafening roar of the fire that sounded like a freight train hurtling down the tracks at full speed. He noticed a rattler slither out of the tangled thicket frantically trying to escape the fiery furnace. It slid swiftly down the mountainside and out of sight.

Poky and Addie Jane made it down to the valley with little Grae, weak and out of breath, frightened, yet happy to be away from the fires. Sitting on nail kegs at Martin's Store, they gulped down the water offered to them. Old man Martin's tall, frail wife filled their glasses again. "I'm here all alone. Gaston an' all th'menfolks fightin' th'fire. That where Barclay is?"

Addie Jane nodded.

"Where daddy?" Grae whined tiredly.

Poky pushed the glass of water at him. "Fightin' that fire, son. Now drink this'ere water."

As the day wore on, the fires increased. The afternoon

passed, the evening, a three quarter moon rose up over the fiery forest, creating an eerie effect as the black billowy smoke blended into the night, and glowing flames danced in the winds, consuming years and years of growth. As the fire moved on its never ceasing path, the weary firefighters moved with it. Exhausted from the fight, they hardly noticed where they were. It all looked the same, the trees, the brush, the smoke, the flames. But suddenly, Barclay looked around realizing where he was, not that far away! It was headed for the stream, the mountain stream that was unusually wide in this area with falls, cold, rushing falls plunging down the rocky mountainside. It was wide, wide enough to stop the monster! With renewed strength, he moved excitedly along the right flank of the charging red front that knew not what it would encounter. Beating incessantly, he tried to keep it from widening while watching anxiously for the water.

"Barclay!" a voice called out. He turned to see a figure whom he could not distinguish flinging a bucket at him, and he laughed aloud. Someone had had the insight to think ahead. There it was! He ran toward the rushing cold stream, the bottom of the cascading falls, and dropped the bucket into its rapidly flowing, icy cold water, filled it up and raced back to the encroaching flames. Reeling with immense satisfaction, he tossed the cold water onto the flames and ran back for more. Thus, he continued, back and forth, laughing aloud and emptying bucket after bucket of water on the hungry flames. Back he ran for more and more and more.

Suddenly he looked up and across the rushing falls. The tall pines on the other side were aflame. The fire had jumped the falls! Barclay threw the bucket down in despair. "You gonna burn up the whole durn mountain!" he yelled out to the roaring fire. "You gonna burn up Oak Mountain!" Tears rolled down his blackened face in little rivulets.

The fire persisted throughout the night, taking with it more and more acres of timber, but more sadly, consuming the innocent mountain life as it proceeded up the mountain while widening its boundaries. More reinforcements came to aid the tired and frustrated firefighters. Some relinquished their places to others, unable to go on, but Barclay fought on, obsessed with a determination to destroy the destroyer. He must save his beloved mountain! His strength was about gone, and his thinking not clear. When man is at war against nature's fury, the only edge he has is his unique brain, his ways to think and outsmart the adversary, but when fatigue destroys this, then he is no match and an easy target for the enemy. Such became the case with Barclay Branham in the middle of the night. As the fires blazed, he fought crazily, beating the wretched flames in a rage, unable to comprehend any longer. While thrashing, he did not notice that he'd entered the danger zone, and the flames surrounded him. Suddenly, he looked up and around. "Oh my God!" he cried out in the heat and smoke as the enemy closed in. Between coughs and gasps, he whispered..."Lord...Lord...."

It was in the early morning hours that the winds ceased, and the flames lost their vigor, enabling the army of firefighters to get the upper hand. By noon, the dirty, smoke covered men stumbled out of the defeated forest and down the mountainside. They came to find water, food and rest. Addie Jane and Poky waited along with the rest. Neither had slept, but watched the fiery glow throughout the night from the window of the little Baptist church in the valley. A number of them had taken refuge in the small clapboard church to watch and pray. Now they rushed out to meet the returning firefighters who staggered in one by one. Family and friends welcomed them with mugs of cold water or hot coffee, then led them to tables set bountifully for them. The afternoon wore on, and soon it was apparent that Barclay was missing. Poky pushed frantically through the crowd of men, women and children, grabbing hold of each tired, dirty firefighter.

"You seen'im? You seen Barclay?"

Always the answer was no. She scurried back to Addie Jane, only to find little Grae sitting all alone on the floor crying. Grabbing him up, she ran to the door just in time to see her disappear into the smoke filled forest.

"ADDIE JANE!" she hollered out. "ADDIE JANE!"

Addie Jane heard nothing and saw nothing but the fear in front of her leading her on, a fear more tangible than the heavy lying smoke, more tangible than the hot cinders on the ground and more tangible than the obvious dangers surrounding her. Barclay was in there!

Deeper into the forest incinerator she forged ahead, with each step sending up puffs of hot grey dust as she tried dodging the hot cinders under foot, occasionally stepping on them, but numb to its pain. The smoke thickened, and she began to feel her chest tighten. The coughing started. Still she ran on wildly, calling out...*BARCLAY...BARCLAY...BARCLAY*...and the name she loved so was eerily echoed back to her over and over. Her vision was significantly impaired by the thick smoke, slowing her down, and if it hadn't been for her innate sense and feel for the mountain, she would have run in circles. Instead, she climbed the familiar ridges, something pushing her onward and upward, higher and higher toward their place, toward the oaks. He would be there! He must be there! Her feet were seared and burning, but all was numb to her. Suddenly, a tall poplar toppled in front of her and lay crackling. Her mind raced backwards, across the miles of life, across the years of living to a different time where there was no smoke, no burning, no cinders...only *ice*. The popping of the fiery branches transformed into ice popping...and she was a child again and so afraid and all alone. But then! He was there, picking her up in his strong arms. *Barclay!* Her heart pounded, and her coughing increased, but still she pushed upward. She could see him now...standing there with his arms outstretched at their place...there in the midst of the oaks...the cool welcoming oaks. He looked so handsome with his broad shoulders, his dark thick wavy hair, his eyes...deep dark pools, and his smile...just for her...always just for her. Her heart pounded harder, sharp pains cut through her heaving chest, and she coughed and coughed. She couldn't breathe, but Barclay was there waiting for her.

Two days later, a steady, fine rain fell over Oak Mountain, sending up smoke streams again, as the cold rain fizzled out the last remaining remnants of burning cinders. A heaviness hung over the mountain, heavier than the black smoke previously. Voices hardly raised above whispers. Poky lay in bed at the church parsonage. The young pastor and his wife tended to her as she sought to escape reality.

At Blackford's Funeral Home, a crowd had solemnly gathered. Just about everyone from the settlement, and they moved silently among strangers, teachers, principals, doctors, lawyers and politicians from far reaching valleys, who had come to pay their tribute, quietly shaking hands and displaying dignified smiles. Artists from Lynchburg and Charlottesville filed in, as well. A heated debate was rising in a far corner of the room, and others crowded close to hear.

"They'd want th'best for him. I know they would, and we can give it to him, too."

"But he belongs *here* on th'mountain!"

"Why? So he can be treated like nothing like the rest of us?"

"They'd want him here. I know they would!"

"But they ain't here, are they?"

There was silence.

A shiny, black car pulled up beside the funeral home. Jon Junior got out, flipped up a large, black umbrella and walked around to the other side. He opened the door for Hallie and Lauralee. Jordan emerged from the back. Solemnly, they walked in.

"Look, yonder goes a priest," a lad pointed toward them,

and all eyes turned their way. Jordan smiled warmly, and they nodded reverently. They walked through the crowd, looking for Poky, and then down the long crimson carpeted runner toward two closed coffins. Hallie was crying softly. Lauralee followed suit. Jon Junior pulled his large, white handkerchief out of his back pocket and began blowing. Jordan quietly witnessed it all, and it was striking the inner sensitivity of his soul. They stopped short of the oak caskets, seeing no family line formed. Instead, there was an air of confusion, discord even, as if this dual death had struck the mountain as a sword, severing ties, exposing hurts, creating acute pains and leaving chaos.

Suddenly the funeral doors flew open, and the cold, driving rain blew in. Poky stood dripping wet, looking all but crazed. She came forward, her eyes riveted to the caskets. She passed through the crowd as if unaware they were there. As she walked past, Hallie reached out for her, but Jordan gently pulled her back. A hush fell over the place as the old midwife stood before the closed caskets. A piercing, painful wail escaped her, filling the building and echoing off its walls as she fell between the caskets and bowed her head. There she remained, and the crowd let her grieve.

The next day, the rains ceased, and the sun appeared as if nothing had happened at all. The valley looked new, cleansed from its washing. And in the valley, spring was everywhere...the dogwoods and redbuds were blooming in full array, spirea was exploding snowy white, and apple blossoms were sending forth their fragrant perfume throughout the deep green valley. If one didn't look up at the beloved mountain, now partially blackened and forlorn, they might not remember the horror. They might not really believe that there would be a funeral at two o'clock.

Almost time, the valley was full of people, cars parked everywhere and even on up the mountainside, any available place. Poky stood stoically beside Jordan awaiting the moment. He remained attentively by her side, quite aware that of all the mourners there that day, including family and friends, none felt the loss as deeply as this dear lady. Her wound was fresh, raw and bleeding.

Jordan looked up at the mountain. Though it was partially darkened with black, skeletal trees climbing it in a ghostly sort of way, it still held its magic spell. He felt its strength, its comforting aura. There was something here that was different. No wonder its people were the same.

Two hearses pulled up, stopping at an angle, and two caskets laden with flowers were brought forth by solemn pallbearers. They were placed beside the gaping holes.

Jordan cleared his throat, and everyone was silent. *"'I will lift up my eyes unto the hills....'"* They all automatically looked toward Oak Mountain.

"'...from whence comes my help. My help comes from the Lord, who made heaven and earth.'

"'The Lord is near to all who call upon Him, to all who call upon Him in truth.'

"'Fear not; for I am with you; be not dismayed; for I am your God; I will strengthen you; yes, I will help you, I will uphold you with the right hand of my righteousness.'"

Poky nodded through her tears. Jordan continued.

"'Jesus said to her, I am the resurrection and the life; he who believes in Me, though he may die, he shall live.'

"'For we know that if your earthly house, this tent, is destroyed, we have a building from God, a house not made with hands, eternal in the heavens.'"

Jordan looked upward and closed his eyes..."Our Father, the light of the world who hung the sun, moon and stars in the heavens to give us light in darkness, now that our minds and souls are darkened, please give us your light in this needy hour.

"Help us, Lord, to let go of these two and leave them in your care, for certainly thy love is greater than all of ours combined. We find joy in knowing that both Barclay and

Addie Jane knew you, had trusted in you and now are with you in Paradise; but it is the human desire to ask why, to question, to wonder, to try to understand...but you said, '*Trust in the Lord with all thine heart; and lean not unto thine own understanding.*' That is what we'll do, Lord. Let us leave this place with the precious memory of these two who shared a strong and binding love, knowing that they now walk the streets of heaven together...and let us leave with the thought that life is too strong for death, and love never fails."

Suddenly little Grae broke loose from Jack Jacob's wife and ran toward Jordan, then he stopped short and looked all around. Poky picked him up and held him tightly.

A subtle breeze lifted over the crowd, leaving the scent of apple blossoms, and softly they sang together...

Beyond the sunset, O blissful morning
When with our Savior heav'n is begun,
Earth's toiling ended, O glorious dawning
Beyond the sunset, when day is done
Sunrise tomorrow, sunrise tomorrow
Sunrise in glory is waiting for me
Sunrise tomorrow, sunrise tomorrow
Sunrise with Jesus for eternity.

(Thirty Years Later...)
October 1995

GRAE WAS SILENT. Poky stared out over the treetops to the far off mountain ridges of varying stages of blue. She'd ceased talking, but her still keen mind kept rolling on as an old silent movie, the reels never running out. They just kept on and on. A cool autumn breeze blew through the open doors of Grae's Cherokee. A car pulled up in front of them, and several people jumped out, running excitedly over to the overlook. The father, apparently, began snapping pictures with his compact Canon. Two children, a small boy and girl, pounced on the crumbling, old rock wall built many years ago by the CCC's and now worn smooth on top from years of mountain winds and rain and thousands of footsteps such as these. The mother was quickly spreading out a red gingham tablecloth on the grassy meadow adjacent to the pull off.

Grae looked over at Poky.

"What do you say we drive over to Oak Mountain?" he asked.

The old woman nodded.

"Why don't you ride up here with me?"

Again she nodded.

He helped her out and up to the front seat, gently closing the door behind her, and walked around to the driver's side. He slowly pulled out on the parkway, and they drove on in silence for several miles, Grae with a pensive expression and Poky returning to her own world.

Again, he noticed the masses of scraggly trees lining the roadside and climbing the steep ridges. What did she call them before... *Tree of Heaven*? He glanced over at the silent old woman, realizing now that she was a walking encyclopedia of these mountains.

"Miss Poky, tell me about these trees...you know...the ones you call *Tree of Heaven....*"

She studied him a moment and then spoke in an alternate high, low pitch, sometimes hardly above a whisper..."them trees, they struggle, ya' see. Struggle for survival. Jest like you say, most folk think they're jest a nuisance, an' cut'em down all th'time. Folks don't think they're pretty, don't think they're worth much, not good as other trees...but God don't think so. He must'a thought them right pretty...else he wouldn't have made s'many!

"...an' t'make up for'em bein' so small like an' fragile, they jest keep on'a growin', multiplyin' an' crowdin' in on th'roads...gonna make sure *somebody* notices'em." She chuckled. "They're fragile on th'one hand, but a hardy bunch on the other. When ya' daddy was growin' up, one day we was sittin' out on th'ridge an' th'sun commenced t'settin'. A beautiful fall day like this'un, it was. That big ol' orange sun jest fell on them lil' trees, lit up their red branches, an' it was jest like th'Lord opened up my eyes. I looked over at yo' daddy, little Barclay, only 'bout six years old at th'time. An' I realized them trees was like them...like th'folks from th'settlement. They would keep on'a strugglin' an' growin' an' multiplyin' 'cause th'good Lord loved'em. He loved'em much as He loves anybody. It was 'bout then I quit frettin' 'bout how folks treated'em, ya' see, 'cause I knew they'd survive, they'd be all right jest like th'Tree of Heaven."

Grae marveled at the old woman's insight, and here he was the psychology major. He looked back out the window at the mass of swaying, spindly trees, suddenly seeing them for the first time. Why hadn't he noticed them before?

Poky's cracking voice interrupted his thoughts, "...they grow 'bout four t'six feet a year!"

"That so?"

"Yes, siree. Ya' see, they's reachin' for heaven, they are. Could be 'cause'uv their struggle. Ya' know, hardships an' struggles 'cause a body to look upward, too. We feel sorry for them that goes through hardships an' troubles, but it ain't all bad...not if they learn t'look up."

Again Grae was quiet with his thoughts as they continued along the winding, picturesque parkway. He thought over the old woman's words, such profound statements. He recalled the nagging thoughts he'd been dealing with in the past year himself, the void he'd felt in his own life. Although, he'd spoken to no one about it, not even Barbara Ann, his fiancée, it was constantly before him. Why didn't he feel content and happy? Why did he feel this void within? He had a hunch Poky had the answers. He might be wise to spend more time with her.

Soon they left the neat and orderly parkway for the real country. A country with rugged roads, overhanging branches and barbed wire fences lining it. Scattered black and white cows grazed, and occasional remnants of summer gardens lay tangled and abandoned, and sparse cornstalks still stood. The countryside was old, rounded and comforting, the land of the Virginia 'hollers' with quaint cottages half hidden in them or precariously perched alongside its steep hills.

"Sure is country out here."

Poky smiled. "And I love it...miss it, I do. My friend, Miss Hallie, always loved it, too. 'Course she lived in th'city all'uv her life, but she said t'me once...'Miss Poky, you a lucky lady 'cause you get to spen' all your days in this'ere beautiful country.'"

"How did that come about? I mean your best friend living in the city and you way out here?"

"Oh, Miss Hallie knew me all'uv my life ever since my mama took me t'stay with'em when I was jest a lil' bitty baby. She was my best friend, an' ever since she passed on t'glory, life ain't been th'same." They bounced over the uneven country road.

ACROSS THE HOLLOWS, the thick autumn forests, the valleys and the ever flowing James, Lauralee was reminiscing as well, as she stared up at the newly erected steeple of the First Baptist Church. Two long years they'd waited for it to be replaced, for it to once again pierce the Lynchburg skyline. The cool breeze caressed her wrinkled forehead and her greying hair, lifting it lightly with its touch. She looked around, and no one was in sight. Good. She sat down on the rock wall adjacent to the church and remembered the days when her mama used to bring her here, hand in hand all dressed up for Sunday school and church. How she missed her! She looked down at the relatively new ABC store now butting up against the beautiful old church...changes everywhere...progress? She turned to the old school building directly across from the church. The large, red brick building hadn't housed any children for years now. It had been converted to offices years ago. She recalled wistfully looking out those large windows and up at the church steeple and wishing she could escape the reading and arithmetic and climb that steeple. She used to think that if she could just reach the top of that steeple, she'd be able to see clear to West Virginia or maybe even North Carolina. My, what children think of. She glanced at her watch. Eleven thirty. Jon Junior would be calling her most likely, checking on her, wondering where she was. She chuckled. He was just like a mother hen. But he'd never understand her need to come downtown and just spend time with the things of her youth. It had been ten years now since her mother had died, and it was October then, too...a lovely October day.

"Mighty pretty, ma'am."

She looked up suddenly at a middle-aged man, who certainly looked older than his years. Obviously, he was one of those less fortunate individuals that seemed to be a part of most downtowns. Unkempt and shabbily dressed with a short tangled beard, he sported a blue Atlanta Braves baseball cap.

"Yes, sir, it is."

"I watched'em put'er up there!" he boasted proudly.

"You did?"

"Yes, ma'am. A great big crane come an' lifted that thing right off the ground an' up she went!"

"That must have been something to see."

"Sho was. Me an' a whole lotta other people watched. Was something. It's ninety feet high, that steeple, you know?"

"Yes, sir, I know." Lauralee gazed up at the ethereal steeple that, along with its massive base, towered almost two hundred feet above Lynchburg's skyline, a pinnacle reaching up to heaven. It had seemed awesome to her as a child. People say when you grow up and grow older, things diminish in size and scope. But not the steeple! It still held her in awe. It had not lost its grandeur nor commanding aura.

"When that windstorm hit't in '93, it come crashin' down all right, right through the roof. I went inside an' seen it. First time I'd ever been in that nice, fancy church."

"You don't say."

"Yes, ma'am. She landed right in th'middle of that great big sanctuary...and the tip of it was almost touching the pulpit. Ain't that something?"

"For sure."

"...an' it didn't stop there, ya' know...in the sanctuary that is. No, siree. It went right on down to the basement. Made a great big mess of things, that wind did!"

Lauralee was quite aware of what the man was describing. On that summer day two years ago, without a word of warning, a ferocious wind, some say tornado, whipped through Lynchburg, tearing its way through, leaving a path of destruction. Trees were felled in its fury, houses were torn through and steeples toppled as the torrential rains fell, accompanied with marble sized hail. Power lines dropped and electricity died. She vividly recalled where she'd been at the time herself, driving along alone. So frightened in the midst of the storm, she had gotten down in the floor of her car and pulled a shopping bag over her head. But after it was all over, the most lasting impression of this savage wind was the toppled steeples. Not only the hundred-year-old steeple of First Baptist, but also its sister church, Court Street Baptist. Its steeple twisted and cracked, ready to fall, as well. Afterwards, both churches, only blocks apart, but with years of history between them, stood naked without their precious steeples. The grand old First Baptist, considered the mother church of the Baptists in Lynchburg, claimed Court Street Baptist, the oldest Black Church in Lynchburg, as its sister church. Some of the old members of First Baptist actually called it their baby because the original black congregation were first members of First Baptist Church before building their own.

"Right after it happened," the man continued, "I poked my nose in there an' couldn't hardly see nothin'. Somebody had a flashlight an' was aimin' it all over th'place. Eerie like. It was a mess. The steeple was smashed to pieces, an' the whole place was covered with timber and plaster an' such. Looked just like a bomb had exploded!"

"You're right, sir. I know all about it. Amazingly, none of those beautiful stained glass windows were broken except for one small one."

"Ain't that somethin'! I can't figure it out neither."

"God intervened, I think."

The man looked at her with curiosity.

"You come here, lady?"

"Yes, sir, all my life, from the time I was a little girl, I can remember attending. It was my mama's church."

"You don't say!"

"I can hardly wait until we can meet here again. It'll be in

December, I think."

He stared at her.

"Why don't you come, sir...and visit with us." She realized he would stand out like a sore thumb in the neat and fashionable crowd, but wouldn't that be what Jesus would do?

He began to shuffle around. "Well, I don't know, ma'am. Ain't never been in such a place 'cept when it was all broken up."

"Please come." Suddenly it seemed the most important thing in the world to have that indigent man attend her beloved church.

A smile lit up his weathered, yellowed skin, and she caught a twinkle in his eyes. "Yes, ma'am. I might just do it." He shuffled off and turned back to wave. A warm feeling flooded over her, and she looked up at the tall steeple again. Mama would be proud. Mama always had a heart for such people. She got up from the rock wall and rubbed her back. Sat too long, she thought. She walked out to the sidewalk and looked back, a feeling of nostalgia overwhelming her. Life was good, life was happy, but life was sad, too...here in the autumn of her years. Oftentimes it was depressing as one watched the changes taking place, and witnessed loved ones and friends pass on. She loved to reminisce...but sometimes it was sad to remember the good times when one was young and now....

"Oh well," she said aloud, calling on her Frederick strength, "I'm going to a movie!" She started down the familiar street before she remembered there were no movie theaters downtown anymore. She stopped and thought, I can catch a bus to the mall. Go to that movie theater, if you can call it that. She'd been once before and was quite disappointed. All the old theaters, her friends, were gone. The last one had been torn down years ago. Even the glorious Paramount had been razed, much to her sorrow. It was certainly an inconvenience since she couldn't drive anymore because of her cataracts. But she was determined to go to a movie, and set out for the bus. Mama must be smiling at me, she thought.

POKY AND GRAE continued on, and were soon climbing the forest covered mountain. Poky was silent. She gazed out the window, noticing the full forest that had reclaimed the mountain where once stood black and bare skeletons. Though it had been many years ago, the memory was as vivid as yesterday.

Grae interrupted her thoughts, "Miss Poky, after living all of ninety-seven years, how do you feel about life? I mean how would you sum it up?"

She looked at the handsome young man, generations between them. "Well, son, when ya' get to th'end...it's a surprise...*it's so short.* Don't seem like no time a'tall I was jest a young'un myself. I don't know what happened to all them years!"

He nodded. "The brevity of it."

"...an' if I had it t'do over, son, I wouldn't'uv wasted s'much 'uv it. Would'a spent more time 'bout th'Master's business."

"I see."

Grae's ears were popping as the Cherokee ascended Oak Mountain. Soon they were there, and Poky tapped him on the arm. "Pull over here." He obeyed and looked around. Seeing nothing at first, he then noticed a few old boards sticking through the tangled brush. He looked at Poky.

"That was your home, son, when you was a baby. A fine lil' place, too, it was."

"I know. It burned."

"Yeah, it burned."

"Mind if I get out and just look around a bit?"

"Go 'head on. I'll jest sit here a spell."

He walked around the site, stepping cautiously through the high, tangled weeds. He stopped and stood scratching his head. It all seemed so alien to him. He had no memory of it. Poky watched him. Soon he got back in and quietly drove on, continuing up the mountain. Then he saw something up ahead. It looked like a grotesque, green figure at first rising up from the mountain ridge. Then he realized it was a house fallen in, a mountain cabin or what was left of it. He looked over at Poky.

She nodded. "Pull over, son." Again he obeyed. She sat there still and quiet, just staring at the little cabin, practically swallowed up with the aggressive kudzu that had wrapped itself up and around it, almost concealing its entire identity. But a window with broken panes peered out at them from underneath its intertwining tentacles, and the remains of a chimney poked through the lush greenery. A tear slid down the old woman's wrinkled cheek.

"You want to get out?" Grae asked reluctantly, and she reached for the door handle.

"I'll get it for you." He hopped out and practically ran around to her side, opening the door and helping her out, handing her the cane she'd brought along. She wobbled over the coarse, uneven mountainside with him hovering close by. As they got closer, they could see that part of the roof had fallen in, and there was a gaping hole left that allowed easy access to the forest creatures. A dead poplar branch straddled the opening, and a squirrel's nest rested skillfully there upon. The decaying cabin seemed to be just another part of the mountain, but Poky stared at it, a kaleidoscope of memories racing through her mind.

She lifted her cane and pointed. "This was *my* home."

Not knowing what to say, he just stood there.

"Still there...least part'uv it...can't get rid'uv them chestnut cabins...tougher'n anything...."

Again she lifted her cane pointing to an ancient grove of twisted and gnarled apple trees beyond the house. "Mama's grave," she said matter-of-factly. It, too, was all but covered up with the crawling kudzu. Grae ran toward it and began pulling away the lush, green vines.

"Leave it be, son," she called out. "Mama don't mind."

He looked up questioningly, and rose slowly, brushing the dirt off his khaki pants. She motioned for him to come on back.

"Only got two things t'ask'uv ya', son."

"Yes, ma'am?"

"When my time comes, you call Miss Hallie's grandson...th' Rev'rend Jordan McKenzie Frederick. He done promised t'say a few kind words over my body. He lives way down yonder by th'ocean somewheres, but he'll come. He's Presbyterian, ya' know. I like Presbyterians jest th'same as Baptists. Ain't much difference."

"I'll be sure to do it, Miss Poky. You can count on me."

"An' I want my bones t'lie right yonder a'side'uv hers."

He looked back at the grown up grave spot beneath the dead apple trees. "Don't they have laws about that now...I mean laws about where you can and cannot bury someone?"

"Don't matter none. This'ere's my land still, an' I wanna be buried right here. You see to it, son." She turned to go back to the car. He followed.

As he started the ignition, she asked rather pointedly, "Can we go to th'mission?"

"Well, sure we'll go, Miss Poky." He glanced at his watch, wondering what time he should have her back at the nursing home. "Can't say that I remember much about it, though. Been so long since I've been."

She was quiet.

"Understand they're converting an old school building to a museum. Probably a good idea. You know, it's good to be *Indian* now. Everyone wants to be Indian...all over the country, even in the northeast."

"Th'museum, son, ain't jest a building. It's t'honor your ancestors an' your heritage. One day it's gonna tell th'story'uv who you are."

He smiled at her and said, "A member of *The Monacan Tribe.*"

She didn't respond, and they drove silently down the

mountain. As they leveled off, she asked, "You draw, son?"

"Yes, ma'am. I paint some when I have time, which isn't a lot. Uncle Jack told me I got it from my dad, the talent, that is."

"You did. Barclay was a fine artist, he was. Don't forget that, son."

"No, ma'am. I won't." He couldn't help but feel like he was about ten again. "I have one of his paintings in my office."

"*The Shadow....*" she murmured.

"Ma'am?"

"You got th'*Shadow...*'cause I gave it to ya' when they took you away."

He'd never heard that part. Uncle Jack had simply told him it had belonged to his dad. He'd often studied the picture. "Do you know what it means, Miss Poky...the picture that is?"

"Reckon I do. Barclay gave it to *me*. That's why it didn't burn in th'fire. Was up at my place when th'mountain burned. My place escaped somehow. They still don't know how."

He waited.

"...folks from th'settlement...from High Peak...your folks, son...lived many years in th'shadow'uv th'mountain...in th'shadow 'uv th'Blue Ridge. A shadow ain't real, ya' know. You can't touch it, feel it. It jest lets ya' know there's a presence nearby."

Grae frowned. "I still have a hard time seeing it. I mean I don't really understand...."

"You wouldn't, son. You don't need a shadow *now*...." she closed her eyes.

He felt a bit frustrated but could do nothing but let her rest. Thoughtfully, he drove toward the mission, not by memory, but with the help of a little map Uncle Jack had given him previously. About half way, she looked down at the map and then back up at him, said nothing and closed her eyes again. Why did he feel like a kid caught with his hand in the cookie jar? Finally, he was descending the hilly, narrow back road and suddenly the small white chapel, St. Paul's, and the row of mission buildings were directly in front of them. Her eyes flew open as if she knew, and a smile flickered across her aged face. He pulled over to the side of the road.

"Let's get out." She was already pulling on the door handle.

"Yes, ma'am." He hopped out and rushed around to help. With her leaning on her cane, they walked up to the front door of the small chapel. She wanted to go in. It was cool and inviting inside, and she sat down on the back pew while Grae wandered about. Her mind slid backwards again...to her first visit...must've been about 1933 durin' th'Depression. An' Barclay...tears fought to surface but couldn't quite make it...she'd shed too many tears...no need now...she was old...too old for tears. But that day, she could remember it now...sharper than th'crack'uv a good rifle on a clear day. That Sunday so long ago, he'd just been born, an' it was a cool autumn mornin'. He was all bundled up in them wraps, an' he'd stared right up at her with those dark, penetrating eyes. She closed her eyes again. Grae looked at her and walked on outside. The sun was streaming through the stained glass windows, casting multicolored prisms across the empty pews, and across the frail shoulders of the old woman. She felt its warmth and looked up, remembering another day...Addie Jane was walking down the aisle...her countenance radiant. Th'preacher was standin' up front there with Barclay...an' th'look in Barclay's eyes! She'd never forget it...love pourin' out. Grae stuck his head in the door again and she jumped. It was confusin' for old folks, she thought. Th'generations jest sort'uv fused together an' you found yourself mistakin' th'grandchildren for th'children, an' th'great-grandchildren for th'grandchildren.

"You ready yet, Miss Poky?"

"Jest about." Grabbing hold of the pew in front, she slowly pulled herself up.

Back outside in the warm autumn sun she hesitated.

"You want to sit down awhile. I thought I'd check out the museum progress."

She nodded, and he led her over to a ledge and gently let her down. "You warm enough?"

She waved him off, and he disappeared around the chapel. Relieved to be left alone, she stared up at the little chapel. It, too, was old. Not as old as she...'bout sixty-five she reckoned. She looked up at the simple white cross that held its prominent place of honor, a symbol of faith, hope and love. The towering poplars provided a startling backdrop, their large, golden leaves floated gracefully downward and around the cross, sliding precariously off the roof on their final descent. The murmuring creek flowed lazily beneath, adding to the unusual scene of tranquillity. She watched the clear, cold water meander down its path between twin banks...and she remembered Barclay throwing pebbles into it, creating enchanting circles. She sighed and thought...a wind's blowin' up from th'valley. She could feel the subtle mountain breeze as it whispered through the granite boulders...and she could hear the soft strains of a guitar...and voices barely echoing through the Blue Ridge...a familiar melody....

Down in the valley
Valley so low
Hang your head over
Hear the wind blow

Roses love sunshine
Violets love dew
Angels in heaven
Know I love you...

THE END

Epilogue

As the year of 1998, and soon the century ends, the small town of Lynchburg, now a growing city with a population of over 65,000, still retains its quaint ambience. As with most urban towns, the focus is on downtown revitalization, and the historic old streets, such as Court, Clay, Pearl are part of a united effort to preserve and protect the downtown, including the riverfront as the James River continues on its path.

As for the Monacans, they received State Recognition in 1989. The General Assembly officially recognized the Monacans as the eighth native tribe of Virginia, and the only one located west of the Richmond/Tidewater area. The book, *Indian Island in Amherst County,* by Dr. Peter Houck and Mintcy D. Maxham (published by Warwick House), which tells the history of the Mysterious Monacans, sparked an "awakening." Today, the Monacan Indian Nation is reclaiming its ancestral land, but more importantly, reclaiming its heritage. On October 3, 1998, a crisp fall day and somewhat overcast, the grand opening of The Monacan Ancestral Museum, located at the Mission in a former school building, was proudly celebrated. The following day, October 4, 1998, the Monacans solemnly honored their ancestors with a reburial of Monacan remains that had been excavated ten years prior from a burial mound northeast of Charlottesville. Not only were the remains put to a final rest, but the event was a way of putting things to rest, as well...a healing for the Monacan people. Today these persecuted people march to a different tune...that of pride. Their struggles behind them, they now reach forward to a "brighter future." Dreams do come true!

Acknowledgments

I would like to express my sincere thanks to all those who've supported me in writing this book, plus my previous novels. Foremost, is my loving husband, Enoch, who over the years has believed in me, patiently allowing my creative work to weave throughout our lives. My three wonderful children's support has been most inspiring and appreciated. Troy has assisted me with photography, and Tara and Bethany have been with me every step of the way, never resenting my research, reading and writing that has many times taken me from them and my grandchildren, Robby, Laura, Sarah and Will. Also, thanks to all of my Tyree family clan, especially Aunt Bessie, my biggest fan. Of course, a big thanks to my mother, Margaret, for sharing with me all those stories of growing up in downtown Lynchburg.

A warm thanks to those who have worked with and for me, often voluntarily, making it possible to realize my goal: To my sister, Rita Argenbright, for reading this book in its awkward manuscript form, to Kim Shoemaker and her father, Ray Gerson, for their valuable editing and creative insight, to John Eller, Attorney, for his editing and legal expertise, to those members of the Monacan Nation who shared their hearts with me and gave me a glimpse into their struggle, to Dr. Peter Houck for taking time out of his very busy schedule to read my manuscript and write the Foreword, to Joyce Maddox with Warwick House Publishing for her careful editing and guidance, also to Becky Driskill-Childress for getting me started in those early days, to the staff of the Lynchburg Public Library for all their help, and for allowing me to tie up their microfilm machine for hours at a time, to all my friends, including those on the Blue Ridge Parkway, who sell, buy and support my books.

Last but not least, a heartfelt thanks to my "readers" everywhere who've encouraged me to keep writing. I especially appreciate all those wonderful cards and letters through the past years. Those have been my greatest reward!

Song Credits

Brother, Can You Spare a Dime?, pg. 36 - Lyrics - E.Y. Harburg/Music - Jay Gorney

Stormy Weather, pg. 267 - Lyrics - Ted Koehler/Music - Harold Arlen

Amazing Grace, pg. 49 - Lyrics - John Newton/Music - Samuel Stanley

In the Garden, pg. 178 - Lyrics and Music - C. Austin Miles

Beyond the Sunset, pg. 372 - Lyrics - P. Brock and Blanche Kerr Brock

Down in the Valley, pgs. 81, 175, 216, 385 - American Folk Song

Carolyn Tyree Feagans grew up in Amherst County, adjacent to Lynchburg, at the foot of the Blue Ridge Mountains.

(P.O. Box 10811, Lynchburg, Virginia 24506)